The Story Hunters

The Story Hunters

A Novel

Karen McGoldrick

DEEDS PUBLISHING

Published by Deeds Publishing in Athens, GA
www.deedspublishing.com

Printed in The United States of America

Cover and interior design by Deeds Publishing

ISBN 978-1-961505-51-3

Books are available in quantity for promotional or premium use.
For information, email info@deedspublishing.com.

First Edition, 2025

10 9 8 7 6 5 4 3 2 1

Dedicated to the memory of my mother, Marjorie Butler Jaffa. If you knew my mom, you would be able to spot her influence throughout this tale. She always had the tea kettle at the ready, along with home baked goods, and an empathetic ear. She loved old houses, ghost stories, memoirs, letters, and oral histories. She was able to do an amazing amount of genealogical research before the age of the internet. So much of what she discovered, I later was able to verify online.

She is always missed, but always with me.

Keeping Track of the Hemings
(A Reader's Guide)

Parthenia (Thenia) Biabaye - slave ship Captain Hemings: Progenitor of the now famous Hemings line in Virgina. She gave the captain's surname to her daughter, **Elizabeth/Betty**, who passed it on to all her line, and they to theirs, male and female, regardless of paternity.

Parthenia's daughter, **Elizabeth/Betty Hemings** (became a mother of 12) had six children with her master **John Wayles** (father of Martha Jefferson). **Elizabeth/Betty Hemings** was "willed" to Martha Jefferson and after Wayles' death and came to live at Monticello. She appears to have enjoyed special status at Monticello, as did all her children.

Elizabeth/Betty Hemings' daughter **Critta Hemings** married a free (and landowning) person of color, Zacharia Bowles. She remained enslaved by Jefferson and had to stay at Monticello, bearing a son, who was by law, also enslaved and the property of Jefferson. After Jefferson's death in 1827 her freedom was purchased by Francis Wayles Epps. She retired to her husband's property north of Charlottesville, and lived to age 81,

Elizabeth/Betty Hemings youngest child sired by Wayles, **Sally**, would become well-known for bearing four living children with Thomas Jefferson. This fact was denied until later proven through DNA.

Elizabeth/Betty Hemings oldest daughter **Mary** had four children at Monticello (daughter is **Betsy**) but then is rented to a merchant in Charlottesville. (While Jefferson is in Paris). In that time, she bore two children sired by the merchant (Thomas Bell). Later Thomas Bell will free **Mary** and their children and live openly with her as a common-law wife.

Mary's daughter, **Betsy,** is rumored to have been fathered by Thomas Jefferson. At age 14, she was given as a gift from Thomas Jefferson to his daughter Maria, and later, after Maria's death, it is rumored, also gave birth to children fathered by Jefferson's son-in-law, John Wayles-Epps. Unusual for the time, **Betsy** is buried in the Epps family cemetery. John Wayles-Epps' second wife is not.

1

Abby shrugged into her backpack and walked out of Pepper Tree Elementary. Right away, she spotted the silver-haired witch sheltered under the feathery canopy of a pepper tree, leaning against its trunk. Next to the witch stood a large black wolf with eyes of gold, intently focused on her.

It was, in fact, her grandma with her black German Shepherd, scrolling through her phone.

Abby smiled to herself. Her grandma *could* be a real witch, and Freddy a real wolf. But Emmaline would never admit either thing, even if it were true. The thing was that Abby just knew her Grandma was something more than she appeared to be. She intended to find out more, and to write a story about it, too.

But right now, Abby needed to square her shoulders and steel herself. Her grandma had been relentlessly drilling her on vocabulary so she would win the spelling bee at camp this summer, but today, it was not vocabulary that had Abby worried.

Emmaline pushed herself off the tree and slid her phone into the back pocket of her jeans. Abby knelt to greet Freddy who began his odd growl and wiggle routine where he snapped his jaws and curled himself around Abby. Freddy was weird, his golden eyes spooky, his body language confusing to some, but Abby adored him.

Emmaline said dryly, "What word would you use to describe your day at school?"

Abby stood up. "Abysmal."

Emmaline frowned. "Define please."

"Wretched."

"Etymology?"

"Related to abyss. As in bottomless pit."

Emmaline made a tsk-tsk sound. "Being a tad over-dramatic?"

Abby shook her head.

"Let's hear it then. Just rip off the band-aid and get it over with."

"I got sent to the principal's office."

"Abby! Why?"

"I told Ms. Pierce that she was wrong. A kid asked her what the word "persecute" meant, and I'm not kidding, she said it was what the law did to you. Persecute. P-E-R-S-E-C-U-TE. It means to harass or oppress."

"Ah. Ms. Pierce confused it with prosecute."

Abby rolled her eyes. "The woman is totally unqualified to teach."

"Abby, you only have two weeks left in the school year. Do not torture poor Ms. Pierce. You are off to camp soon. Let's focus on winning that spelling-bee."

"Oh, I'm going to win. I just hope Kat Portman is at camp again so I can see her face when I beat her."

Emmaline said sternly, "Mastery begins with humility."

Then Emmaline added, "But come back to why you were sent to the principal's office."

"I told you."

"Only the part that made you look right, and Ms. Pierce look wrong."

Abby shrugged, "Um. Well. Maybe she was having a bad day before that. I mean, her neck gets red and the red kind of crawls onto her face when she gets…" Abby paused a moment, "addlepated. A-D-D…'"

"Don't change the subject."

"It means confused, flustered."

"I know what it means. Why was she flustered?"

"We're studying ancient Egypt. I gave my oral report. It was excellent."

Emmaline shook her head and sighed.

Today the air was crystal-clear, not a trace of smog, and so the San Gabriels looked as if you could reach out and touch them. Emmaline turned her gaze north for a moment and drew a deep breath.

She said, "Stunning, aren't they?"

"What?"

"Our mountains. Rugged. Timeless."

"Just like always."

Emmaline nodded, then turned south. "Let's go get our croissants."

Abby and Emmaline and Freddy began their short walk to the village. When they got to their favorite bakery, Abby plopped down at one of the iron tables with Freddy laying down on the pavement beside it. Emmaline stood looking down at her.

"Our usual?"

Abby nodded.

Emmaline sighed, "Okay, I can't believe I'm asking, but why did Ms. Pierce become addlepated?"

"I guess she didn't like my report."

"On?"

"Embalming."

"Oh."

"No one else looked upset. In fact, I think I hit it out of the park."

"Don't boast. It's off-putting. Perhaps Ms. Pierce felt your treatment of the subject was inappropriate for sixth grade. Some people are squeamish. And then later, you added insult to injury by correcting her misuse of a word, and that was the final straw. Am I close?"

Abby nodded slowly, as if the idea might have merit. "Maybe. But I think she just hates me."

"I feel sympathy for Ms. Pierce. Even though I agree she should know the difference between 'persecute' and 'prosecute.' The thing is, Abby, that you won't always be right or do right, and when you get caught, well, you'll wish others showed you more mercy than you've shown Ms. Pierce."

Emmaline turned abruptly and went into the bakery, leaving Abby to absorb her grandmother's words. She knew Ms. Pierce hated her. And even though her audience had seemed rapt during her report on embalming, she knew the other kids hated her too.

The three of them ate their after-school baked goods. The bakery sold home-made dog biscuits too, so Freddy was not left out. People stopped by their table to chat with Emmaline about her latest historical novel, "*Sharp Elbows, Loud Voices*" which was about women fighting for the right to vote.

Abby always felt proud sitting next to her grandma when she had fans. She wanted that to be her one day.

Once done, they started back up the hill the few blocks to "the big house." The big house had been in Emmaline's family for years. It was only three blocks north of the village. It had been built for the Sparks family in 1908. It was a two-story house with a deep front porch and sturdy rock and timber accents, Arts and Crafts style. But Emmaline and Abby did not go into the big house. Emmaline let them in through a side gate, and they made their way to the guesthouse. After Abby was born, Emmaline had insisted that her daughter and son-in-law move into the big house, and she moved into the guesthouse.

Emmaline unlocked the door, and Freddy went straight-a-way to his water bowl, splashing water all over the floor.

"Grandma, you filled it too full again. Do you want me to clean up the spill?"

"No. I want you to get your homework done so you and Freddy can do your training session. I've got reading to do."

* * *

Abby got her homework out of her backpack and Emmaline went to the bathroom. The guesthouse was its usual mess. Books were stacked on the floor as well as on most flat surfaces. Abby walked into the tiny kitchen where Emmaline had left dirty dishes on the counter. Abby tried to pick up a mug off the counter, but she could not budge it. Stuck.

She heard Emmaline come out of the bathroom, so Abby ducked back into the living room. But Emmaline did not come into the living room.

Emmaline had gone into her bedroom.

Abby walked around the living room as if she were look-ing for something, but really, she was just looking for a reason not to do the stupid busy-work assignment for Ms. Pierce. School was basically over. Besides, Emmaline was doing re-search for her new book but had not told anybody what it was going to be about.

Emmaline had her enormous desk pushed up against a wall. The living room had become Emmaline's office. Gone were the days when the room had a proper sofa.

Abby walked over to her grandma's desk. There was the usual stuff, the colored markers, the sticky notes, the lined notebooks full of Emmaline's scrawling cursive. But there was also an obituary printed off the internet. Abby picked it up and read it. The lady was very pretty. Her name was Delia. Weird name. The photo looked old. Abby put the clipping down and picked up one of Emmaline's notebooks, scanning the page for clues.

Emmaline was suddenly at her elbow, startling her. "Aren't you supposed to be doing your homework?"

"Yes."

"Chop, chop. Dog waits for no man."

"Ha-ha Grandma. That's not how it goes."

"Not according to Freddy, who would like to have his training session."

Once Abby finished her homework, the three of them headed out again. This time they headed east to walk the paths and lawns of the college campus that was the heart and soul of the town. The college kids were already out for the summer, which meant Freddy had fewer distractions for his training sessions.

Freddy had been a rescue, found by animal control, dragging a chain, a collar deeply embedded in his neck. The animal rescue organization had saved him from certain death.

Their vet had surgically removed the collar, and the rescue organization had begun his rehabilitation. When Abby and Emmaline met Freddy, Abby had just finished a book report on Frederick Douglass. She made the connection between the two and insisted they get him, because, as Abby noted, Freddy had emancipated himself, just like Frederick Douglass.

Freddy was a spooky looking dog, with phobias that made him unstable and potentially dangerous. As they were warned, aggression is often fear-based. Emmaline was hesitant. But it was Abby who persuaded her. Abby made a solemn oath to be responsible for training Freddy under the guidance of a professional. For Abby and Freddy, it had been love at first sight, and she would have gladly written and signed her oath in blood.

Freddy's visible wounds had healed well, but the trauma he had endured had made a different kind of wound. Maybe the sort that would never fully heal. He was prone to panic attacks, and in the throes of one, he had caused property damage, one time destroying the upholstery in Emmaline's car while they shopped. And although the attacks came less frequently these days, they were not completely under control. Freddy did not always accept restraint or confinement.

He was oddly terrified of cats. Abby had learned that a long pull against his collar would create aggressive posturing by Freddy, not toward her, but he would find an external focus, often a person, where he would direct that aggression. It was intimidating. Short tugs were okay. A long pull was not. She met with the trainer once a week and practiced with Freddy daily. Things had progressed. Even though Abby's dad, Jim, still worried that Freddy could be a liability.

Freddy knew "heel," "sit," "down," "stay," and "come." They had graduated to a long leash for recalls, and now that the college kids were gone, they had started working off leash. Freddy's reward was to chase a tennis ball. Abby was terrible at throwing the ball. Emmaline was far better, even though she was a grandma, so Emmaline usually did the honors.

While Freddy wore himself out, Abby asked her grandmother about her research. Abby and her mother, Belva Ann, had been asking for details, but Emmaline had been stubbornly silent. Emmaline said, "I'm digging out a wonderful story."

"Hidden history?"

Emmaline nodded, "Stories of the powerless. Stories the powerful did not want told."

"Kind of like Freddy's story."

"But I'm telling a story about human history."

"Freddy's story tells a lot about humans, too."

"Touché."

Abby was strangely silent.

Emmaline noted, "Ah. An unfamiliar word. Spell it."

"T-O-U- um, S?"

"T-O-U-C-H-E. French. It comes from the sport of fencing. When your sword tip touches the opponent, you score a point. You just made a good point. Now, perhaps that's a sport you would like."

Abby frowned, "Not a chance."

Emmaline said, "Nonsense. You debate a point like an

adult. Debate is not unlike fencing. A bit of thrust and parry, linguistically speaking. Sport is a metaphor, is it not, for far more serious things?"

"Grandma, you're lecturing."

"Of course, I am. So, sport is a metaphor. Stories about animals are too. Both inform us about the human condition, do they not? You asked if my new story was from hidden history. Yes, in a way. History is written by the winners, not the losers, not the powerless. It is often curated to hide the unsavory bits, the bits that are felt to be shameful.

"I go digging up those bits. But hiding those bits, even if well-intentioned, does make the historian, in a way, guilty of distortion. Too many historians write hagiographies. H-A-G-I-O-G-R-A-P-H-I-E-S. Do you know what that means?"

"No. You think that word might be in the spelling bee?"

"Could be. Start with the root."

"Graph means to write."

"Good. Keep going."

"Hagia? Sorry."

"From the Greek, Hagia, like a halo."

"So, is a hagiography when you put a halo on the person you are writing about?"

"Yes. It's making your subject into someone saintly."

"Oh."

Emmaline sighed, "Sometimes of course, I get things wrong. I try not to go too far afield of the evidence. I at least provide a hypothesis for the real historians to consider. Fiction gives me leeway to write dramatically what I believe to be true, and I think I have found a promising thread, some unheard voices, and even some important truths. We shall see."

Abby said, "I want to write stories like you grandma. Except I want to have witches and wolves and maybe even dragons in my stories."

Emmaline grinned. "Then you should do that! Just remember that even a dragon can be a metaphor."

* * *

Belva Ann and Jim Woods believed in eating dinner as a family every weeknight. Emmaline and Freddy seldom joined them.

Abby's mother, Belva Ann, worked full time writing ad copy for a company that built senior living communities. She had found a hundred ways to describe the same place, and she had a stack of stock photos of old people playing tennis, golfing, and swimming to go alongside her copy. It was not the kind of writing she had imagined doing. Still, even working full time, she managed to put together a dinner each night which had become more complicated since Abby had declared herself vegan.

Jim Woods scouted new sites for fast food restaurants. It often meant travelling. It also was a career choice he never imagined for himself. He never cooked. But he usually did the washing up.

Abby had helped her mom set the table and had slipped the note from the principal under her plate. She knew she had to get it signed by both parents and return it to the principal, or there would be a dreaded phone call. She needed to wait for the right moment.

Jim looked across the table at Abby's plate. "Young lady, I expect you to at least try the chicken."

Belva Ann said, "She doesn't have to. The potatoes have protein. There's cheese in them."

Abby asked, "Is the cheese Vegan?"

Belva Ann said, "Yes, I was surprised how good it is."

Jim shook his head, "Still in that phase? I blame Emmaline."

Belva Ann said, "Hey, Mom's lowered her cholesterol and her blood pressure. You know heart disease runs in the family."

Abby frowned, "Is Grandma okay?"

"Of course she is, darling. Anyway, Jim, how was work?"

Abby tuned out her mom and dad and toyed with her food. It had never occurred to her that her grandma didn't eat meat for health reasons.

Jim scowled. "I work for an idiot. I really had to bite my tongue today. I get tired of the travel, but when I have to be in the office with all those low-IQ types, I just want to get back in my car and go somewhere else, anywhere else."

Belva Ann said, "It can't be that bad. We had such a good time last summer at the company softball game. You were the superstar. Everyone was so nice."

Jim nodded, and was quiet for a moment, enjoying the memory of his performance. He never played anymore, but he still "had it."

Abby seized the moment and slid the note out from under her plate. "Um. I had a little problem at school today."

Abby handed the note to her mother, who read it silently and handed it over to her husband, who read it aloud.

"Abby is an incredibly bright student who is a high achiever academically. However, her teacher has found her to show a lack of respect toward authority. Abby also tends to pass harsh judgments on others. This has caused disruptions in the classroom. These continued disruptions impact her teacher's ability to maintain a positive learning environment. We are nearly finished with our academic year, and my hope is that Abby can be helpful to her teacher and finish the school year on a positive note."

Jim Woods looked up from the note at his daughter. "Nobody likes a know-it-all, Abby."

Abby lifted her chin and said, "I never pretend to know everything. Today I did not know the word "touché'" or "hagiography.'"

Belva Ann chimed in, "You learned that at school today?"

Jim shook his head, "Of course not. That's not in any 6th grade curriculum."

Abby said, "Grandma taught me."

Belva Ann said, "Jim, Emmaline is helping her prepare for her summer camp's spelling bee."

Jim said, "I wish she wasn't going back to that snobby camp for nerds."

Belva Ann said, "Stop calling it that. It's for kids who want an academic experience."

"No. It is a camp for parents who will not let their kids be kids. She should be doing team sports."

Abby raised her hand. "Hello. I am here. Right here. I liked the spelling bee. And I hate sports. I suck at sports. All sports. If it's a sport, I suck at it. I'll never win anything playing sports, but I can win a spelling bee."

Jim said, "Do not use the word suck."

Belva Ann ignored him. "Abby, I wasn't good at sports either. Sports aren't everything. I ran the school newspaper, and I even won a short story contest."

Jim added, "But you were socially awkward and had few friends. That had to be miserable. Sports teach you how to work with others. Your team is *your* team. It's a great way to make friends."

Belva Ann shook her head, "Jim, you have no idea how painful sports are for those who are bad at that sort of thing. Let Abby do Abby. And sure, I was socially awkward. I admit it. But not so much that you didn't fall for me. Right?

Abby grinned, "Touche', Mom!"

Belva Ann did a funny snorting laugh and pulled the note out of Jim's hand and turned to Abby, "Get me a pen, please."

Abby returned and Belva Ann signed the note, then handed it to Jim who did likewise.

Jim said to Abby, "At least take the sailing class this summer at your egg-head camp."

Abby should have nodded her head. But she did not have the good sense yet to throw her dad a bone. She said, "No way. The water is too cold. But I did have mom sign me up for riding lessons. Grandma said I would be a natural since I'm such a good dog trainer."

Belva Ann raised a warning eyebrow at her husband. And whatever he was going to say, he did not say.

Belva Ann instead asked, "Any news on Mom's new book? You're better than I am at picking up clues."

"She's digging up something. It's another story the 'winners' don't want us to know."

Belva Ann said, "Clearly it will not be a hagiography."

Abby said, "Good one, Mom. You're hot tonight."

Belva Ann winked at Jim, "Did you hear that? I'm hot tonight."

And Abby, brilliant Abby, missed the double-entendre, which was too bad, because Emmaline, had she been present, would have explained the meaning of "double-entendre," made Abby spell it, and then taught her its etymology.

* * *

In only a matter of days, Abby found herself, once again, sent to the principal's office by Ms. Pierce.

The principal pushed his chair back from his desk and crossed his arms.

"Well, Abby Woods, we find ourselves once again in a thorny situation. Ms. Pierce tells me you disrupted class once again, this time by announcing that she had her facts wrong. You then proceeded to argue with her and derailed the whole lesson."

Abby mirrored the principal's posture by crossing her arms too. "Ms. Pierce clearly had not read the assignment."

The principal snorted, "Good grief. This is sixth grade, not a college symposium. You do not get to argue with your teacher in sixth grade. So, here we are again, and I am supposed to discipline you. And you are supposed to react to the discipline by reforming your behavior. How would you rate our success at this point?"

"Hmmm. Wait. How about "Execrable?" E-X-E-C-R-A-B-L-E. It means very bad."

Abby rolled her eyes up toward her forehead, then added, "It comes from the Latin word for curse."

The principal tapped his pen on his desktop. "Yes, well, I didn't know that. I mean, the etymology."

Abby announced, "I'm going to win the spelling bee at camp this year."

"I have no doubt, but somehow you have to finish this school year without being expelled."

"So don't expel me."

"You don't seem the least bit intimidated."

"Execrable is not like a real curse, is it? I won't turn into a beast or fall into a coma. But if I get expelled, that's okay too. If I get expelled, I go home and hang out with my grandma, and work on writing my story."

The principal shook his head. "Defeats the purpose. It is supposed to be punishment. You want to be a writer? Your grandma writes historical fiction as I recall."

Abby nodded proudly sitting up a little straighter.

"My wife raved about the one about the suffragettes."

"*Sharp Elbows, Loud Voices.*"

"The very one."

Abby added, "I give her feedback. I help her catch mistakes, too."

"Is that so?"

There was a gentle knock on the door, which had been left ajar, the principal's secretary sat just outside and obviously had been listening to every word.

"Excuse me. I could not help but overhear and had an idea. I wondered if I could put Abby to work in my office. I always have so much paperwork piling up at the end of the year. Besides, I have it on good authority that Ms. Pierce is on her last good nerve, which makes me inclined to think she would agree to the arrangement."

The principal tipped his head and made eye-contact with

his secretary. Then nodded. He said, "Abby, how about you work here in the office for Ms. Wilson as her assistant? You'll still need to finish your assignments for Ms. Pierce in addition to the work you have to do for Ms. Wilson."

Abby shrugged, "Beats drinking hemlock."

The principal shook his head and looked over at his secretary, who was grinning. "Are you sure you can take ten days of this?"

Abby smiled at the principal. "You got the joke." She gave him a thumbs up.

Ms. Wilson winked at Abby, then turned to her boss. "Emmaline Sparks and I go way back. She was insufferable at this age, smug and far too sophisticated. My parents never liked her. Most adults and our classmates felt the same way. But even then, she could tell a story. Her ghost stories were so scary that she got into trouble for them."

The principal said, "Apple didn't fall far from the tree."

Abby brightened, pulled out her notebook and wrote the phrase down while Ms. Wilson and the principal looked on.

Abby added, "Like a chip off the old block?"

Ms. Wilson smiled, "Exactly."

As the two left the principal's office, Ms. Wilson was saying to Abby, "This spelling bee sounds like serious business. Do you have money riding on the outcome or something?"

Abby shook her head, "You get your name engraved on a plaque that goes on this huge trophy that sits in a locked glass case forever."

Ms. Wilson said, "Ah. A bid for immortality, then? So much better."

Abby said, "Wow. You totally get it."

* * *

Abby, Emmaline, and Freddy were enjoying fresh baked (vegan) treats at their usual spot. Abby was enthusiastic, "The files were a mess. I got everything back in alphabetical order. Then when the filing was done, I got to make labels with this cool machine. I wish you would get one, Grandma. I'll make files for you and label each one. It would be so much easier for you to find stuff."

Emmaline blew on her coffee. "You don't approve of my floor filing?"

Abby rolled her eyes, "I've seen you spend half an hour looking for some paper and still not find it."

"Time is fleeting and once gone, never to be recaptured. Use it wisely."

Abby narrowed her eyes, "Kind of my point."

Emmaline continued, "I think it is important to keep one's eyes on the prize. I now refer to your prize, not mine."

"The spelling bee?"

Emmaline laughed. "Well, in the short term, sure. But you can't spend the next calendar school year in the principal's office. The world will not change for you, you must move forward in the world in which you live. What is your goal? What do you want? And how do you plan to accomplish those things?"

Abby thought about this for a moment. She stroked Freddy on the top of his head, and he looked up at her, panting. His amber eyes were partly hooded, he was relaxed and drowsy, secure with his two favorite people in the world.

"The women in your last book..."

"What of them?"

"'Sharp Elbows, Loud Voices.'"

"They were not sharp or loud just to be irritating. Those women had a clear idea of their goal. Their cause was noble. But to get there, to struggle to the front of the line, for not only themselves, but for all women, they needed sharp elbows, and loud voices."

"People hated them for it, didn't they?"

"Abby you are being intentionally obtuse. Making people dislike you is not a virtue! O-B-T-U-S-E. Maya Angelou famously said, 'People will forget what you said, people will forget what you did, but people will never forget how you made them feel."

Abby picked up her backpack, pulled out her notebook and carefully wrote the quote, while Emmaline looked on silently. When Abby was finished, she slid the notebook over to Emmaline who checked it with a nod.

Then Abby said, "I get so confused sometimes. I mean, I know a lot of stuff, stuff that I think is cool. And I work hard to learn it too. It does require 'affixing the seat of my pants to the seat of the chair.' I spend hours learning new stuff. I crack jokes and people laugh. I am not trying to make people hate me. But my teacher hates me, and the kids hate me, and the principal hates me too. At least Ms. Wilson seems not to hate me."

Emmaline leaned toward Abby, "There is a time for sharp elbows and a loud voice. Until then, hold your fire. Abby, you have the power to turn this around completely. Not this school year, but next year. You will be in middle school, with new teachers and new kids. You will have new chances to make friends and not enemies. So, I need you to listen carefully to what I am about to say."

Abby's eyes got wide, and she leaned in, ready to hear some pearl of wisdom, some bit that Emmaline, for whatever reason, had been holding back.

Emmaline dropped her voice, "I'm a story hunter. Right?"

Abby wilted. She had somehow thought this was going to be something completely different. Like a special incantation her white witch of a grandmother would pull out of a secret book of magical spells. But it was going to be the same old lecture.

Emmaline said, "Don't look like that. This is important. Everyone has a story to tell. Everyone. And once you make it your raison d'etre to hear what it is, it changes everything."

"Raison d'etre."

Emmaline wrote it down on Abby's notebook page, and then said, "Look it up." Then slid the notebook back across the table.

Abby said, "That sounds like a waste of time."

"Abby, really? When you dig for buried treasure, you do not always find it right away. But that does not mean you do not dig. No one wants to share their personal stories with someone who is judgmental or looks down on them or treats their stories as a waste of time. Receiving a person's story is a gift not to be disparaged. It is an enlightening, even intimate, experience. The kind of experience that makes life rich and rewarding.

"It is a gift received, but also a gift exchanged, because in the process you will come to know someone, have made real friends. I am not giving you permission to skip that 'seat of the pants to the seat of the chair, time.' That is critical. All worthwhile pursuits require work. Still, you will make mistakes, you will make many, sometimes terrible, mistakes, those are equally important. They keep you humble. And..."

Abby remembered, "Mastery begins with humility."

Emmaline said, "Well done. But do you understand what that means? I suppose I didn't at your age. It takes some hard scrapes to free yourself from arrogance and pride."

"So, your big secret is to listen to people tell their stories? That's it?"

"It helps to serve coffee or tea and offer baked goods. But yes."

Abby nodded. "Okay, I've seen you do that. But Grandma, you're always asking people to tell you their stories, but it seems to me that you never tell anyone anything about yourself."

Emmaline paused before saying, "Just promise me you'll think about what I just said."

Abby nodded. But she wasn't focused on what Emmaline had just said, but rather on what she, Abby, had just said about her grandma. Because it was true. Even an epiphany. Epiphany was one of her spelling bee words. But she couldn't remember its etymology.

2

Abby was putting Freddy through his paces on the college green, showing off for her mom as well as her grandma.

Both Belva Ann and Emmaline rewarded Abby with high praise.

Freddy was rewarded by an enthusiastic tennis ball session.

It was clear when Belva Ann stood next to Abby that indeed the "apple had not fallen far from the tree," in a physical sense at least. The two were tall and squarely built while still being spare of flesh. This used to be referred to as being "raw boned." The sharpness of their frames, however, was softened by more delicate facial features. They had large hands and feet to go with their long legs. Belva Ann joked that her large feet meant she "would not tip over in a strong wind." And there *was* something anchoring about being in Belva Ann's presence.

Someday, Abby and Belva Ann would have silver hair like Emmaline, but that day was far in the future. Emmaline's silver mane, thick and wavy, was a distinctive feature. Belva Ann and Abby had the same thickness and wave, but in a light brown shade. Abby and Belva Ann also shared the same fair complexion that required repeated applications of sunblock all summer long. Emmaline did not. Emmaline never seemed to get sunburned.

In other families, it might be said that Abby and Belva Ann's complexion took after Emmaline's husband's family. But that was not something ever mentioned by Emmaline or Belva Ann because Emmaline had never married. Belva Ann never knew her father or his family. This mystery intrigued Abby. But she had long since learned not to ask direct questions. This was a mystery she would need to solve by other means.

As usual, Abby kept one ear open to Belva Ann and Emmaline's conversation while they strolled along College Avenue toward home. Freddy was still carrying his tennis ball lightly in his mouth, his tongue lolling out the side.

Belva Ann was saying, "Abby says you've made some decisions about the topic of your new book."

Emmaline replied, "Not exactly. I am still waiting for that moment that always comes. The moment where I choose whose story needs me the most."

Belva Ann smiled. "The voice in the night?"

"You remember."

"I miss those days."

"Darling, you were the best research assistant ever. I miss those days too."

Abby interjected, "Voice in the night? Grandma, is that like communing with the dead? Like a séance?"

Belva Ann realized Abby was listening. "What? No, dear. Grandma has a process."

Emmaline explained, "It's like this. When I read diaries, letters, interviews, and so on, I often feel people are speaking directly to me, telling me the trauma they lived, the injustices they endured, the dramas of their time.

"I can't undo the harm or injustice that was done to them

in their lifetimes. But I can try to give them a voice in my own time, even if it is only in the form of a story, a work of fiction. But it's not easy to decide whose story to tell. Sadly, there is no shortage of injustices from which to choose."

Belva Ann added, "Part of a researcher's job is to help find those compelling stories. Stories that matter. It can be overwhelming, narrowing the field. Someone's voice will be central. Others will become subplots or supporting characters, and some will get left out."

"Grandma, how do you decide?"

Emmaline said, "A voice in the night. The answer seems to come to me in the night. And that voice is often insistent, nagging even. And then I know."

Abby said, "I'd like that to happen to me."

Just then Freddy stopped up short, and he dropped his precious tennis ball. The hackles rose on his back, and he began to tremble and growl.

Emmaline warned, "Kitty-cat, three o'clock. You know what to do."

Abby gave a short upward tug on the leash and said, "SIT, STAY!" Freddy obeyed but began to mix whining into his growling. Abby stepped in front of him and tapped her own nose. "Look at me, Freddy." Freddy quickly looked at her then tried to peer around her.

Emmaline softly crooned, "Freddy, Kitty-cats are our friends. Kitty-cats are our friends."

Freddy tried to get up, Abby commanded, "SIT!" And he tried. But he was so rigid in his joints that he looked like it had become impossible, his tail was curled tightly between his legs while urine dripped on the pavement.

Emmaline walked over and picked the cat up, cradling it against her body. She walked over to a short rock wall and placed the cat on the other side of it.

"Out of sight, out of mind."

Abby commanded, "HEEL." and the party marched off. Emmaline retrieved the tennis ball as Freddy was far too anxious to do so.

Once they had "made tracks," Freddy and company slowed down. Then Abby gave him a moment to squat like a puppy on the grass. He emptied his bladder while looking nervously over his shoulder. Then they proceeded at a more leisurely pace.

Emmaline said, "Good work, Abby."

Belva Ann said, " I'll never understand why that huge dog is afraid of cats."

Abby said, "A memory. Terry says that animals think in pictures. Seeing a cat brings up a traumatic picture that produces the same chemicals in his body as if the trauma is happening again."

Emmaline added, "PTSD. Like he's watching a scene from a horror movie over and over again, except he was part of that scene."

Abby continued, "Terry said we can't block every bad memory. And we can't stop the bad chemicals from flooding into his bloodstream. But by giving him something to do, we can distract him from his bad memory and replace it with something better. Over time, it will get better. Terry said when it's 100%, Freddy will obey without thinking. That's why I must train, train, train, train, until he obeys without thinking."

Emmaline said, "PTSD is exactly the same for humans. Except of course, humans have more understanding of what is happening to them."

Belva Ann added, "And more guilt about not being able to cope."

Emmaline said, "He's improved a lot. He used to nearly knock Abby over, pee all over himself, and make a lot more noise."

Emmaline added, "You watch… someday a kitty is going to be his friend. For real."

Belva Ann said, "You really think so?"

Abby said, "Maybe if we started with a kitten."

Emmaline sighed, "Abby, we are NOT getting a kitten, even though I'm quite fond of cats. Freddy is more than enough for the both of us."

Belva Ann laughed, "Don't look at me either. I love cats, but your dad is not a cat person."

Abby looked dismayed. "Did I say I wanted a kitty?"

Belva Ann said, "I really wouldn't mind, it's just it would be terribly unfair to both the dog and the cat."

Abby added thoughtfully, "Well, I'm not asking for a kitty, not now, only when I know for sure that Freddy would accept a kitty as a member of the family."

* * *

Emmaline and Belva Ann sipped coffee at the small kitchen table in the guest house, while Abby pulled out a notebook from her backpack and sat sideways in an upholstered chair.

Abby said, "Okay, I'm ready, Grandma."

"I'll say them, write them down the best you can, then look them up. Okay?"

"Okay."

"Learn the difference between Semantic and Semitic. Adverse and Averse. Compliment and complement. Principal (he is your pal, so spell it that way) and principle. Systemic and systematic. That's enough for now."

Abby intently scrawled away, Freddy at her feet working assiduously with his tongue at a rubber toy stuffed with peanut butter.

When she finished, she showed her notebook to Emmaline who nodded distractedly.

Abby then got another notebook out of her backpack and flipped to the middle.

Emmaline was saying to Belva Ann, "You hate your job. Quit."

"I can't make that kind of money doing anything else."

Emmaline pressed her lips together and looked at the ceiling for a moment. Then said, "You could start by co-authoring a book with me or strike out on your own. I can help make up the difference if your expenses exceed income."

"That would go over like a lead balloon with Jim. He already thinks you do too much. We live in a house that is rightfully yours, rent free, and you provide free childcare, too."

"Don't be silly. That mortgage was paid off decades ago. You pull your weight with expenses and taxes. Besides, I don't want to live alone in that big house. I love the privacy and size of the guest cottage. But my point is that you should be engaged in writing what interests you. You are talented. As far as my afternoons with Abby, well, I am the luckiest grandma I know, getting to be part of Abby's daily life. That is not childcare."

Belva Ann placed her large hand over Emmaline's smaller one and squeezed it. She said, "To be honest, Mom, I think he is jealous of how close we three are. But, in a way, that's why I don't feel like I can quit that mind-numbing job of mine. It's a concession to Jim. And even though he blows hard, he worries about his own job security. I just don't think the time is right."

Belva Ann looked over at Abby, who appeared deeply absorbed in her work, her pen flowing over the page at top speed. Then she looked back at her mother. "Abby is dead serious about this spelling bee."

Emmaline said, "She hated coming in second place last summer."

Belva Ann leaned in and lowered her voice. "Do you think it's healthy? The way she wants to beat last year's winner seems, oh, like revenge. And then this stuff at school where she's doing office work for Joy Wilson, instead of being in the classroom. Abby isn't kidding when she claims the teacher hates her. I think she might be right. I don't get it. To me, Abby is this great kid who inherited our love of words and language. She has more discipline than most adults I know."

Belva Ann lowered her voice to a whisper. "Jim thinks she's socially maladapted."

Emmaline shook her head, "Absurd. And I don't think there is anything worrisome about her investing so much energy into winning the spelling bee. She may win it. Or better yet, she may lose again. Life has a way of doling out lessons in humility. Either way, she's expanding her vocabulary. She also has an affinity for aphorisms, just like we do. Sometimes she exhibits a remarkably sharp wit for her age. Granted, she is socially awkward, which isn't necessarily a terrible thing, at least with the boys. Repelling boys and men is a protective superpower."

"Was I that cocky?"

"You? Never. Me? Oh, yes. Afraid so."

Abby was reading over whatever it was she had been writing. She had been furiously scratching away at her notebook, drawing lines through, and rewriting, filling the page. She scratched something out and drew an arrow to the margin, turned the notebook sideways and kept writing.

Emmaline said, "Abby, did you look up those words?"

"I finished that a long time ago."

"What are you writing?"

"A story. I'm rewriting. It's like my third draft."

"Care to share?"

Abby pressed her lips together, then said, "Well, okay, since this bit is pretty polished. But don't judge."

Belva Ann turned her head slightly so that Abby would not see her smile at her mother who was suppressing a laugh.

Emmaline took the notebook and said, "I would never! The important thing is that when you have an idea, you let it run free across the page. We tame it later."

Abby nodded her head, her brow furrowed. She said, "I know. You taught me that. In the first go-round, the words wanted out. I let them out and they took off running. I could barely keep up."

Emmaline said, "I love it when that happens!"

Emmaline's first read through was done silently, with

Abby at her elbow. As she read, she placed her hand around Abby's waist and drew her close. Then she passed the paper over to Belva Ann.

Emmaline smiled, "This is great. You've got the gift."

Then she said to Belva Ann, "Let Abby hear you read it aloud. You're a talented voice actor."

Belva Ann first read it silently to herself. Then she cleared her throat, and her eyebrows lifted. She began to read in a voice Abby had not heard since the days her mom would read her a bedtime story.

Belva Ann was good.

But Abby was too.

Belva Ann read, *"The witch drew the hood of her cape over her wild grey locks and slowly twirled while she chanted in low tones. She was not sure if her incantation was correct, as she mouthed the words, words she had been carefully gathering these long winter months.*

Her black wolf began to circle her in the opposite rotation. He curled his body around her legs. His growls, low and continuous, like a song, were punctuated by howls as he lifted his chin toward the sky, his golden-eyes glowing.

As woman and dog continued to rotate in opposite directions, the sun set behind the horizon, and the moon appeared, as golden as the eyes of the wolf. When it broke free of the shadow of the earth, the dog and the woman stopped turning.

No message, no magic occurred. She had failed yet again. The witch removed her cloak and spread it on the ground. Then wolf and witch sat side-by-side upon it, to gaze at the golden orb.

The witch spoke to the wolf, "Am I still unworthy? I once was worthy. But that was a long time ago."

And then she stroked the wolf upon his head, which he rested on her thigh, sighing.

She said, "There was only one who I was ever bound to, and I must regain his favor. But how? I released him once. Perhaps I gave away all rights to him forever. Or not. We will try again, for the sun will set and the moon will rise, and each day is but another chance."

The wolf continued his gaze, absorbed in her words, whether or not he caught their meaning."

Belva Ann had finished and was struck dumb as she set the notebook on the table.

Emmaline said, "I'm the witch?"

Abby grinned. "And Freddy is the wolf."

Belva Ann finally found words. "Abby this is amazing. Do you have any idea where the story is going?"

Abby said, "I don't. I'm working on it. But I'm thinking there will be a dragon, a fire-breathing dragon. I know that much."

* * *

That night at dinner, Belva Ann looked grim. She said she had an announcement.

"Oh, Abby, bad news. I had a letter from camp. They sent back our deposit. They've had trouble this year with staffing. So, they've had to reduce the number of campers. They gave preference to campers according to seniority. Since you've only attended one time, I'm afraid you had no seniority."

Abby shrugged her shoulders. She said, "That's OK."

Jim frowned. He said, "Well, knock me over with a feather. You've been laser focused on the spelling bee and how you were going to have your name on that perpetual trophy, beat the girl who beat you last year. You don't seem all that upset that now you're not going."

Abby looked annoyed, "Dad, I was going to win and sure, I was going to get my name on that trophy. No question. But I never really liked camp, so I'm okay with no camp this summer."

Her dad was shaking his head, "Your mother and I can't just leave you at home all summer. You are going to a summer camp; it's just not going to be this camp."

Abby crossed her arms, "Mom used to help Grandma by being her research assistant. I don't see why I can't do the same thing this summer."

Jim said, "Out of the question. I'm going to find you a camp. I don't care if it's soccer, tennis, badminton, volleyball, water sports, you're going to go somewhere."

Belva Ann's shoulders slumped in disbelief. "Abby, I can't believe you didn't like camp. I mean, last year I understood your anxiety about going. It was all new. You got homesick. But I was under the impression that you were enthusiastic this year."

"There were parts that were okay, like the spelling bee. But I didn't like any of the kids and they didn't like me. The best part was getting to play Lady Macbeth. You know I like acting."

"You played Lady MacBeth? You never said."

"We got to pick excerpts to act out. Just short bits."

"Out, out, damned spot?"

"No. I did the part where she's making MacBeth murder the king."

31

Jim was scowling. "For God's sake. That's gruesome stuff. Maybe it's a good thing she's going somewhere else."

"Dad, I'm not going to go to some camp for dumb jocks."

Jim replied, "Abby, if I'm lucky enough to find one that can take you, you're going. End of discussion."

Abby leaned back in her chair and said, "Nope."

Belva Ann reached across to touch her daughter's hand.

"Sweetheart, we'll figure something out that works for everyone."

Belva Ann changed the subject. "Jim, Abby and I had a lovely day with Emmaline. I'm so proud of how well Abby has trained Freddy. And mom is getting closer to starting her new novel. It's exciting. And Abby is writing, too! And she is *so* good!"

Abby shook her head at her mom. Belva Ann understood Abby did not want her to go there.

Jim was tapping his fingers against the tablecloth. "Emmeline is about to get very busy. Once she starts writing, she spends hours sitting in one spot completely absorbed in her task. The last thing she needs is to babysit Abby all summer. Plus, it is not healthy for a young person to spend the summer stuck inside. Kids need to be out moving."

Abby whined, "Dad, we take long walks; we throw the ball for Freddy. Grandma believes in physical exercise. I can be her research assistant. Mom used to do it. Grandma didn't send her off to camp, and she turned out okay, right?"

Jim said, "Abby this is not your decision. Help your mother clean the kitchen. I need to look online for options."

Belva Ann tried to reassure her daughter while they cleaned up the kitchen that things would sort themselves out.

But Abby, in return, had set her jaw. She held up a dish like Scarlett O'Hara brandishing a turnip and announced dramatically, "I am not a jock, I will never be a jock, and sending me to a sports camp would be child abuse and probably cause permanent psychological damage."

Belva Ann laughed so hard she had to lean against the kitchen counter and then blow her nose on a paper napkin.

Belva Ann wiped her eyes with the same napkin and said, "I bet you were a great Lady Macbeth."

Abby said meekly, "I thought I was great. The other kids, not-so-much."

When Abby went to bed, she turned off her light but then got up and went into her closet. The walls were thin at the back of her closet. It had probably been a later addition to the room, because she knew that in the olden days, rooms didn't have closets. Instead, they had big pieces of furniture called wardrobes. Abby knew this because she had read, "*The Lion, the Witch and the Wardrobe*" series by CS Lewis, multiple times. But she had learned by chance that if she went into her closet and the air conditioning duct was open, she could hear what her parents were saying. Or at least she could hear what her dad was saying. Belva Ann had a softer voice. But once her dad got rolling, his voice was loud. Especially like now, when they were having a heated discussion.

Jim was saying, "Stop calling it camp 'Ship-'em-off.' Good God! Summer camp is a privilege, not child abuse."

Abby could hear a bit of her mom's reply.

"...Mom's research assistant... not a bad thing. ...time and energy... Mom ...spelling bee. I haven't seen you... vocabulary, etymologies, definitions, spelling."

Then her dad said, "Annie, your mother has been very generous. I realize those historical novels of hers have been successful commercially, that's great. But Emmeline focuses on unsavory bits of history. Salacious. Violent. That's what Abby would be helping Emmaline research. Our kid should be out with other 12-year-old girls kicking a soccer ball and playing with dolls. Isn't that what most normal 12-year-olds do?"

Abby couldn't hear what her mom was saying.

Then she heard her father say something she had never heard before, and it was a bombshell.

"Emmaline is not exactly some harmless old granny. Why the big secret about who your dad is? She always says you were no oopsie. That she is not ashamed of being an unwed mom. That she got pregnant with you on purpose. It's all so insane. I'm sorry to bring up a sore subject, but it does say something about the impulsiveness of your mother."

Abby could not hear what her mother said in response.

Her father said, "I know she loves Abby. And yes, she's helped Abby achieve straight A's. Well of course she's educated, but she never finished her dissertation. Why is that? Who quits that close to the finish line? Close but no cigar! She should be Dr. Sparks and teaching full-time at a college. Instead, she got pregnant and then came back home to let her parents provide everything... and never left."

Belva Ann said something.

Jim raised his voice in exasperation, "You don't get it. She wants you to quit your job and depend on her entirely, just like she did with her parents."

Abby found herself leaning even closer to the vent. She felt her face warm, because as much as she wanted her dad to be wrong, on that point she knew he was not wrong. Still, she wanted to hear her mother defend Emmaline. But the only voice she could hear clearly was her dad's.

"Honey, Emmeline clearly has a problem with men. What she did was self-sabotage. What your mother did was bonkers. She's bonkers."

Abby knew her mom's daddy, her mystery grandpa, was a subject that was off-limits. But being off-limits had made Abby even more determined to know more. Belva Ann had a father. Emmaline had made her mother with someone. Didn't her mom want to know more? Abby wanted to know Emmaline's story. She felt certain that in time, she would know. She would piece things together. Abby now had new information. Her Grandma had stopped short of finishing her PhD. That did sound bonkers. But she also knew her Grandma wasn't bonkers. Her dad was wrong about that. Abby also didn't think her grandma had a problem with men. Just because she hadn't found someone else, it didn't mean she had a problem.

Her Grandma had written *"Sharp Elbows, Loud Voices"* about women fighting for the right to vote. Abby knew that Emmaline had been named for Emmeline Pankhurst, the suffragette. Emmaline had even joked that writing that book had been pre-ordained. Emmaline had carried on the tradition by naming Belva Ann after one of the first female attorneys in America, Belva Ann Lockwood. Abby was named for Abigail Adams, who had told her husband John to "Remember the ladies" as the Founding Fathers enshrined the rights of citizens into the Constitution. But John Adams had NOT remembered the ladies, had not enshrined equal rights for women in the Constitution.

As a man of his time, he was incapable of understanding the need. But Emmaline and Belva Ann and now Abby, *they* would remember. All of that meant that all of them were destined to be strong women. Her Grandma had told her so. None of that meant any of them had a problem with men. No, her Grandma was not bonkers.

But what had happened to Emmaline that had made her give up her degree and not stay with Belva Ann's daddy? Emmaline had not yet told her story. Which only caused Abby to make up her own. She imagined her grandma had been separated from the love of her life somehow. She imagined he could have been a famous man, a movie star even. And for sure, very handsome.

Abby realized a couple of things. First, that she was not going to hear anything more from her parents tonight. But she also knew she was not going to sleep much either. She had work to do on her own behalf. She had no intention of attending any new "camp ship-em-off." But she needed to state her case convincingly to her dad without blowing her cover as a spy.

When Abby woke up, she was relieved it was Sunday, because after an exhausting night of research and writing and then rehearsing what she would say, well, she was pooped. As soon as she cleaned up this mess about going to camp, she could have a walk with Grandma and Freddy and then nap.

Her mom and dad were sitting at the breakfast table when she came down. Dad had his laptop on the table with a notebook open next to it. He held a pen that he was nervously tapping on the paper as he read from the screen.

Belva Ann looked up from her coffee, "Hey, sleepyhead."

Abby flashed her the peace sign.

"You want eggs?"

"Nope. I'm having a bagel with vegan cream cheese and blueberry compote."

Her dad finally looked up from the screen. "Hey, look at this." He rotated the laptop to show her a photo of kids' white-water rafting. Abby was about to roll her eyes but stopped herself. Instead, she went into the kitchen and put a bagel in the toaster. She let her parents whisper to each other while she waited for the bagel to toast and made a cup of hot tea with honey. Once her bagel was done, Abby took her time to spread her cream cheese and blueberry compote.

When she sat down, Belva Ann said, "Wow, that looks good."

"There's more if you want one."

"Thanks, sweetheart. I've already eaten."

Jim took a conciliatory tone, "I'm sorry about your camp. I realize it was a shock for all of us last night. We had counted on you going. That's all. Life throws us a curve ball from time to time. We can adjust. We can make new plans."

"Daddy, I've adjusted, and I've made new plans."

Belva Ann said, "But what will you do this summer? We need childcare of some kind, at least during the day when we're at work."

"I'll stay here with Emmaline and Freddy. Just like I do now. I want to write a novel. Like Grandma."

Jim said, "Abby..."

Abby said, "It'll be age-appropriate; I promise."

Jim looked at Belva Ann "Do other twelve-year-olds use terms like 'age-appropriate?'"

Abby said, "I'm just repeating your own words."

Belva Ann fought back a smile. "Jim, let's wait and see what Mom says."

Jim put both palms on the table and pushed his chair back. "Abby needs to learn how to relate to her own peer group."

Jim turned to Abby, "Who is your best friend at school these days?"

Abby answered with a question, "Who is your best friend at work?"

Jim threw up his hands.

Abby said, "You once told me it's lonely at the top."

Belva Ann stifled a laugh.

Jim said, "It wouldn't hurt to have friends."

Abby said, "'To thine own self be true.' Right? That's Shakespeare, too, I think."

Belva Ann said, "Hamlet? We can look up the entire quote."

Jim moaned.

Belva Ann said, "Later."

Belva Ann sat up straighter and asked, "How about we find a camp for young writers? Or drama? Is there such a place? Abby, would you be open to that idea?"

"I'd consider it."

Belva Ann turned to her husband, hands in the air, "I'm a genius. Okay, Jim, you work on that angle, but as it is still a long shot, especially at this late date, let's be sure to talk to Mom STAT. She expected Abby to be at camp for the entire summer, too."

3

Belva Ann and Abby walked across the backyard to Emmaline's cottage.

Belva Ann was saying, "Let me explain to Mom what's going on."

"I don't see why it's a big deal."

Belva Ann stopped Abby by putting a hand on her shoulder. "Sweetheart, Grandma adores her time with you, but she also has a life of her own. This is a big ask. It's not her job to be responsible for you all summer, and you can't be responsible for yourself yet. That time will come soon enough for us all. But for now, you have us. Of course, I promise to take your wishes into consideration, I always do."

"Dad doesn't."

"He's trying to do what's best."

"Except that he doesn't know what that is."

"Promise to let me do the talking, you stay out of this for now."

Abby nodded, and they continued to walk to the guest house and knocked on the door.

Before Freddy could start barking, Abby opened the door, and Freddy came bounding out. Abby sat down and let him do his weird greeting ritual, "grrrrrr. whoooooo. eeeeeeee. grrrrrr." Freddy went through his various vocalizations. Some sounded fierce, some funny. The display always made Abby laugh. Freddy wrapped himself around Abby in a frenzy of happiness, then flopped over on the grass, kicking his legs in the air as Abby rubbed his tummy.

Finally, he quieted, tongue lolling out the side of his mouth, head tipped up so he could see Abby. His golden eyes gave him a look of utter derangement. He pushed a front paw against her thigh.

Abby was cooing, "I was going to miss you so much. But now I won't have to leave you at all."

Emmaline had come to the door, but the whistle of her electric tea kettle caused her to turn around.

Abby and Freddy got up and followed Belva Ann into the house.

Emmaline said, "Tea anyone?"

Abby thought the place was even messier than usual, if that was possible.

Belva Ann had noticed. "Did we catch you in the middle of something?"

Emmaline ignored her, "You still like Constant Comment?"

Belva Ann smiled, "Of course. Ever since you told me it was named after me."

Abby said, "Hey! Grandma, you told me it was named after *me*!"

Emmaline pulled out three mugs from her cabinet and said, "What did I teach you about novelists?"

Belva Ann and Abby answered in chorus, "They're liars."

Emmaline called for the second verse, "But liars who..."

Again, together, "Reveal great truths!"

"Well done! Milk, no sugar. Here you go."

Emmaline placed a plate of ginger snaps on the table alongside the tea and sat down.

Belva Ann asked, "Any voices in the night yet?"

Emmaline took a nibble of her cookie and followed it with a sip of tea. "Not yet. But I'm meeting some fascinating characters."

"You can't reveal more than that?"

Emmaline smiled, "Ideas are shy things before they are fully formed. Can't scare the muse away, and all that sort of rubbish."

Belva Ann shrugged, "You don't believe it's rubbish, neither do I. But by the stacks of papers and books around here, I can tell you are hot on the trail of some story."

Emmaline nodded, "True."

Freddy had his head on Abby's lap. She had quietly fed him a ginger snap. He rolled his bright amber eyes up at her and slowly wagged his tail, hoping for another. Abby kissed him on the top of his head.

Emmaline changed topics, "Abby, I thought we could go over roots again today. I've found a few tough words for you. I know you can noodle out the meaning and the correct spelling if you rely on your knowledge of roots."

Abby looked over at her mom and raised her eyebrows to give her the prod she clearly needed.

Belva Ann announced, "Spelling bee is off."

Emmaline's mouth fell open, her hand went to her chest. "What? No! How can that be?"

Belva Ann said, "Our deposit check for camp was returned to us yesterday. The camp is so understaffed this year that they had to reduce the number of campers."

Emmaline huffed, "A likely story!"

"Mom, I have no reason to doubt the story. There's a labor shortage everywhere. Anyway, that's that. They gave priority to those children who had been attending the camp the longest. We're out."

Emmaline turned to Abby. "I'm sorry to hear it. But none of that work we did was a waste of time. And if you want to compete in another spelling bee, we can find one for you next school year."

"That's okay, Grandma. I've decided I want to be a writer. That's my focus now."

"So, you want to join the family business?"

"Not the kind of writing Mom does. No offense, Mom. I want to write stories like Grandma."

Emmaline smiled at Belva Ann. "Your mother writes stories, too. Wonderful stories."

Belva Ann said, "Used to. But they were rejected by basically everyone."

Emmaline swatted that comment away, "So, then, what's the new plan for your summer, Abby?"

Belva Ann answered for Abby before little Miss "Constant Comment" could take over.

"No decisions yet. What about your summer, Mom?"

Emmaline took a long sip of tea, draining her cup. Then she said, "Anyone up for a second cup? Or should we take Freddy to campus? He's been restless all morning."

Abby said, "C'mon, Freddy, let's go."

Abby grabbed a tennis ball, then clipped Freddy's leash on his collar, and the three left their teacups on the table and headed for campus with a bouncy German Shepherd.

Abby strategically gave her mom and her Grandma some space as she and Freddy led the walk. But not so much space that her ears wouldn't catch their conversation in case she felt the need to intervene on her own behalf.

Emmeline said, "I have news, too. I *did* make plans for the summer."

"What kind of plans?"

"I rented a house outside of Charlottesville, Virginia."

Abby had to force herself not to turn around, not to look at her mother. Because the prolonged silence was hard to interpret. Her mom, the other "constant commenter" was not commenting. Abby found herself slowing Freddy's steps, sensing her mother had stopped walking.

Emmaline said, "Is that a problem?"

Belva Ann said, "Who goes to Charlottesville in the summertime? It's hot and humid. Not to mention what went on there in recent history. Oh my God, Mom. You are *not* writing about that, are you?"

"Calm down. No. I'm writing historical fiction. Which *is* relevant to current events. Always true, although one doesn't have to make those connections. Not all readers do. Mostly I hope to write a compelling story. But if you're asking if the place I've chosen to spend my summer has relevance to my project, it does."

"Why not wait and go in the fall? Virginia is beautiful in the fall."

"This summer seemed like perfect timing. I expected Abby to be at camp. And I thought the University grounds wouldn't be as crowded during the summer. Anyway, the house is special, historic, and available. They'll let me bring Freddy. I totally overpaid for it and made a huge non-refundable pet deposit. People back east always add a 'California surcharge.' They know we pay higher rents here and won't question it. And I didn't. I'm excited. I haven't lived there since graduate school."

Belva Ann sighed, "I've never been. I've read a lot on Jefferson, and watched so many documentaries and movies, probably because of you. Remember when the DNA evidence came out about Sally Hemings? Her children carried Jefferson's DNA, that got passed down through the generations. Wild."

"You'd love the house I rented. You love history as much as I do. Surely you can get away for a visit. The house is spacious."

"Our vacation days are limited. In the meantime, we'll need to find another camp for Abby to attend."

Emmaline added, "You should try one of the private schools."

Belva Ann said, "A boarding school?"

"Certainly. Or a day school. You might have to juggle it with a babysitter filling in the gaps."

"Jim's been looking at sports camps."

Emmaline shook her head. "You'll have a rebellion on your hands."

Belva Ann was silent.

Emmaline said, "Now, drama classes would be just the ticket. Drama, studying history, or writing. That's where our girl would thrive."

"Jim's in the house right now working the phone, trying to figure something out. Perhaps I need to go monitor him to prevent him from signing Abby up for girl's rugby or some such."

Emmaline laughed.

Belva Ann joined in.

Abby wilted.

Her mother had not asked.

And Emmaline had not offered.

She was doomed.

* * *

Later when they returned to the big house, they found Jim sitting at the dining table, laptop open, coffee mug at his elbow.

Belva Ann said, "Any luck?"

He shook his head.

"Emmaline suggested private schools. Most have summer sessions of some kind."

"Yes, I thought of that, too. I found a program that looks excellent, but even if we could get her in, the tuition is exorbitant."

Abby couldn't help herself, she said, "That's a great word, Dad. "Ex' means out of, and 'orbit' means orbit. So, 'exorbitant' means out of orbit. Does the word end with 'a-n-t' or 'e-n-t'?'

Jim Woods looked at his daughter as if he just noticed she was present. "What?"

Belva Ann answered, "I believe it is 'a-n-t,' but I recommend you look it up. I'm not always right."

Jim scowled, "Those sorts of prices are exclusionary by design. Keeping out the hoi-polloi."

Jim looked at Abby and said a bit smugly, "Go look *that* one up."

"Grandma already taught me that one. It means 'the many' but it has come to mean 'the great unwashed,' or the common people. Grandma taught me to remember the meaning by saying that the hoity-toity always look down on the hoi-pol-loi."

Belva Ann smiled, "Mom has really expanded her vocabulary!"

"Grandma says that words are like a painter's palette. A writer needs a large palette of words. I'm going to be a writer."

Belva Ann said, "And choosing the right words to paint a vivid picture is a craft as well as an innate gift."

Jim said, "Emmaline down in the cottage busily painting away, is she?"

Belva Ann said, "Actually, she told me she's rented a house for the summer in Charlottesville, Virginia."

"Why would she do something like that?"

Belva Ann said, "Charlottesville is one of her old haunts. That's where she did her undergraduate and most of her graduate work."

Jim said, "What's that got to do with the price of bread?" Then he shot Abby a look that said, "Don't even dream of interrupting."

Belva Ann said, "It has something to do with her top-secret project. She won't say yet what it is."

"Afraid spies are listening in?"

Belva Ann replied, "Now you're just being snarky."

Jim said, "She could have let us know before now."

"Mom doesn't have to ask our permission to rent a

house elsewhere for the summer. With Abby going to camp, her taking a house in another town, well, it would have given us a bit of privacy. Did it occur to you to think of it like that?"

Jim looked at his computer screen. It had timed out and shut down. "Sorry. I'm just flummoxed about what to do for Abby. Could you work from the house this summer? You can do that easier than I can. I have to be able to travel to sites."

"I can't work from home and be engaged in activities with Abby at the same time."

Jim sighed, "We'll just have to hire sitters."

Abby had taken a seat, crossed her arms across her chest, brow furrowed. She thought her parents were useless.

She was going to have to take the matter into her own hands.

* * *

Monday afternoon, Abby walked out of Pepper Tree Elementary to see the silver-haired witch leaning against a large and gnarly tree of the same name. Her large black wolf had already spotted Abby, fixed his glowing eyes on her, and had started to dance from paw to paw, throwing his head back and singing to her. "whoooooooo-whooooooooo-whoooooooo!"

Emmaline pushed herself from the tree, and Abby, who insisted she had no athletic ability, in one swift and fluid motion, sprinted to Freddy, threw her backpack to the ground, and slid to her knees. Freddy began his wiggly circle-hug with a chorus of vocalizations.

Emmaline said, "Last week of school. You going to make it?"

Abby grabbed her backpack and got up, taking the leash from Emmaline. "Of course. I have perfect attendance, and I'm a straight A student."

"One who is not welcomed to return to the classroom. You omitted that bit."

"I like working for Ms. Wilson."

Emmaline smiled, "I like her, too. She has a great sense of humor and the patience of a saint. But she is not certified to teach. You may glide over the finish line this year, Abby, but unless you learn how to be a help and not a hindrance to your teacher, well, you know what they say the definition of insanity is?"

"Wait, I know this one."

Emmaline didn't wait. "Doing the same thing over and over again, expecting different results."

"Oh."

"My point being that it is *you* who must change, not the entire structure of American public education."

"Oh."

They both got quiet.

Emmaline smiled again, "Let's go get our croissants."

Emmaline, Abby, and Freddy began their stroll to the village. Emmaline worried that she had hurt Abby's feelings. But when she looked over at her granddaughter, she noticed a slight upturn to the corners of Abby's lips.

They got to the bakery and Abby and Freddy took their usual places at an outside table. Emmaline brought out the croissants and Freddy's biscuit and their teas.

Once they were sorted, Abby said, "Some girl scout camp is going to be a total waste of a summer."

Emmaline tipped her head, "Ah. Is that what is planned? You might like it."

Abby frowned, "Not a snowball's chance in hell."

Emmaline said, "Where'd you hear that one?"

"Dad."

Emmaline suppressed a smile.

Abby said, "You know, we make an awesome team, you and me, prepping for the bee."

"You and I."

"See. You are always teaching me something!"

Emmaline sat back in her chair and took a sip of tea, narrowing her eyes. "Buttering me up?"

"And you're smarter than anyone else I know."

"Definitely buttering me up. Where is this going?"

"Grandma, it's about 'who' as much as it is 'where.'"

Abby could see "the penny drop." But Emmaline was not smiling.

"If you're asking what I think you are asking, the answer is no."

"I could take care of Freddy for you."

"I don't think that's necessary."

"But what if you have to go somewhere where he isn't welcome? You know he hates to be left alone. Who is going to keep up his obedience sessions?"

"Hmmm."

"And I could be your assistant, just like Mom used to be."

"Hmmm."

"You ask Ms. Wilson about my labels and filing. You've

seen how fast I am on the internet and on the keyboard. I type as fast as you do. Let me type up all your notes and put them into labelled file folders."

Emmaline gently shook her head, then some woman stopped by their table with a copy in her hand of Emmaline's latest. She even brought a pen with her. Emmaline signed the book, while the woman said flattering things about the novel before saying good-bye. Abby had seen this happen before, and it always made her proud of her Grandma.

Emmaline and Abby then finished their snacks and made their usual trek up College Avenue. Then they walked to their favorite ball tossing quad. Freddy chased down the tennis ball, thrown by Emmaline, until he flopped down on the grassy bank, not so tired that he didn't merrily slide down on his side. But he was ready to walk back to the guest house with Abby and Emmaline.

When they entered the guest house, Abby looked at the many piles of papers and books scattered all over the floor and stacked on shelves and tables. She said, "You've needed an assistant. And a housekeeper too. Let me do it, Grandma. It would be fun."

"It's only fun for a very short time, dearest."

"I won't complain. I promise."

"You'll be bored silly. Not just in my rental house, which is not in town but in the boondocks, but on the trip itself. It will take three days there and three days back. A real marathon."

"We can listen to audiobooks and music and have sing-alongs."

Emmaline smiled, "You make it sound like summer camp."

Abby said, "It will be OUR summer camp."

Abby reverted, just for a moment, to the twelve-year-old she really was, saying, "Please, Grandma? Please, please, please. I won't be bored. I have my own writing to work on."

Emmaline smiled because every now and then, Abby forgot to try to sound like a PhD candidate. And it was in those moments that Emmaline's heart melted, and she was afraid it showed. That would only encourage Abby.

It did.

Abby became even more dramatic, "Don't let them send me away to some awful camp, where I have to sleep in a cabin named after some indigenous tribe. A tribe whose land was stolen before they were marched off to a reservation or were forced to convert to Christianity."

Emmaline snorted, "If you say that kind of stuff in front of your father, there truly will not be 'a snowball's chance in hell' he would allow you to come with me. He knows exactly where you get those sorts of ideas. Anyway, I am not your parent. It's not my decision.

Abby paused a moment, then firmly announced, "Grandma, I'm going to load and run your dishwasher."

"Abby, I can do that."

"You do your work, and I'll try to be quiet."

Emmaline sighed. Then nodded.

Abby was delighted. She was going to prove to her Grandma that she was indispensable. I-N-D-I-S-P-E-N-S-A-B-L-E!

The countertops were cluttered, as usual, with dirty mugs and bowls. Abby rinsed them off and loaded them into the dishwasher. Then she wiped down the sticky counters. It was then that she noticed a shard of China on the window ledge by the sink. She picked it up to have a look. It was white and blue, an intense blue. Why would her Grandma keep a broken bit of China? Abby put it back and started the dishwasher.

Then she found scouring powder and sponges and attacked the stove top. She briefly looked inside the oven, but realized it was beyond her skill set. But she found the broom and mop and scrubbed the ancient linoleum floor. She cleaned up her mop and put it and the broom back in the utility closet, then stood back to admire her work. Clean as a whistle. Whatever that meant. She would have to look that up.

Abby picked up the piece of broken China and walked over to her grandmother sitting at her desk and peered over her shoulder. She was writing in a spiral notebook; a hard-bound book was held open by a weighted bookmark next to her.

"I cleaned up your kitchen."

"Thank you, darling."

"Grandma, why did you save this piece of broken China?"

Emmaline swiveled in her chair and took the bit of China from Abby.

Emmaline said, "I didn't save it, I lost it, or thought I had. I had forgotten all about it. It just reappeared. That color is called cobalt blue. Pretty, isn't it?"

"Yes."

"Let me show you something. Here look when I hold it up to the light. See how the white part glows."

"Um."

"It's bone China. Bone China is translucent."

"Grandma, is it made from bones?"

"Actually, as I recall, it has bone ash mixed into the porcelain."

"Human?"

"I should hope not."

"That's spooky."

Emmaline rolled the piece of China around in her palm, then said, "I hadn't thought of it in those terms before. You make it sound sacred. To some folks this is just a bit of trash. For others this bit of broken China could hold meaning."

Emmaline set the piece on her desk, then she rolled her neck around, and said, "I've got such a kink, right here," as she rubbed the base of her neck. "Can you massage that spot?"

Abby may have been a child, with a child's hands, but they were large for her age and very much like her mother's, and as she had seen her mom massage Emmaline's neck, she knew what to do. She rubbed her hands together to warm them, then did her best to mimic Belva Ann.

Emmaline said, "Ooh, that feels great. Deja Vu. You know what that means?"

"Sort of."

"It's a sense of familiarity, although the conscious mind knows the experience is new."

"Okay."

"Belva Ann was my regular masseuse, so to speak, for many years."

"Just like she was your research assistant?"

"Clever girl."

"Did she clean the kitchen so you could work?"

"I see a case being made here."

"Grandma, you need me."

"I've never said that I didn't."

Abby placed her hands together, as if in prayer. "Yes!"

"It's not my decision, just as it's not your decision."

Abby said, "Mom would totally let me go."

"Your parents will make the decision together."

"After you make it sound so good, educational, that they'll agree. If I ask, they'll say I'm like, 'holding a gun to your head' or something like that."

"Oh dear. That does sound violent."

"Grandma, it's an aphorism. I learned it from you!"

"Sounds more like your father."

"Maybe."

Emmaline looked thoughtful. "Well, then, I'll speak to them. But don't count your chickens before they hatch."

"Grandma, 'Time is of the essence.' 'Strike while the iron is hot.'"

Emmaline laughed, "Or before your father puts another deposit down."

Abby said, "Or that."

"Tonight then."

Abby looked serious as she nodded, "Tonight."

4

Emmaline, Abby, Belva Ann, and Freddy stood in the yard between the guest cottage and the big house. Belva Ann was saying to Emmaline, "Oh she already had me sold on the idea, Mom. But this is your summer vacation, and I thought it presumptuous to ask you to change your plans to include a twelve-year-old, even though I know Abby's your all-time-favorite twelve-year-old."

Emmaline said, "To be honest, I hadn't entertained the idea until Abby argued her case so persuasively. I know she wants to be a writer, but I think she's also got the chops for appellate argument, or she could be a judge. I can almost see it. I could crochet her one of those lacey chokers to go over her robes, ala' Ruth Bader Ginsberg."

Emmaline winked.

Belva Ann looked at Abby and said, "What say you, counselor? You could stick up for the little guy, take on powerful evildoers? Be a superhero?"

"Mom, being a lawyer is not like being a superhero."

Emmaline said, "Maybe you need to reconsider what a superhero really is. The greatest good deeds are done without the need for recognition or any kind of fame or fortune. That's why superheroes are portrayed with masks on."

Belva Ann laughed, "Mom, don't write off the benefits of fame or fortune! Consider that most of the fictional superheroes are independently wealthy. Nothing wrong with Abby achieving financial security before she expands her goals to becoming a do-gooder."

Emmaline looked at Abby, "Fair point. Abby, please make enough money so that your folks don't have to sell the house to provide for their old age. It's a grand old house."

Abby shook her head, "I'm twelve. You people are some kind of crazy."

Emmaline said, "Hey, careful who you call crazy, you're 'cut from the same cloth.'"

Abby exclaimed, "I'm going to be a writer!"

Belva Ann touched her mother's arm, "Jim just drove in."

Abby looked at her mom intently and said with feeling, "Mom, screw your courage to the sticking place."

Belva Ann said, "Okay, Lady MacBeth, let's not be too dramatic. We're talking summer vacation, not murder."

Belva Ann called out to Jim, "Hi dear. I just invited Emmaline to join us for dinner. I've got vegetarian chili in the crock pot."

Emmaline rarely ate dinner with them. Even Abby understood at some level that Dad was not a fan of their living arrangement, smack next door to his mother-in-law. Although to Abby it was perfect in every way. But she had noted that her grandma was careful around her dad, and her dad was careful around her grandma. Prickly. A word that sounded exactly like what it meant.

Emmaline and Freddy ran back to the guest house to prepare a treat ball for Freddy. She stuffed it with peanut butter so he would be occupied and calm. Jim was only marginally okay with Freddy coming inside the big house. He shed a lot.

But Freddy was always happier with his family than separated from them. So, Emmaline brought him anyway.

They soon got settled with their bowls of chili at the big oak dining table, with Freddy curling up with his treat ball at their feet.

Belva Ann said to Jim, "Honey, I don't suppose you had time to work on Abby's summer plans today."

Jim shook his head, "I had to put out fires all day. I work with idiots. In fact, my neck is killing me."

Belva Ann said, "I'll be happy to give you a massage later."

"That would be great."

Emmaline pulled out a folded-up piece of paper from her back pocket.

"Have a look. This is the house I rented for the summer. The home was built in 1832."

She slid it over to Jim, who was saying, "Must have been off the beaten path for the Union Army not to have burned it down."

"It is. Plus, it's brick. Brick is so durable. Painted white at some point. The red brick shows through the white paint in a way I find fetching."

Jim said, "Why would a fancy historic house like that be available for rent?"

Jim slid the page over to Belva Ann who said, "Wow, Mom. You've rented Tara!"

"Not Tara, but a fine example of Federal style antebellum architecture. But to your point, Jim, it's been used for student housing for a very long time. That's why it just so happens to be empty this summer. For a history buff like me, it's magical. I'll be basting my prose in its ambiance."

Abby said nothing, but was leaning forward slightly in her chair, spoon hovering over her bowl of chili.

Belva Ann added, "Jim, Mom has graciously offered to take Abby for the summer."

Jim scowled, "How's that going to work?"

Emmaline said, "Ah, there's the operative word, 'work.' I propose that Abby work for me this summer. Of course, I can't pay her. Think of it as an apprenticeship."

Jim looked at each of the women in turn. Then he said, "I see the die has been cast."

Belva Ann said, "Don't be angry, hear us out."

Jim crossed his arms across his chest. Freddy came out from under the table, sat down next to Abby and glared at him.

Jim added, "Good God, even the dog is in on it."

Abby said "Daaaad!" in a way that dragged out the vowel and sounded very much like a dog whining.

Jim added, "I can't help feeling like I rank below the dog around here."

Emmaline said, "I'd be putting her right to work. I've got a lot of packing and cleaning to do before I can leave. Then I've planned a three-day drive and although Abby can't drive, she can keep me alert. But the real work begins after we get to the rental house."

Jim said, "I'm all ears."

"She'll be my dogs body. She's already scrubbed my kitchen better than it's been scrubbed in years. But it will be educational too. Monticello is right there. And the University. And of course, Abby will still oversee Freddy. She can make sure Freddy gets enough exercise, keeps up with his training and avoids Kitty-cats. Freddy will be an asset, too. He looks intimidating at least. He'll keep us quite safe."

Belva Ann said, "Jim, I may take a week off to join them, once they get settled, I mean."

Jim sighed, "I was hoping Abby would mix with her peer group this summer. Maybe even make friends with someone her age. I made lifelong friends at camp. I really feel she is missing out on something important. Abby, don't you want a friend to play with?"

Abby said, "I have Freddy. He's my best friend."

Jim looked defeated.

Belva Ann said, "Darling, Abby will remember this summer for the rest of her life. And frankly, I'm so jealous I can barely stand it."

Jim pushed his chair back and stood up. He said, "Abby, don't make me regret this. Go. Have fun. Be safe."

Abby jumped out of her chair and flung her arms around her father's neck, saying, "Oh Daddy, thank you, thank you, thank you! And Grandma promised to teach me to throw a frisbee, you'll like that because frisbee is a sport. Grandma says she did a lot of it when she went to school there, and she's really good at it, too."

Emmaline laughed. "I may have overstated my prowess to Abby. Not sure I still have the knack. But it was 'de rigueur' back in the day, of course I mostly played with the requisite beer in my other hand."

Jim said, "Scandalous Emmaline. Just scandalous. No beer for Abby, please."

They all laughed, and Freddy barked at the joke too.

* * *

Abby came out of Peppertree Elementary School for the last time as a sixth grader. Her favorite witch and wolf had already spotted her. The other kids were right behind her, loud and giddy with excitement. Girls were hugging other girls, some tearfully.

Abby was not distracted by the displays. She was out of there. She had allowed Ms. Wilson to hug her, but ugh, the woman wore way too much perfume. It nearly closed her throat down.

Next year she would be at Peppertree Middle School. She dreaded going. Why attending such places was compulsory, Abby did not understand. She guessed it was a way to ware-house kids while grownups did real stuff. She could certainly get a better education elsewhere. She hated school and as far as she could tell, the feeling was mutual. But she shook off the thought the way Freddy shook off the rain.

Abby threw her backpack onto the grass with more than her usual vigor, knelt, and opened her arms wide. Freddy snapped his teeth and yodeled the song of his people. Then he performed his ritual dance and curled himself around her. He was welcoming back to the pack a returning member.

"Freddy has been very restless. Funny, but he sensed today was different."

"Freddy, I'm free! I served my time. I'm hanging tight with you and Grandma all summer long!"

Freddy responded by leaning into Abby and slurping her across the face, and Abby hugged him and gave him a loud kiss on top of his head.

Emmaline said, "You two pull yourselves together. Show a certain level of decorum when in public, please."

"Grandma, you are funny."

"Utter abandon has its proper place and time."

"Careful, Grandma, that kind of talk will get you in trouble with dad. I'm only twelve and utter abandon is something I'm not allowed to know about."

"Poppycock. I've seen some of the same movies that you've seen. Far too many of them, I'm sorry to confess."

"What's the etymology of 'poppycock?'"

"I don't know. Why don't you look it up?"

Abby looked down at her phone while she and Emmaline walked toward the village. "Grandma, this is gross."

"Let's hear it."

"It comes from the root words, 'pap' and 'kakka.'"

Emmaline laughed, "Kakka? As in poop?"

"Yup. And 'pap' as in mush."

"Mushy poo?"

"Uh-huh."

Abby and Emmaline laughed together, and Freddy joyfully pranced alongside them.

Suddenly, Freddy skidded to a halt.

Emmaline whispered, "Kitty-cat, twelve o'clock."

Freddy had spun around, knocking into the back of Abby's knees.

"Grandma, oh no, Kitty-cat six o'clock, too."

The two cats were in a crouched position, and growling.

Emmaline said, "For goodness sakes, we are in the middle of a 'shoot-out at the O.K. Corral.' We've got to get across the street."

Freddy had gone rigid with fear, urine puddling beneath him as he cowered against Abby.

Still, Abby knew she could not pull hard on Freddy without sending him into a frenzy. She touched his nose lightly and then touched her own. "Freddy, look at me."

Freddy glanced nervously at Abby. She commanded firmly, "Freddy, heel!"

Abby turned sharply and marched across the street. Emmaline marched too, and Freddy, tail tucked tightly between his legs, with glances over his shoulder, and bumping into Abby's legs, scurried across the street with them, leaving a trail of urine. Abby walked with determined steps toward the village and away from the cats. Behind them, the growls had escalated into shrieks.

Emmaline said, "It sounds serious, keep moving."

Abby said, "I hope there aren't kitty-cats in Virginia."

Emmaline said, "There will always be cats, real and metaphorical. Most are harmless. Some you can befriend. Others you better just cross the street to avoid."

"And if you can't cross the street?"

"Try words."

"And if words don't work."

"Run. Hide until it's safe to come out."

"Grandma, heroes don't run away. They fight."

"No, Abby. No. Sometimes the most heroic action is not to fight at all. True heroism is always based on selflessness. And survival. Not just your own, either."

Abby frowned but said nothing. She knew her Grandma was not just thinking about kitty-cats. The witch and her wolf, well, it seemed they both had fears.

* * *

Abby and Emmaline were hard at work when Belva Ann knocked gently on the door and walked into the guest house.

Abby was sitting on the floor, Freddy sprawled out next to her. Abby had her notebook computer open with several stacks of books on either side of her.

Emmaline too was on the floor, picking up notepapers and looking at each one. Some went into a "keep" pile and some went into a trash can, and some got ripped apart and put into both piles.

"Wow, look at you two."

Emmaline said, "I've allotted three days to pack before we hit the road."

Belva Ann frowned. "Only three days?"

"I think with Abby's help, we can do it."

Abby said, "Most of these books are staying. I'm downloading e-versions for Grandma. The few that aren't available, we ship."

"Very wise, if not exactly inexpensive."

"Abby very kindly gifted me one of her notebook computers. She says it's an extra. I hope you don't mind. She's a whiz about electronics. She was able to get the thing completely set up for me."

"Is there anything I can do to help?"

Emmaline looked up from her paper. "I'm afraid I'm the only one who can decide which of these notes and articles are important."

Belva Ann started to pick one up, but a glance from Emmaline caused her to put it back down. "Still top-secret?"

Emmaline smiled, "Not top secret exactly, just on a 'need to know' basis."

"I'd like to help. If I can."

Emmaline said, "Abby needs your help getting herself packed. The weather, as I recall, is hot as Hades, so mostly shorts and tee shirts, but by the late afternoon there are often incredible storms that cool things down. So, pack jeans, rain gear, and appropriate footwear."

"I suppose it will be no different than packing her for camp. I'll throw in a bathing suit, just in case."

"They have big box stores in Charlottesville. Anything we forget, we can purchase."

Belva Ann looked down at Freddy, "And you, young man, I see you are right in the thick of things." Freddy thumped his tail. "I'm counting on you to be security detail. You are to protect these two from all threats, foreign and domestic."

Emmaline poked a finger in the air and said, "As long as it's not a 'Domestic Short Hair,' we should be fine."

Belva Ann turned to Abby, "Are you really prepared to live with this 24/7?"

Abby grinned, then typed another title into her search box. She said, "Another one that's only ninety-nine cents, Grandma."

Emmaline pumped her fist. "Score!"

Belva Ann asked, "Seriously, isn't there anything I can do?"

Emmaline nodded, "Yes there is. Abby keeps trying to clean. But we need to focus on our task. So, I was wondering if you could hire professional cleaners once we're gone. I can pay them from anywhere, what with this new app Abby set up for me on my phone."

"I can do that."

"Thank you, dearest."

Belva Ann said, "Abby, time to come in for dinner."

"Can I stay awhile and finish these stacks?"

"No. You need to come now."

It pained Belva Ann to see Abby look at Emmaline to confirm she had to obey her.

Belva Ann said, "I'll give her back to you right after breakfast."

Emmaline said, "Wish you were coming with us."

"Me, too. I'll be stuck at my desk, copying and pasting the same boring old text, next to the same boring old photos, in yet another advertisement."

Emmaline raised her eyebrows, "My offer still stands."

* * *

Freddy was hanging his head out the window of the back seat and whining. He was eager to get going.

They had, in fact, packed in three days and were ready to roll.

Dad had helped load the cargo area, arranging and rearranging things so that they fit together snugly, and so that Emmaline and Abby could get their overnight bags out easily when they got to their hotel.

Dad closed the hatchback and said, "You'll call tonight so we know you got safely to the hotel?"

Belva Ann added, "Anything you forgot, let me know and I'll send it STAT."

Hugs were exchanged, and as soon as Emmaline started the engine, Jim banged on the roof of the car twice, then used both arms from the elbow to point the direction out in a way that made Emmaline laugh.

"Your Dad makes me feel like we're on the deck of an aircraft carrier."

Emmaline put the car into neutral, just to gun the engine twice before actually putting the car into gear. She rolled the windows down so they could both wave goodbye.

As she drove away, she said, "Please tell me they're laughing."

Abby twisted in her seat to look.

"Well, Dad has his arm around Mom and she's still waving manically."

Emmaline said, "Manically is better than maniacally. You understand the difference? They are quite close."

"Grandma, we don't have to study for a spelling bee anymore."

"Says you. You just entered the *classroom of the car,*' and there is no exit for three whole days."

"I thought we were going to sing songs and listen to audiobooks."

"You said that, not me. 'Manic' refers to excitability. 'Maniac,' well, that refers to insanity."

"I wasn't calling Mom insane. So, other than vocabulary, what kind of classroom activities have you got planned?"

"I have people for you to meet. Dead people."

"Your night voices?"

"Yes. You'll be the first, other than Freddy, to hear of these people from me."

"But lots of other people knew them, met them, and know about them already."

"Quite true. But few written records survive. We do have oral history, passed on from one generation to the next. Some survive, but often the thread gets dropped. History gets lost. And often those threads that survive, they'll be discounted by persons who had or have authority. They will get buried. And the truth is, that truth is elusive. Not all oral history is accurate. Tricky business. But as a novelist, I can shape a story to speak to what was happening to many and not just one notable case. That's why my story can't just be about one of my voices. The story is larger than one voice."

"But what's the story about?"

"Ah, the big question, the deep question. You know about slavery?"

"You know I do. I got an A+ on my report on Frederick Douglass!"

"Well, we're going to a state where the enslaved used to make up close to half the population. Slaves were the economic engine of the state for a very long time. They were not so prevalent in the mountainous areas, but in the areas with large arable land, they were essential to wealth building, so that's where the enslaved were mostly to be found. We're going to a state that contained the capital of the Confederacy. On the eve of the Civil War, Albemarle County, where we are headed, contained more enslaved people than free people."

"But what's the story about?"

"At the moment, it's about four women. Betty, Mary, Sally, and Betsy, all related to each other. It's about the reality, the prevalence, of what I call 'shadow families.' Families that were not recognized by law or customs. But they were families, nonetheless, because the law is not always right or moral or just. Sometimes in fact, the law supports gross injustice. You know that from *"Sharp Elbows, Loud Voices."*

"Yes."

The 'silver-haired witch' was finally, finally, letting Abby into her story. And Abby knew instinctively that although her grandma wrote about other people, every story she wrote provided a clue about herself. No one can write a story that doesn't say something about its author. Abby almost felt that she should not breathe too loudly, or Emmaline would clam up.

Emmaline said, "Shadow families existed but were rarely acknowledged, because to do so would violate the stated moral codes of a people who considered themselves aristocratic, refined, and honorable. Virtue was central to their self-perception."

Emmaline continued, "However, legally the enslaved were either denied full humanity or deemed to exist as an inferior form of humanity. Race 'mixing' was loudly decried and legally forbidden. Did you know that the word 'mulatto' comes from the Spanish word for mule? A mule is a hybrid between two species, a horse and a donkey."

Abby wrinkled her forehead, as encouragement for Emmaline to keep talking.

"You don't know about mules. Mules, and indeed most hybrid animals, are sterile. A mixed-race child is of course, not sterile. But you see how the label was demeaning? As if enslaved Africans and whites were different species and a mixed-race child was a hybrid? Absurd and clearly a lie easily disproved by the abounding evidence that lived and breathed in their very own households. And at least a quarter of all African Americans today have some European DNA. So, words and deeds did not match.

So, you see; to publicly embrace one's shadow wife, one's own flesh and blood children, would mean acknowledgment of breaking the moral and legal codes. It could mean social ostracism. And yet these shadow families usually co-existed with the white family, sometimes in close proximity."

Abby said, "Close proximity?"

"Proximity means nearness. There is a letter from a visitor to Monticello, who describes an enslaved person who was the spitting image of Jefferson, serving them dinner. Even Jefferson's own grandson, who denied any blood ties to his grandfather's shadow family, admitted that they all *looked* like his grandfather. Yet, no one would have dared mention it in front of any of the white members of Jefferson's family. That would have been considered an attack on his honor."

"So, they zipped their lips?"

"To a point. It was an informal social norm, a silent pact among many white male slave owners. But never, never were white women given tacit approval to use their male property in the same way men used enslaved women. You may already understand the reasons why that would be so."

Abby nodded. "Control, right?"

Emmaline nodded. "White women were duty-bound to produce a male heir for their husbands. Child mortality was high, so, even better, she should produce an 'heir and a spare' to inherit the whole shebang. Her progeny had to be unquestionably his."

"Shebang?"

"The whole ball of wax. The whole enchilada. You capiche?"

"Oh, Grandma. I get it, yeah."

Enslaved women had no more rights to their own child

than a cow or a horse has to their 'get.' We don't know how Betty or Mary, or Sally, or Betsy felt. Not exactly. But I'll try my hardest to give them a voice that is supported by the thin facts I can gather. They did manage remarkably well for themselves and their children, especially considering that the power they wielded was minimal."

"Grandma, what about the white families, the wives and kids? The ones who had proximity."

Emmaline nodded, "There had to be a tremendous amount of tension and bitterness. But not much they could do about it. Women had few rights. When they married, the men had legal control over them. The power legally passed from fathers to husbands. It was called 'coverture.' And what power they had they used to protect their own children and their own standing in society. They wouldn't want folks to know about their shadow family. Remember when I said it was the winners who write history?"

"Yes."

"These shadow families got written out of the historical record by those who had more power than they did. Their ties, especially to important families, got passed off as 'fake news.' By and large, the women were protecting their own honor, which was tied tightly to the honor of the white men in their lives, by making darn sure the shadow families stayed in the shadows. They 'circled the wagons' to protect their lineage. They meant for the historical record, as best as they could impact it, to obliterate any blood ties to the shadow families. They denied ties to people they often knew on an intimate basis."

Emmaline paused for a moment before adding, "When a

woman has no power, and is dependent on men, it's amazing what she will endure, what lies she will tell, to protect men who deserve no such protection. A tale as old as time."

Emmaline got quiet. She seemed to be focused on the road.

Abby said, "You're not just talking about slavery-times."

Abby repeated herself. "Grandma?"

"Hmmm?"

"You're not just talking about slavery times, are you?"

"No. I suppose I'm not."

5

"Abby darling, have you *ever* been outside the state of California?"

"I went with you and mom that time to Tijuana."

"Oh, that hardly counts. Although it was fun."

"Speak for yourself. You and mom just bought cheap stuff."

"Well, I was trying to make a point here, look at that sign." Abby read aloud, "Welcome to Arizona."

"You aren't in California anymore. Prepare yourself for a journey of discovery!"

"Just looks like the same-old-same-old."

"My point is that travel expands your world, in so many ways."

"Why do I sense a lecture coming on?"

"Mark Twain said, 'Travel is fatal to prejudice, bigotry, and narrow mindedness....' You'll have to look up the rest of it."

Emmaline continued, "It's human nature to think that the way we do things is the right way to do things. But even in our own country, we are foreigners when we travel to different regions. And if you think there is only one way to think and dress and speak and eat and live and pray that is American, then you haven't traveled enough."

Abby frowned, "But you never go anywhere."

"I suppose that's fair. I mean, you only know me as your grandma who lives in your backyard with a silly old dog."

"Freddy is not silly or old. You're going to hurt his feelings."

"Not a chance. Freddy has been 'sawing logs' back there since lunch."

Abby was quiet for a beat, then said, "But you're right. I only know you as my grandma. And I guess, where we're going, I'll be a foreigner, but you won't be."

Emmaline sighed, "Perhaps, perhaps not. You cannot step into the same river twice."

"What does that mean?"

Emmaline continued, "Rivers, like time, keep flowing. So, it's never the same river, and you are never the same person."

Abby said nothing in reply. And Emmaline too, got quiet. The lecture, it seemed, had ended.

But Abby was intrigued. She saw in her mind, her grandma, the white-haired witch, stepping into a river, her lips moving, the golden-eyed wolf sitting on the bank watching. And as she spoke, the river stopped its flow, eddied around her ankles, then changed direction, flowing upstream, and as it did, her grandma too changed, into someone much younger, hair now dark.

She stopped her incantation to gaze up the incline to where the light broke through the trees. And there he stood, bewildered. He had come, perhaps against his will, tall and straight backed, young. He whispered her name. But then the light dimmed, his image breaking apart, like the reflection on water broken apart by a skipping stone. The enchantment was broken. The water once again circled her ankles, then began to flow downstream. He was gone.

Abby couldn't wait to write it all down. Later.

* * *

Before they went to the hotel that night, Emmaline found a park off the road where Freddy could stretch his legs and chase the tennis ball for half an hour. They did admire the view of the San Francisco Mountain range, and the dark sky brilliant with stars, before checking in to their room.

Later, when Abby invited Freddy into bed with her, Emmaline did not object. She was too tired.

Abby stroked the head of Freddy and said, "Grandma, you started to tell me about those women. Those women who speak to you in the night. I know a lot about slavery. I know about a lot of bad things. I read that book about Frederick Douglass. Heck, I named Freddy, Frederick Dog Douglass, because I was so proud of how Freddy escaped his chains. Don't you think Frederick Douglass was scarred for the rest of his life? Like Freddy, who has those scars on his neck, but scars in his mind, too."

Abby put her arm around Freddy and pulled him into her, so they were like two spoons in a drawer.

She continued, "And I know you said those women were brave and determined and made good lives for themselves, despite all they went through. But I thought you were going to tell me about bad things that happened to them. And now I think you don't want to tell me about what happened to them because it's so bad. I can handle it, just like I can handle Freddy. The scars aren't mine. You need to be able to tell me the bad parts. I'll be okay when you decide to tell me. Okay?"

There was no reply because Emmaline was fast asleep

* * *

Emmaline said, "We've got to make tracks today. All the way to Amarillo, Texas. That's our goal."

"Is it named after the animal that looks like an armored possum?"

Emmaline laughed, "No dear. That's an Armadillo. Amarillo means yellow. As in the song 'The Yellow Rose of Texas'. Texas was once its own republic, after it separated from Mexico. It has its own culture."

"Are you telling me that Texas was once Mexico?"

"I am."

"And then Texas was its own country, and not part of the USA?"

"Also, true. And as you know, it seceded from the US in the Civil War, too. There's still folks who are bitter about how that turned out."

"Now you're being funny."

"Only a little bit. Once we get on the road we can play, 'spot the cowboy hat, confederate flag, or gun rack."

"And win valuable prizes?"

"Does ice cream count as a valuable prize?"

"Grandma, ice cream is not vegan."

"I think we should 'fall off the vegan wagon' for the summer."

"No way."

"I'm not saying we're going to start eating the flesh of animals."

"Because that would be gross and bad for your heart and the planet."

"Let's not wax too poetical about climate change or carbon footprints or methane from cow burps, this summer, either."

Emmaline's eyes seemed to sparkle; her lips turned up slightly in the corners.

"Are we really going to eat ice cream?"

"Well. It's full of sugar and saturated fat, and nature meant for cow's milk to be consumed by baby cows, not people. But…"

"Grandma! Cowboy hat, passing lane."

"Oh. He also has a gun rack. You win the prize!"

"Prize?"

"You and I are having ice cream."

"Whoa, who is this person I thought was my grandma?"

* * *

After lunch and ice cream, all three of them got drowsy. Emmaline had to pull over for a coffee. She said, "That sugar rush was amazing, but now we pay for it by experiencing the crash."

Abby yawned.

Freddy, who had only had dog biscuits and no ice cream, seemed to catch the mood. He was already dreaming, twitching, and puffing out his cheeks with muffled barking.

"Grandma, ice cream is intense."

Emmaline had a giggle fit.

"What?"

Emmaline made a funny snorting sound and had to put her coffee in the cup holder.

"Grandma, don't crash the car."

"That stuff is, indeed, intense. Refined sugar is addictive. It lights up the pleasure sensors in the brain. Not only that, but you have to eat more and more of it to get the same rush."

"Oh, please. It's not a drug. They serve it at kids' birthday parties."

"Au contraire. It's all chemistry. Not my best subject in school, but I have a general grasp on the concepts. We need sugar to live and function. But except in serious medical situations, it's better to eat less of it, and eat sugars that elevate glucose in the bloodstream more slowly. That means eating your sugar in whole foods that add fiber that slows down absorption. Plus, fiber is good for your heart. It fights inflammation. But I admit, I do love it."

"Grandma, I'm okay with *not* eating ice cream. I thought it was yummy, but it did make my brain hurt. So, I don't think I'll eat it again."

Emmaline said, "Don't be so sure."

They soon fell back into the doldrums.

Emmaline tried to take an upbeat tone, "So, let's examine what went wrong last year in school, because I don't think we've really gotten a handle on it yet."

Abby crossed her arms, "Do we really have to do this?"

Emmaline said, "I see no reason not to."

"Let's go then. Number one, Ms. Pierce was an idiot."

"Seems an awfully harsh assessment to me."

"Grandma, she was *anti-semantic!*"

"Do you mean antisemitic?"

"No. anti-semantic, not semitic. I learned the different meanings when we were preparing for the spelling bee. Ms.

Pierce slaughtered the English language so badly on a regular basis that I decided she had something against it."

Emmaline guffawed. "That's so good I may have to steal it."

"Thank you."

"Now you've distracted me. I'm sure Ms. Pierce has other admirable personal qualities."

"I doubt that. I really hated how she spoke down to me."

"Oh, my goodness, Abby, she spoke down to you because she's your superior."

"All men are created equal."

"That refers to the equality of mankind and not insubordination by a student toward a teacher."

"She was a terrible teacher."

"While that may be perfectly true, you seem to have misunderstood power dynamics."

"Which are?"

"A classroom only has one Captain, the rest of you are the crew. She gives the commands, you follow."

"But Grandma..."

"Choose your battles wisely, Abby. We only die once. Is this the hill you wish to die on?"

"What does that even mean?"

"Fighting every tiny wrong, every little dig, every slight... well, it gets you nowhere. If the battle is for something larger than yourself, a battle that really matters, then it is an act of courage to dedicate yourself to the battle. Otherwise, you are just a thorn in everyone's side, the skunk at the garden party. You win yourself no friends. Don't waste your energies and time tilting at windmills."

"Tilting at windmills?"

"Look it up. Next year, instead of being a boil on the backside of your teacher, be solicitous. Help the teacher, help the kids who are struggling. Try not to draw attention to anyone's errors, because it is wrong to humiliate anyone, and certainly unwise to humiliate your superior in command. That includes the classroom as much as the army."

"Grandma?"

"Yes."

"Between the ice cream and your lecture, my brain's having a bad day."

"I'm not trying to be unkind; I just want next year to be different for you. Better."

"I can't think about school anymore. I can't think about Ms. Pierce anymore. Tell me a story. Tell me about one of the women who you hear in your sleep."

Emmaline did feel sorry for Abby. She patted her on the knee.

"Okay. Where shall I begin? Elizabeth? She's mostly referred to as Betty. But just to keep things straight, since so many of the names get repeated through the generations, I'll call her Elizabeth. And unlike so many of the enslaved, Elizabeth had a last name. It wasn't the name of her master. It was Hemings.

Elizabeth Hemings never knew her father. But her mother made sure she knew his surname, which was Hemings. He was not a slave, and he was not her mother's master. But he was a white man, an English sea Captain. He was the Captain of an English slave ship.

But wait. Perhaps we should start with Elizabeth's mother because she is the root of the famous American Hemings line. Elizabeth's mother was African. Captured and brought to America to be sold and enslaved for the rest of her life. And she *was* sold. To a famous and wealthy Virginia planter by the name of Francis Epps.

We shall never know for certain what Elizabeth's mother was called in Africa. And there is no record of the name she was given in Virginia. But there is some oral history that it may have been Parthena, 'Thenia' for short. So that is what we shall call her.

Thenia was pregnant with Captain Hemings child when she was sold. And the oral history passed down recounts the captain's efforts to purchase his child, and when Epps refused to sell, to attempt to kidnap mother and child.

The only benefit to Thenia from this drama, is that she was brought into the house for safekeeping, to be a housemaid, rather than sent into the field, and her daughter too, would in time, be trained as a housemaid. Because Epps brought them inside the house, they probably led an easier life than a life of hard labor in the tobacco fields."

Abby said, "Still, poor Thenia."

"Indeed. For many reasons. Imagine having survived the middle passage, with all its horrors, including providing sex to the captain, and then being sold like livestock into an unknowable future, pregnant with the child conceived on the journey."

"Grandma, I read about the middle passage. It was like months, packed below deck so tightly that you couldn't move."

"I wonder about Captain Hemings, choosing Thenia to be his concubine for the voyage. Did he choose her for her beauty? Did she get special treatment? Did she stay in his quarters? Get safer water and food and fresh air? And in that time, those 80 some days, did he recognize her humanity? Was he violent? Or even kind? Did he form an attachment? Why didn't he buy her and his own child before Epps did? I suppose we shall never know."

"Grandma, when Thenia got bought by Mr. Epps, and he took her back to his farm, did Thenia find other slaves that knew her language?"

"I don't know. Africa is a huge continent made up of many different countries and peoples and languages. I'm sure there were many slaves at Mr. Epp's plantation, Bermuda Hundred."

"Weird name."

"It was. It was an important place for inspecting and selling tobacco and then shipping it to England. Slaves were needed for cultivating tobacco, and Virginians got very rich through their labor."

Abby nodded. "So, Thenia got sold and taken to the place with the weird name where she couldn't understand what anyone was saying, and they couldn't understand her."

"Maybe Captain Hemings had taught her a few words. Maybe there were other enslaved people there who spoke her language. We just don't know. But we do know Thenia had endured capture, sexual assault, and enslavement. She was in a strange land where she did not speak or understand the language, at least not much of it."

Emmaline continued, "I wonder if by giving her child the surname Hemings, which was then passed on, perhaps she felt some small gratitude to Captain Hemings, even though Hemings had used her for his own pleasure. Or perhaps, she knew that he had tried to purchase their child, even perhaps to kidnap them, perhaps to give them their freedom, and she wanted to preserve the name in case he tried again later, to locate them and free them. We can only speculate here."

"Did Captain Hemings come back for them?"

"Not that we know of."

"Grandma, why didn't Thenia teach her children her real name?"

"Who says she didn't? But who writes history?"

"The winners. Those with power."

"I have seen claims online that her real name was Biabaye, and that she was captured in what we now call Nigeria. But I couldn't find the source. It's likely it was gleaned from oral history, which should not be discounted. But often in oral history, facts get lost or muddied over time, and unless they get written down in a near contemporaneous time, they are often unreliable, or difficult to confirm. A contemporaneous written record, ledgers, letters, interviews, well, those are mighty important and powerful. Nothing quite like first-hand knowledge."

Abby added, "The pen is mightier than the sword."

"Yes. That was one reason it was against the law to teach an enslaved person to read or write. Those who depended on the slave system fully understood the danger of literacy. Thenia's real name is not recorded anywhere, as was true of nearly all the people captured and enslaved. Their names were lost because they were not recorded. Who they were before being captured was intentionally erased. They were only given first names, English names. We don't know for sure her name was Biabaye. We do not know what tribe she came from, or what language was her native language."

Abby said, "But she knew her own name. Her real name. I bet it was Biabaye. I bet she told her children."

"I'm certain Thenia never forgot her African name."

"I bet her daughter never forgot it either."

"But remember her daughter, Elizabeth, only ever heard her mother called Thenia. Elizabeth was born in Virginia. That was her native country. And so, Thenia, not Biabaye, was the name that Elizabeth would pass on to her first daughter, along with the surname Hemings. And that Thenia would also have a daughter named Thenia Hemings."

Abby noted, "The white Captain's name got recorded, but her real name got lost."

"And when Francis Epps' daughter, Martha, married John Wayles, well, Thenia and her teenage daughter, Elizabeth, became wedding gifts to Martha."

"People given as a wedding gift?"

"They were part of a thing called a dowry. Upper class marriages often included legally contractual items of wealth as part of the marriage contract. Slaves and land were both worth a lot of money."

"Wow. Harsh. Like you had to pay to get rid of your daughter."

"You have to understand the laws of the time. Before laws were changed, the colonies followed English law. Entail and primogeniture were two such laws. Entailed property could not be divided between children. The oldest male, and by that, I mean white male, inherited everything. Entailed estates had to, by law, be kept intact and not broken up. It was a way to protect the ruling classes, the aristocracy, and keep them land rich. That meant that the other children had to be provided for by marriage, or through gifts, or be dependent on the eldest son's largesse."

"I think I learned that watching a movie with you."

"That was *Pride and Prejudice.*"

"Crazy."

Emmaline mused, "It must have been a huge relief to Thenia to not be separated from her daughter when they became wedding gifts. I think of her years at Bermuda Hundred, whatever their number, to be as a young woman, a young mother, with no women she knew to give her love and support. She would have been traumatized, lonely, confused. And yet, she survived.

"I think becoming a mother gives her a reason to survive. I expect at some point she accepted that Captain Hemings was never coming back. And that this strange land and people who thought her inferior, who thought of her like livestock, well, this place was where she would spend the rest of her life. Instead of succumbing to despair, she made a place for herself and her child. And looking through the lens of history, she prevailed. Years later, she would become the property of Thomas Jefferson, along with her daughter and grandchildren."

"Whoa, Grandma. Thomas Jefferson?"

"Yes. The Hemings family were exceptional in many ways. Partly through luck. Partly through character. Where was that character formed? Well, talking out loud to you about it, I see Thenia is the foundation. She is key to understanding all the Hemings to follow. But there is hardly any historical record to build upon. But she was there. She had influence over her daughter and her grandchildren. I think you've helped me see where this story really begins."

"How long until we make Amarillo?"

"What? Oh. Still a way to go, I'm afraid."

"Grandma, can we listen to an audio book now?"

"Can you find one that is relevant to our field of study?"

"Really, Grandma?"

Emmaline smiled, "You must steep yourself in the world of your subjects as much as possible. You wanted to come along, so where I'm going, you're going, and I don't just mean physically. I mean metaphorically. It's hard, from the perch of this time and place, to do justice to your characters. But we have a moral duty to try. What I don't know, I must invent. But knowing that, I want what I invent to hit close to the truth. Some research will be tedious. We may not achieve all that we hope. We must be willing to take the risk of being wrong, of being called out by someone who may know more than we do. You trust me?"

"Of course, I trust you. You're my white witch."

Emmaline smiled. "I like being your white witch. I suppose that writing *is* a form of conjuring, Words can be magical. But one never gets the spell right the first time, or the second. Failure is simply part of the process. Failure is part of life, part of everyone's story. Failure is something you live with; you take out and dust off and examine and reexamine."

Abby nodded, knowingly. She'd been paying attention. She had been doing a bit of her own conjuring. Abby didn't pay attention to the part about failure, certainly not her own failures. But it did make her wonder about the failures of her grandma.

She asked, "Grandma, tell me about your failures; your story?"

Emmaline reached over and patted Abby on the thigh. "We are researching the Hemings story. Your job now is to find a relevant audio book."

6

At dinner, Abby was about to send her stuffed baked potato back, but Emmaline made her pick all the bacon off the top instead."

Emmaline said, "Never complain, never explain."

Abby countered with, "Squeaky wheel..."

Emmaline said, "The nail that sticks up gets hammered down."

"But Grandma, we don't support the killing of pigs."

"Eat your potato. Save the bacon bits for Freddy. That pig is past caring."

"Um, okay."

After dinner, Freddy was thrilled to gulp down Abby's bacon bits, along with the overcooked green beans and fatback that Abby had pronounced "gross."

They made it to the motel, dragged themselves up to the second floor, took hot showers and fell into bed. Emmaline had forgotten entirely about getting her promised massage. Emmaline had also forgotten to set an alarm, and the blackout curtains had been effective.

Emmaline had to shake Abby to wake her up. "Wheels need to roll, STAT!"

Abby grumbled, "I don't get why we have to rush."

"Only those not paddling have time to rock the boat. You need to paddle, and paddle now."

"I'm technically not paddling. I'm twelve, remember."

"Yes, and if you would like to turn thirteen, I suggest you pick up your pace."

Abby slithered out of bed and stomped to the bathroom.

At least she could zone out once they got on the road. They had begun listening to a twelve-hour audiobook on Sally Hemings and Thomas Jefferson by a highly respected Jefferson scholar. Abby had expected it to be boring. But since she had learned about Biabaye, AKA Thenia and Elizabeth, AKA Betty, she found she wasn't bored. Not at all.

Every now and then, Emmaline would turn it off to add information.

Abby asked, "Grandma, what did they look like?"

"Well, there's very little about Sally Hemings' appearance that made it into print, some of it was meant to damage Jefferson, and should be taken with a grain of salt. But some descriptions of Sally were from interviews with former slaves or in letters by people who had seen her. But about the other women I mentioned, there's nothing. Sally was, of course, the granddaughter of Thenia, and the daughter of Betty, and Betty's white master, John Wayles. John Wayles was Martha Jefferson's father, too. That meant Sally was Martha Jefferson's half-sister. She may have resembled Martha, but we know precious little about Martha Jefferson's appearance. Sally *was* described as attractive with straight hair that hung down her back."

"Grandma, why aren't you a historian like the lady who wrote this book?"

"Water Under the Bridge."

"Are we going to 'Cross that bridge when we come to it?'"

"I burned it down."

"I thought you weren't supposed to burn your bridges?"

"Do you know the etymology of that aphorism?"

"No."

"Well, say you are running from an enemy. You cross a big river, and as soon as you are safely on the other side, you burn the bridge so the enemy can't come after you by crossing."

Abby said, "So, why is the aphorism telling you *not* to burn it?"

"The way back is gone."

"Grandma, why can't you simply build a new bridge?"

"You could. Or you could keep marching forward."

"You burned your bridge?"

"I kept marching down a new road. I write novels. And I base them on historical facts. I depend on historians to give me the facts, and their interpretations of those facts. Fiction has a way, though, of reaching people on a gut level, an emotional level, in a way that non-fiction rarely does. Well-told fiction can open minds and hearts to a point of view they otherwise might not entertain."

"You're not going to tell me why you burned your bridge and kept marching?"

Emmaline smiled a sly smile. "Nope."

Abby was quiet. But again, her witch and wolf appeared in her mind's eye. They had come to a deep ravine where the blackened ruins of a bridge remained. And although the witch had long ago been the one to curse the bridge into flames, she failed, after many attempts, to conjure it back to wholeness. She was going to have to find another way back.

* * *

Emmaline and Abby ate biscuits and drank hot tea on the road

Emmaline was exclaiming, "Little Rock, Arkansas. Site of a famous struggle in this former Confederate state over desegregation, back in the fifties. Ugly stuff."

"Like what happened in Charlottesville, where we're going? Mom said that was ugly."

"You know about that?"

"Mom tried to tell me about it."

"Well, just because slavery ended, legally I mean, as an institution, with the 13th Amendment in 1865, doesn't mean things were made right and equal for those whose ancestors were enslaved."

"Grandma, spit it out, what are you trying to say about Little Rock, Arkansas?"

"The Federal government told states that they were no longer allowed to force black children to go to different schools than white children. That happened in 1954. They had to let the black students attend what had been whites-only public schools. The states in the south fought it, and they fought it hard."

"Blacks had to go to different schools?"

"Even after it was declared illegal."

Emmaline continued, "In Little Rock, in 1957, nine brave black students decided to test the law. They enrolled in a whites-only public high school. The governor of the state used the Arkansas National Guard to stop them. White people did not want black students to mix with the white students. Miscegenation. The Latin root 'miscere' means to mix. That word goes right back to the heart of my story."

Emmaline continued, "So, anyway, President Eisenhower

sent in federal troops to escort the children safely to school. Look it up, Little Rock Nine, 1957. Then look up Charlottesville, 2017 rally. Look at the photos from both events. Look at the faces. Remember those photos, darling. They say so much about the legacy of slavery that still haunts us today."

Abby was about to ask her grandma to spell miscegenation. It would be one heck of a spelling bee word. But she wasn't going to compete in any spelling bees. She let it go.

As they drove, the flat dry land greened up. Abby began searching road signs for a lunch spot. Everything was about beef. They drove past Stockyard City. Emmaline explained that was where the cattle went to be butchered. To Abby, the idea of killing and eating cows was sickening.

"Grandma, looks like we'll have to live on potatoes."

Emmaline nodded, "Worked for the Irish. Until the great potato famine."

"Now you're making things up."

"I'm not."

Abby said, "I was kidding. Man cannot live on potatoes alone."

Emmaline said, "Man cannot live on bread alone. But potatoes, that's a different story."

"So, what happened to the Irish?"

"Living on potatoes kept body and soul together in Ireland, until the potato blight. Then there was mass starvation. What's the moral of that story?"

"Don't put all your potatoes in one basket?"

Emmaline smiled, "Touché Although, in the aphorism the word is eggs, because *if* you put all your *eggs* in one basket, you could lose them in one 'fowl' swoop!"

"Haha, Grandma. I have an idea; we find a grocery store and buy real food. There must be grocery stores with fruits and veggies. Even here in cattle country."

Emmaline said, "We can have a picnic somewhere. Freddy can get out and chase his ball. Until then, put the audiobook back on."

It was almost midnight before they were able to get to bed. Abby felt better. She had stuffed herself with fresh bread with hazelnut spread and blueberries and strawberries.

Tomorrow would be the last long drive and stay in a hotel room. They were driving to Knoxville.

Emmaline and Abby found good coffee and bagels for breakfast.

They were taking a Freddy break at a rest stop when Emmaline said, "'Look at the sky. See the rain moving our way?"

Freddy had his nose up, sniffing the air

The wind is blowing the smell our way. Petrichor. That is what the smell is called. It's the smell of rain hitting the ground. Let's get in the car."

As they sat in the car, fat rain drops began to smatter against the windshield, wind began to buffet the car.

Emmaline mused, "You'll discover, someday when you are older, that smells are evocative. I love that smell."

The fat raindrops became sheets of water blowing over the car. It alarmed Freddy, and Abby was nervous too. Emmaline looked serene. Her silver hair was loose and wavy, falling over her shoulders. She was wearing a flower print dress and a silver bracelet with little turquoise beads.

"Grandma, were you a hippy?"

Emmaline laughed. "No. Whatever made you ask?"

"I saw some show on TV once about hippies, and I wondered. You kind of look like one."

"Me? Sorry, no."

"I don't believe that because they look so cool, and you are way cool."

"Let me assure you that my coolness, if I possess any such thing, was late in arriving."

"Are you trying to tell me that I'm not hopeless?"

Emmaline had to raise her voice over the rain on the roof.

"Is that what you want, Abby? To be cool?"

"Doesn't everybody?"

"What does it mean to you, to be cool?"

Abby got quiet. The rain began to slow down. Freddy was panting nervously. He may have enjoyed the smell of the incoming rain, but the sound of it hitting the parked car continued to be a cause for anxiety.

"I guess, I'm not sure."

Emmaline said, "To me it's a person who has attained a relaxed confidence in themselves. They no longer have the insecurity of those who are either trying too hard or are eaten up with self-doubt. All of that is hard won."

Emmaline continued her musing, "Feeling secure, feeling prepared for the world, moving freely, joyfully; well, these things make you cool. It's like the unselfconsciousness of babies. We lose it, though. And then spend our lives trying to regain it, and never fully do. But to whatever extent we do, ah, that's what cool is to me."

The rain lightened up.

Emmaline said, "Darling, check the radar. Do we dare get back on the road?"

93

"Yeah. Looks okay. Only light green bands."

Emmaline nodded, "Wiper blades are brand new. We should be fine."

Emmaline started the car, and they pulled back out onto the interstate.

Emmaline added. "Understand that confidence comes from the gradual process of gaining knowledge and skill. Add to that, the wonderful uniqueness of you, and that adds up to a kind of cool no one else can replicate."

"I'll be cool, then?"

"You'll be incredibly cool, but by that time, it won't matter."

* * *

Knoxville had a vegan restaurant where they ordered take-out. Knoxville had a pretty river, too, and everything was green. You could look up and see the Great Smoky mountains, which did look smoky. When the sun was setting, they almost looked like they were on fire.

Emmaline pointed out that the air was different. She made Abby take deep breaths.

They went to the hotel, and ate take-out in front of the TV, watching a movie Emmaline called vapid. Between listening to the audio book and Emmaline's 'classroom of the car' lectures, Abby needed to let her brain float in shallow waters. Even if the content was vapid. In fact, things that were vapid, banal, jejune, seemed to Abby to have a valuable role to play in life, especially if you were road weary.

Emmaline shook Abby awake far too early the next morning.

"Abby, this is it. This is the day we arrive in Charlottesville!"

"Couldn't we arrive in Charlottesville an hour later?"

Emmaline ignored her and pulled the covers back. Freddy eyed her suspiciously, but jumped off the bed, yawned and stretched.

"Let's roll!"

Once they got back on the road, Abby began to catch her grandma's excitement. She pulled out the picture of the rental house. It looked like something out of a history book.

"Grandma, does the house have a name? Like Tall Oaks, or Tara, or Monticello?"

Emmaline said, "We can give it one."

"But it wouldn't be its real name."

"It can be our special name for it. It's not like we get to keep it."

"Grandma, I can't remember why we're doing this. You want me to travel, so I won't turn out like the people Mark Twain criticized. But you didn't decide to do this for me. I'm kind of a last-minute addition."

"But what a valuable addition you are!"

"Remind me again why we're driving across the country to live in an old house?"

"Because your grandma wants to feel the same earth beneath her feet as the women in her story."

"That's the reason?"

"Well, that's one reason. The earth, places, they remain a constant. There is something magical about standing in a place where interesting people and events have taken place. It's like holding two severed pieces of a rope and finding a way to let the two frayed edges touch."

"A frayed rope?"

"Past meets present. To experience the magic, you must study your subject first. That's the seat of the pants to the seat of the chair part. Study until you get a sense of character and even voice. Then you stand where they stood. You take what you know about the person, one end of the rope, and let it touch, through you, the place, another end of the rope. You become the conduit. The connection when it happens, even if the moment is fleeting, is transcendent."

"Grandma, you *are* a witch. I knew it."

"Well, it is a form of conjuring. It's giving history back its humanity, summoning back the heartbeats that made history, at least the shadows of those hearts. That's how I think of it. These were people as complicated as we are. They too were full of insecurity, ambition, and made compromises and experienced failures."

Abby had a fleeting chill that made her hair stand up on the back of her neck. She thought briefly about Mrs. Wilson telling her that Emmaline's ghost stories were too good and that parents had complained.

Abby shook off her chill and pointed to a sign, "Grandma, look! We're in Virginia!"

Emmaline grinned, "Now we climb, up, up, up, up, to mountainous Lexington, Virginia. Then, we zig-zag our way back down into the Piedmont. Thomas Jefferson country."

The road suddenly got bendy but opened to spectacular views. Abby was gazing out the window at deep green ravines with loud rushing water below her.

"Grandma, I do think it's beautiful here."

"I can't wait to show you 'The Grounds.'"

"What's that?"

"Mr. Jefferson's University. Thomas Jefferson designed the original grounds himself. It's never called 'campus.' It's always referred to as the grounds. For those of us who enjoy mind-tripping our way into the 18th century, it's a magical place."

"Is that where you played frisbee?"

Emmaline smiled. "Yup. On the lawn and Mad bowl, as well as other spots. I wonder if Freddy would catch a frisbee?"

"I think he'll be better at it than me. But Grandma, I still don't get why you had to come all the way across the country to come to college."

Emmaline smiled again. "Now you sound just like my mother!"

"It's a long drive."

"I didn't have a car until I was a third year."

"Man. That had to be rough."

"It wasn't."

"But why come to school here?"

"Test myself, I suppose."

"But why UVA?"

"I was enamored with the Founding Fathers, especially Jefferson. I admit when I got here it was quite a culture shock. But I grew to love it. That first winter! I wasn't prepared for how cold it would get in Charlottesville. It wasn't long before I splurged on a long down coat."

"Really?"

"Winter in Charlottesville is unlike anything you've ever experienced in southern California."

"And you wouldn't have done your college tour in wintertime."

"I never stepped foot in Virginia until orientation."

"That's crazy."

"It was just the way it was."

"Hey Grandma, look! That's the first sign we've seen that says Charlottesville!"

"We won't be going into Charlottesville proper today. We're going around Charlottesville to get to our rental house. The rental house is in the country. I can't wait. There's lots of room for Freddy to run, and peace and quiet and long walks. There are endless paths around the fields and through the woods. The hunt club has kept them cleared for fox hunting."

"That's still a thing?"

"Oh yes. But not now. Season is over."

Abby was thoughtful. "Why would anyone hunt a fox? No one eats foxes."

"Ever hear the saying, 'Don't put the fox in charge of guarding the hen house?'"

"Nope."

"If you raise chickens, ducks, geese, well, foxes were a threat to your flock. So, if you needed an animal to guard the poultry house, a fox would be a very bad choice. Kind of like hiring a bank robber to guard a bank."

"Oh."

Abby said, "I've seen it in movies. I didn't think it was a thing in real life anymore."

"Well, maybe you and I will see a fox this summer. Maybe even some kits if we're lucky. I know we'll see plenty of deer, likely groundhogs too. Oh, and the birds! You've never seen a Bluebird, a Titmouse, Pileated Woodpecker, or a Cardinal!"

Abby laughed, "A Titmouse. Are you joking?"

"A Tufted Titmouse. We'll have to get a bird feeder. Put it where we can sit and watch."

"Grandma, we're turning in a mile."

Emmaline grinned, "Aren't you excited!"

Abby said, "I am. But I really have to pee."

"Well, I'm not stopping this close to our destination. Grab my purse, look for the envelope with the keys and all the important information I printed from the email."

Abby dug through Emmaline's bag, which was big and deep, with dog hair and a collection of ink pens and highlighters in the bottom. But Abby found the one item she was assigned to retrieve, although it was not the only piece of mail in the bag. She knew it was the right one because it clearly contained a house key and a smaller key without any sort of key chain attached to them, and they had caused the corner of the envelope to tear.

"Grandma, you could have lost the house key!"

"Nonsense. It would have been in my bag."

"You mean this dark hole you call a handbag?"

"Pay attention. We're looking for a gravel road on the right. Mr. Taylor said the road doesn't have a proper street sign, but there's a concrete post with the road name on it."

Emmaline slowed down to an embarrassing crawl. A pickup truck zoomed around them. But they didn't go past the turn, which was almost invisible. They did see the post. And as soon as they made their turn, they passed what was once a shack of a house. But now it was nothing but a ghostly hump of kudzu.

"Grandma, that vine has swallowed a house."

"Kudzu. An invasive non-native plant."

Freddy had begun to whine, his head poked over the seat-back. He had noticed right away the different sound of the wheels as they left the pavement for gravel.

"Grandma, we're supposed to take a slight right. I don't see any right turns."

Emmaline ignored her, "The night sky will be fabulous. We can stargaze!"

The road did bend to the right, and the woods gave way to cleared fields, covered in bright green vegetation, the edges bright with exposed orange clay soil. Ahead was a large white farmhouse. But it wasn't the grand house in their photo.

But what caught Abby's eye was the barn next to the farmhouse and the black board fenced field next to the barn. That field had horses in it. Lots of horses.

Abby exclaimed, "Wow. Look at all those horses!"

As they drove past the house, a dog in the yard barked enthusiastically. Freddy did a soft growl and then yawned nervously. He probably had to pee as badly as Abby did.

The GPS showed they had only a thousand feet left to go. And soon the voice announced, "You've arrived."

On their right was a battered mailbox, and what must have been their driveway.

Abby's voice dropped. "What if we're at the wrong place, and like we drive in there and get stuck and can't turn around, and we have to call a tow truck, and the tow truck can't get here for hours, and it gets pitch black, and we have to sleep in the car."

Emmaline laughed out loud. "You've got the chops to spin quite a tale. But look at the numbers on the mailbox. That's us."

Emmaline put the car in gear, and they drove on, weeds brushing against the sides of the car. They bounced through a few ruts and the bottom scraped against some rocks as they climbed a hill. And finally, they saw the house, sitting on a rise, seeming to peer down at them through dark wavy glass windows.

It *was* the house in the photo that Emmaline had shown Abby. But in some ways, it *wasn't*. It had a neglected and unhappy look about it. It was two-story with red brick showing through the thin wash of white paint. It had four columns and a front porch. The upper story had a smaller porch. Over that was a peak with a fan shaped window.

Emmaline enthused, "Hello, you grand old lady!"

Abby frowned, "Grandma, it's looking at us the same way Ms. Pierce looked at me."

Emmaline took a serious tone. "She probably thinks we're northern carpetbaggers. You know this house survived the Civil War? Imagine that! Imagine Union troops coming up this driveway. Imagine the terror of those in that house at the sight."

"Were there enslaved people here, too?"

"Maybe not so many as before the Emancipation Proclamation. After that, many of the enslaved men left to go find Union lines and join the fight."

"Are we carpetbaggers?"

"No darling, we are not."

"What exactly are carpetbaggers?"

Emmaline continued to slowly bump her way up the driveway. "After the Civil War, unscrupulous opportunists flooded into the region."

Abby frowned, "We need to let the house know we come in peace."

They pulled right up to the front door, and Abby let Freddy out of the back.

Freddy only went a few feet from the car before squatting like a female dog to relieve himself on the dirt drive. Abby took the key to the front door, walking on a large but sagging front porch. She put the key in the lock, but it would not turn.

"Grandma, are you sure this is the key?"

"Of course it is. The landlord said to pull and then turn."

Emmaline stepped up to the door and took over. She was saying to herself, "Pull, then turn. Pull, then turn. But she too, had no success."

Emmaline stepped back and took a deep breath, and when she did the door swung open, all by itself.

Emmaline lifted her arms, "The portal opens! Now, Abby, we cross the threshold. Are you ready?"

Instead of answering, Abby bolted past Emmaline. Her bladder had urged her through that portal, over that threshold without hesitation. She had spotted a door to what she correctly assumed was a powder room and made a beeline.

But Abby did yell as she ran, "Thank you, house. I promise we are NOT carpetbaggers!"

7

As soon as Abby had emptied her bladder, she focused on her surroundings. The powder room was tiny with a sloping ceiling. That made sense. It was under the staircase. But the newest and most pressing problem was that there was no toilet paper. No TP and no cabinet or shelf to find a spare roll.

Abby cracked the door and yelled, "Grandma! There's no TP!"

Freddy pushed his nose into the space and then his head, and soon he was halfway in the tiny space, panting with concern.

Still, no grandma.

"Grandma!"

Abby heard water rushing through the pipes in the wall. She exhaled. Of course, Emmaline had used a bathroom that was upstairs. She thought she ought to count to ten before hollering again.

Before she tried again, Emmaline was sticking one of those little travel packs of tissues over the top of Freddy.

"Be sparing. I've only been able to locate half a roll upstairs."

Abby washed her hands with rust colored water with no soap and no way to dry them. She wiped them off on her shorts.

Emmaline had gone out to the car and was walking back

in, pulling her wheeled suitcase. She walked to the foot of the stairs, and letting go of the suitcase, she enthused, "Look at this staircase, Abby."

Emmaline's suitcase slowly began to roll away from her back toward the front door.

"Grandma! The house wants us to leave!"

"Oh Abby, don't be silly, it's the foundation. It's not level. It happens all the time in old houses. The ground shifts and settles, and whatever sits atop the ground shifts right along with it."

Abby said, "I don't know, the way the door swung open, too. Creepy."

"Ah, that. The door frame is so out of plumb that the deadbolt isn't matching up to the plate."

Abby stage-whispered, "This house is a mess."

Emmaline frowned, "It was once someone's pride and joy. A symbol of wealth. Oh, well. Let's get our stuff out of the car and make our beds. I packed fresh linens, towels, and pillows."

Abby and Emmaline emptied the car and carried their suitcases up the grand staircase. The bedrooms had high ceilings and large casement windows. Emmaline got first dibs on the room in the middle of the hall. It was larger and had a door to a small porch. Although Emmaline said it was no longer safe to use it. Besides, they now had air conditioning, unlike the old days where folks would sleep out on the porch in the summertime to escape the heat.

At the end of the hall, there was a narrow door that looked like a closet door, but Emmaline said it went to the attic. Abby wondered how Emmaline would know that. But she went and opened the door to find a dark, dirty set of stairs. Abby closed the door.

There was one central bathroom upstairs for four bedrooms. It had a clawfoot bathtub that had a funny shower in it with a curtain that ran around the tub on a suspended ring, like a halo. One wall had cubby holes. In one of the cubby holes someone had left a pair of flip flops and a bar of soap.

Abby said, "I could have used that soap to wash my hands downstairs."

Next, they went downstairs to empty their cooler. The kitchen had a linoleum floor with places that were worn all the way through. But it was huge, and it had the biggest walk-in pantry Abby had ever seen.

Abby wrinkled her nose, "What's that smell?"

"Insecticide. Be glad they sprayed. The roaches are big and plentiful in this part of the country. Let's open the windows and get some fresh air in here."

Then Abby and Emmaline tried but couldn't open a single window.

They opened the back door instead, then fed Freddy and watched him gobble down his kibble while leaning against the Formica countertops, sipping on half-chilled bottles of green tea.

Abby then began to open the cupboards. There were plates and glasses and bowls. The drawers contained mismatched silverware. There were pots and pans and spatulas and a couple of burned and stained potholders.

Abby asked, "Are we going to eat off this?"

"It'll be fine. All we need is hot water and soap."

They watched as Freddy got a drink from his water bowl,

and then they all walked into the living room. Emmaline practically fell into an armchair, pulling an ottoman close and leaning back with her feet up. She reached over to her handbag, which was resting on the floor, and pulled out the photo of the house.

She said, "How old do you suppose this photo is?"

Emmaline passed it over to Abby. "Really old. It's black and white. Could it be from the Civil War era?"

Emmaline began to laugh in a loopy sort of way.

"Don't laugh, I've seen photos of Abraham Lincoln."

Emmaline couldn't stop giggling. "Grandma!"

"I'm sorry. Forgive me. Of course this is quite an old photo. But *not* "antebellum," which would make it over 150 years old."

"Didn't you check on Yelp or anything?"

Emmaline shook her head.

"I thought you researched everything, Grandma."

"Let's not mention this to your mom or dad."

"Isn't Mom coming out later to visit?"

"Later is the operative word."

"Grandma, I feel sorry for the house."

"I feel that way, too."

"I bet it was once beautiful. I've never seen a fireplace like that one."

"Stunning, isn't it? It's marble. Look at the acanthus leaf design and ornate scrollwork."

"It's so dirty."

Emmaline waved her arm though the air. "Don't focus on the dirt. Look at the woodwork. The arched doorways. These floors, even if they are unlevel. Even the baseboards are special. And did you notice the wainscoting in the dining room?"

"What sorts of people have been living here?"

"The sort who needs a wall of cubby holes in a shared bathroom."

"Why did someone leave flip flops in a cubby?"

"What?"

"There were old flip flops in that cubby space."

"Oh. You don't want to be barefoot in a dirty shower. Someone with athlete's foot might have been standing there."

"Athlete's foot?"

"A fungal infection."

"Ew."

Abby nodded, "Poor old house."

Emmaline agreed. "It's down on its luck."

"Grandma, when it saw us coming up the driveway, I think it was scared of us. I think it was afraid we were coming to rip out its marble fireplace to sell like carpet baggers would have done."

Emmaline raised a finger. "The final indignity!"

"It shouldn't be scared now. The front door might not lock, but Freddy isn't going to let any old carpetbaggers in. We'll look after the old lady while we're here."

Emmaline responded, "I was taught that we should respect our elders, respect those who raised us and loved us and nurtured us. We should return to them, in their old age, the love and care they gave us in our youth. This house was a special place to someone. But clearly it has lost its friends and family."

"Grandma, that's so sad."

"Yes."

"Grandma, we can love this old lady of a house while we're

here. You know how good I can clean. I'll clean it from top to bottom."

"Why don't you start with the bathtub."

"The bathtub?

"Then we throw away those flip-flops."

* * *

Abby and Emmaline ate their dinner out of containers and then threw the trash in the trashcans they found in a shed outside. Emmaline noted the trash was mostly beer bottles.

Abby helped Emmaline make the beds with new mattress pads and sheets. They struggled but did get the windows opened and turned on the ceiling fans. Things were looking up.

The cubbies were practical, in that Emmaline and Abby each had a place of their own to hang a towel and keep their toothbrush and toothpaste and sundry other bathroom items. Abby did notice that her grandma had pill bottles in her cubby. She didn't ask what they were for but seeing them did give her a moment of anxiety that she quickly brushed off.

Emmaline turned on the spigot in the tub, and the water came out brown.

"Let it run, Abby. The pipes haven't had water run through them in a while."

Abby and Emmaline stood with arms crossed and let the water run. It finally cleared up.

Emmaline said, "I'll go first. You take Freddy for a short walk, okay? Stay close to the house."

"I'm not afraid, Grandma."

"It's so quiet here, I'm expecting the wildlife may resent our intrusion."

Emmaline had a short shower and found Abby sitting on her bed with Freddy stretched across it.

"The shower is all yours!"

"Grandma, you were right about the stars. They're bright here. And I heard a sound that I thought was an owl."

"Lovely."

Abby was careful getting into the tall bathtub, and she felt claustrophobic pulling the curtain closed on the ring above her. But the water did feel good. She soaped herself up and began to rinse off when suddenly the water went cold. She tried to step outside the flow of water, but there was nowhere to go. She turned the water off and yelled as loudly as she could, "Grandma!"

Freddy came first and poked his nose inside the curtain.

Then Emmaline was there.

"What is it?"

"No hot water!"

"I had hot water."

"I had hot water at first."

"Let me try the sink."

"Grandma, I'm all soapy!"

"I can't get any hot water in the sink either."

"What am I supposed to do?"

"Did you wash your hair?

"No."

"You'll just have to rinse off with cold water."

"Grandma, we need hot water."

"Tomorrow, darling. Tomorrow, I call the landlord and get the water heater fixed."

* * *

The next morning, Emmaline couldn't get the stove to work. So, they made their tea in the microwave oven. They fed Freddy then took their breakfast to the front porch and sat on the rusted patio chairs to enjoy the morning and the view.

They watched Freddy, nose down, run circles around the yard. Once he had inspected the area to his satisfaction, Freddy bounced up the stairs, greeted them, and then positioned himself like a secret service agent, his back to them both, with a good view down the dirt track that served as their driveway.

Emmaline said, "Try to see that track the way it used to be. It's empty now, but it once was busy. In slavery times, the overseer would ring a bell before daylight. Then the enslaved would make their way to the barns, harness the mules, and get out to the fields to be ready to plow when the sun broke over the horizon. Can you see it? Can you see a horse and rider coming along that track?"

"I *can* see it. Wow, Grandma, you are a witch!"

"Be careful who you call a witch. At one time, witches got burned at the stake."

Freddy woofed and then ran down the stairs.

Emmaline tipped forward in her chair and squinted.

Abby stood up and was halfway hiding behind one of the columns, when she turned to Emmaline and whispered, "Sometimes you scare me. You summoned it; you did."

Emmaline stood up too. "I have to admit, it kind of feels that way. But I can see it's a girl on a horse; it's a young black girl. She's wearing jeans and she's carrying something. She's no ghost."

Abby stayed behind the column until the girl rode up to the steps and slid off the horse who was not wearing a saddle. Freddy was doing a wiggle dance to greet her, slightly crouched down with his head lowered and his ears back, more nervous than excited.

The girl leaned over and patted Freddy without hesitation, as she said, "Hey. My Mimi asked me to carry these to you. Fresh baked biscuits. My name's Sissy."

Emmaline gestured to Abby to come out of hiding, then stepped off the porch and took the sack. "Pleased to meet you, Sissy. Thank your Mimi for these. My name is Emmaline Sparks, and this is my granddaughter, Abby Woods."

Emmaline opened the sack and inhaled. "I'm guessing your Mimi can make a mean biscuit."

"Yes, ma'am. You got butter and honey? Daddy, he got honeybees."

"Well then, I suppose we'll be buying some of his honey."

Abby said, "Freddy likes you. He doesn't like just anybody."

Sissy said, "Looks like a wolf."

Emmaline smiled, "He's a German Shepherd."

"He been fixed?"

Emmaline said, "Yes."

"I got a hound bitch. She ain't fixed. Hunt gave her to me since she didn't suit them. But she suits me, just like this horse here. She suits me too."

Abby said, "Can I pet her?"

"Sure."

Abby walked down the steps and up to the face of the horse, lifting her arm to pet the horse on its face. The horse backed away from her.

Sissy said, "Not like that. See, horses don't see good right in front of them, nor right behind them. You going at her like that, right at her face, well, she's a tolerant girl, but that ain't the way to do it."

"Oh. I don't know anything about horses."

"What you want to do is come up on their left-hand side. That's the side we lead them from and get on and off their backs, so that's normal to them. They got real good wide-angle vision. She can see you good from there and she can figure out you ain't no threat. Now you go on and pet her on the neck and introduce yourself that way."

Abby did as she was instructed. The horse seemed huge, but sweet, and so very soft to the touch.

Abby asked, "What's her name?"

"Bunny. Cause of those ears."

Abby saw nothing special about her ears.

Sissy explained, "They're big for a horse. Even for a mare."

"Oh."

Emmaline interrupted, "That must be your home we passed on this road."

"Yes, ma'am."

"You do have a lot of horses."

"We run a retirement home for hunt horses. They're mostly my job. Daddy, he works at the University. I take care of them, and I get to hack them out if I want to. Well, the ones that are still sound. Bunny is my favorite. Long as she don't hear the huntsman's horn, she's as gentle as a kitten."

Emmaline asked, "And what is your father's name?"

"Francis Taylor. And my Mimi is Bernice Taylor, but everyone calls her Mimi."

"Well, Sissy, please tell Mimi we say thank you, and send our greetings to your father, too. We are sure going to enjoy these biscuits and I look forward to returning the call as soon as we can. Right now, we have a little problem in that we have no hot water. But as soon as we get that sorted out, I plan on stopping by to introduce myself, and my granddaughter Abby, to your family."

Sissy nodded, then she tapped the ground with the toe of her boot. "Bunny" put her head down, and Sissy climbed up on her neck. The mare lifted her neck, and Sissy slid down Bunny's neck and landed in the right spot for riding.

Emmaline said, "Well, that's a neat trick if ever I saw one."

Sissy said, "When I was little, I couldn't get up on the horses by myself. Daddy showed me how to train the horses to allow a neck mount. I learned Bunny how to do it myself."

Abby blurted out, "Taught."

Emmaline pressed her foot into Abby's foot.

Emmaline said, "I wonder if you could, I mean, if you were interested, would you consider teaching Abby about horses? You clearly are an expert. You've already taught Abby the proper way to introduce yourself to a horse."

Sissy looked serious. "I'd have to ask my Daddy about it."

Emmaline said, "Of course."

They waved as Sissy turned Bunny around and headed back down the track.

Abby said, "Wow, did she ever slaughter the English language."

Emmaline murmured, "When the student is ready, the teacher will appear."

Abby tipped her head, "You mean I'm supposed to teach that kid?"

Emmaline smiled, "I didn't say that."

* * *

After Emmaline and Abby had polished off the biscuits, Emmaline called the landlord.

Abby watched Emmaline speak into the phone.

"Propane tank?"

Then, "It's in the rental agreement?"

"Oh."

"Yes, I'll make that call. Can you come have a look at the front door? The deadbolt is not functioning."

"Thank you, Mr. Taylor. Anytime is fine."

"Bobby. Thank you, Bobby."

"Call me Emmaline. Thank you."

When Emmaline hung up, she walked out the back door and out into the yard. Abby and Freddy followed.

Emmaline pointed, "And there it is. How did I not notice?"

Abby said, "What?"

Emmaline sighed. "That is a propane tank. We were supposed to have it filled prior to our arrival."

"What is it for?"

"Instead of natural gas, our stove and water heater use propane that runs from that tank to the house."

"If you say so."

"And it has to be filled. Like when we fill the car. Except the gas station has to come to us instead of us going to the gas station."

"And it's not the same kind of gas, right?"

"Right. The salient point here is that I neglected to order the service prior to our arrival. Now I must beg forgiveness and see how quickly we can get the propane delivered. Until then, it's cold showers for you and me."

Abby pointed to a different thing that looked like a miniature house. "What is that?"

Emmaline inhaled and exhaled deeply. "It's a well. We also have a septic tank somewhere. But that's underground."

Emmaline went back into the house and grabbed her purse. Abby watched as she dug around, pulled out another envelope, and then paced back and forth in the living room with the sheet of paper she had pulled from it.

While Abby and Freddy looked on, she placed another call.

"We just have the house for the summer. I neglected to have the tank filled before we arrived. Evidently, it's empty. We really need your services right away. The account has an overdue balance? Isn't that Mr. Taylor's responsibility? No?"

Emmaline was silent while the propane company person spoke.

Then she said, "They must have been the prior tenants. How much? How much? Oh, for goodness sakes. Well, that's not the hill I'm going to die on. If you can get out here today, I'll pay it in full. We've been on the road for days. Yes. We drove all the way from California."

Emmaline hung up and turned to find both Abby and Freddy staring at her. She waved the phone at them, "Ignorance carries a surcharge. Remember that."

Abby grimaced. "Bad?"

"I'll never say. But some young person is going to stop getting harassed by a collection agency. It's their lucky day."

"Grandma, the salient point, as you would say, is when will we be able to have a hot shower and put the kettle on for tea?"

"If promises made, turn out to be promises kept, we'll have hot showers before bedtime."

The propane truck arrived before lunch. Emmaline was giddy with excitement.

Abby barely recognized her grandma, as she breezily chatted with the driver as he filled their tank, and weirdly, Abby noticed, her grandma seemed to have acquired a southern accent.

She was saying, "I confess it never occurred to me we were on propane."

He grinned widely, and Abby was shocked to see his teeth were crooked and brown.

"Ma'am, don't feel too bad. I once had a university student tell me propane tanks were third world. Can you believe that?"

Emmaline seemed charmed, "Well, thank you for telling me that. Now I don't feel quite so stupid!"

Emmaline paid with her credit card, but as he was climbing into his cab, she handed the man with the brown teeth a twenty-dollar bill.

Emmaline looked him in the eyes and said, "You have a bless-ed day."

Emmaline and Abby, with Freddy by their sides, watched the propane tanker truck bounce down their overgrown track.

Abby looked up at her grandma, who looked the same as she always had, but looked different somehow too. She said, "Bless-ed day?"

Emmaline shrugged. "You've never heard that before?"

Abby lifted her eyebrows, "Not from you, I haven't."

"It's just a polite way of saying good-bye."

"Weird. And the way you said it. Weird."

"Whatever do you mean?"

Abby put on a syrupy southern accent. "You have a bless-
ed day."

Emmaline said, "You make me sound like Elly May
Clampett."

"Who?"

"A caricature of a southerner."

"But that guy was weird. And you sounded weird."

"But I got our propane tank filled on very short notice,
didn't I? And while you may have thought the delivery man
was weird, he could have felt the same way about us."

"We are *not* weird."

"How do you know that?"

Emmaline did not wait for an answer but flicked her hair
over her shoulder and with a small smile, turned and walked
toward the back door.

Abby frowned at the retreating back of her grandma, the
witch. Freddy, instead of following Emmaline, or staying by
Abby's side, pricked his ears, then spun around and darted
into the tall grass where he slowed down to a crouching,
stalking sort of walk Abby had never seen him do. He looked
just like a wolf.

Weird.

8

Emmaline was focused on setting up her office in the room she was calling 'the library' (it had a built-in bookshelf). It had a window that looked out the front of the house, which she said gave her a mental resting place, and bathed the room in natural light. It had a beat-up table and chair that was perfect for her laptop, and she found a side table in one of the upstairs rooms she and Abby carried down for her printer.

The library had a smaller version of the grand fireplace in the "parlor." The fireplace in the library shared a wall with the dining room, which was in bad shape and had no furnishings. The dining room had a fireplace, wainscoting, now covered in layers of paint, and peeling wallpaper that when Emmaline gently lifted a corner, revealed older wallpaper beneath it.

Abby took on the job of cleaning out the refrigerator. Emmaline wanted to get groceries, but Abby was adamant that nothing was going into the 'nasty' fridge until she could sanitize it. Abby located scouring powder and rags under the kitchen sink. She attacked the filth with enthusiasm.

Freddy watched the proceedings for a time. But as both Abby and Emmaline became absorbed in their tasks, Freddy lost interest, disappearing.

Time passed, and Abby was feeling proud of the clean white interior of the refrigerator, which had lost its funky odor. She had chucked sundry moldy jars of condiments and packets of sauces from Chinese and Mexican take-out into the trash can out back.

Freddy startled them both with furious barking. He was upstairs. Emmaline and Abby both made it to the bottom of the staircase, to find themselves nearly bowled over by Freddy in full and rapid retreat, flying straight towards them, ears flattened, tail tucked.

In hot pursuit was a squirrel.

Abby shrieked, which did nothing to calm the dog, the squirrel, or the situation.

"Abby! Quick, grab Freddy! Shut him in the kitchen. Go!"

The squirrel seemed to be defying gravity, having plastered itself on the wall, frozen.

Freddy, now plastered against Abby, was also frozen, but for the fact that he was trembling all over.

Abby tapped Freddy's nose, then touched her own, saying his name, "Freddy." He did not lift his head but rolled his eyes upward at her.

She commanded him in as serious a tone as she could muster. "Freddy, heel!" His tail tucked, back arched, and head down, he obeyed, and they made it to the kitchen.

Poor Freddy didn't want Abby to leave him alone in the kitchen. He was glued to her side. Abby was pretty freaked out, too. She'd never seen a squirrel chase a dog before. She cracked the door and stuck her head out to check on Emmaline.

Emmaline was speaking to the squirrel in low tones, and Abby could have sworn her accent had gone full 'Elly May' again.

Emmaline drawled, "There seems to be a misunderstanding. You see, we've rented this house for the summer. You must now find other accommodations. Now then, I'm going to open the front door while you compose yourself. And then I shall step aside to give you the space you need to depart with dignity."

Emmaline walked partway toward the kitchen door. Abby had her foot in the door to hold it open a crack, while Freddy cowered behind her.

Emmaline glanced at Abby and put her finger to her lips. Then she turned to look toward the front door, her lips curving upward into a smile.

She whispered, "He did it. In a dignified manner too, just as I requested."

"Grandma, you spoke to the squirrel kind of like you spoke to the propane guy. And the squirrel understood you, too."

"Well, he is a Virginian."

Abby opened the kitchen door, but Freddy stayed behind her legs. So, she walked into the hallway toward the front door and he tip-toed behind her, ears down, back hunched, tail tucked.

Emmaline shook her head at Freddy, "Squirrel phobia?"

"It was *kind* of like a cat. A cat that was after him."

Emmaline looked at Freddy again, "You let a squirrel chase you down the stairs?"

"Grandma, I screamed too."

"Oh, for goodness' sake, Abby. Squirrels are cute. They have those bushy little tails. And big eyes. And sweet little hands and toes."

"Not that one. He was like, a Ninja warrior, and going after Freddy."

Emmaline looked thoughtful before saying, "I did think of rabies. But the squirrel calmed right down and listened to me. It took direction. I don't think a rabid squirrel would do that. Hopefully, that's the only one."

"You think there's like a pack of them?"

Emmaline said, "I don't think squirrels travel in packs. The thing is, that squirrel has been living here. It is we who have invaded "Squirrel Manor." Hopefully, this squirrel will tell the others, if there are others, he's been given his eviction notice."

Abby mentally added, "squirrel whisperer" to the white witch's magical powers.

* * *

Abby and Emmaline found a good grocery store. Emmaline went on a crazy shopping spree. Abby had to get a second cart. Emmaline announced they were going to make poppy seed loaf cakes. Not just one or two. They were going to make a bunch of them in little aluminum disposable pans.

Abby said, "Whoa, Grandma, I like other kinds of cake, too."

Emmaline explained that one was going to go to the Taylors. They would make one for themselves, and the rest would go in the freezer to have on hand to give away.

Abby was told this was the neighborly thing to do.

Abby thought maybe that was what other people did, but she'd never seen her grandma do such a thing before.

But then Abby remembered that baked goods were part of Emmaline's plan. It was how she got people to tell her their stories. It was how she had extracted information from Abby every day after school. Abby realized the Taylors would be Emmaline's first target.

They left Freddy in the car in the shade with the windows halfway down while they shopped. Thankfully, he appeared to have fully recovered from his squirrel encounter.

When they loaded the car with the groceries to go home, Emmaline said, "Let's drive through Charlottesville."

"Grandma, we have groceries. Lots of groceries. Like half the store."

"I just want to believe I'm really here."

Emmaline pulled into a parking spot on University Avenue. She was looking up the rise at a building Abby thought looked vaguely familiar.

Emmaline pointed, "That's the Rotunda. That's Jefferson's statue, right out front."

"Okay."

Emmaline waved at the statue. "Hello, Thomas. It's Emmaline. I've come back. Just for a visit, mind you. Remember me? I was among the first of your lady scholars."

Emmaline had a faraway look in her eyes, gazing at the Rotunda.

Emmaline said, "I need to buy a frisbee."

"Grandma, what's that got to do with the price of bread?"

Emmaline ignored her. "Another time. Our dance card is full for the day. We've got groceries to put up. Then we'll have a baking spree. And then we make our mushroom burgers for dinner on the porch. And then..."

"And then what, Grandma?"

"Hot showers! Hot showers with our newly purchased lavender body wash. I think I'm going to sleep well tonight!"

Abby said, "Maybe *you* will. I read online that we could have squirrels in the attic. And if we do, that squirrel will be coming right back in."

"I don't like the sound of that."

"You're going to have to call the landlord guy."

"I suppose I will."

"On the internet, it says you have to find out how they're getting in and block it. Otherwise, they just come right back."

"You don't think Freddy is a deterrent?

"Really, Grandma?"

Emmaline nodded, "He's a paper tiger, our Freddy."

Abby defended Freddy. "Not with people, he's not. He was amazing the time he went after the guy breaking into the big house."

"True. He was a hero that night."

"It's just cats."

"And squirrels."

Abby thought a moment, then said, "Which you have to admit are kinda' similar."

Emmaline said, "They aren't. A cat is a predator. Squirrels aren't. They eat nuts and fruit and stuff like that. They don't hunt and kill other animals."

"Well, *that* squirrel was going after Freddy. Why would a nut eater be going after Freddy?"

Emmaline's jaw dropped. "'There is no greater warrior than a mother protecting her child!'"

Abby looked excited. "Grandma, we have baby squirrels!"

Emmaline put up a finger. "And no, we cannot keep them."

They drove home and Abby and Emmaline put the groceries away. Except for the ingredients for the lemon poppyseed cakes. Emmaline wanted those to come to room temperature.

Once that was done, the two of them took veggies and dip and crackers out onto the front porch for a break. Freddy was given a carrot as his treat.

Emmaline said, "Let me tell you a story. A true one."

Abby settled back in her chair.

"There once was a slave girl who ran away without really running away at all. You see, her master had repeatedly tried to force himself on her. But each time she had managed to thwart his advances. Her mistress was no dummy, in that she sensed what was going on. But it made her heart bitter toward the girl instead of toward her husband. The girl received many senseless beatings for made-up offenses."

The story had many twists and turns, but to shorten the tale, Emmaline skipped to the part where the slave girl instead gave herself sexually to a white lawyer in the small town in hope of his aid and protection.

"Yet, seeking the aid and comfort of a different white male, one who did not own the girl, enraged her master further. The girl was his legal property, you see? To legally do with as he saw fit. The lawyer had no legal standing to use the girl as he had. The white lawyer could not help her, although he continued to use her, and she bore him two children. Sadly, her master became the legal owner of her children, too. That was the law.

"Eventually, the slave ran away. Except she had nowhere to run. And because her brother had tried and been captured, and been sold to a slave trader because of it, she did not dare to make a run for it.

"What she had done was hide in a crawlspace under the eaves of her grandmother's roof, while the word went out that she had run away.

"She made small holes in the wall to serve as her windows for a view, and for light and air. It's hard to believe, but she stayed in that cramped space where she could not stand up, for seven long years."

"Seven years!"

"She watched her children grow up through those little peepholes."

"Grandma, how did she not go 'stir-crazy?'"

"She could read. 'Literacy is a bridge from misery to hope.' She read, and she found hope. Her only book, a Bible. She also had her grandmother. I expect she would have lost her mind but for that Bible and the love and care of her grandmother. Finally, an opportunity arose, and with help from white folk, she made it north, to freedom."

They finished eating, quiet and thoughtful from Emmaline's story.

This was the grandma Abby knew. Her voice was serious, stern really with no hint of Elly May.

Emmaline stood up, breaking the spell. "Now, Abby, *you* will demonstrate an alternative meaning of 'stir crazy.'"

"How?"

"There's no electric mixer in this kitchen. But there *is* a great big wooden spoon and an enormous mixing bowl. If the butter is soft, you should be fine. I bought a sifter, a juicer, and a zester."

"Grandma, you could have bought us a mixer!"

"I didn't see one."

"Oh."

Emmaline mused, "I hope the oven is true."

"What does that mean?"

"A true oven is one that accurately heats to the temperature on the dial. If that oven lies to me, and my cakes come out dry, it will break my heart."

Emmaline set Abby to squeeze lemons while she sifted flour and mixed in the baking soda and salt.

Then Abby had to cream the butter and sugar until it was pale and fluffy. This was no easy task. Abby complained, and Emmaline promised to buy a hand mixer before they tried this again.

Emmaline refused to let Abby go to the next step until she was satisfied, and in Abby's opinion, her grandmother was being incredibly picky. Finally, Abby passed muster and was allowed to mix in the eggs, the juice, the zest, and the poppy seeds. Once that was done, they added the flour mixture and the milk a bit at a time until it was all mixed together.

"Now, melt some butter in the microwave and then coat the pans with the melted butter."

Once they got the cakes in the oven, Emmaline watched them like a hawk. When she was satisfied the cakes were done, but not overdone, they got pulled out and placed on the counters to cool.

Emmaline crowed, "Perfection. I tell you these cakes are perfection! Tomorrow, we make the icing!"

"Grandma, 'the proof of the pudding is in the eating.'"

"True. I hope I didn't jinx us. Now we need to make dinner."

"Grandma, I don't think I can cook anything else tonight."

"All we need is a good hike with Freddy to reinvigorate us."

And so, the three of them strode out the front door and walked down the rutted drive toward Sissy's farmhouse. It was nice out. Not too hot, as the sun was dropping behind the hill. The board fencing had a few bluebird houses affixed to its posts.

Emmaline said, "Bluebirds are the harbingers of happiness."

"That makes no sense."

"They make *me* feel happy."

It occurred to Abby then, that her grandma *did* seem happy, and they hadn't even seen a bluebird. Just boxes nailed to fenceposts. Her grandma even looked different. Abby noticed, maybe for the first time, that for an old person, her grandma was very pretty.

Emmaline stopped walking, and pointed, "Abby, look!"

They saw Sissy and Bunny galloping up the hillside, away from them. A dog was following along at a run."

Emmaline looked at Abby. "How does that make you feel?"

"What?"

"Looking at Sissy flying up that field."

"I don't know."

"Surely *you* are not at a loss for words."

Abby shrugged. She had words she could have used. They would have been accurate too. But for once in her life, she stopped them before they could pass her lips. Abby Woods, who was never jealous of other children, was, in that moment, undeniably jealous.

When Abby and Emmaline and Freddy returned from their walk, they headed straight for the kitchen. But as soon as they entered, a mouse made a kamikaze leap from the kitchen counter and ran past them into the pantry.

Freddy made a high-pitched yelp before spinning around and slamming into Abby's knees to run back into the hall.

Mentally, Abby added mice to squirrels and cats as creatures that terrified Freddy.

Emmaline flew past them exclaiming, "Not my cakes!"

Abby walked over to the counter. "Grandma, the mouse only got to one of them. I'll eat that one."

Emmaline scowled at Abby.

Abby added, "What I mean, is that I'll cut the part off that has the teeth marks on it."

Emmaline then patted Abby on the head, which Abby thought was weird. It was like her grandma was petting Freddy or something.

Freddy was now barking in the hallway.

Emmaline wearily said, "Go check on Freddy. I'm putting these cakes into the cold oven. At least the mice can't get to them there."

Abby went to settle Freddy, only to find a man standing on the front porch.

Abby commanded, "Freddy down! Stay!"

Freddy looked relieved to hit the deck, panting and gazing at Abby. He only stopped panting when he looked at the man, who Abby had allowed to cross the threshold.

"Grandma, we have a visitor!"

"Coming!"

The guy standing in the hallway looked sketchy to Abby.

But then again, she had been the one to open the door and let him in.

He said, "Is that one of them wolfdogs?"

"He's a German Shepherd."

"You got him under control?"

"Freddy is very well trained."

Emmaline walked up to the man with her hand extended, "Emmaline Sparks. This is my granddaughter, Abby. And I suppose you've met Freddy."

"I'm Bobby Taylor. You get your propane tank filled?"

"We did. You are so kind to stop and check on us."

She turned to Abby. "Abby please be a darling and put the kettle on for tea."

"Mr. Taylor, we just baked lemon poppyseed loaf cakes. Can I offer you a slice with a hot cup of tea? They're not iced yet, but I bet they're still warm."

"You don't say? Well, I'm not supposed to eat sweets, but I won't tell if you don't."

Emmaline had Abby serve them in 'the parlor' and whispered in her ear to be sure and cut off the parts nibbled by mice.

Bobby Taylor enthused, "This here don't need a lick of icing. It's about the best thing I've ever put in my mouth."

"You're too kind."

"It's true. Well, I'm glad to hear you got propane. I guess I told you this place is near as old as these hills. And you being into stories, well, too bad these walls can't talk. They'd give you more stories than you could write about in one lifetime."

"You must tell me everything you know."

"'Course, I didn't grow up in this house. My Daddy wanted to, but Momma put her foot down. This here area got taken over by the coloreds after the war. It wasn't a place Momma wanted to settle. You know the sayin' 'location, location, location.' She didn't want her children going to school out here neither."

Abby was shocked to see that Emmaline did not correct the man. What was that about?

Emmaline said, "You mean the Civil War?"

He said, "We call it 'the war of northern aggression.'"

Emmaline said, "I see."

The man shook his head, "See here, you're not far from the capital of the Confederacy. And folks around here are real proud of their heritage. We got kind of a thin skin when outsiders tell us what we ought to think and feel about that conflict."

Emmaline nodded, "Well, I'd be fascinated to learn more about this grand old house."

"I'm the one who knows. The place was built by the Taylors, and I'm the current Taylor on the deed. It got built in stages in the 1790's. Roof caught fire once and it was only by divine providence that they got it put out before it took the rest of the house. Chimney fire. Story goes the heavens opened and doused the fire. You can still see the water damage from that dousing in the dining room."

Abby asked, "Are there ghosts?"

"Sugar, if there are, they ain't ever bothered nobody."

Emmaline put her mug down. "Mr. Taylor..."

"Aw, you can call me Bobby."

"Well, Bobby, then please do call me Emmaline."

"What can I do for you, Emmaline."

"Bobby, I'm not a bit worried about ghosts in the house. But we *did* have an indoor encounter with a squirrel. And today we saw a mouse."

Bobby's smile was patronizing. Abby was once again surprised to see her grandma's face looking serene.

"Well, Emmaline, an empty house is gonna' be like that. That is a fact. That's why it ain't good to ever let one sit empty. But you got that scary wolfdog who ought to run out the wildlife lickety-split."

Emmaline sighed dramatically. "Sadly, he is no terrier."

Bobby said, "You want me to set some traps? I think there may be some in the shed out back. Course, I won't be here to empty them. Traps don't always kill 'em clean."

Abby blurted out, "We don't want to kill them!"

Bobby laughed, "You want me to politely ask them to leave?"

"That's what grandma did. She asked the squirrel to leave, and he did."

Abby watched as her grandma winked at Bobby.

Abby looked offended. "You did. I watched you do it."

Bobby said, "Well, ain't that somethin'?"

Emmaline said, "The squirrel was obliging. But I don't think the mice will be."

Bobby grinned widely. "You just need one-eared Tom to come out. He'll take care of your mouse problem. Works cheap too."

"One-eared Tom?"

"I'll see if I can scare him up. Meanwhile, if my memory serves, there's a pie safe in that pantry. It'd be a damn shame if them mice got into this cake."

"Oh, that's good to know. Thank you so much."

Emmaline managed to look Abby straight in the face, without even a twinkle in her eye, and said, "Abby, please get Bobby one of those loaves to take home with him."

Bobby grinned, "I won't say no to that."

Abby jumped up to do as she was asked, and although no one could see her face, she was smiling. She realized she had just witnessed her grandma's "baked goods strategy" at work.

That night Abby dreamed of squirrels and mice. There was a mama squirrel who was trying to put her babies to sleep in Abby's bed. Their little heads all in a row on her pillow. Abby was there, trying to explain to the mama that this was now her bed. Freddy appeared in the doorway as if to summon her. Then she heard a crash. She and Freddy ran down the stairs to find a sea of rampaging mice. They were drinking beers! Tiny little bottles that looked like the ones in the trash bin. Some were fighting. Some were chasing each other around. Abby woke up smiling.

9

Abby and Emmaline located the pie safe, and along with it, a cache of nuts and fluff on the pantry shelves, evidently put there by the resident squirrels. After cleaning up that mess, they iced the cakes, made mushroom burgers, and even had extra-long lavender scented showers. Then they collapsed into bed, exhausted.

At breakfast, Emmaline burned their bagels, trying to use the broiler in the oven because they had no toaster.

"Abby, we need an electric mixer *and* a toaster. Oh, and a frisbee."

"Frisbee?"

"Little things can make big things happen."

Abby furrowed her brow trying to connect big things happening from throwing a frisbee or eating lemon poppy-seed cake. At the moment, none of it felt big, or even the least bit interesting.

Emmaline said, "What's bothering you this morning?"

"I don't know. Aphorisms."

"But you love them as much as I do. I've always been enchanted by their pithiness. They are designed to deliver the essence of a profound truth. And I suppose I have taken comfort from them over the years. They bubble up constantly in my mind."

"Sorry. I think I'm just in a bad mood. Maybe it's this

burned bagel. Maybe it's because that man yesterday was vile. Why were you so nice to him?"

"Our landlord?"

Abby made a face and mimicked his voice, "Call me Bobby." "Vile?"

"You know, wicked, morally despicable."

Emmaline shook her head, "I know the definition of the word. And yes, I see why you might think that of Bobby. But he is our landlord, he liked our cakes and seemed happy to sit and chat. Besides, we need his cooperation in getting rid of the mice, and any other requests we may make this summer. If I had insulted him, how obliging do you think he would be the rest of this summer?"

"You didn't have to act all helpless."

"I had hoped you thought I was disarming. To be disarming is to be someone who defuses situations. Rather like defusing a bomb. It's a skill you might consider acquiring. Remember, 'you catch more flies with honey than vinegar."

"Bobby is more like a jackass than a fly."

"You have a talent for snappy comebacks. But they do not qualify as disarming."

Abby seemed to consider that. "Disarming. Hmmm. So, like taking away their guns so they can't shoot back."

Emmaline sighed as an answer, then said, "Load the dishwasher so we can take a cake to the Taylors."

"Which Taylors?"

"Sissy and Mimi and Francis."

"You go. I don't feel like being disarming."

"Nope. You are coming. They are our only neighbors. We are going to get to know them better."

They put Freddy on a leash and walked to Sissy's place. Sissy was driving a gator utility vehicle into the herd of horses in the field, a dog sitting on the passenger side. Abby and Emmaline stood and watched as she put the gator in park and cut open a bale of hay in the back. She put down flakes of hay in a line, and the horses began to jockey themselves into position. Sissy pulled the gator forward and opened another bale and repeated the process.

Abby said, "She's too young to drive."

Emmaline said, "Not on a farm."

Freddy was on his leash, seemingly curious about the horses, but not trying to run away or hide.

Sissy turned her utility vehicle around, saw them and waved. When she got closer, she yelled, "Can you get the gate?"

Emmaline opened the gate wide. As Sissy pulled through, the dog jumped out of her gator.

Sissy said, "She's real friendly."

Sissy's dog was a large hound, mostly white with a black and tan saddle with tan points over her eyes. She was wagging her tail and wiggling side to side, her body scrunched down in a submissive gesture.

Surprisingly, Freddy bowed, lowering his shoulders, butt up in the air.

Sissy yelled, "You can turn him loose. They's going to play."

Abby looked at Emmaline who shrugged, "Why not?"

Sissy went to park the gator while Emmaline and Abby watched the dogs' romp. They had never seen Freddy play with another dog.

Emmaline enthused, "Abby, look! Freddy has a friend. How wonderful!"

Sissy joined them and said, "Belle is the best dog ever. And to think she's a cull."

Abby said, "A cull?"

Sissy said, "The hunt club don't keep all the hounds they breed. Some gets traded in drafts to other clubs. And some, them that won't hunt..." Sissy drew her forefinger across her throat.

Emmaline said, "Surely not these days."

"Not like they used to do. Otherwise, she wouldn't have landed here. Same with these old horses. Knackers. They used to butcher them and feed them to the hounds."

Abby gasped.

Sissy said, "It was supposed to be an honor. But I 'spect it's an honor the horses sure can do without. So Daddy, he let me run the retirement home for them. The folks in the club, the ones that own the horses, pay me every month to take care of them. The ones that can still hack-out, they let me hack-out."

Emmaline said, "We saw you riding Bunny yesterday. You seem to be a natural, Sissy."

Sissy grinned, "Bunny is like sitting in an easy chair."

Emmaline lifted her bag with the loaf cake in it. "We baked these yesterday. Lemon poppyseed loaf cake. Hope you'll like it."

"Go on and knock on the door. Mimi's in there. She'll be glad for company. I'll bring the hounds when I come in."

Abby was surprised to see that Freddy and Belle were side by side in a thicket, tails wagging and noses down, absorbed.

Abby reluctantly followed Emmaline, who did not seem hesitant at all to leave Freddy.

Emmaline knocked on the doorframe, the door being ajar. The knock was answered with, "Come in, come in, neighbors."

Emmaline said, "You must be Sissy's Mimi. We devoured your biscuits! They were delicious, and we didn't yet have a thing to eat in the house when they arrived, so the timing was perfect."

Mimi was dark and petite, with closely cropped hair, and a broad smile.

She said, "I'm glad you enjoyed them. I make 'em from scratch every morning."

Emmaline said, "I'm not a baker like you, but I did try my hand at Lemon Poppyseed loaf cake, and I confess I think I got a pretty good do."

Abby detected a hint of Elly May in Emmaline's voice. Disarming the neighbors?

Mimi smiled, "Ooooh, I do love anything lemon. Thank you. Now you folks come on in and sit down. I got coffee in the pot. How you take your coffee?"

Emmaline said, "Cream and sugar for me. Abby doesn't drink coffee yet."

Mimi said, "Sissy, she drink it like she fifty. But somedays she do think she fifty!" Mimi laughed. "Course, every so often, I brings her down to reality."

Mimi sliced the cake and brought the coffee to the table. She said to Abby, "Child, you want a glass of milk to wash that down?"

Abby said, "Thank you."

Abby had not had cow's milk for years, but a side glance at Emmaline told her she had answered Mimi's question correctly. "When in Rome..."

It was then that Abby noticed a small plate hanging on the wall, like it was a piece of art. And it was white with a rim of cobalt blue with flowers in the middle. In her mind's eye, she held up that broken bit from Emmaline's kitchen window ledge as if it were a missing piece of a jigsaw puzzle, but of course, Mimi's little plate was whole, still. She kept her voice as natural as she could. But she felt a small rush.

Abby said, "That plate. Is it bone China?"

Mimi was standing at the kitchen counter, pouring Abby her glass of milk. She turned to look at the plate on the wall.

"Why yes. Now, how is it you know such a thing?"

Emmaline answered without looking at Abby, "From hanging around her grandma too much! It is very pretty. Cobalt blue. Beautiful."

Mimi said, "It's real old. Came down through the Taylors. That's all that's left. I sure wish I had the set."

Mimi served them, then sat down, "How's it you two ended up in that derelict old house of Bobby's?"

Emmaline said, "Well, I write novels, and this area of the country figures heavily in my latest project. It started when I got interested in the story of Sally Hemings and Thomas Jefferson. I've been reading some of the oral history around that. And as you know, the oral history, and the first-person accounts of those who had been enslaved, well they had been discounted, ignored, brushed aside, dishonored. And the lies, the rationalizations, the cover stories by relatives and others wishing to hide the truth, they were believed, while the other stories were not. But I put a great deal of store by the oral tradition among the formerly enslaved."

Abby had another bite of cake followed by a gulp of milk.

She found that she liked it. It didn't taste all that different from Almond milk and it was nice and cold.

Mimi nodded, and added, "That's real interesting."

Emmaline continued, "And then came the DNA evidence. And it got me to thinking about all the stories that had been handed down over the generations about other such families that had been denied or hidden. Maybe people who weren't as famous. I call them the shadow families."

Mimi said, "Plenty of them, too."

Emmaline continued, "Oral histories need to be given their due. I know that oral histories aren't perfect. That's why I choose to write fiction, in case I get something wrong. But I want to try to tell unacknowledged truths through story. And I find this sort of tale to be an essential truth about America, the way it was. I want to tell the story of those shadow families that had no legal or social standing but were real as real could be."

Abby stayed silent, scraping a bit of icing off her plate with the edge of her fork. But she had heard every word. And two words, "unacknowledged truths' repeated in her mind. What about the unacknowledged truths Emmaline was hiding? Her grandma was always different, magical, a witch, but one who had clearly lost her wizard a long time ago. Abby would search for the truth through story, just like her grandma. She might not get it all right, but she intended to get close, to get to the essential truths.

Emmaline smiled and took a sip of her coffee. "That's good coffee."

Mimi said, "Thank you. But listen here, you choosing to go walking' through a briar patch. Just saying'."

"Don't worry, Mimi. I have no reason to speak of such things around Bobby Taylor."

"Bobby Taylor? I don't care a whit if you speak such around Bobby Taylor. Bobby got no real power. Now, a book, that can be a mighty powerful thing. Even I knows that."

Emmaline nodded, "True that."

Mimi sat back in her chair and nodded at Emmaline, "Well, if you interested, I got stories and you're welcome to them. I don't mind telling' them true. I's worked in white women's kitchens since I was nine years old. I got pulled out of school, and nobody done nothing about it. I hear things working in those houses that would make your hair as curly as mine. You think it's better these days… course, in lots of ways it *is* better. But they's a meanness these days that makes me think of some mighty bad times in the past. People gets so heated up, they's bound to boil over. And that be exactly what some folks be wanting. I do worry about that. 'Specially after events that were fairly recent."

Sissy walked into the kitchen with two happy dogs, both panting heavily.

Mimi tsk-tsked, "Sissy, what you thinking, bringing those curs into my clean kitchen?"

Abby stood up and walked Freddy to the doorway. She said, "Freddy, down! Stay."

Freddy with extra flair, hit the deck. He had a delirious grin on his face, tongue lolling out the side of his mouth.

Sissy took Belle by the collar and placed her next to Freddy where she stayed.

Mimi said, "Sissy, Abby got the touch with animals, like you! Now, you sit down, and I'll cut you some of this fine cake Emmaline baked."

Abby said, "I can't ride a horse though."

Sissy said, "I can learn you if you want. It ain't hard."

Emmaline clapped her hands together, "Oh Sissy, do you really have a horse that Abby can ride?"

Mimi brought Sissy a slice of cake and turned to pour her a glass of milk.

Sissy said, "Buttermilk is near impossible to fall off. She's fat and she so short even if you find a way to fall off, you don't have far to fall. Just know your jeans will get real dirty since we don't have a saddle for her."

Abby's cheeks had gone pink.

Emmaline answered. "How about *that* Abby? Sissy is going to teach you how to ride!"

Sissy said, "'Come on then. We can take the dogs, too."

Abby said, "Now?"

Sissy said, "Soon as I finish this cake. Ms. Emmaline, this is yummy!"

Emmaline said, "Abby, jump on that offer. Go have fun."

Then Emmaline turned to Mimi. "Mimi, I don't want to make a pest of myself, but I would love to hear your stories."

Mimi grinned, "If you really want to hear them. This old gray head of mine is right full of them. They ain't all pretty though."

Emmaline put her palm on her chest. "I *really, really*, do want to hear them. But I also want to learn how to make those biscuits."

"All right. But only if you share this recipe with me. 'Cause I must admit, you sure did get a good 'do' on these here cakes.

Sissy made fast work on her piece of cake. Then she chugged her milk. Sissy stood up and nodded at Abby.

Emmaline made a shoo-ing gesture at Abby, who suddenly felt nervous. That was a new sensation.

* * *

Sissy led Abby through a herd of horses who had stopped grazing and were a bit too close to Abby for comfort. Sissy pointed out Buttermilk.

Sissy said, "Come on, Abby! You gotta' just walk on up to her on the left side. The left side. Remember what I said? Okay, watch me. See, Buttermilk is an old girl who knows what's what. But she still ain't gonna' put the bridle on herself."

Sissy threw reins over the head of Buttermilk, then slipped the bit into her mouth. She fastened what she called a throat latch, and then the noseband.

"Hang onto her. I'll catch Bunny."

Sissy got the bridle on Bunny, then they led the horses out of the field, closing the gate behind them. Sissy put Buttermilk up against a tree stump and told Abby to climb up on the stump. Abby stood on the stump and although she heard Sissy speaking, it might as well have been a foreign language. Although Buttermilk stood still, only flicking her long tail at flies, there didn't seem to be an obvious way to get on a bareback horse.

"Go on. Grab a hunk of mane, get a good grip. Just go on. Grab her mane with your left hand. I can hold the reins for you 'til you get aboard."

Abby began to sweat. "Shouldn't I know more about, y'know, controlling a horse, before I get on one bareback?"

Sissy had her own aphorism, she said, "Experience is the best teacher."

Abby quipped, "Experience is something you don't get until just *after* you need it."

Sissy giggled, "I guess that's true, too. Just pull yourself part way on by laying on your belly right behind her withers."

"Withers?"

"That high bone where her neck come into her spine."

Sissy pushed Buttermilk even closer to the stump. "Look here, she so short, you only got to flop over."

Abby did. It was uncomfortable. "Now what?"

"Now you just swing your right leg over and sit up."

Abby managed to scrunch her leg up and over and sat up.

She noticed the two dogs were sitting side by side, watching, mouths hanging open.

Abby said to the dogs, "I'd like to see you get on a horse."

Sissy said, "You're funny! Now take a rein in each hand, but you ain't allowed to pull on the reins unless you're trying to stop or turn. Buttermilk don't like a heavy hand."

Sissy, quick as a wink, did her fancy neck mount onto Bunny.

She instructed, "Give her a cluck to get her going. Follow Bunny. We's just going for a walk. Don't worry. I'm just going to show you around is all."

Abby looked down at her horse. "I love her color. Buttermilk, I mean."

"She's buckskin. Black legs, black mane, tail, yellow coat. Kind of unusual for a hunt horse. But she was a good field horse for a couple of ladies. Then she just got old. Sometimes one of her ladies comes out with apples or carrots to visit."

"How old is she?"

"I believe she be twenty-four."

"That's old?"

"It is. Bunny be twenty-two. Nobody better tell her that, though."

Sissy grinned. "I do love this old mare."

Abby said, "The world does look different from up here."

"We turn here. I'll show you a real pretty view."

They turned onto a worn path along the edge of a hayfield.

Sissy said, "That's our hay. We got to stay to the edge until it gets cut and baled. After second cutting, we got enough for us. Sometimes we get enough to sell."

"How much of this land belongs to you guys?"

"Most of what you see. 'Cept some around Bobby's old home place. But most of that went to us long time ago."

"Are you related to Bobby?"

Sissy laughed, "Do we look related?"

Abby felt incredibly embarrassed. "Oh. Um."

Sissy said, "Made you squirm, didn't I? Like you couldn't have noticed that we be black folk and old Bobby, he be lily-white?"

Abby started to be a smart-ass. But thought of her grand-mother and managed to stop herself.

Sissy laughed. "Got you! I was just teasing. You ain't dumb and you likely ain't wrong. Now, Bobby, he'd likely slap you if you said such a thing. But we got the same last name for a reason. And that reason is that his people owned my people. And somehow, when the deck got reshuffled, we got more of the land in our name than he got in his name."

"There must be a story there. Something big reshuffled that deck."

"You'd have to ask my Mimi. She knows more than any-one about just about everything. She is the smartest person I ever know'd. And my Daddy is real smart, just a different sort of smart. Mimi, she don't read or write so well, but dang, she remember everything and then some. Now, you grab a hunk of Buttermilk's mane and hang on. We gonna' climb up to that ridge. Don't go sliding off her butt."

Sissy turned up what seemed like an impossibly steep track, but the horses did not hesitate, and neither did the dogs. Abby felt the back muscles on Buttermilk rise and fall, flex and relax, her hind legs pushing up under her belly, her neck reaching down and forward. Abby was gripping the mare's mane harder than she needed, but she sure wasn't going to embarrass herself by sliding off.

They got to the top and Sissy and Bunny stopped and stood on the ridge, and Abby and Buttermilk came to stand next to her.

Abby exhaled, "Wow. That *is* beautiful. I have to bring my grandma up here. She'd go nuts over that view. It's so green. And look, there's a lake over there."

Sissy said, "I bet you got pretty views where you come from too."

"We do."

"But this here view, well, I feel like it's mine. Course it ain't. Just like I feel like Bunny is my horse. But she ain't."

Abby said, "Ownership is an illusion. Everything we have is on loan, to be enjoyed while it lasts."

Sissy frowned, "Where the hell did that come from?"

Abby grinned, "You're not the only one with a smart grandma."

* * *

Later, upon seeing Abby, Emmaline laughed, "Oh, my goodness, Abby! I've never seen such a sight. Take those jeans off and we'll throw them in the wash. "

Abby pulled off her jeans right there in the kitchen and handed them to Emmaline who turned them around and held them up for Abby to see the backside.

There was a perfect crescent shape on the seat made up of horse sweat and dirt.

Emmaline said, "I think Buttermilk could use a bath."

Abby covered her mouth for a moment. "Please tell me that will come out. Those are my favorite jeans."

"I'll spray them with stain remover. You go put on some shorts. Then I'll show you what I bought."

Abby came back downstairs to find that Emmaline had purchased a lot more stuff. It wasn't just her purchases, though. A bunch of boxes had been delivered to the front porch. All the stuff they had shipped had arrived. Abby was tired, and her inner thighs were so fatigued they were almost trembling.

When Emmaline served their lunch salads, Abby was propping her chin up in the palm of her hand.

"Abby darling, I bought a Frisbee, and I thought maybe this afternoon I would teach you how to throw and catch it."

Emmaline tipped her head in the direction of Freddy, who was snoring and twitching. "Clearly, this is not the optimal time."

"Grandma, Buttermilk is so cool. We climbed a steep hill to a beautiful view. You would have loved it!"

Emmaline leaned back in her chair, "Did you enjoy Sissy's company?"

"Yeah, but Grandma, why doesn't she know how to speak properly? And no offense, but her Mimi is just as bad. At least they don't seem vile like Bobby."

"Judge not, lest ye be judged.'"

"Do you even think she knows?"

"Knows what?"

"The way she speaks. She's worse than Ms. Pierce."

"Abby, her speech is what is called a dialect. I'm enjoying hearing it again. To me, much of the regional dialect seems musical. Music I've not heard for a very long time."

"But people will think Sissy is stupid if she goes around speaking like that."

"Then 'people' would be wrong. Sissy is a smart girl. If Sissy finds that she needs to change the way she speaks for certain audiences, say for professional or academic goals, I think she'll ask for the help if she needs it."

"Do you mean me?"

"Never assume, never presume! Just be a friend. I think *you* could use a friend for the summer."

"Grandma, I don't think we have enough in common to become friends."

"Phooey. You just need to get to know each other. I have an idea."

"That's scary."

"I'm going to unpack some of these boxes and then we're having mac and cheese with broccoli and picante sauce for dinner.And then tomorrow..."

"What?"

"I think we should invite the Taylor family over for dinner."

"Pushing it, don't you think?"

"Not at all. We'll have a little dinner, and then I'll teach you girls, and maybe the dogs too, all about frisbee."

"You are obsessed with this frisbee thing, aren't you?"

"It's a life skill, darling."

"Uh, a useless one, if you ask me."

"I never found that to be true."

"Grandma, really, what possible use could it have?"

Emmaline gave a sly smile. "Well, it's a way to spend time with a guy, where you can chat and learn about each other, while keeping a decent buffer zone."

"Grandma, I've never seen *you* throw a frisbee. I've never seen *you* with guys. Besides, I can't even throw a tennis ball. Frisbee won't change my life."

"There are more things in heaven and earth than are dreamt of in your philosophy."

"Grandma, I don't get it."

"Just because you haven't seen the evidence yet, does not mean I'm not right. You should look that one up. It's from Hamlet."

Emmaline had a twinkle in her eye. And Abby saw the witch again. But she could not imagine, not yet, how the witch tossing a disc back and forth, (and she did remember Emmaline mentioning holding a beer in her other hand) could figure into her own tale.

But then it struck her that for Emmaline, everything was a metaphor. Although Abby did not yet understand the significance of this one, the twinkle in her grandmother's eye felt like a command to keep trying.

10

Emmaline and Abby moved the kitchen table into the formal dining room.

"Grandma, this will only seat four people and there's going to be five."

"We'll make a children's table for you and Sissy."

"A children's table? From what?"

"From the porch furniture. That's what."

Abby frowned, "That Bobby Taylor ought to be ashamed of himself, calling this a furnished house."

Emmaline suppressed a laugh. "You sound like your father. We have been bamboozled. Perhaps I was too enchanted by the history of the house to ask about specifics. Regardless, I *am* enchanted. A lack of dining room furniture is not going to dampen my enthusiasm."

There was a light rap on the front door. Freddy rushed to the door, first barking like mad, but then seeing who was there, began his silly dance.

Sissy was standing there holding a pie, and behind her was Mimi and her Daddy, Francis. Emmaline took the pie and ushered everyone into the parlor. Sissy had dropped to the floor to greet Freddy, who was snapping his jaws, and curling around her and yodeling.

Sissy was crooning, "Ain't you the silliest beast? What kind of language is you speaking? Well, Miss Belle, she think you the greatest. Nearly broke her heart to get left behind."

Abby said, "I wish you would have brought Belle."

"Mimi wouldn't have let me bring her. She said that would be an impolite thing to do."

Emmaline poked her head out of the parlor. "Abby, please set the tables. Sissy can help you bring in the porch table and chairs."

Emmaline had made one of her favorite summer pasta dishes. Chopped summer tomatoes, fresh basil, garlic, and brie cheese torn into little bits. All of it she had let come to room temperature with salt and pepper in olive oil. After a time, the brie liquified in the oil. Then she tossed it into a bowl of hot spaghettini. Along with that went warm French bread and butter.

After everyone was seated and served, Mimi took a bite and crowed, "Mmmm-mmm. Emmaline, you got yourself another good 'do' girl! You got the touch."

"Thank you."

Everyone made small talk while the pasta disappeared and the plates were wiped clean with bread.

Emmaline said, "I'm looking forward to a piece of that sour cherry pie, myself. I'll put the coffee on, but while it brews, I want the girls to carry that porch furniture back out, because I think we should have our dessert out there and watch the sun go down."

Once they got settled on the front porch, Emmaline went back into the house and came out carrying a new, very large, Frisbee.

"Did I mention that I was among the earliest classes of women at The University?"

Freddy had put his head across Abby's knees, and she had been silently stroking him on his head. She looked up, interested in this new fact. But Freddy took his long snout and pushed it under her hand to get her back on track, so she did not get to ask any questions.

Sissy's Daddy, Francis said, "That would have been early 70s?"

"Yes. While there, I got more than proficient at Frisbee. There weren't many women yet, so finding a date was like shooting fish in a barrel. Still, there were few women who could toss a disc like I could and as I was not socially adept, it became a valuable tool."

Francis nodded, "Aw, Emmaline, I bet you couldn't beat them off with a stick. But I do remember how Frisbee once was the thing. I wasn't too shabby myself. Of course, I didn't go to school there or even work there like I do now."

Emmaline smiled, "It was a magical time. I thought I would see if I still had the touch, and if I did, if I could teach these girls how to toss a Frisbee."

Abby was all ears, imagining not her grandma throwing a Frisbee, but her grandma with a long stick like a sword, fending off the men.

Mimi said, "Francis, I seen you toss that thing around with your friends. You was better than good."

"Daddy, is that so?"

Emmaline shook the Frisbee in the air like she was shaking a tambourine.

She said, "Francis, I double-dog dare you."

He got up and turned to his mother, "Mimi, you sure you want to see your son make a fool of himself in front of his daughter?"

Abby said, "I won't think less of you, Mr. Taylor, if you aren't good. I can't hit or catch a ball or run fast. Grandma thinks maybe Frisbee will be different. But I doubt it."

Emmaline and Francis stood about fifty feet apart and began to toss the disc back and forth. They managed to catch nearly every throw. Freddy barked once for each toss and followed the flight with his eyes, dancing back and forth on his front paws.

Sissy said, "Hey! Ya'll ain't too bad! Daddy, you even got a bit of style."

Emmaline bragged, "Abby, your grandma's still got it!"

Mimi said, "Now you girls try. Emmaline, maybe you got some pointers?"

Abby looked at Sissy. "Hate to break it to you, Sissy, but when it comes to anything athletic and me, it's a lost cause."

Sissy said, "That can't be so. You sat up there on Buttermilk real good. In fact, I think tomorrow we get you trotting and maybe even cantering."

Emmaline had gestured for Abby and Sissy to come over to her. "It's all in the wrist. You hold it so and flick your wrist. Let your arm follow your eyes." Then she tossed it to Francis, who tossed it back to Emmaline.

Emmaline added, "The secret of success is being willing to really suck at something long enough that suddenly you don't."

"Grandma that can't be a real aphorism."

"Sure, it is. It's pithy and it expresses an elemental truth about life."

"You just made it up, didn't you?"

"Nothing is original, dearest. Go on now, you girls enjoy sucking at Frisbee without our help while we sit and chat."

Abby was terrible.

Sissy was terrible.

They truly did suck at Frisbee.

But Freddy kindly fetched the Frisbee from all its "far-flung" locations and brought it back to Abby.

The adults were hardly paying attention.

Sissy said, "My daddy and your grandma must have spent a whole lotta' time sucking at this to get as good as they are."

"My grandma is also pretty good at chucking tennis balls for Freddy to retrieve. But this Frisbee thing is news to me."

Sissy called over to the porch. "Miz Sparks, you think Freddy could learn to catch this thing?"

"Sure. We can try."

Emmaline got up from her chair. "Abby, take Freddy a bit further away, and I'll send him a gentle floater. You tell him to go get it while it's still in the air."

Freddy caught it on the first try! Everyone applauded. He stood stock still, Frisbee in his mouth, mystified at all the fuss. Emmaline repeated the exercise, and Freddy caught every single one, and each time, they applauded. By the fourth catch he greeted the applause by dropping the Frisbee and barking along with the clapping.

Finally, everyone was tired, including Freddy. The girls sat back on the porch with the adults.

Emmaline was saying, "So, Bobby Taylor has never lived in this house?"

Mimi shook her head, "After the Civil War, the white Taylors stopped living in this old house. But the black Taylors stayed. You see, after the war, this area here was a place the freed slaves made a community. But they come here because it had already been a place for free people of color. Now, that's a story. It goes all the way back to Monticello."

Emmaline leaned forward, "No kidding?"

Mimi nodded, "One of the Hemings girls married a free person of color who lived out this way. But that's only part of the tale."

Francis interrupted his mother. "But our original bit of land, back in Antebellum times, it come from a white Taylor putting aside something for his mixed-race children. There was a time he had both white and black women, and two sets of children living here. Those mixed-race children of them times, well he didn't give them freedom. They's was all enslaved back then, his very own children. But he made sure them children learned trades and in time they bought their own freedom. It was a tricky thing to do back then. For the longest time, you free a slave, by law the freedman had to leave the state. Whites knew a free slave could give the enslaved ideas, you know? They feared an uprising."

Emmaline leaned forward in her chair. "Fascinating. This is exactly the kind of thing I want to know more about."

Mimi said, "I got more. But I want to hear what stories you've gathered."

Emmaline said, "What I have I've gathered from reading. What you've got goes far beyond that. But I'm happy to share what I've got."

Sissy added, "You two can make a project out of swapping stories but I got my own idea for a project. I'm gonna' make a rider out of Abby."

Francis nodded, "That's a fine idea, Sissy. And I think you and Abby also ought to work on throwing that Frisbee. While you're at it, you can make a fine Frisbee dog out of that wolf-dog."

Abby and Emmaline made a chorus saying, "He's a German Shepherd!"

* * *

Later when the Taylors had gone home, Abby got to work cleaning the kitchen, while Emmaline sat and wrote notes at the kitchen table, now back in its proper place.

Abby said, "You're writing down what Mimi told you?"

"Oh yes. In fact, I'm thinking of recording her stories. You think she'd mind if I did?"

"No. I don't think she would. But I was thinking of you two trading stories."

"Yes?"

"And Sissy teaching me how to ride Buttermilk."

"I'm excited for you. What an opportunity!"

Abby said, "I need to do something for Sissy, too. I just wish I could fix the way Sissy speaks. And I understand what you said about dialect. But it doesn't change that people are going to think she's stupid."

"Did you think she was stupid?"

"I did at first. Until I got to know her. But there are a lot of people won't give Sissy a second chance if she speaks like that to them."

Emmaline looked thoughtful. Then said, "You're right about that."

Abby raised her eyebrows. "I. Wow. I am?"

"We judge people by how they speak all the time. Using

'Standard English' is taken as a sign of social class and education. But people learn to tone down their dialect if they feel they need to. Because linguistic profiling is a reality most of us recognize. It's only natural. We humans feel the need to make quick assessments through superficial observations. And speech is one way to do so. As is race. As is sex. As are other aspects of appearance. But of course, doing so is often wrong and unjust."

"Grandma, you told me I was right, but I still feel like you're saying I'm wrong."

"Hmmm. I have an idea. How about you invite Sissy for a sleepover?"

"I don't know that she'd come."

"What if you tell her she can bring Belle? Then Freddy can have a friend, too."

"Grandma, you're pushing things."

"I was thinking I could read to you guys. You used to love that. This house would make a perfect backdrop for ghost stories. I'm sure the house is full of ghosts."

"I'm sure it's full of squirrels and mice."

"True."

Abby shrugged. "Sure. Okay. Why not?"

* * *

The next morning Emmaline winked at Abby before performing an incantation over the new toaster.

"Toaster, toaster, hear my pray-er, no burned bagels, now or lay-ter.

Toast 'til tawny,

Then call out 'ping!'

when perfection is their thing."

"Now, Abby, Watch this." Emmaline split a bagel and put it in the toaster, pushing down the lever.

Emmaline said, "I've poured our tea and it's steeping. I also gave Mimi a call to ask if you and Freddy could come down this morning to hang with Sissy and Belle. She said to come on over as soon as you've had breakfast. Sissy is picking up the field, whatever that means."

"Are you getting rid of me for a reason?"

Emmaline flicked her hair over her shoulder and looked off in the distance. It was sort of like she was posing for a photo or something.

Emmaline said, "I'm meeting an old friend."

"Hmmm. An old friend?"

She turned back to look at Abby, "You'll have more fun with Sissy than having to sit while two old people rehash college memories."

"You never said you still had friends here."

"A friend. Sissy is welcome to come back to the house with Belle after your ride. But only if Mimi says it's fine. I expect you two can find something to eat between the two houses."

"How long are you planning to be gone?"

"I'll be home before dinnertime."

"All day long?"

"We have a lot to catch up on."

"Ping."

"Grandma, who is this person you are going to meet, and why didn't you mention them to be before now."

Emmaline pulled the bagels out with a pair of tongs. "Oh, would you look at our bagels, Abby. It's magic."

"Grandma, it's a toaster. That's just a toasted bagel."

"Never let your senses dull to those small miracles that make up an ordinary day."

"You are so weird."

"I take that as a compliment. Now, eat your perfect bagel and drink your perfect tea, and go ride horses with Sissy. That's sure to wake up your senses."

Emmaline had shut down her questions. And Abby wanted to ask more questions, but just mentioning riding horses made her tummy go flip-flop, as Sissy had said, "Today, they would trot and maybe even canter." Abby wanted to. But she also did not want to. She knew her senses were not dull; in fact, they were wide awake. Her inner thighs were screaming at her just from yesterday's walk on Buttermilk.

* * *

When Freddy and Abby found Sissy, she was in the pasture with the horses, driving a little tractor that was pulling a thingy behind it. The thingy seemed to be throwing stuff behind it as Sissy drove. When Sissy saw her, she waved.

Abby stood at the gate with Freddy. Belle came loping over and the two dogs wiggled and sniffed butts and then began a game of chase. Abby stood alone by the gate and felt out of place.

As she stood there though, her eyes were drawn to the horses, all lined up munching the hay on the ground that Sissy had set out for them. She spotted Buttermilk right off. Easy. Buttermilk was the only Buckskin in the herd.

But then she was able to spot Bunny. Sissy was right. Her ears were larger than the ears of the other horses.

Mimi came out on the porch and greeted Abby. "Hey young'un." It still sounded odd to Abby to have someone greet her with "Hey." When in Rome. "Hey, Mimi."

"We sure did have a fine meal with good company. You tell your grandma we said thank you. And don't you go home without taking a jar of Francis' honey."

"Will do."

Mimi nodded toward the field, "Sissy been hard at work this morning, picking up that field and spreading. She'll be done soon. Then ya'll be free 'til supper."

"Grandma said to tell you that Sissy and Belle are invited to a sleep-over anytime."

"I'm sure Sissy would like that. She still gots to do her job though. Them horses are Sissy's paying customers."

"Mimi, can I ask you something?"

"Sure, child. Go on."

"How is it that you left school? Kids that ditch school in California, they get hauled into summer school, or alternative school."

"I had to go to work."

"Um, that's also against the law. Child labor and all."

"Children in the country work. Sissy, she drive the tractor and the gator as soon as she could reach the pedals. But that's here at the homeplace. But even still, it's like this see, things that been doing a certain way for a long time, kind of get accepted even when they's wrong. And that goes for a lot more than a child working in a kitchen or not showin' up to school. The world changes a lot slower than the law. It sure do."

Abby, young as she was, could feel the weight and regret of Mimi's words.

"Mimi, does it make you sad that you didn't get to go to school?"

"It do. And I try real hard to get Sissy to see she need to try harder. She need to do better at school because her poor granny never did get the chance to try. But she don't listen to me. Me and Emmaline talked about it. And we's both hopin' that you can help Sissy. But don't you let on I said so."

"Help her how?"

"Sissy, she read real slow. And she get embarrassed at school when they make her read aloud. It only make her hate going all the more."

"Grandma said if Sissy sleeps over, she'll read stories to us. When grandma reads, she does all the different voices and even does the sound effects."

"Bet your grandma is a regular actress. Well now, that makes me want to come too. Being able to pick up a book, and get them words to come out of it, through your body, and out your mouth, them different people, places, and happenings, is sorcery of a kind, aint it?"

Abby said, "Wow, Mimi, I think so, too! But my grandma would say it's an everyday sort of magic."

Mimi looked sad, "For some."

Abby said, "But you're right, it is magic. Some days my grandma seems like a witch, even to me."

Mimi smiled, "Emmaline was certain you would be the one to teach Sissy."

"I'm not sure about that."

"You know what I'm thinking? I'm thinking when this summer be done, you gonna' look like a natural on a horse. And Sissy she going to let the words flow through her from them books. Maybe she'll read them Bible stories to her poor old granny, who can't read enough to save her soul."

Abby thought Mimi was making a joke. But her face was serious.

* * *

Once Sissy got Abby on Buttermilk, she had no problem shifting into full teaching mode. Sissy explained, "See trot goes like, 'bump-bump-bump-bump-bump' up and down, and you just go with it. Long as you stay centered, where you gonna' go?"

"Um, the ground. Ow. This is painful."

"Go with the movement, instead of fighting it. Don't go gripping with your legs so. Can't lean forward neither. Kiss of death."

"This can't be right. Ow."

"You'll bloody your knees like that. Jeans will scrunch up and rub you raw."

"I think it's too late for that. Inside of my knees are burning."

"Okay. Take a break and walk. Old Buttermilk got a back like an easy chair. All soft and padded with fat. So, y'know, sit back on your butt on that cushion of fat. You can grab some of her mane and kind of pull on it to hold yourself upright. It don't hurt her, and she don't care. But I'm promising you, if you lean forward and grip with your knees, you ain't going to be able to take a shower or a bath for days."

"What? I don't understand."

"Reckon you will soon enough."

"Do you mind if we leave cantering for another day? I really suck at this."

"Guess that's true. But not nearly as bad as we both suck at Frisbee."

* * *

Abby and Sissy, along with Belle and Freddy, got back to "Squirrel Manor" for a late lunch. Abby had promised Sissy iced tea and avocado toast with pepper jack cheese (she wanted to use the new toaster).

When they walked into the kitchen with the dogs, there was a large paper bag sitting on the table.

Abby opened it and looked inside. "Weird. Look at this. There's a bag of dry cat food in here."

Sissy said, "What's that note say?"

"A week or two of One-eared Tom ought to fix you girls up right, Bobby."

Abby said, "Oh, that is not good, not good, not good at all."

Sissy said, "Looks like you got you a cat here somewhere."

"Freddy hates cats."

Sissy shrugged, "Any cat called 'one-eared Tom' has learnt how to take care of hisself."

"I'm not worried about the cat. It's Freddy."

Sissy laughed and looked down at her dog, "Belle won't let no kitty hurt your wolf!"

"He's a German Shepherd." Abby sighed, "Freddy will freak out."

"You serious?"

"He loses his mind when he sees a cat."

"Belle can learn him about cats. She's a hound, but she don't hunt nothing. She ain't scairt and she don't chase 'em, neither. We got a barn cat and Belle likes her. She was even gentle with Ginger's kits."

"Grandma needs to come home, now."

"Where's the fire? Besides, I thought you were going to feed me some California specialty for lunch. I'm hungry."

"Shouldn't we find the cat before it finds us?"

"Naw. Let's eat."

Sissy had never had avocado toast or pepperjack cheese.

Once she had taken a couple bites she said, "Hey, this is tasty."

Abby and Sissy polished off the toast and then found leftover pie. They ate every bit of it. Sissy got up and said, "I need to go and do chores, but I want to hear your grandma tell more of her stories. I think my Mimi might want to listen too. I mean if it's suits ya'll, maybe we can come by later. No need to feed us dinner, or for me to stay the night. I can run us over on the Gator. I bet Mimi would bring more pie to go with a story."

"You're going to leave me and Freddy alone with that cat roaming around in here?"

Sissy and Belle were already heading down the hall toward the front door. Sissy turned around and grinned, "Look-it! Bobby wasn't kidding. That cat already left you a present!"

Abby froze, "Oh, barf. Is it dead?"

Freddy was already shrinking behind Abby's legs. But not Belle, and not Sissy. Sissy bent down and picked up the dead thing by its tail. "I'll just chuck it out back."

"What? I don't want to step on it or something."

"Okay. I'll go put it in the bin."

"Outside. Out back. In the shed."

"Cat won't need dinner tonight. He done ate all the squishy parts."

Abby put her hands over her ears. "Too much information, Sissy. Way too much."

Sissy laughed and headed out the door with Belle trotting at her heels.

Abby looked down at Freddy who was more nervous than she was. She said, "It's in the house somewhere. Where's Emmaline? She'd be saying, 'Kitty cats are our friends.' But you never bought that line, did you?"

Sissy and Belle walked back in, and Abby said, "I hope you're going to wash your hands. I bet you can get all sorts of diseases from a gutted dead rat."

"That was a mouse."

Abby said, "Whatever. I don't get the difference."

"You sure would if you saw a rat."

Still, Sissy walked to the little powder room under the stairs and washed her hands with the fancy bar of scented soap that Emmaline had placed there. She went to dry her hands, but called out to Abby, "Am I allowed to use these towels?"

"Yes. Use them. We have a washing machine."

"Mimi would skin me alive if I used her good hand towels. They's only for company."

"You're company."

Just then all hell broke loose. Freddy sounded like he'd been shot. Belle began barking like mad.

At that moment, Emmaline walked through the front door with a bag of groceries. The cat had streaked through the room with his next victim clenched between his jaws, and seeing the dogs, had sprinted up the stairs with it.

Sissy called Belle, who came to her.

Then Emmaline, Abby, Sissy, and Belle, followed the trail of urine back into the kitchen to find Freddy plastered in the back corner of the pantry.

Emmaline said, "What the hell was that?"

Abby said, "You didn't see?"

Emmaline put her bag of groceries down, while Belle went into the pantry and began licking Freddy in the face. Freddy was whining and moaning and whimpering while Sissy and Abby stood watching.

Sissy said, "Weren't nobody but one-eared Tom. Bobby was right about him. Slick fella. He'll clear out your mice lickety-split. Mice aren't stupid. Word will get out this house has a killer on the loose."

Abby said, "A killer on the loose! Poor Freddy."

Sissy said, "I never seen a dog so scairt of a cat."

Emmaline exhaled loudly, "Freddy has a few quirks."

Abby handed Emmaline Bobby's note.

Emmaline shook her head, "This presents a challenge."

Abby was shocked, "A challenge? Are you kidding me? This will be a disaster. Chaos. Freddy will get an ulcer. Or maybe commit suicide. I'll get an ulcer. I mean, who can sleep with that cat skulking around assassinating mice. The cat is a professional killer."

Sissy began to laugh.

Emmaline joined in.

Freddy did not get the joke.

Abby definitely did not get the joke.

Emmaline wiped her eyes and said, "This might be a good thing, Abby. Not an easy thing, but a good thing, nonetheless. Freddy may have some rocky days ahead, but maybe he'll finally believe me that 'Kitty cats truly are our friends.' I have had many kitty cat friends over the years."

Sissy said, "I don't get y'all. Cat's doing his job, just like Bobby said he would. Mice are dirty. They poop their little pellets everywhere, they'll get into any food you leave out, and they'll chew up clothes and make little nests, places to have babies. Cats are predators. Just like dogs."

Emmaline added, "And people."

Abby said, "But we don't eat animals, Grandma. We aren't predators."

Sissy added, "Because ya'll are weird."

Emmaline held up her hands, fingers curled, "Nature *is* red in tooth and claw."

Sissy nodded, "Miz Emmaline, that's true. You just come up with that?"

Emmaline said, "I'm quoting the poet Tennyson."

Sissy said, "Might want to hear more from him."

Emmaline clasped her two hands together in front of her smiling mouth and looked down at Sissy with affection. "You have excellent taste!"

Sissy looked as proud as proud could be.

Abby said, "Sissy thinks she and Mimi should come by after dinner with more pie and you should tell us about the women in your story."

Emmaline said, "Not a sleepover?"

Sissy shook her head, "Mimi wants to hear your story. So, I think I'll run us up in the gator, and afterwards I'll take us back home. And if Daddy wants to come too, is that okay?"

"Absolutely. How wonderful! We'll have all the elders. We shall convene a council of elders."

Sissy said, "A what?"

"Well, tender young things, when you convene a council of elders, you draw collective wisdom from those who have a long experience of life. Listen and learn. and bring Belle. I don't want her to feel excluded. And besides, Freddy may need some moral support if he catches sight of the mouse-assassin."

11

They sat on the porch, sipping coffee, having polished off another one of Mimi's sour cherry pies. Emmaline had added a scoop of vanilla ice cream. Ice cream. They had for sure fallen off the vegan wagon.

Everyone had turned up in the gator, Francis, Mimi, Sissy, and Belle. Freddy and Belle had played but were soon stretched out and dozing.

Emmaline rose and turned to face them, leaning against one of the pillars. She made a sight, with her silver hair loose around her shoulders, wearing a long flower print skirt and gauzy black blouse. She was wearing her silver and turquoise bracelets, and they clinked musically as she moved her arms. Abby settled back in her chair and made eye contact with her grandma, who winked at her.

"You all know I write novels. And I've come here this summer for inspiration, because I've become intrigued with a bit of local history. I've been researching the lives of five of the Hemings women, as well as the general subject of mixed-race families, before emancipation. I call these families shadow families. These 'shadow families' were not acknowledged by law or custom but they weren't uncommon. It was a terrible thing, to be an enslaved person. It was especially hard for women. The WPA slave narratives from the 1930's, well, they give a clue what it must have been like. Some of the stories are bone-chilling.

"But I can't write the stories of these Hemings women, Parthenia, Elizabeth, Mary, Sally, or Betsy Hemings, without talking about their enslavers. They are critical to the telling. I can't talk about any of them, without talking about how the laws and customs of the time enforced injustice and immoral acts using rationales of false justice and corrupt morality. So, I may digress from time to time.

"These women, well, we can piece together their stories because they, and their extended family, became the human property of Thomas Jefferson. These shadow families were made up of the sons and daughters of white men and enslaved women. They were not anomalies among the Jefferson clan, or among the slave-owning class. There are still some who try to deny this."

Mimi was nodding her head, "Folks get mad if you call it legalized rape. But no enslaved women had legal power to resist. If an enslaved woman had a husband, the master could sell him, their children too; siblings could be broken apart. There were ways to punish women other than whippings."

Emmaline said, "You're right. And yet, even under these terrible circumstances, the enslaved managed to form families. One of the many things that moved me in my reading was the desire, upon emancipation, for formerly enslaved couples to obtain legal marriage certificates. It struck me how much the legal certificate mattered to those to whom it had been denied. Legal marriage was a statement of liberation. No more 'jumping the broom' for the master. No more producing babies that the master could sell or use as collateral to get a loan from the bank. A marriage certificate for a formerly enslaved couple was as legally binding as that given a white couple. The irony being that it would still not be legal in the state of Virginia to marry across the same color barrier that the white masters had long been crossing. That wouldn't happen until 1967."

Mimi asked, "Why you think you're drawn to write about these enslaved women? How is it you find you care so much about them?"

"That's a good question, Mimi. I'm not sure I can give you a good answer. But I do care. I'm drawn to these women who survived and even thrived somehow. I came here to feel them, to be closer to them. But you live here. You are far closer to these women than I can be. I want to know what you know, what you feel."

Mimi nodded, "You mean that?"

"I do."

"Okay. You tell me what you know. Maybe I'll learn something new. Then I got something to share with you. But you go first."

"I guess I'll start with a white woman, Martha Wayles, who would later marry Thomas Jefferson. Martha Wayles never knew her mother, who died two weeks and three days after her birth. Against the heavy odds of the time, baby Martha Wayles survived. I bet you can guess who fed her, held her, rocked her, and changed her nappies. No child thrives, and some do not survive without love. She was fed, loved, and nurtured by the very same enslaved women who had known and cared for her dead mother.

"When her mother, Martha Epps, married, she did not come to her husband's plantation, 'The Forest,' by herself; she brought enslaved women with her. She brought the African we know as Thenia, along with her mixed-race daughter, Elizabeth, who we will know later as Betty.

"Thenia had been captured, enslaved, and sold to Martha's father, Francis Epps. There is oral history that her real name was Biabaye, and that she likely was captured from Nigeria. But like most Africans sold into slavery, her former identity was not recorded. Enslavement erased her past.

"The English captain of the slave ship had used Thenia on the journey. And so, when she was sold, she was pregnant. The English captain was named Hemings. How he felt about Thenia and his child is impossible to know. But the story goes that he tried to buy the pregnant Thenia back from Colonel Epps but was rebuffed. Then he tried to steal them, but again, his attempt was thwarted.

"He sailed away without them, never to return. The fact that Thenia passed Captain Hemings' name on to her daughter does indicate, I think, that Thenia wanted his name to remain attached to his child. Perhaps Thenia wanted him to be able to locate his child in the future.

"Thenia's baby was named Elizabeth Hemings and would later be known as Betty Hemings. Betty was raised inside the Epps house, so Betty had known her mistress, Martha Epps, all her life. Thenia was about a year younger than Martha Epps. As I mentioned, Thenia and Betty would move with Martha to the Wayles plantation, 'The Forest,' as wedding gifts before her pregnancy and death.

"Imagine the grief at "The Forest' when Martha died. Martha Epps Wayles was only thirty-six years old. Imagine if you will, Thenia holding that newborn child of her mistress. Thenia's own daughter Betty was only 13 years old but still would have been expected to help her mother care for babies. Imagine that newborn babe, gazing up at these two women who would be with her at the start of her life, and later, Betty would be bedside at the end of her life. Martha Wayles Skelton Jefferson would die young, from childbirth, just like her mother, and Betty would be there."

Mimi asked, "You assuming that these enslaved women loved the white lady they was bound to?"

"No. I don't assume that. But enslaved or free, a woman's heart is still a woman's heart. And a tiny orphan babe surely bonded with those who held her, fed her, and rocked her cradle, even if they bore no love for the mother. I think it no stretch that the bond between a newborn babe and the women who cared for her was forged."

Sissy asked, "What happened to Thenia and Betty?"

"I'm afraid I have more questions than answers about Thenia. When she was kidnapped from Africa at around the age of twenty-two, did she leave behind a husband and children? After having Betty, living at the Epps', did she have more children? Was she forced to separate from them when she was given as a wedding gift to Martha Epps? I don't know. It would have been unusual if she had no other children besides Betty.

"As noted by Jefferson in his diaries, an enslaved female was considered an asset, not just for her labors in the house or fields, but through producing children. Jefferson looked to increase his slave population, and by that his assets. He wrote that he expected a female slave of childbearing age to produce a child every two years. It is likely that John Wayles, who traded in slaves, would hold a similar view.

"We know more about Betty. Betty would name her first daughter Thenia. We see that name repeatedly given to other Hemings children. Betty would go on to give all her children the surname of Hemings, six of which were fathered by Martha Jefferson's father John Wayles.

"Because of that, I think of Thenia as an important and revered woman among all the future Hemings', but sadly someone we know little about."

Francis spoke up, "What you mean is the white folk didn't care to leave a record. But you know those Hemings likely passed on more than just her name."

Emmaline nodded, "You're right. What little we have was passed on through oral history. What records we have come from farm books and legal records. Like we know when Martha Jefferson's father, John Wayles, died, one hundred and thirty-five slaves, which would include Thenia and Betty, became the enslaved property of Thomas and Martha Jefferson. And we know that eventually the Hemings clan came to live with Thomas and Martha Jefferson on the mountaintop estate we all know as Monticello."

Sissy asked, "Miz Emmaline, about these enslaved women you studying?"

"Yes."

"It's the story of women who looked like me, right?"

"We don't know what they looked like. Not really. We do have photos from descendants, some of their children's children, and some of the extended family."

Sissy continued, "Ms. Emmaline, what I'm saying is they all black folks. And no offense, but you're real white."

Emmaline nodded her head. "I think you're addressing,

perhaps obliquely, something called appropriation, which is different from appreciation. Appropriation is to take something that doesn't belong to you. But this story, it's American history and it's a story about women. So, it's also connected to me as well as to you, although perhaps not as close."

Sissy looked unconvinced.

Emmaline continued, "I want to study American history in all its complexity, including the parts that don't necessarily make those who looked like me, look good. That can't be done if I only studied the people who lived, and struggled, and endured, who looked like me. In fact, it's been too long that the historians only wrote about the people who looked like me."

Abby added, "The winners write history, but it's the stories the winners don't want told that interest my grandma."

Francis, who didn't talk much said, "You and others like you, sure make folk like Bobby madder than a wet hen. He think you disrespecting America when you tell history that shame folks. He think you trying to make the little white children ashamed to be white."

Mimi nodded her head. "People get blood in they eyes."

Emmaline asked, "I know one thing for sure, a person who has blood in their eyes trying to prevent me from knowing about or telling a story, is NOT the good guy."

Francis said, "Around here, folks would call you a troublemaker, Emmaline Sparks."

Emmaline smiled, "I've been called worse. Besides, think of it as "good trouble."

Francis slapped his thigh, "You're quoting John Lewis. Now, that man was an inspiration and a harbinger of hope. He was nearly beaten to death on that bridge, by the police.

But he always believed in the future and that it was worth fighting for."

"I don't mean to compare myself to John Lewis. That man is a civil rights icon. I'm not brave and I'm no orator or organizer. I just try to write good historical fiction that tells stories that no one else is telling. I try to paint an authentic picture."

Sissy looked at her Daddy with pride and then back at Emmaline, giving her a nearly imperceptible nod.

Abby piped up, "Grandma was named for Emmaline Pankhurst."

Mimi asked, "Who is that?"

Emmaline said, "Another icon. A suffragette, fighting for the right for women to vote."

Mimi said, "Bet your momma chose that name 'cause she was fighting for women's rights and all."

"And my grandmother before her. I suppose it runs in the family."

Mimi asked, "Abby, you interested, too?"

"I don't know. I like stories. Grandma is almost like a witch, the way she finds things out and then weaves them into a story. That's what I want to do."

Emmaline said, "I think that's enough storytelling today. I'm ready to see if you girls are any better with that frisbee."

Sissy grabbed the frisbee and trotted down the front porch stairs. Abby got up more slowly, glancing at her grandmother, who had cut her off before she could tell the Taylors about voices in the night and muses and conjuring.

Emmaline looked at the sleepy dogs, "Freddy, Belle, you two better get out there, because I bet that frisbee will get lost in the weeds and you'll need to go fetch it back."

The dogs did not look enthusiastic. Freddy stretched and yawned, then watched the frisbee go off into the grass in an unintended direction. The dog sighed, and then both dogs walked down the steps and into the yard.

Mimi laughed. "Freddy don't have a bit of faith in those girls learning to throw that thing."

Francis said, "Now, Momma show some yourself."

Emmaline asked, "I don't mean to pry, but how long has Sissy's Momma been gone?"

Mimi said, "She passed when Sissy were six years old. She got the cancer. I think that be why Sissy hate school so. She knew something was wrong and didn't want to leave her Momma. Now the boys, they be lots older. It was hard on them, but hardest on Sissy."

Francis added, "My boys both went into the service. One already was serving when Gay died. One was in high school."

"I'm so sorry."

Mimi asked, "Abby have both her folks?"

Emmaline nodded, "She does. She was supposed to go to summer camp but when that fell through, I said I'd keep her this summer. My daughter, Belva Ann, and her husband, Jim, work full time. I live right behind their house, in a guest house, so I am lucky to see Abby nearly every day."

"No Mister Sparks?"

"Afraid not. Just Freddy."

Francis switched the subject, "You sure that ain't a wolf or one of them wolf-dog crosses?"

Emmaline smiled slyly, "Freddy is a German Shepherd."

Mimi said, "I see."

Francis raised his eyebrows and nodded.

Emmaline added, "That dog may look fierce, but he is terrified of cats. And Bobby, bless him, to rid us of mice, tossed a one-eared tomcat into the house.

Francis said, "Is it working?"

"Well, the cat is a regular assassin who leaves eviscerated carcasses everywhere. It's been on a non-stop killing spree."

Mimi looked impressed. "The mice will get the message. You watch."

Emmaline frowned, "That's exactly what Sissy said."

Mimi added, "Let the cat do his job."

"The problem is, well, other than freaking me and Abby out by gutted bodies littering our floors, well, it's Freddy. He freaks out more than we do. He even loses bladder control."

Mimi nodded, "Maybe he don't have any wolf blood after all. Sounds more like my sister's chihuahua."

Francis said, "What you ought to do is ignore that dog when he gets afraid."

Emmaline asked, "Why?"

"When that dog see you get excited, you just confirming what he already think."

"But Freddy is truly traumatized when he sees the cat. It seems cruel to subject him to something that creates that kind of fear."

Francis shrugged. "It ain't cruel if you let the dog keep whatever distance he needs. I'm just saying you ignore the cat. And ignore the dog while you're at it. Unless you think he gonna' hurt hisself."

"Even if he's shaking like a leaf and peeing on the floor?"

"You think he gonna' damage *those* floors?"

Emmaline laughed, "Not likely."

Francis continued, "I worked with horses many years. And you can help a scared horse get over a fear by letting them decide how much distance they need. But they got to see that you ain't afraid. Then they begin to relax, and then they gets curious. Pretty soon they got theys nose on it and feel like they is the bravest creature on the planet."

"I suppose I could have some hellacious nights ahead of me."

"Just shut the cat out of your bedrooms at night."

Just then Abby tossed the frisbee and it floated in a perfect arc, where Sissy plucked it easily out of the air.

Abby and Sissy screamed and jumped up and down and hugged each other.

Emmaline softly said, "Brilliant."

* * *

After everyone had gone home, Emmaline said, "Well, that was fun. Abby, please help me put the kitchen to bed, and then we can do the same."

"Grandma, was it a fluke, do you think?"

"Of course not! I was once a killer frisbee player, it's in your DNA. You keep it up and you'll have a brand-new skill to take back home and show off next year to your friends at school."

Emmaline continued, "Funny, how I haven't touched one in years. But it was effortless. As soon as I tossed it, it was all there like I had never stopped. The frisbee was like a talisman."

"Grandma, what's a talisman?"

"Hmmm? Oh, look it up."

Emmaline did that weird thing again, tossing her hair over her shoulder and looking at nothing. But Abby, looking at her grandma, realized Emmaline *was* looking at something. That something was inside her head.

Emmaline's weird spell only lasted a moment, and then the three of them walked into the kitchen. Well, Freddy walked partway into the kitchen before he yelped, backed out of the room and fled.

Sitting on the counter, staring at them with intense amber eyes, was 'one-eared Tom. He really *was* missing an ear.

Abby said, "Poor Freddy!" And she turned to go after her dog.

"Abby. Let him go. If you follow him, you'll reinforce his behavior. Francis said we can't act like there is anything scary about the cat."

"But he's afraid and alone."

"Let Freddy take as much space and time as he needs. We shouldn't make a big deal over it. That just reinforces that the cat is something stressful. Francis thinks over time he'll need less safe space between himself and the cat. He may even get curious."

The assassin in question said, "Meow." And then looked directly into Emmaline's face.

Emmaline walked over to the counter and the cat put his tail up in the air and walked over to her. She stroked it along its back, and it turned a circle, and she stroked it again.

Abby said, "It likes you."

"We didn't set out cat food or any water for it."

"Or a litter box."

Emmaline said to the cat, "We have been remiss. And here you went straight to work!"

Emmaline poured a dish of the dry food that Bobby had brought, and the cat went for it. She then set out a bowl of water, saying, "Bobby didn't say anything about a litter box."

"Maybe we're supposed to let it go outside."

Emmaline said, "Tom, I expect you need to go out." The cat looked up at Emmaline, jumped off the counter and trotted to the back door, tail up and vibrating. Emmaline opened the door, and he was gone like a streak.

Abby said, "I'll go tell Freddy he's gone."

Emmaline smiled and pointed. Freddy was peeking into the room from the hallway, silent, but ears slightly flattened back.

"He knows."

Freddy bounced into the room, and Abby knelt, and he did his magic dance, curling around her and snapping his jaws and yodeling. "Oh Freddy, you survived!"

"Abby, he came back all by himself to check on us. Wasn't that brave?"

"Or he heard you open the door and knew the assassin had left the building."

Emmaline tipped her head, "Or that."

* * *

Abby had put on her pajamas and was getting ready to get into bed when she heard Emmaline on the phone. She knew she was talking to her mom and felt a pang of guilt because she hadn't been homesick at all. Not like at camp last summer.

She walked into Emmaline's room and interrupted her to ask, "Is that Mom?"

Emmaline nodded but held up a hand. She was saying, "That would be lovely, darling. Text me those dates."

Abby sat on the edge of Emmaline's bed to listen.

Emmaline continued, "No. We have not seen another squirrel, although we do still call the house Squirrel Manor. But the cat is the new drama in our lives. Yes. Freddy is terrified. It *is* disgusting the way the cat leaves the gutted corpses everywhere. We refer to the cat as our mouse-assassin."

"She's right here, and desperate to speak to you."

Emmaline handed Abby the phone. "Mom, I threw a frisbee!"

Belva Ann said, "And you have a new friend?"

"Uh-huh. Her name is Sissy. She lives at the end of our driveway. But I'm the one who made the perfect throw. It was me."

Abby found herself unable to slow down or barely take a breath to catch her mom up.

"Sissy has horses and let me ride one named Buttermilk. Bareback. It's harder than it looks. And more painful too. And she has a dog named Belle, and Freddy likes both of them. Is Daddy coming?"

"I'm sorry darling, but Daddy doesn't think he can afford to take time off."

"But I want him to see me ride and throw a frisbee and mix with someone from my peer group."

"I'll make a video when I'm there."

"A video isn't the same."

"I know he'll be so sorry to miss out."

They said their farewells, and Abby handed the phone back to Emmaline.

Abby thought her dad should come with her mom. He had come last summer on parent's day at camp. Then she had pretended to be okay with the camp when she really hated it. This time she would not have to pretend.

Abby had trouble falling asleep. She reached for her phone and looked up the word "talisman." It read, "An object that is believed to have magical powers." A frisbee? It was made of plastic. That seemed wrong for a talisman.

She thought about the silver-haired witch and her wolf companion. She thought about her story. Or the story she still had to finish. It was Emmaline who was giving her clues about the witch and the wolf, and the arc of her yet to be finished tale. But a frisbee? That would not work. But now she thought her story would need a talisman of some sort. She even liked the way the word sounded. She'd have to think about that.

She must have been dreaming when she saw Emmaline and Freddy walking down a snowy path through a field. Then she saw the house, Squirrel Manor, at the end of the path. Emmaline was not wearing a witch's robe, but one of those puffy winter coats that go all the way to the knee; it was black. It had a hood with a fur trim. Freddy's black coat contrasted sharply with the snow. A person came out of Squirrel Manor. She could not see who it was, but Freddy got excited and ran to the person, who Abby saw now was a man, not a shimmer of a man, but very solid and real. Emmaline began to run too. Except that didn't seem right. Emmaline never ran. And as Emmaline ran, her hood fell off her head and onto her back.

Her hair was black, not silver.

* * *

Emmaline placed the perfectly toasted bagel in front of Abby. "Today we have honey from Francis' hives!"

"They're not hives, they're boxes. I saw them behind their house."

"I know nothing about raising honeybees. I know it is important for the planet. But one thing I do know is that we are tasting this specific ecosystem. This honey is from the flowers and fields around us."

Abby took a big bite of bagel, and then a swig of her tea.

Emmaline explained, "The bees make it from nectar from the plants around them."

"How does the nectar become honey?"

Emmaline shrugged, "I bet Francis can teach us."

"Grandma, do you own one of those big puffy coats?"

Emmaline looked puzzled, "That's a non sequitur."

Abby tapped at her phone to check the definition, before replying.

"Fair enough, Grandma. It was a non sequitur. It's just that I had a dream, and in it you were wearing a big puffy coat."

"I wonder if you had kicked your covers off and were cold."

"You said it gets cold and snowy here in the wintertime."

Emmaline got that distant look in her eyes and flipped her hair over her shoulder. Abby noticed and thought her grandma was once again watching some kind of movie inside her head.

"When I went to school here, we had a blizzard. I'd never experienced anything like it. But it was kind of fun, to be honest. For a few days at least."

"Did you have a long black puffy coat?"

Emmaline smiled, "Everyone had a coat like that, back-in-the-day. Mine is likely still in the back of a closet some-where in your house. It was filled with real goose-down, with a fur trimmed hood. It was warm. I loved that coat."

"OMG, it was in my cool dream. Freddy was in it, and Squirrel Manor was in it too."

Emmaline sensed manipulation. "Abby, our rental agree-ment is only for the summer."

"The snow was pretty. I bet Freddy and Belle would like to play in it. Bet the horses like it too."

"I bet you're right."

"Grandma, the part of my dream I remember the clearest, is that when your hood fell down, your hair was black. Kind of looked like Freddy's hair."

"You had to use your imagination there, darling. It's been silver since before you were born."

"And some man came out of Squirrel Manor to greet you, and you and Freddy were so excited to see him that you both ran."

Emmaline got up so abruptly she startled Freddy. But all she did was put her plate and teacup into the dishwasher.

Emmaline exclaimed, "Look, Abby!"

One-eared Tom was at the back door, staring through the glass at them. Freddy followed their stares and began to back away slowly, never taking his eyes off the cat as he backed all the way out of the kitchen, a low whining growl fading as he made more distance between Tom and himself.

Emmaline said, "I'm going to let him in."

"Now? Are you sure?"

"I expect he would like to be fed."

"Grandma, Freddy may never come into the kitchen again. It's now been cursed by the mouse-assassin. Way bad vibes."

"Nonsense. Come on in, Tom."

Emmaline opened the door, and he came in, tail up and talking.

Emmaline stroked his back a few times before picking him up and feeding him on the counter. She said, "At least Freddy was quieter this time. Francis knows his stuff. I looked up how to desensitize fearful dogs. But you must go slowly and expect setbacks. But in the end, letting him choose the distance himself is the kindest method."

Abby said, "I'm going to get him out of here and head over to Sissy's. If you don't need me that is."

"That's fine. I'm meeting my friend in town again."

"Again?"

"We have things to discuss. And I'm picking up something from the bakery. Tonight, we meet at Mimi's for her turn at storytelling. You be sure to bring the frisbee. Practice makes perfect."

"It's your talisman, not mine."

"Maybe so, but remember, it's in your DNA. So, don't look a gift horse in the mouth.

"Grandma, what does a horse's mouth have to do with anything."

"Have Sissy explain it to you. She has forgotten more about horses than you or I will ever know."

"I would gladly give up my frisbee gene for a horseback riding gene."

Emmaline laughed. "Just because I don't ride and your Mom and Dad don't ride, it doesn't mean that you don't possess such a gene."

185

"Really? Where else should I be looking?"

"Have fun at Sissy's."

"Meanwhile, the assassin has the run of the house?"

"It's his job."

Emmaline seemed to dance up the staircase. When she came back down the stairs, she was wearing another skirt. She had on a different piece of turquoise jewelry. And Abby noticed that her grandmother was wearing makeup.

12

Sissy said, "All you gotta' do, see, is hold on to her mane. Lean back against it if you got to. Buttermilk ain't going to run off with you or nothin' like that. When I stop Bunny, she'll stop too. So, don't pull on her reins."

"What will happen if I pull on the reins?"

"You told me Freddy don't like you pulling on him. Well, Buttermilk don't like it either."

He gets aggressive if I do it. Like an attack dog."

"She won't attack anyone, but Buttermilk will toss her head and pull right back."

"Okay."

"See that hill?"

"Yes."

"We gonna' make tracks up that hill. Get you a fistful of mane."

Sissy watched as Abby, her mouth set in a grimace, grabbed mane. Sissy gave an approving nod, then pointed Bunny up the hill and clucked.

Belle and Freddy got the message along with the horses. The four animals charged up the hill, like some kind of stampede. The dogs soon scampered to the side as Bunny shifted into a faster pace, flinging a clod of red dirt at Buttermilk, it hit her in the nose, and she tossed her head and accelerated. Abby did not like the head-tossing.

Abby was gripping her hunk of mane with all her might, while thinking, "Don't pull on the reins, don't pull on the reins, don't pull on the reins, don't pull on the reins." She was also trying hard not to grip with her legs, but it was useless. The inside of her knees and her inner thighs were on fire. Yet Abby realized that Buttermilk was not hard to sit, not really. Her back moved in a steady rhythm; her feet hit the ground with a self-assurance that was palpable.

Sissy had turned around to check on Abby, a huge grin on her face. Sissy dropped her reins and put her hands up in the air. She yelled something unintelligible, but Abby thought it looked and sounded like some kind of battle cry. Before Sissy turned around and took back her reins, she yelled, "Best feeling in the world!"

Abby, despite the pain in her legs, and the cramping in her hands, said nothing in reply, but she was thinking. "Yes. Yes. Yes. Yes, it is."

The horses broke into a bouncy trot that made Abby pinch with her knees. Abby thought for sure her knees must be bloody. Blessedly, they dropped to walk as they crested the hill. And there it was again, a stunning view of green fields below. Even though the inside of her knees were on fire, Abby could marvel as the green grass rolled in the breeze almost like water. And the red clay of the field's edge was like nothing she had ever seen back home. The dogs caught up to them, mouths open, tongues lolling.

Belle threw her head back and bayed, "Whooooo-oooooo." For what reason, Abby had not a clue. Freddy just looked at Belle with adoration and wagged his tail.

Abby said, "My first canter."

Sissy said, "Girl, that was a gallop. 'Course, Bunny, and Buttermilk, are old and don't gallop as fast as they used to. Back in the day when they were bona-fide field hunters they flew. But they haven't forgotten."

Abby found herself petting the side of Buttermilk's neck, the way she had seen Sissy do with Bunny.

Sissy sat on Bunny upright while also sort of draped around the horse, like she was part of Bunny. But Sissy was also a part of this hill, this view, and a little bit wild herself. Abby felt a wave of jealousy again.

Abby said, "That was kind of scary, but I liked it. And I didn't touch the reins."

"You did real good."

"The inside of my legs are likely rubbed raw, though."

Sissy grinned, "I expect they are. Don't take a shower to-night."

"I know I'll never ride as well as you do. But even though it was scary, I loved it."

"Bug bit ya'?"

"I think so."

"You should keep it up. Just so you know, there's all kinds of riding out there. And all kinds of horses too. And there's some real bad snobs who think money can make a horseman. But that ain't so. Buttermilk and I will teach you what we know. But if you want to become a real horseman, it means you got to commit to keep learning. It means you got to find a way to ride when you go home. Sometimes barns will trade lessons for mucking out and such. You should try and arrange something. There's always a way."

"I know my grandma would let me, but it's my mom and

dad I'll need to convince. My dad wants me to play team sports, and I hate team sports."

Sissy said, "Maybe you can try out for the frisbee team."

They laughed.

Abby had a daytime sort of dream. She saw an Abby who was a frisbee-throwing, horseback-rider Abby, an Abby who was cooler than anyone else she could think of back home. In fact, this very moment, after one gallop up the hill on Buttermilk, this moment in time, she was probably the coolest she had ever been in her entire life.

* * *

That night, they were having dessert at the Taylors. Sissy came to pick them up in the Gator. Abby and Emmaline, carrying a bakery box, climbed aboard while Freddy trotted alongside.

Emmaline said, "Careful over the rocks, Sissy. It would break my heart to drop this cake."

Francis greeted them on the front porch. "Good evening, ladies. Mimi insisted I have on offer both coffee and tea. What will you take?"

Emmaline said, "You are so sweet. Abby and I will have tea."

They went into the house and Emmaline went straight to the kitchen, announcing, "Mimi, when I show you this dessert, you'll think someone was pulling my leg. They told me it is supposed to look this way."

Abby said, "Grandma wouldn't let me peek."

Abby and Mimi watched as Emmaline opened the bakery box and pulled out what looked like someone's flop.

Mimi said, "What in the Sam hill?"

Emmaline grinned, "It's burnt."

"I see that."

Abby added, 'It won't win any prizes for its looks."

Emmaline announced, "It's called a Basque Burnt Cheese-cake."

Mimi said, "They do that on purpose or are they pulling your leg?"

Abby blurted out, "Well, you know what they say, 'The proof of the pudding is in the tasting!'"

Mimi grinned, "Abby, you got a point, there. The prettiest cakes displayed in the window are nothing but colored lard on cardboard."

That got a laugh.

Everyone settled down with the burnt cake and tea and coffee in the living room.

The cake was proofed and declared delicious. The burnt part tasted like the top of a Crème Brulée and the rest of it was creamy and lighter than most cheesecakes.

After the cake had been dispatched, Emmaline said, "Mimi, it's your turn. I want to hear your stories. I bet you have a lot to tell."

Mimi nodded, "I'm gonna' tell you what I learned from Mother Taylor. And Francis, he know all this too. But it will be Sissy to carry them forward, and she ain't heard this before but it's about time. So, listen good, child, even though these are grown up kind of stories.

"Emmaline, I expect you'd like to know more about that old house you call Squirrel Manor."

"I would. I wonder what it was called, back in the day when it was grand."

"It's not been called anything at all for as long as I've been around. But I heard it was once called "Chickasaw House" for the Chickasaw horses that used to be bred there. Tough ponies, mostly used to pull carts and such. I expect you curious how it is that Bobby Taylor owns it but never has lived there. And how it is that we be Taylors, like Bobby. You might want to know how it come to pass that we own all this, but we don't own that old house, or the land it sits on."

"I do."

"Well, I told you about the one Hemings that did live out this way."

"Was she connected to Squirrel Manor?"

"Not directly. But freedmen continued to settle this way because of what changes had already gone on here. Changes that come about at your Squirrel Manor. That decrepit house, it was once a beautiful house, long time ago, and was lived in by a bachelor man name of Robert Taylor. He owned a lot of land. He also owned a good many people. And he took one of his enslaved women into that house, like a wife, you know? Lucy. And he got many a child off Lucy. But as rich as he was, legally he had no heirs."

"Did people accept this arrangement?"

"The ladies surely gossiped but could do nothing about it. Besides, many a father encouraged their sons to engage in such behavior, as a sort of rite of passage, which kept the young men at home. That's the truth. But Robert Taylor of old, he took it too far, see?

"The story goes, as the oldest son, he had inherited the bulk of the family estate. He had a duty to wed a white woman and get sons off her.

"The story also goes, he was resistant to change. But when he was in his thirties, he took him a white wife who was barely grown, name of Charlotte. Brought her to live alongside Lucy, under that one roof."

Emmaline said, "And how well did that work?"

"Charlotte, who went by Lotty, had a rude education. For Robert, it is said, showed real affection for Lucy and her brood. Besides that, Lucy ran the house and kitchen and carried the keys. She was in charge of it all, not the young Lotty."

Emmaline said, "What was he thinking?"

"Lotty, she did one thing right though, she produced an heir and a spare. Once she felt she had done her duty, she demanded that Robert get rid of Lucy and her children, sell them away. And when he refused, it was said she got crazier by the day. She wrote her sister saying that Robert had been put under a spell. That Lucy was a real-life witch, an evil conjure woman. She wrote that she was afraid for her life as long as Lucy was there. She wrote that Robert would no longer be welcome in her bed if he kept his black witch and her spawn on the property. She would not be forced any longer to endure the indignity of it all.

"Course I see her side of it. She didn't know what she was gettin' into. She was too naive to wonder about a man that old never been married, and he was wicked not to let her know the truth."

"What happened?"

Mimi lifted her eyebrows and pursed her lips in a crooked smile, "Well, Robert got rid of the one woman who was trouble to him.

"He moved Lotty to another one of his farms. Built her

a house. Not as grand as this one, mind. Think Robert never was welcomed back to her bed, though. Lotty never did have more children."

"What happened to Lucy and her children?"

"Things went back to how they'd been. As Lucy's children growed, Robert carved out connected lots of land for the boys to farm and made sure they learned trades. In time, those boys bought their own freedom. He deeded those lots to those boys before he died. After old Robert died, Lotty had Lucy kicked out of the house. Lucy moved in with a son. Could have been worse. She could have sold her, could have even had her whipped to death.

"But Lucy had her revenge. Lucy did play up the notion that she was a witch, she told Lotty, that if she or her boys moved into the house, they would die within a year. And if they did harm to the house, on purpose-like, or sold it away, it would come back on them."

Abby said, "A witch? And a curse? Oh, Grandma, our old lady of a house has been protected by a curse!"

"Did Lotty believe her?"

"I expect it made her ill at ease, but she did move in. But sho 'nuff, she passed not long after. Spooked them white Taylors so bad, they never did live in the house again. Superstitious lot. And spiteful. Neither Lucy nor her kin ever got the house back. But bit by bit, the black Taylors bought slices more of the land. I guess they needed the money. You'd think after all this time some Taylor would have sold that house. I suppose the rent is good income. Bobby sure doesn't use any of it for upkeep."

Mimi paused a moment, then added, "Lucy and old Robert are said to haunt the place, and I think many a student has had fun reporting seeing ghosties. Bobby doesn't discourage the rumors. It tends to attract students who go in for that sort of thing. But one day that old heap will crumble to the ground, it's been so neglected. And I don't think Bobby Taylor will mind when it does."

Abby said, "Chickasaw House?"

Emmaline added, "I love the name. And wow, what a story. Mimi, you are a born storyteller. It means so much to me that you shared this. I wonder if you mind if I copy it down when I get home. It should be recorded somewhere."

"Course I don't mind. You just write down that you heard it from Mimi Taylor, one of the black Taylors, as was told to her by her mother-in-law, who got it from her mother-in-law."

"Oh, I will!"

Abby said, "Grandma, maybe we'll see old Robert and Lucy. I'll bet they could tell us stories not even Mimi has heard."

Sissy shook her head. "You wouldn't be scared?"

Abby smiled, "No. Maybe if I was a Taylor. But I was a little scared today, and weirdly enough, a little scared felt good. Really good."

* * *

The next day, after their ride, Abby and Sissy found Emmaline in the library. She looked rough but was also excited, arms wide, the room was its usual disaster, but now with colored index cards taped to the walls.

She said, "I'm using the walls instead of posterboard. So, expansive. There is no limit to the number of cards I can add. I just love this space."

Freddy and Belle were not looking at the walls, instead they were snuffling around the floor. Freddy sat down against a pile of notebooks, and went after a flea, and the notebooks toppled over. He was non-plussed, as this was his normal. He yawned and then stretched out on the floor.

"Grandma, now this room looks just like the guesthouse."

Emmaline ignored Abby, and directed her remarks to Sissy, "So, let me show you something. To the left of the window is Act One. The wall between the windows is the first part of Act Two. To the right of the window is the second part of Act Two. And this wall over here will be Act Three."

Abby scolded, "Grandma, you've taped all these cards directly to the wall."

"Yes?"

"It ruins the paint."

Emmaline picked up a roll of tape from the floor, and waggled it in the air, "Painter's tape. Won't damage the paint."

Sissy walked over to Act One.

Emmaline said, "These cards are the bones, the skeleton of the story. And then I add the flesh to the bones. The beginning is so important. I need to entice my readers to come and to stay for the telling. If I don't do a good job here, then it won't matter what part I tell next."

Abby said, "Like casting a spell."

Sissy added softly, "When you and Mimi tell your stories, it feels that way. Like my heart slows down, and my body goes heavy, and I don't see what is in front of me. My mind goes where your words go."

Abby leaned closer a read a card, "A white baby is cradled against a black breast. A white man stands near, tears streaming down his face. Start with the death of Martha Epps (age 36) and imagine the house of John Wayles that day. The woman cradling the babe will be Parthenia. The young woman with her will be her daughter, Elizabeth (Betty) Hemings. The babe, of course, is the future Martha Wayles Skelton, Jefferson. This is both a starting point, and a foreshadowing of what her own fate will be 34 years later."

Sissy nodded, "Abby, you read smooth. It's like them words and you are one thing, moving together."

Abby said, "Wow, that's exactly how I feel about watching you ride Bunny."

Emmaline said, "I know Abby would like to ride like you. Would you like to be able to read like Abby?"

Sissy looked very serious. "Nah. I mean, sure. But I sure hate looking and sounding a fool."

Abby said, "When people force you to do stuff you suck at, in front of people who are good at it, the kind of people who you know are making fun of you, well it's sick, isn't it? Sadistic."

Sissy said, "Sadistic?"

Abby took a serious tone, then turned her eyes upward as if reading from a cue card. "'Sadistic' means deriving pleasure from inflicting pain and suffering on others. Derives from the Marquis de Sade, a man known for his cruel sexual practices."

Emmaline said, "I don't recall teaching you that word."

Emmaline then turned to Sissy, "I do agree that while one

is learning, it helps to learn in a safe and encouraging environment. But oh, let me tell you, there is a great deal of pleasure to be had in finally breaking through incompetence to competence. It's wonderful to have others there to cheer for you when that happens."

Abby said, "I haven't fallen off a horse yet. But Sissy said I will in time. I won't mind if Sissy sees me fall off. I still want to learn. Bad. But man, I get that pain is part of the process. I already took the skin off the inside of my knees. It hurts every step I take. Sissy said not to take a shower for at least three days."

Emmaline said, "Three days? Really?"

Sissy took a solemn tone, "Those legs of hers are chewed up."

Emmaline sighed and turned back to the wall, "We are *not* sadists here. Sissy, go on and try to read the next card. You don't have to read it out loud. If you find a word you don't know, ask your smarty-pants friend there, the one with the chewed-up legs, the one who somehow knows about the notorious Marquis de Sade, a sexual pervert, even though she is only twelve years old and not allowed to read that sort of thing."

Abby protested, "Grandma, you're telling me stories about sex all the time, like it's basically in all your stories."

"I suppose I am."

"And you tell me to look stuff up if I want to learn more about it."

"True."

"And I'm researching for you all the time and making notes about bad behavior."

"Also, true."

"So, I didn't just fall off the turnip truck, now, did I?"

"Pretty sure I didn't teach you that aphorism either."

Emmaline's phone rang as she was laughing. She picked it up. Sissy was reading the next card, silently.

Abby realized right away that Emmaline was talking to her mom and was gesturing to let her have the phone. After exchanging pleasantries, she handed the phone to Abby and walked over to Sissy at the wall.

Belva Ann said, "Abby! I miss you so much. Tell me everything. How is Freddy doing?"

"Freddy has a girlfriend. She's a foxhound named Belle. But poor Freddy, we now have a beat-up old Tom cat. He has only one ear. He is a mouse assassin. He leaves half-eaten bodies around the house. Well, that's his job, so we don't hold it against him, although it's gross."

"Freddy must be terrified."

"Yeah, he is, but Francis said just to pretend we don't notice, and that in time Freddy will decide to close up the distance all by himself."

"Francis?"

"Mom, I'm riding horses. I suck at it."

"I'm happy for you, but please, that word, Dad doesn't like it when you use that word."

"Grandma uses that word all the time. It's not a curse word. Not the way grandma uses it, anyway. Grandma says being willing to suck at something means embracing something new, outside your comfort zone. Then, by hanging in there while you suck, you build resilience and find joy in the journey as you seek competence. And when you finally are competent, you no longer suck. That's a win."

"Well, while all that may be true…"

"What word would you prefer I use?"

"Can't you just say, 'I'm not good at this yet?'"

"Oh, Mom. That's weak language. Doesn't pack the same kind of punch. But whatever."

Abby then sighed dramatically, "Please tell me Dad is coming. I have so much I want to show him."

"I'm sorry, sweetie. I wish he could."

"But I want him to see me throw the frisbee. I really su… I mean I'm not good at it yet. But I can throw a floater now. And I can canter Buttermilk."

"Buttermilk?"

"Mom, that's the horse's name. Oh, and we found out that this house was once called Chickasaw House. Pretty cool, huh? But just so you know, it's a dump. And even though it's a huge old house, Grandma has it looking like the guest house. Like it's been hit by a tornado."

"I thought you were there to keep things clean and orderly."

"There's only so much a twelve-year-old can do."

Belva Ann laughed.

"Laugh all you want, but it's true. I can't even drive a car. Although Sissy can. Sissy is twelve too, but she drives a Gator and a tractor."

"And who is Sissy?"

"Sissy Taylor. She's my friend."

"You have a friend? And she's twelve? Darling, that's wonderful."

"Be sure and tell Daddy. It will make him feel better."

Belva Ann was quiet for a long beat. Then she simply said, "Will do."

13

Abby woke up to find her room bathed in light. She sat up in bed and gazed at the tree outside her window. Emmaline said it was an oak tree, but it didn't look anything like the oaks back home. Abby's oak trees had prickly leaves, but these trees had different leaves, softer ones. Nothing was the same here. Not the air, the light, the dirt, the trees. Freddy, curled up at the foot of her bed, lifted his head briefly to look at her, and then put it back down, stretched and rolled onto his back.

"Belly rub? Okay, but then we need to get up."

The house seemed oddly quiet when Abby and Freddy made their way to the kitchen. They found Emmaline sitting at the kitchen table, perfectly upright in front of a cup of tea, but with her eyes closed. She was still wearing her pajamas, her long white hair was unbrushed, forming a halo around her head and shoulders.

"Grandma?"

Emmaline opened her eyes and sighed. "Ah. There you are."

"You okay?"

"Better than okay. It happened. That voice in the night moment."

"Whose voice?"

"I dreamed of Robert and Lucy and Lotty and of this house."

"I want to hear all about it."

"I'm so tired."

You want me to make you some toast? A fresh cup of tea?"

"That would be lovely. Then I need a toes-up."

"What time did you get up?"

"I think it was around three am. I had to write down the fuzzy bits of my dream. I had to write down everything I remembered about Mimi's story. And oddly, it brought back other memories, long forgotten. And all of it felt urgent to get down in print, the way it does sometimes when I'm writing."

"You had to chase it all down before it got away from you."

"Darling, I love that you understand. And dreams, well they are especially slippery."

"Did you see them? Robert and Lucy and Lotty?"

Emmaline nodded.

"Oh my God, Grandma. Tell me!"

"Mimi's story lit a fire in my brain, and now I see her story as central to my new novel, of course, only if Mimi and Frances agree. And there's one other thing, well maybe two."

"What's that?"

"It's Mimi. I would like to use her as the basis for a character, the narrator. She is, as she said, a storyteller in a long line of storytellers. Just as you and Belva Ann are born to be storytellers because I am a storyteller."

"Like inherited?"

"Yes."

"Okay, but why Mimi?"

"She's the story-keeper for the Taylors. Frances carries the bloodline, as does Sissy, but Mimi is the historian of the family."

Abby nodded. Then asked, "And the other thing? What's the other thing?"

Emmaline continued. "This house. It is also a character, just like any other character. Think of what this house has witnessed. And like all homes, it has an origin story, and wow, what a story it is. And through no fault of its own, the house fell upon hard times but miraculously survives."

"Grandma, when I sit on the front porch, with my back to the house, well, I imagine it like it must have looked when Robert Taylor was living here. I imagine what went on here and feel somehow that the house absorbed it all and now it's like a giant talisman."

"Yes. Oh, yes. Darling, on this we are sympatico."

"Sympatico?"

"Like-minded."

"We see it through 'rose-colored' glasses."

"Perhaps that's true, too."

"Grandma, what about all the work you've done, all the research you did on the Hemings women? Those women need their stories told. That's why you chose them."

"I have not forgotten them. There is a pattern of resilience and strength among all these women who did their best to survive and thrive under a social system that was unjust. I'm in the process of drawing connecting lines between them all. But we now know that a child of Betty Hemings was able to settle near here with her husband as free people. It says a lot about this area. And right here where we sit, Lucy and Robert's children became free people, people who owned land, this land around us, well, the lines do intersect."

Abby was silent a moment. Then said, "I think you've

already figured it out. How to use all your research, all the Hemings women. All those stories lead up to this one, right here, to Mimi and to this house."

"Yes. This house. It's a wonder it still stands. But what did you think about the fact that Robert left nothing to Lucy?"

"Um, I didn't think about it."

"Or that he didn't free his own sons, but made them buy their freedom?"

"I don't know."

"We should be careful about our rose-colored glasses."

"What are you thinking?"

"I'm thinking, 'Time flies over us but leaves its shadow behind.' That's Hawthorne, by the way."

"Grandma, what are you trying to say?

Emmaline smiled. "Just that my visions last night of Robert and Lucy, and Lotty, those shadows, well, they were dark. Anyway, how about that hot tea and toast. Then I'll catch a few z's before my lunch date."

"Date? Again? What the heck?"

Emmaline deflected, "Oh, and you won't believe it, but Belva Ann and I talked late last night. Well, it was late here, not in California. She said Jim has agreed to come along to visit us."

Abby's face lit up. "Daddy is coming? Mom told me he couldn't make it.'

"He's coming, and I'm afraid I may have oversold your frisbee skills. I suggest you and Sissy increase your practice sessions."

Abby sighed, "Why would you do that?"

She shrugged. "It worked better for my narrative."

* * *

Abby and Freddy found Sissy and Belle standing at the pasture gate while all hell seemed to be breaking loose in the field. The horses had their heads up, their tails up, and were in a scrum, moving at a trot and canter around the field as one. They would skid to a stop and stare off into the distance and then make deep woofing noises from the bottom of their lungs, blowing hard through their nostrils, before twirling and moving off into a new spot from which the performance was repeated.

Abby asked, "What the heck is going on?"

Sissy grinned, "Ain't they something? Bunch of old arthritic fools. But they sure do look fancy when they get their blood up. You heard it, didn't cha'? The horn. It's cubbing season. They heard the huntsman's horn. That's all."

Abby didn't hear anything. The horses were now frozen in place, heads high, tails high, searching the horizon.

One horse made that odd woofing noise again, deep and loud and long, "Woooooof!"

It was a noise Abby had never heard before. TV and movie horses were always whinnying and snorting and such, but never, not ever had she heard the noise these horses were making.

Abby said, "That noise. It's so weird, isn't it?"

"They's my fire-breathing dragons."

Abby stared at the horses. "I love dragons. But I've never seen one. Not in real life."

"They's real as real can be, even if they's horses. Sensitive, powerful strong and able to take flight like, that." Sissy snapped her fingers. "They got a strong flight reflex. Daddy told me long ago never to forget it. I don't cause no horse ever did. They survived through time by running away from danger. They hard-wired to run at the first hint of danger, get a head start, before discovering if it's real danger or not. But in this case, they ain't scared. They's excited."

Abby nodded. "When they blow through their noses like that, I can almost imagine flames shooting out."

"That's the alarm call. It's a big sound." Sissy pointed at one of the horses. "And look how high they carry their heads and tails." She continued; "Gotta' look big."

Abby understood. "Like a puffer fish. It's a defense mechanism."

Sissy looked sideways at Abby. "I don't know about fish. But that sounds right. Also, horses got to lift their heads to focus on distance. They lower their heads to focus on stuff that's close. It's how their eyes work. Neck up high, distance, low for close. Different to how our eyes work."

"So, they're looking for the huntsman?"

"Yeah. They heard the horn. For years that horn meant something. Time to move off, follow them hounds. But I think the huntsman must be moving away from us. I don't hear it no more. But bless 'em, it got their old hearts beating faster."

"Sissy, that makes me feel kind of sad. They remember. They don't like being left behind."

"No herd animal does. But they have each other. And ain't they grand, still?"

"Yes. Man, you've already taught me a lot about horses. Like the first day when you taught me that Bunny couldn't see right in front of her nose."

"Behind too. Two blind spots."

"And now, how they can't focus without moving their heads. So, horses can't see all that great."

Sissy made a sound that signified disappointment. "Ain't what I said. They might got two blind spots, and they might need to move they head up or down, but they see all around them, almost like they got eyes in the back of their head. Like way better than we do. And they see movement, even a little, tiny movement. Cause in the wild they had to be able to take a drink of water, but see the branch move on a bush way off to the side where some old lion is hiding. They see that branch move, and they is off like lightning before that old cat can get traction."

Abby could see that the horses were relaxing. Heads came down, tails came down. The herd began to spread back out again. One horse went and rolled, and when it got back up, it put its head back up and scanned the horizon, then gave a mighty shake, the dirt making a small cloud around it, then it put its head down and began to graze.

Abby said, "They have each other, so they aren't upset now."

Sissy said, "No horse is a loner. Just like people. Everybody needs friends."

"I guess that's true."

Sissy nodded, "Shows over. Let's ride."

* * *

Sissy had wrapped Abby's legs with horse bandages. She called them polo wraps. They were made of polar fleece. They created a nice cushion between the scabs and chafes on her inner knees and Buttermilk's hide. It made the ride bearable. And Abby even forgot about how bad her legs had stung when she decided she had to take a tub bath the night before.

The two girls walked side by side around the field. Abby's voice was animated. "Robert and Lucy and Lotty, they all visited Grandma last night!"

Sissy's eyes were wide. "What you mean? Like ghosts?"

"I like to think maybe they were ghosts. She said they came to her in a dream. But my grandma lies. She's a good liar. She says all writers are. It's just that they lie in order to tell truths."

"That don't make no sense."

"There's no law that true things, real things, have to make sense. It would take all the mystery out of life if there were. Grandma says that human beings just have limitations on understanding."

"Half the time you don't make sense either, Abby Woods."

"And I'm real, aren't I?"

"A real smart-ass. That's for sure."

Abby grinned, and said, "For someone who pretends not to be smart, you sure are a smart-ass too."

Sissy laughed. "Must be why we go together so good."

"So well. We go together so well."

"Ain't that what I just said? Tell me about them ghosts your grandma saw or didn't see. Tell me them truths or lies. I want to know either way, 'cause I sure like a good story."

"Me, too."

It wasn't until Abby and Sissy had gotten the horses good and sweaty, had galloped up the hill, the dogs loudly panting, that they returned to the story of Robert and Lucy.

Sissy said, "That Robert, he were a white man, and Lucy, what you suppose she looked like?"

Abby said without thinking, "Like you."

"Me?"

"Sure. I mean, she was the Matriarch of your line, right?"

"Matriarch?"

"Your founding mother."

Sissy was quiet for a moment. "I forgot about that. She's my blood. That's something."

"Didn't Mimi tell you that story about her before?"

"No, I heard only that this land come to us from former slaves, Taylors, a long time back. I heard that the white Taylors didn't want nothing to do with us."

"Well, that's right, far as it goes. I mean, that's just not the interesting part of the story."

"My Mimi never told me anything about curses. Now that's the interesting part. Guess she didn't want to scare me."

"And you didn't know about the white man who fathered those former slaves. That white man is your ancestor, too. He's your blood too."

Sissy grinned, "Could be true, or not. Maybe I got some white way back in my blood, but what I know for sure, lookin' at you, is I don't think you got a drop of African blood you can claim."

"Alas, I think you're probably right."

"'Alas?' Girl, I don't hold nothing against you for being white. But maybe I got a problem with you saying words like 'Alas.' Who talks like that?"

Abby sat taller on the back of Buttermilk, "That's nothing, listen to this" Abby lowered her voice, and raised one hand up in the air, "Screw your courage to the sticking place, and we'll not fail!'"

"Now you talking straight-out crazy."

"Not crazy. It's Shakespeare. I memorized Lady Mac-Beth's speech last summer for summer camp. Lady MacBeth was trying to convince her husband to murder the king. And she basically shames him into it by making out that he's a coward."

Sissy and Abby were now strolling back toward the barn on two tired and sweaty horses. The inside of their jeans were damp and dirty, the horses were relaxed and needed no direction or attention from their riders.

After getting the horses put up, Abby and Sissy drank lemonade on Mimi's back steps. Then Mimi fetched them a comb, not for themselves, but to rid the dogs' coats of 'hitch-hikers' which were seed heads of some sort that stuck like glue to the dogs' coats. Belle wasn't so bad, but Freddy, with his longer hair, was covered.

As they combed out the seed heads, Abby talked Sissy into pretending they were Robert and Lucy. With a little prodding, she got Sissy to pretend she was Lucy, while Abby acted the part of Robert. They imagined what the two would have said to each other about his marriage to Lotty. And every time Sissy said something anachronistic, Abby would protest.

But what shut Abby up, was when Sissy said, "If you think I look like Lucy, I betcha' I sound like Lucy too. When I speak, you likely hearing what she sounded like."

Abby said, "Wow. Touche'." And then explained what touche' meant, and told Sissy the origin of the word, even though Sissy did not ask to be told.

Even to Abby's own ears, she sounded kind of condescending.

But she was struck by Sissy's point. It was valid. Sissy's voice was the echo of the history of this place, and the people who once lived here. Sissy gave the figures in this story an authentic soundtrack. That was something you couldn't find in a book. Abby may have read a lot, but she was just a kid from California.

Sissy didn't call Abby weird for using the word touche'. She let Abby be Abby. But she did notice that Abby had given her props for being right. And she was right. She knew she was.

* * *

After Abby and Sissy had raided Emmaline's fridge for lunch, they practiced frisbee. The dogs had stretched out in the shade of the front porch of Chickasaw House (formerly known as Squirrel Manor) and were deeply asleep, occasionally twitching and exhaling small barking noises. Abby and Sissy were missing more than they caught.

One-eared Tom had silently made his way to the porch too. He found a spot balancing on the porch railing and looked like someone spectating at a tennis match, following the frisbee with his head as it went back and forth, as well as into the weeds to be retrieved.

Abby said, "Grandma told my parents I was good at frisbee."

"Good? When we nail one, it's dumb luck. That don't qualify as good."

"We need to practice. Like a lot."

"When they coming?"

"Around a week from now."

"Hah. We got a snowball's chance in hell of either of us being good in a week's time. Why you gotta' be good at this?"

Abby frowned, "My dad thinks I'm weird."

"Well, he ain't wrong there. But I like you fine anyway."

"He thinks I should be out playing sports and interacting with my own peer group. But I like hanging out with my grandma and playing with my dog."

"I expect he'll think I'm weird, too."

Abby tossed a floater, and it landed right in Sissy's open hand.

Abby said, "Oh my God! I did it again!"

Sissy tossed the frisbee back, but she shanked the disc into the grass, so Abby had to run to scoop it up.

Sissy said, "And if you show your dad that you can throw and catch this thing, he won't think you're weird anymore?"

Abby's voice got small. "Maybe. Maybe a little bit. But also, he'll like my grandma more."

Sissy looked puzzled. "He don't like Ms. Emmaline?"

Abby exhaled loudly. The dogs sat up, and One-eared Tom jumped down off the railing and darted off into the brush. Freddy stood up; the hackles rose on his back. He sniffed the air, then sat back down, looking anxious, but not panicked.

Abby said, "That's the best Freddy has ever done around Tom."

"He only smelled him. Didn't see him. But still..."

Abby added, "Grandma had a date in town. Again."

"Uh, okay. That's nice."

"She puts on makeup and jewelry, too."

"For an old gal, she's real pretty. So why shouldn't she have a date?"

"I don't know. It makes me feel anxious. I mean, my mom and dad are coming, and if they found out that she was dating, it might make things worse for both of us. My dad for sure would say it was inappropriate."

"Naw. That ain't so. The way I see it is that your grandma isn't just hanging out with kids. She's going out and mixing with her own, what you call it?"

"Peer group?"

"Yeah. And with Mimi, too. That's good for them both. Everybody needs friends."

"But a date is different. My dad would see it that way. Maybe I should warn her to keep it on the lowdown."

"You met this fella?"

"No. But I saw him in my dreams."

Sissy shook her head, "That's you just making up stories in your head."

Abby nodded. "Yeah, that's what writers do. See, I wrote a story, where my grandma is a witch and Freddy is her wolf, and she is summoning someone to come to her."

"Freddy sure do look to be a wolf, But Ms. Emmaline a witch? Don't know where you got that summoning idea."

"See, Emmaline never had a husband. But someone was mom's daddy. What do you suppose happened to him? No one ever told me. I know not to ask. In my story, he wouldn't come to the witch's summons, and he never has. And I think that's why she's here. I think he's here."

Sissy nodded, "You may be weird, but you ain't stupid, Abby Woods. You figured out any particulars?"

"No. Grandma's a hard nut to crack."

"You treading where you ought not to tread. I say you stick to the ghosties. Ms. Emmaline is a grown-up; she knows what's what. You best not say a peep. And she knows your daddy and your momma before you did, and likely better than you do."

"But she doesn't know what they say about her behind her back?"

"And you do?"

"Well, I'm not supposed to, but…"

"But?"

"I spy on my parents."

"How you do that?"

"There's this heating vent."

Sissy looked surprised. "Abby, I knew you were weird, but I didn't peg you as sly. You shouldn't spy. And for sure you shouldn't tell Ms. Emmaline things she weren't meant to hear. That's called 'tellin' tales out of school. Even I know that's bad."

"I haven't. But it doesn't stop me from knowing stuff."

Sissy said, "Seems to me that learning to throw and catch this frisbee ain't gonna' fix what needs fixing. And it also seems to me that what needs fixin' needs fixin' by the grownups. Not you."

"I still want to get good at this, though. Frisbee."

"Tell me why. And tell me without talking about your dad."

"Okay. I will. Emmaline told me that one summer she was walking in our village past the park, when she saw a couple of boys tossing the frisbee back and forth. She was in high school at the time, and these were college boys, handsome boys. She thought they were far too handsome and mature to look twice at her. But she got an idea. She got one of them to teach her how to toss it. Turns out she was good at it, too. He asked for her number. My Grandma won't say much more than that, except that it turned out to be a good social skill that served her well once she got here for college. She thinks it is especially good for people like me."

"You mean weird?"

"People who don't interact with their own peer group or play team sports."

Sissy began to laugh.

"What's so funny?"

"Emmaline is sly too. Guess you didn't 'lick it off the grass.'"

Abby giggled.

Sissy said, "Okay, so, learning frisbee is going to get us dates someday. Dates with handsome college boys?"

"According to Emmaline; yeah"

Sissy grinned, "Toss me that frisbee."

14

Mimi exclaimed, "Ooh, ain't that the purtiest cake ever!

Emmaline looked a bit sheepish, "Confession. I didn't make it. It's from a bakery straight on from the corner."

Abby scowled, "Grandma, you're talking gibberish."

Sissy corrected her. "No, she ain't. The corner is a place certain, right there on the grounds."

Francis chuckled, "I bet I know the bakery. Main Street."

Emmaline nodded, "Did you know that in England, every dessert is referred to as a pudding? Even a cake?"

Mimi said, "Emmaline, I don't know how you know so much about so much."

Emmaline spoke rapidly, "I forgot about Yorkshire pudding! That's a savory popover served with onion gravy next to your slab of roast beef. Plum pudding is a dense cake, soaked in rum and lit on fire when it is served. I don't know why in the USA the term pudding got narrowed down to custards."

Emmaline paused and then added, "I do love a custard."

Abby interrupted, "Grandma, you've got the zoomies from too much coffee. Can we eat now?"

"I guess I do have the zoomies. I'll cut the cake. Abby, you take coffee or tea orders."

Once they got settled, Emmaline began to 'hold forth.'

Emmaline slowed down and lowered her voice. Abby felt herself drift into that quiet space. It was nearly a dream state, but a waking one. Even the dogs seemed affected as they stretched out on the porch, bellies flat against the planks. Her grandma was doing that thing she did that put everyone under her spell. Everyone else saw Emmaline, but Abby saw her witch.

Emmaline said, "I'm going to set the scene. Look down this drive toward your house. Then cast your mind back to the year 1837. Maybe the grass was tall like it is now, maybe it was mowed. Maybe it had livestock on it to keep it grazed down. Maybe not. Maybe the enslaved people who lived here kept it groomed as a show of wealth.

"Imagine a small dark woman driving a farm cart pulled by a sturdy small horse, a Chickasaw horse. As she gets closer, we can see that she's old, but not ancient. She's come on a social call to visit her friend Lucy.

"She's Critta Hemings Bowles. Once the property of Thomas Jefferson. She was a slave until the age of fifty-eight. Her freedom was purchased for the pittance of fifty dollars by Jefferson's son-in-law, Francis Epps. Critta is married. Slave marriages were not legally binding until after emancipation, but that did not make Critta's marriage less real. Her husband is Zachariah Bowles. He had once worked at Monticello, where he had met a young Critta, who had no power to leave Jefferson and live here with her husband. Not for a very long time.

"Zachariah had been born free, as his mother was a mixed-race indentured servant and not a slave. Zachariah must have been a good man. Why do I say that? Well, he was somehow able to raise a slave child as if it were his very own. It was the child of Critta's niece, Martha Ann and Burwell Colbert,

Jefferson's butler. Critta and Zachariah also had one child of their own, James, born to Critta when she was the property of Jefferson. Under the law, her son James was a slave, Jefferson's property. When he was only seventeen, he ran away. He was pursued, found, but ran again.

He was mentioned years later in Jefferson's records as being paid to do a service for him. Paid. Just like a freed person would be paid, although he was never formally freed. I imagine him, at seventeen, working for his father, Zachariah, in a state of uneasy liberty. Imagine if you will, the complicated negotiations that left James unpunished and living away from Monticello.

"Zachariah's mother was not only free, but landed, owning 224 acres of land, right near here, and 96 of those acres became Zachariah's at her passing. Then those acres became Critta's at his passing. Just as Mimi told us, after the Civil War this area drew newly emancipated slaves, because freedmen already lived here. Some settled, some later moved northward in the great migration. But sadly, and in time, a struggle ensued between whites and blacks over ownership of this bit of turf. But that is not the moment I want to imagine tonight.

"Critta is coming to visit.

"Lucy comes out onto this very porch to greet her. A black child comes out from behind her and Lucy tells the child to unhitch the horse and give it hay and water, since she intends to keep company for a spell with Critta. They have a lot of news to catch up on, because now that Lotty is gone, Lucy can preside as mistress of Chickasaw House. She can now speak freely. She can entertain her friend. She has won. At least that is as it stands for this moment. She and Robert have much to decide and to plan to see to the benefit and well-be-ing of their children, though the law sees them only as slaves, his property, never to reach the age of majority in the eyes of the law and attain the rights and obligations of adulthood."

Sissy spoke quietly, as if it might not be proper to inter-rupt Emmaline.

"Excuse me, Miss Emmaline, is it okay to ask what that word mean?"

"Of course. When children reach the age of majority, the state declares them to be able to make their own legal choices. They are no longer children in the eyes of the law."

"And the law tries you as an adult if you break the law?"

Emmaline nodded, "That's true. Yes. I hadn't thought of that."

Mimi turned in her chair to Emmaline. "You been think-ing on my story."

"Oh, yes. I have been. A lot. It's made more powerful be-cause it was all right here. Right where we sit. On these old planks. I can see Critta, and I can see that Chickasaw horse. And I understand why Critta and Lucy would be friends. Critta would have had sympathetic ears to Lucy's situation. Critta's big sister is Sally Hemings, mother of four of Jeffer-son's children. Critta's mother is Betty Hemings, mother to six children by her owner, Martha Jefferson's father.

Now Emmaline focused on Mimi. "Mimi, all of this came to me last night. It woke me up from a deep sleep. These amazing Hemings women, there were so many of them, many generations of them. Not just at Monticello, but living at Jef-ferson's quarter farms, and living with his daughter Maria, and here is Critta living by Chickasaw House. The Hemings women are well known now and were well known then. But what you told me is new. Your story is unknown. So, here is what came to me, and I will only pursue this with your blessing. May I develop your Lucy and Robert and Lotty story and the story of Chickasaw House in my work of fiction? Will you allow me to base a fictional story upon what we do know? Do you trust me to do it justice?"

Mimi looked thoughtful. "I suppose I do trust you, but I sure wish I could tell you more."

Francis piped in. "I trust you, Emmaline. You are a respectful person, and I know you respect those who come before us."

"Thank you, both of you. I have one more thing to say, here. Mimi, I told you about that "voice in the night" moment. It's when some character speaks to me, directs me, inspires me. Writers speak of their "muse" speaking to them, directing them. Sometimes the voice is urgent. It has something very specific to say, and sometimes it is more visual, like watching a movie inside of my head and I must describe what I am seeing, get it down into print. But what woke me up at three am, was a voice. A very clear and distinct voice."

Mimi tipped her head. "Emmaline, what you trying to say, girl."

"It was your voice, Mimi. Your voice. And maybe it wasn't you exactly, maybe it was someone who came before you. Someone in my imagining, but it was your voice. I want to use you as a character in my story. I want you to be the narrator. I'll let you read everything I write, and I want you to let me know if I get something wrong or if it just feels wrong to you. This is Taylor land. This is the land of Chickasaw House and

Chickasaw horses, and a place that was home to free blacks and those caught in between that state of enslaved and truly free, much earlier than the date of emancipation. I can write the words. I can create scenes and dialogue, but the stories belong to you, and the Taylors and the Hemings' and untold other families. Although to be honest, they belong to us all, as Americans, acknowledged or not. But it's a lot to ask. Please if you need to think about it..."

"Honey, I don't need to think on it. I'd be honored. I just hope people know that it ain't just fiction, even though you gonna' call it thus."

"Those that read the acknowledgment page will hear how the story came about. But the thing about fiction is..."

Abby broke in, "That you can tell great truths."

Everyone nodded in unison.

Including Sissy.

* * *

Emmaline continued to have the zoomies. Every day.

Abby knew she was excited about her writing, which Emmaline said, now had structure and characters and theme, but had yet to be written. But Abby knew her Grandma's zoomies went beyond that. Yeah, her parents were coming to visit. But she wondered if Emmaline was planning to finally open up about her 'friend.'

Abby wasn't sure how Emmaline got Bobby Taylor to mow the weeds that lined the dirt driveway and then weed whack around the foundation, but it got done. Emmaline, as Sissy had observed, was sly. She had found a way.

Emmaline had also put up a pole and two bird feeders outside the kitchen. When the birds were at the feeders Emmaline raved euphorically over Cardinals and Tufted Titmice, Woodpeckers, and the funny little Nuthatches. She seemed determined that Abby learn her birds, even hanging a "Backyard Birds of Virginia" poster in the kitchen.

Emmaline had purchased new mattress pads, sheets, a duvet, pillows and blankets, along with new towels, for Belva Ann and Jim's bedroom. Abby found scented soaps had been placed by all the sinks and the tub.

Abby usually found Emmaline already up each morning when she and Freddy came down, coffee cup in hand, scribbling on lined paper her plans for the day. This morning was no different. Emmaline was writing away, a half-eaten piece of toast sat next to a mug of coffee in front of her. Her gray hair was piled up on top of her head, with bits that had escaped her butterfly clip hanging down the back of her neck.

She looked up and said, "Are you excited? They arrive tomorrow!"

Abby picked up Emmaline's mug, ignoring the question. "This is stone cold."

"A fresh one would be lovely, thanks."

"Grandma, you're kinda' scaring me. I mean, I'm excited about seeing Mom, and to be honest, I'm a little nervous about seeing Dad, but you look freaked out."

"Do I?"

"Um, yeah."

"Well, I suppose I'm used to Belva Ann and Jim having their space, and I have my space. And now, I'm hosting them here, at Chickasaw House."

"And it's a dump."

"It's a grand old house."

Abby looked thoughtful, scanning the kitchen. "Look at this kitchen. It's shabby. The whole house is. And even though I've cleaned, it always looks dirty."

"Don't swear. Shabby? Do you know the origin of the word? It comes from the old English word for scab."

"Gross."

"And that isn't how you feel about the house either."

"No. But Mom and Dad won't be here long enough to get to know her. The old lady. The house."

"We should make the effort."

"The soaps and towels can't hide the…"

"The scabs?"

Abby nodded.

"Scabs form over wounds. You're right, scented soaps and new towels don't hide anything. We can't cure time. We can't remove time's shadow. And maybe I *am* a bit freaked out. But that will all change once Jim is here."

"Because?"

"Your Dad adds ballast."

"Ballast?"

"Boats need ballast. It's added weight, usually a tank of water down in the hull. Ballast is about creating stability. Something we Spark's women are not famous for possessing, although Belva Ann one-ups me on that score. Imagine a boat, where all the passengers suddenly rushed to one side. Without ballast, what happens to the boat?"

"What?"

Emmaline flipped her hand over.

"Oh."

"I think that's why Belva Ann was attracted to Jim."

Abby nodded, "We don't provide ballast, and we get the zoomies."

"Afraid so. But your dad has many fine qualities beyond stability. He loves to read, and he loves history. I just know he will be very interested to hear about the history of this house and this place. If..."

"If what?"

"It's just that he's been so unhappy these last few years. He wasn't always like that."

"Why?"

"He's worried."

"It's my fault, isn't it?"

Emmaline looked shocked. "What! No. Whatever makes you say such a thing?"

Abby shrugged. She realized she had said too much. She said, "Because of what happened at school. Because I don't play sports or hang out with other girls my age."

"Rest assured, he has plenty of other things he worries over. Besides, although you have your flaws, you're no more flawed than anyone else in this world, including your father."

"Including you, Grandma?"

"Oh, my goodness! Especially me."

"But you never talk about your flaws."

"Abby darling, we all have scabs."

* * *

Freddy was frantic with joy when Belva Ann and Jim got

out of their rental car. He forgot himself and jumped all over them. He nearly made it impossible for Belva Ann to get to Abby to give her a hug.

Belva Ann hugged and kissed her daughter over and over until Abby started to get embarrassed. "Mom, it hasn't been that long!"

"But you're my baby!"

With her hands still on Abby's shoulders she stepped back to get a good look at her. "You're sunburned. You've forgotten to put on your sunblock."

Jim protested, "Aren't I going to get a hug?"

"Daddy! You came; you came! You are never going to regret letting me come with Grandma."

Emmaline broke in, "Come inside. I'll show you to your room, then you need to relax with us on the front porch. I made lemonade."

Abby was feeling buzzy as they sat on the front porch. She thought to herself that she too had the zoomies. Even though she was sitting still, she might as well have been jogging, she was almost breathless.

Emmaline said, "Anyone hungry?"

No one wanted food.

Abby came back with the pitcher of lemonade. Freddy was leaning up against Belva Ann, who was stroking his head.

Belva Ann said, "This must be heaven for Freddy. So much freedom."

Abby answered, "He's got a girlfriend. Her name is Belle. She's a foxhound."

Belva Ann answered, "That must be Sissy's dog."

Abby's zoomies were about to be on full display.

Abby talked non-stop for the next thirty minutes or so. She told them about Sissy, Belle, Bunny, Buttermilk, riding bareback. She told them that Sissy drove a gator, worked and made money caring for retired foxhunters. She told them about Frisbee, Mimi and Francis. She told them about desserts and story time. She even told them, on the lowdown, that Sissy had trouble reading and her language was ungrammatical, but that she and Emmaline were tactfully helping her increase her skill level.

Abby didn't even notice Emmaline and Belva Ann exchanging glances with faint smiles. But what she did notice was that her dad seemed to be listening to every word.

* * *

They ate dinner in what had once been the beautiful dining room. Now they ate from a folding table and sat in folding chairs. Emmaline had put a tablecloth over the table.

Jim said, "I thought you said the place was furnished."

Emmaline did not take offense, "Well, this room was furnished by me. I bought the table and chairs, elegant as they may be."

Abby added, "She purchased them just for you guys. We've been eating in the kitchen or on the front porch."

Belva Ann said, "You didn't need to do that, Mom. We would have been fine eating in the kitchen."

"True darling, but I wanted you to appreciate the charms of this room. The fireplace, the woodwork, I believe is original."

Abby gave her father a stern look. "Dad, don't say mean

things about the house. We're supposed to respect our elders. And the house worries enough as it is."

Jim objected, "It's an inanimate object."

Belva Ann glanced at her husband before saying. "Abby, you are right about showing respect for old things as well as old people. But why do you think the house is worried?"

"What if Bobby Taylor got desperate for money, he could rip out those marble fireplaces and sell them at auction. It would be like selling off body parts. You might not think a house worries about such things, Dad. And maybe that's not the right way to describe it. But Grandma and I felt it right away, didn't we Grandma? We're strangers here, and we had to convince the house that we were better tenants than the squirrels who were living here."

Jim's eyebrows went up, "Squirrels?"

Abby said, "Don't worry, Dad. Grandma charmed the squirrels into leaving. I saw it with my own eyes. Now we set out shelled peanuts for them in the yard." Abby nodded solemnly, "Compensation."

Belva Ann said, "A squirrel charmer? And here I thought I knew everything there was to know about you, Mom. "

Emmaline said, "Not even close, dear. A child should never, ever, know everything about a parent. Abby did witness me talking a squirrel into vacating the premises, I had no such effect on the mice. For the mice we had to hire a professional."

Abby chimed in, "One-Eared Tom."

Jim mock scowled, "Now you two are toying with us."

Emmaline laughed, "When Bobby Taylor told us he was sending 'One-Eared Tom' over, well, we were expecting an odd-looking fellow."

Abby said, "Then he moved in with us!"

Emmaline looked at Abby and grinned, "Shall we tell him?"

Abby said, "Daddy, it's a cat."

Jim said, "A cat?"

Emmaline added, "A regular assassin. Gutted mice corpses were strewn about the house for days on end."

Jim shook his head. "You women look gleeful. Bloodthirsty lot."

"Grandma pets him and praises him, too, meanwhile, poor Freddy."

Emmaline said, "I've grown quite fond of him. And he's been an instrumental part of Freddy's desensitization program."

Jim looked interested, "How's that going?"

Emmaline put her hand in the air, palm facing the ground and tipped it back and forth."

They ate gelato on the front porch and Emmaline began to tell them what she had learned about the house. Jim was leaning slightly forward in his chair. He looked genuinely interested.

He said, "That happened here? In this house?"

Emmaline answered him, "You just ate in the dining room of Robert Taylor. You're sitting on the front porch he built all those years ago. You're looking down his front drive. I expect that view has not changed since the day he pounded in stakes to site this home."

Jim crossed his arms and stared down the driveway, he scanned the area in a slow way, then turned his head to examine the house behind him.

He then looked at Emmaline, exhaled slowly and said, "Fascinating."

Emmaline nodded back, a serious expression on her face.

Abby looked at her dad and then looked back at her grandma. Her grandma clearly no longer had the zoomies. Maybe this had something to do with ballast. Or maybe her daddy had lowered his metaphorical anchor. Stability, either way. He was there for Abby. He was there for Belva Ann; he was even there for Freddy. But something told Abby, he was especially there for Emmaline. And for whatever reason, she felt it, what her grandma had said about her daddy. For this moment at least, she felt relaxed and safe.

* * *

Belva Ann and Jim were slow to come downstairs in the morning. Abby was getting impatient.

Emmaline said, "Remember, it's three hours earlier in California."

"Can't I wake them up? I told Sissy I'd be by this morning. I want to show them the horses."

Just then Freddy jumped up and ran out of the kitchen, scooting past Belva Ann's legs as she walked in.

"What's with Freddy?"

Emmaline walked to the back door and opened it. Tom slipped in, stopped and rubbed himself against her legs.

"One-Eared Tom."

Belva Ann leaned over to stroke his back. And he looked up at her, his tail vibrating.

"Mom, he likes you."

Freddy peeked around the corner to have a look, his head lowered, his ears flattened.

Emmaline scooped up the cat in her arms and placed him on the counter. Jim walked in, stared a moment at Freddy, and then pointed at the cat. "Is that sanitary? A cat where you prepare food?"

Emmaline retrieved the cat food from the pantry while Tom walked to the end of the counter, following her with his eyes. She returned to place his full bowl on the counter.

"You never had a cat, I take it?"

Jim shook his head, "No. Not a fan."

Belva Ann said. "You and Freddy both must have had a traumatic experience."

Emmaline said to Jim, "Cats prefer eating high."

Then she said, "Don't you, Tom?" The cat made some sort of noise in reply, without stopping his attack on his dry food. It came out a sort of "yam-yam-yam" as he chewed. If he had been a person, you would have said he was mumbling his agreement.

Belva Ann said, "Too bad about the ear."

Abby said, "You can see a bit of what's left of it, stuck to his skull; mummified."

Jim winced, "Good God, please, I haven't even had my coffee yet."

Abby added, "Dad, you're lucky you weren't here when we had eviscerated mouse bodies everywhere."

"Glad I missed it."

Jim raised his eyebrows and pointed at Freddy.

Emmaline said, "Huge progress. We're proud of him. He's not running away, and he isn't dribbling urine on the floors."

Emmaline raised her pitch and enthused, "Aren't you the best boy! Yes, you are! Yes, you are!"

Jim said, "Why not put the leash on and do your obedience thing, Abby?"

"Francis said to let the dog close the bubble himself. He'll close the space up when he feels safe to do it. If we force it now, we'll only confirm his fears by flooding his system with adrenaline. And that stimulates the flight response."

"The neighbor? He's a dog trainer?"

Abby shrugged, "He mostly trains horses."

Emmaline added, "It's clear to me that it's working. Slowly, but working none-the-less. You'll meet Francis tonight. But this morning you'll meet Mimi and Sissy, as soon as you finish breakfast. Abby wants you to see her ride a horse, and then later, show off her frisbee skills."

* * *

Later, they walked down the long drive to the Taylor farm, Freddy happily trotting at their side. Emmaline had left One-Eared Tom in the house to do his mouse patrol.

Belva Ann was saying, "It's so beautiful here, Mom. I thought it would be hotter. The air is warm and soft and there's a breeze."

"It's been pretty mild. We have some hot afternoons. But I don't mind."

Abby said, "There's Sissy!"

Jim said, "Is she driving a tractor?"

Abby said, "Yeah. She's pulling the tine harrow around the pasture. It breaks up the manure piles, helps it degrade into the soil. The sun can help kill the parasites."

"Parasites?"

"And if you don't spread the manure into the ground, they'll only graze where they don't poop."

"Sounds sensible." He turned his head to smile at his wife.

Abby continued her lecture. "Horses are selective grazers. They won't eat weeds either. Cows and goats do. Not horses. So, Sissy has to keep after the weeds. Otherwise, the horses will graze the good grass down to the crowns and kill it, while the weeds keep spreading. She says pretty soon there would be no grass, only weeds."

Jim muttered, "She seems awfully young to be driving a tractor."

"Francis doesn't let her drive the big one with the bucket."

Emmaline explained, "Farm kids are exempted from labor laws. And that herd of retired horses is Sissy's job. Each one pays a monthly fee."

Mimi came out of the house holding a dish towel.

"Welcome! Welcome! Ya'll sure have come a long way."

Belva Ann stepped forward, "I am so pleased to meet you, Mimi. Abby can't stop talking about you and Sissy and Francis and all your animals. I've never heard her so happy about anything in all my life."

"Well, we've all grown partial to both Abby and Emmaline, and that wolfdog, too."

Jim said, "We're already impressed with Sissy, just watching her drive that tractor. What an enterprising young lady."

"Soon as she could reach the pedals, she was game. She takes care of these horses serious-like. And Francis, he puts whatever is left over as profit into a special account at the bank with her name on it."

Jim said, "That *is* impressive."

Emmaline added, "That work ethic, learned early, will serve her all her life."

Sissy started toward the gate, and Abby stepped forward to unlatch it and hold it open as Sissy pulled through, driving around the back of the barn to a storage shed.

Sissy came out of the barn with bridles. Abby excitedly said to her parents. "Wait until you see how Sissy gets on Bunny!"

Then the two girls walked into the herd of horses, Bunny lifted her head and came to Sissy, who dug something out of her pocket to give to the mare. Then Abby found Buttermilk and did the same. They led the horses out of the field, and through the gate. Sissy gave Abby a leg up on Buttermilk. Bunny put her head down, grabbed a mouthful of grass, while Sissy got onto her neck, then Bunny lifted her head, and Abby slid down her neck into a riding position.

Belva Ann applauded. Mimi said, "You showin' off now."

Jim said, "That is a neat trick."

Abby said, "Come walk with us and the dogs. It's worth it for the view."

Mimi stayed back, but it was quite the party, with Jim, Belva Ann, Emmaline, the two dogs, the two horses, and two chattering girls walking around the hayfields and skimming along the woods. The dogs chased rabbits out of the grass and even flushed deer out of the woods, but soon returned to the hike.

Sissy said, "See that hill, it's our favorite place to let 'em rip. Not that these old gals go all that fast. But we do it every day, and it would hurt their feelings if we skipped it."

Jim wrinkled his forehead. But he said nothing. Abby and

233

Sissy had already moved away, breaking from walk to trot. Belva Ann put her hand up over her eyes as a shade.

They turned a corner, and the horses picked up a canter. Sissy in front. Abby behind, holding onto the mane, leaning a bit forward. Then they visibly accelerated. And off they flew.

Jim said, "Shouldn't they be wearing helmets?"

Emmaline said, "Probably."

Jim added, "And saddles?"

Belva Ann said, "I'm sure when we find a place for her to ride in California, they will provide both saddles and helmets. But not here."

Emmaline said, "Here is a magical time and place that will be part of Abby's memories when she is old as dirt and none of us are around anymore."

Belva Ann said, "Oh. Oh, yes. I think so too. Just leave it, Jim. Don't you dare say a word about helmets and saddles. Not now."

Jim said, "It makes me uneasy."

Belva Ann said, "Everything makes you uneasy these days."

Emmaline looked at Jim, "I haven't asked either of you how things are going at home."

Belva Ann said, "Not much to report, Mom, but thanks for asking. I still hate my job, and Jim still hates his co-workers."

"Annie, really? I don't hate anyone."

"Oh, come on! Every night you tell me they're idiots. To be precise, you recently called your boss a 'bungling idiot.'"

Emmaline said to no one in particular. "Bungle is an interesting word. Not sure of the etymology. But it means clumsy."

Belva Ann replied. "I've met him, and he didn't give me the impression of being an idiot or clumsy."

Jim sighed. "Maybe my word choice was imprecise. I appreciate your interest, Emmaline, but if I start thinking about work…"

Emmaline said, "Don't say another word. I don't want you to worry. 'Worry never robs tomorrow of its sorrow, it only saps today of its joy.'"

Jim nodded. "I don't want anything to sap my joy. Not on this trip."

15

Jim said, "I confess that I've never had banana pudding."

Mimi looked shocked, "Now, that can't be right."

Belva Ann interjected, "Jim has had to expand his palate since he met me."

Jim said, "My mother was not much of a cook. Dessert was ice cream or cookies."

Belva Ann added, "Store bought cookies."

Emmaline said, "Well Jim, you are in for a treat."

Jim added, "I can't think of any other desserts made with bananas. I mean, it is rather unusual, right?"

Emmaline said, "Bananas Foster."

Mimi said, "I've never had that one. Is it good?"

Emmaline grinned, "Oh yes. You saute' the bananas in butter, brown sugar, and cinnamon. The original adds rum and then you light it on fire for effect. Then it gets served over ice cream."

Mimi said, "My, that does sound good."

Sissy said, "Daddy says banana pudding is his soul food."

Francis grinned. "So, Mimi, when you scoop mine out, don't be stingy!"

After the first spoonful, Jim smiled and turned to Mimi, "Banana pudding, where have you been all my life?"

Belva Ann said, "Mimi, you have a convert."

Emmaline said, "Mimi, this is not your average banana pudding. What's your secret?"

"Homemade vanilla pudding, made from scratch, for one thing. It's easy to make. All you need is ripe bananas, eggs, milk, cream, sweet, condensed milk, and vanilla wafers. I don't mind sharing the recipe. It ain't no family secret."

Francis said, "It'll cure what ails ya'."

Everyone had scraped clean their bowls, and Abby and Sissy had let the dogs lick theirs clean. (Belva Ann kicked Jim's leg under the table to prevent him saying anything).

Belva Ann asked a question to get the conversation rolling. "Emmaline tells me your family tree is rooted deeply on this very spot."

Francis nodded, "It sho is."

Mimi said, "All the way back to that old house y'all are staying in. That house was built way before the war."

Sissy added, "The Civil War."

Francis said, "That's right. But that old house went to the white Taylors. They don't claim us as kin. But we are. Way back, that is."

Abby said with enthusiasm, "We could prove them wrong with DNA testing. They'd have to believe it then. Just like that DNA test proved that Sally Hemings' son, Eston, he had Jefferson male DNA. And Jefferson was the only Jefferson male present at Monticello nine months before each and every one of Sally's births. He kept all those dates in his books. And all those years Jefferson's children and grandchildren made all that out to be a lie. Turns out it was them doing the lying all along."

Jim turned to look at his daughter.

Abby got defensive. "What? You don't believe me?"

"No. It's just, well, as well as having developed a knowledge of DNA testing, you seem to have developed a regional accent and a comfortable use of colloquialisms."

Sissy giggled. Mimi glared at her.

Sissy said, "Sorry. I ain't trying to be rude, it's just I was thinking Mr. Woods is for sure Abby's daddy. That's all."

Francis said, "Speaking of DNA. Y'all ever considered getting that dog tested. I know you say he's German Shepherd, but I seen a lot of German Shepherd's in my day, and I never seen one that looks like that one."

Mimi said, "Maybe he's one of them wolfdogs."

Belva Ann looked at Emmaline. She said, "Mom?"

Emmaline took a sip of her tea, sat back in her chair, and drew a long breath.

"Did you know that in most places in the United States, it is illegal to own a wolf hybrid?"

Mimi put a hand over her mouth.

Emmaline continued, "When we decided to adopt a rescue dog, we wanted to adopt one that not only needed us, but one that was unlikely to be adopted by anyone else. We wanted to save a life. Freddy had been found dragging a chain, his collar embedded into the flesh of his neck."

Francis nodded. "Sorry to say, I've seen such things."

Emmaline nodded back at Francis, "Abby had just done a book report on Frederick Douglass. She told me that Freddy had liberated himself, like Douglass, so he was named in his honor. The rescue organization had been working hard to heal Freddy, to rehabilitate him. They wanted to be very careful in placing him. They said he had the potential to be dangerous, in the wrong hands, that is. They also wanted to be sure he didn't go back into the sort of situation he had fled. We had to sell ourselves to them, promise that we could manage. But really it was Freddy who sealed the deal. Freddy chose Abby. He literally threw himself into her lap. It was clearly a match. They read us the riot act on adopting him, didn't they Abby?"

Abby nodded, "Yeah. We practically had to sign in blood, promising to pay for professional training, because he has PTSD and panic attacks, and because he gets aggressive if you pull on his leash."

Francis scowled, "But he's not aggressive. Not that dog."

Emmaline said, "He cannot stand tension against his neck, against those old scars. He remembers the pain, even though outwardly he's healed. And then there is his fear of cats. But Francis, you were right, by allowing him to decide on the distance, he's getting braver."

Jim said, "He still won't stay in the same room with that tomcat."

Emmeline said, "Better is good enough for now."

Francis said, "Might be he was a failed fight dog. The fact he looks like a wolf or maybe is half wolf, made him cost money to them sort of people, thinking they got them a wild one. But he ain't no fighter. Not Freddy. The cat thing? Some people who train fight dogs use cats as bait. Sometimes the cats inflict damage, fighting for their life."

Belva Ann said, "That is horrible. Poor Freddy."

Francis said, "Not poor Freddy, lucky Freddy. As a failed fighting dog, he would have been used as bait hisself. Would have been killed in time, just like the cats. He got out and got a good family. But don't blame him for wanting to give a cat a wide berth. He got his reasons."

Sissy said, "Freddy ain't scared of Belle. They's best of friends."

Mimi said, "Belle never has met a stranger."

Francis said, "Dogs need friends, just like people."

Jim added, "What Abby and Emmaline haven't mentioned is that Freddy has twice caused significant property damage. Once when they left him unattended in Emmaline's car, he shredded all the upholstery. Right down to the metal frame."

Abby said, "That was early on."

Jim added, "Once when we all went out to the movies, he broke a window, ran off, and we couldn't find him for hours."

Belva Ann said, "And when we did find him, there he was, waiting for us back at the house. But he's so much more secure these days."

Emmaline said, "We knew he would be challenging, and we made a commitment. And he's turned into a wonderful dog. And he's a dog who would protect us. He makes me feel secure too."

Abby frowned, "Grandma, you've always said he is a German Shepherd. You always tell me to tell people that, too. Isn't he a German Shepherd?"

Emmaline shrugged, "Who knows, but why would I want to pay money to do a DNA test to find out that he is in fact, not a German Shepherd?"

Jim said, "Plausible deniability?"

Emmaline nodded.

Sissy said, "But if Freddy ain't a German Shepherd, and you telling everyone he is, then that's a lie."

Abby picked up the thread, "Maybe when people ask if

he's a wolfdog, we should just say we don't know. That wouldn't be a lie."

"Dearest, sometimes it is best to lie."

Jim said, "Really, Emmaline?"

Emmaline continued, "Jim, you are a student of history. You understand fully the concept of the 'noble lie.'"

Sissy said, "But *I* don't, Ms. Emmaline."

"Well, what if you were living in another time, say in slavery time. What if you were hiding Frederick Douglass somewhere on your farm when the slavecatchers came looking for him? They ask if you have seen him? They ask if you know where he may be hiding? Would you tell the truth?"

Belva Ann said, "Mom, that's such a heavy example."

"Okay. How about this one? What if a friend is crying because some mean children have called her a fat pig? Maybe she is a full-figured child. Maybe she needs to lose a few pounds. Would you tell her she was fat? Even if she was?"

Sissy said, "I'd lie."

Emmaline said, "Of course you would because it would be wrong in both instances to tell the truth. Not all lies are bad. Sometimes to protect those we love, or simply to do the right thing, we tell a lie, but it is a noble lie. The situation must be considered, the right and wrong of it weighed. And the decision must be self-less, rather than self-ish. There is nothing noble about telling a lie merely to benefit ourselves."

Abby asked, "So even if we found out that Freddy was part wolf, we would lie, because lying would protect Freddy."

"Freddy, if he *was* a wolfdog, could be confiscated and placed in a wildlife sanctuary, or simply be destroyed by the state. We are better off not knowing for certain, and if asked, stating *as if* we knew it to be a fact, that he is indeed a German Shepherd. Which of course, he certainly *could* be."

Belva Ann looked thoughtful, "Mom, do you believe that Thomas Jefferson's children and grandchildren knew that all four of Sally Hemings children were in fact, his children."

"I think they had to know. Of course, they couldn't have dreamed about science one day challenging them. Like many before and likely many to come, they believed they were taking secrets to the grave, believing those secrets would stay buried with them. They most certainly believed they were protecting Jefferson's reputation, protecting his lofty place among the founders, that they understood would grow with time. His granddaughter called such an accusation a "moral impossibility. Such language, the language of high dudgeon, is meant to put a stop to further inquiry. Of course, it was not only possible, but it was also probable."

Abby said, "High dudgeon?"

Emmaline explained, "A state of intense indignation. Offended that anyone would dare 'go there' about her esteemed grandfather."

Sissy said, "You people sure got a lot of words."

Emmaline said, "We do."

Jim said, "Were they willfully telling a 'noble lie' and was such a thing an agreed conspiracy among them?"

Emmaline said, "Who knows? People can tell such convincing lies, and pass them off as truth to willing ears, until they at last come to believe them themselves. Look at what people today are willing to accept as facts, despite mounds of evidence presented to the contrary. A mass agreement, even of a lie, is a powerful barrier, difficult to breach. And until

DNA testing, those who tried to breach it with evidence, were often excoriated by historians. Especially by esteemed historians who wrote hagiographies. But for those who lived in the neighborhood, who knew the Hemings family and her four children? Yes. Of course, they had to know, no matter how discreet Jefferson was. Monticello was like a small village. You know how small villages are. And Charlottesville was small too. Jefferson himself never denied it.

"Remember, Jefferson took the out-of-character step of freeing all of Sally's children, he arranged the two oldest to officially "run away," his cash placed at his request in their pockets. They went to Washington, DC, and there they "passed" as whites. They were fair skinned enough to do so. Tragically, they could never return to their home, Monticello, or see their parents again. They too had to lie about who they were to protect both themselves and the stature of their father. They both married whites according to an interview in 1873 with Madison Hemings, who was the third of Sally's children."

Jim added, "DNA has been a game-changer. Look at all the times it has been used to solve crimes. And what about those wrongfully imprisoned who have finally been released due to DNA evidence. Some with years of their lives spent in prison. The DNA evidence was not available at the time of their trials. But nowadays, it's available even to test Freddy."

Belva Ann leaned a bit forward in her seat, looking at Emmaline. "Wow, I hadn't really ever thought about that. This stuff is now available to anyone. Mom, this is really interesting stuff. Does it have anything to do with your work-in-progress?"

"Well, yes, in that I absolutely believe Thomas Jefferson

was the father of all four of Sally Hemings children. It supports other facts about the Hemings women. It adds to what I've learned from Mimi. Mimi has been an amazing help to me. I hate to give away too much this early on. But the Taylors have a story to tell. And I want to use their story as a source material."

* * *

By the following day, Emmaline seemed to have lost her zoomies and was cool as a cucumber. Abby briefly wondered why cucumbers were cool. Did cool as a cucumber refer to the kind of coolness she envied? Or did it mean cool as in temperature? Because usually when someone looked really good you called them hot, not cool. You could even say it was cool to be hot.

Abby realized it was she who now had the zoomies. Abby needed to calm herself down if she had a snowball's chance in hell of showing off her frisbee skills which Emmaline had arranged for Abby and Sissy to showcase before lunch.

Emmaline brought out a pitcher of lemonade. She had made veggie kale and cream cheese rollups for lunch with kettle chips. She also placed a platter of mini cupcakes on the table. But she wagged a finger at Abby and Sissy. "Before we eat, I want your mom and dad to see you toss the disc."

Emmaline turned to locate Jim and Belva Ann who had taken seats on the front porch, "Then I want to see if Belva Ann remembers how. Jim, do you play?"

"Well, I suppose I did as a boy. But it was a long time ago."

Emmaline said, "Well, I'm sure you'll do fine."

Belva Ann and Jim exchanged a knowing sort of glance, that made Abby feel like they had rehearsed this scene.

Sissy said, "C'mon, Abby, throw it, don't stand there sweating all over it."

Emmaline called out, "You've got to dance like nobody's watching!"

Abby said, "Grandma! Really?"

Abby turned around and put a hard spin on the frisbee. It went sailing off into the weeds.

Freddy and Belle flew after it.

Freddy brought it directly back to Abby. This time Abby was able to put a float into her throw, but it was so weak that even though Sissy ran for it, Freddy got it first, plucked it right out of the air.

Jim said, "That's the most useful thing I've ever seen that dog do."

Belva Ann said, "Hush."

Sissy and Abby kept it up, and their tosses got better. Abby had one ear on the discussion that was ongoing on the porch. Although she could not hear every word, she did notice her dad had his eyes on Sissy and her. Mom was talking to Emmaline, and she sounded animated. Abby heard her say, "If this deal goes through for Jim, I can quit. Finally. He should know soon."

Emmaline said something, and Belva Ann said, "Oh, yes. Soon. You know Jim, he wasn't going to say anything to me until he felt it was a done deal."

Abby's felt like her next toss was in slow motion. The frisbee went high and straight and then seemed to lower itself right into Sissy's hand. She was amazed. She had been paying more attention to her mom and Grandma than the frisbee. If Mom could quit her job, she and Grandma could be a team again, writing.

Emmaline said something again, and Belva Ann replied, "Maybe I can come back to help you make that horrible drive back. We could even sightsee a little on the way. Road trip. Like in the old days. Well, with the addition of Abby and Freddy."

Emmaline called out, "Very nice job, ladies. Now, I want to see if the grown-ups have still got what it takes. Belva Ann, as I recall, you could put a pretty good spin on the disc back in the day."

"Mom, it's been a hundred years."

Emmaline winked, "I've recently learned that this frisbee winds back the clock. Time travel, anyone?"

"Really?"

"It's actually a talisman."

Belva Ann laughed, and the sound of her laughter was like music to Abby. Even Jim was grinning.

Belva Ann said, "Jim, if I'm doing this, you're doing it too!"

Emmaline took the frisbee from Abby, and said, "You two help yourselves to lunch. And be sure that the dogs don't eat any of our rollups."

Abby and Sissy got lemonades and rollups and sat down on the porch steps.

Sissy said, "Your Grandma is funny. And I think we done real good. After you stopped flinging it like it was made of hot coals, that is."

Abby smiled, "I don't know why I was so nervous. I don't think my dad actually cares if I can throw a frisbee or not."

"He thinks you hung the moon, regardless."

"I wouldn't go that far."

Sissy shook her head. "He's just one of those folks."

Abby said, "What's that mean?"

"My Mimi would say, 'He's as nervous as a long-tail cat in a room full of rockers.'"

Abby couldn't help herself; she laughed. And when she did her dad turned his head and the frisbee went right between his hands.

Emmaline said, "C'mon, butterfingers! Run and I'll shoot you a long one."

Abby couldn't remember ever seeing her dad run like that. He looked like he was in a football game, searching for a pass. Emmaline aimed at him, then threw it hard and it went sailing over his head. But Jim jumped for it, neatly plucking it out of the air. But he evidently had not planned his landing. You could hear the air expelled from his lungs as his side met the ground. He stayed down a moment too long.

Emmaline and Belva Ann ran to his side. Abby yelled, "Daddy!"

Jim sat up and waved the frisbee over his head, saying, "Touchdown!"

Belva Ann said, "Are you okay?"

"Yes. Fine. Forgot that this wasn't football, and I had no pads."

Emmaline said, "That was an awesome catch."

Belva Ann said, "Let me help you back up."

"Annie, don't be ridiculous. I can get up on my own steam."

Then he smiled at Emmaline and said, "That talisman of yours was turning back the clock just like you said, right up until the moment I hit the ground!"

No one had the zoomies after that. Not Abby, not Emmaline, not anyone else, including the dogs. One-Eared Tom waited until the dogs were asleep and then cruised right up to them. He even gently reached out with a paw and touched Freddy. Emmaline had put her finger to her lips as they watched Freddy twitch but not open his eyes. Tom turned and looked at Emmaline straight on, like he knew the plan or something.

Emmaline said to the cat, "Well done. Now come and sit in my lap and I'll give you a taste of cream cheese. Actually, it's vegan, not the real stuff."

Emmaline put the cat in her lap, and he licked the stuff off the tip of her finger. Then he began to purr and butt her chin with his head. Freddy began to dream, to twitch, and then he woke up, looking worried. He saw Tom sitting in Emmaline's lap and jumped to his feet. He looked confused.

Emmaline murmured, "Kitty-cats are our friends."

Freddy moved off the porch, put about fifty feet between himself and the cat, and then sat down, his ears at half-mast. He was studying the situation, not relaxed, but not panicked either.

Jim said, "Well, it's not much to hang your hat on, but I agree it's progress."

Sissy said, "Thank you for lunch, Ms. Emmaline. That was good. And man, can you throw that thing, even if you is old."

Emmaline laughed out loud.

Sissy said, "I got to go take care of my horses. Wanna' come?"

Abby turned to her mother. "I won't be long."

As Abby and Sissy walked down the long drive, Sissy said, "I like your folks. Both of them."

Abby said, "I didn't realize how much I missed them. Not until they got here."

"You're Daddy clearly misses you."

"Why would you think that?"

"He was showing off for you, just as much as you were showing off for him."

"Nah. I think he didn't want Emmaline to best him. He's competitive."

"Could be true. I think it could be he's jealous of her."

"Why would he be jealous of her?"

Sissy shook her head, "You really don't get it, do you?"

Abby stopped abruptly. "That's so patronizing."

"I don't know that word. And I bet you know I don't know that word. Which I suspect means that it's you who are being pat-ron-iz-ing."

Abby was about to get defensive but instead absorbed what Sissy had just said. "I'm sorry. Wow. You're smart. Like really smart."

"That ain't what the teachers tell my Daddy."

"Your teachers are wrong."

"Thanks, but look here, don't be getting a kink in your tail because I think maybe your daddy is jealous at how much time Ms. Emmaline gets you to herself. None of that is a bad thing. Not really. You real popular with your folks."

"Thanks, Sissy. I guess I do have cool parents."

"Did I say that? Cool? No, I did not. They ain't cool. Not like I think you mean."

"What do you mean?"

"Well, I mean like you the sun, and everything orbit around you. And don't go assuming I know all about that, but that's exactly what my brothers say about me and my Daddy and my Mimi. They jealous too."

"They do? They are?"

"Yeah, but it don't make my Mimi or my Daddy cool. And if they ever were, they sure ain't going to let on to me that they were."

Abby made a small noise of agreement.

Then Sissy grinned. "You sure are your Daddy's girl, though."

"What?"

"Soon as he began to speak, I could tell. You look more like your Momma. Same color skin and hair. You got her long legs and big feet and hands."

"Hey!"

"Nothing wrong with any of that. Works in your favor as a rider. But you sound just like your Daddy. Yeah, just like him. And he didn't like it much when you sounded otherwise. You starting to pick up the local sound. Like Emmaline. She flows back and forth between the two. It sounds easy as water."

"It's so fake."

"I don't see it that way. I see it like speaking another language."

Abby thought about that a moment. And then she saw Sissy's point. "She's trying to fit in."

"She speaks like us to make us feel good, instead of trying to make herself feel good."

Abby said, "She's not patronizing."

Sissy said, "Can you write that down somewheres so I can look it up proper.

16

Abby surprised herself by getting emotional saying good-bye to her mom and dad. As they drove away in their rental car, Freddy leaned against Abby's legs. He looked sad too.

Emmaline squeezed Abby's shoulder. She took an upbeat tone, "Belva Ann offered to help us drive home at the end of the summer. That sounds like fun."

Abby shook her head, "That wouldn't work. Freddy has the back seat, we made it like a deck for him, and our luggage has the way back. There is no room for Mom."

"We'd figure it out."

"Besides, she has to work."

"Ah, but now she's finally decided to give notice. Isn't that wonderful?"

"She's quitting?"

"Well, yes. It's such a waste of her talents. It always has been."

Abby frowned, "Daddy won't let her."

Emmaline mocked outrage. "I can't believe a granddaughter of mine, in this day and age, would think a woman needs permission from her husband to do anything."

"Grandma, you know that's the only reason she hasn't quit already. Daddy wouldn't let her."

"Let me reframe it for you in a way that gives your mother agency. Remember we discussed the meaning of that word.

Jim has convinced her to stay in that job for various reasons. But since he has a huge deal about to close, well, he has relaxed. I'm sure they engaged in negotiations, and now he is on board with her decision. And I, for one, am thrilled. She will feel so incredibly liberated."

"Grandma?"

"Yes, my darling."

"I didn't hear you or Mom mention any of this in front of Daddy."

"No need to poke the bear."

"Um. But I thought you just said he had relaxed about the idea."

"I didn't want to be a buttinsky."

Abby said, "Buttinsky?"

"Means exactly how it sounds."

Abby was silent for a beat, then offered, "Daddy lost, you won. It was a contest. And you weren't going to give up until you won. Because Daddy had been against Mom quitting her job for so long. And you had been after Mom to quit her job."

"Abby, your mother is the one who told us on a regular basis that she hated her job, that it was 'death to her spirit.' But I can't appear to be overstepping boundaries. If I did say something in front of him, it could give your dad a reason to dig up other bones he has to pick with me. Bones that honestly, are better left buried."

"What bones?"

"I'd rather not dig them up for your inspection either."

"Like why you never finished your PHD?"

Emmaline was momentarily speechless, her eyebrows

raised in surprise. Finally, she nodded. "Have you ever heard the saying, 'Never complain, never explain?'"

Abby said, "No. But you live by that one, don't you, Grandma?"

* * *

One-Eared Tom had decided that Emmaline was his person. She called him her writing partner. Although she had to make clear to Tom that sleeping on the keyboard was not in his job description. Mostly he found a corner of Emmaline's desk, or another elevated spot. Freddy rarely went into her office, or exited quickly once he spotted the cat. But he no longer flattened his ears or hunched his back or curled his tail between his hind legs. And Tom ignored him. Tom had nearly become part of the furniture.

Emmaline had started writing, because she could see scenes, and she could hear Mimi's voice. And she said that a writer had to be willing to chuck all the planning in the world if a character demanded to speak or act or pull the story in an unexpected direction. She had to get it written and only later decide if it was true enough to keep.

And so, even though she only had a fuzzy idea about how her story would end, she wrote. She wrote like a fiend. She scribbled things down at breakfast, she scribbled at lunch, and at dinner, and the rest of the time she sat at her laptop and typed. Most of the time she looked sleep deprived and disheveled. No more makeup and turquoise jewelry or flowery skirts. No more dates.

Abby tried to take on all the other chores to help, lend

an ear when Emmaline wanted to read something out loud to her, or bring her tea or coffee. Mostly though, Emmaline just wanted to be undisturbed. Abby cleaned, she cooked, she made shopping lists. But of course, she could not drive. And so, the cupboards had become critically bare, including such essentials as toilet paper. Freddy too was now out of dog treats.

Abby finally had reached her breaking point. "Grandma, we have to go shopping."

Emmaline barely paused in her typing, "Sure. Okay."

"Now."

"You mean right this minute?"

"Uh, yeah."

Emmaline rolled her chair back to look at Abby. "Where's the fire?"

"Grandma, you look terrible."

"Flattery will get you nowhere."

"You and me, the grocery store. STAT."

Emmaline sighed, "Do you even know what that means?"

"You taught me. It's a medical term that means urgent."

Emmaline nodded, "From the Latin, 'statim' which means 'immediately,' but I fail to understand why a trip to the grocery store would be urgent."

"Toilet paper."

"Oh. I suppose we don't have cornhusks or an old Sears catalogue at hand."

"No. Eww."

Emmaline jumped up, grabbed her purse, and headed out to the car, Freddy and Abby trotting behind her. Emmaline's hair was a wild mess on top of her head, only partially contained by the plastic butterfly clip. She had no makeup on, was wearing jeans and a loose blouse she called a peasant's blouse that Emmaline said was nearly as old as she was. She had slipped into her clogs that had been on the floor next to her desk.

Emmaline called over her shoulder, "I hope you can hold it until we return. If it gets really urgent, you can use the toilet at the store."

"Grandma, I'm not going to poop in my pants, if that's what you mean."

Emmaline had already started the engine. "You're the one who used the word STAT. You two get in, Abby, buckle your seat belt."

"Wait, Grandma, I made a list!"

Abby ran back into the house and grabbed her list. She barely made it into her seat before Emmaline was rolling.

* * *

Emmaline was pushing the buggy down the aisle of the grocery store, while Abby flew back and forth with items from the list, tossing them into the cart.

Abby dropped a huge armload of toilet paper in the cart then asked, "Wait, is this our cart?"

"Of course, it is.

"Are you sure you didn't grab someone else's? Look at all this junk. Potato chips? Candy bars? Are those Tootsie pops?"

"When I am on a writing streak, I give myself a dispensation."

"Do I get to eat this stuff too?"

Emmaline shook her head, "Are you writing?"

"I could be."

A voice behind them called out "Emma!"

Then the man said, "Don't pretend you didn't hear me. I'd recognize that old threadbare excuse of a shirt anywhere."

Emmaline turned around, again, a sheepish look on her face.

"William!"

His eyebrows went up, "Dear God, I see you're on a writing jag."

Emmaline nodded.

He continued, "Well, I must say I'm relieved. I've been calling and texting, but you've given me the cold shoulder. I thought it must be something I'd done or said. But one look at you and I can tell exactly what you've been up to."

Abby cleared her throat dramatically.

Emmaline seemed surprised to find Abby standing by their cart. She said," Where are my manners? Abby, this is William Campbell. He was one of my professors when I was a graduate student here."

William Campbell reached forward and took Abby's hand in both of his large hands, giving her hand a gentle squeeze. "Pleased to meet you...?"

"Abby Woods."

"Pleased to meet you, Abby Woods. And may I ask how you are connected to my old friend, Emma?"

"She's my grandmother."

William said, "Is that so? Well, your Grandmother Emma was my brightest student ever. Always could write. I was sure she was headed for a career in academia."

William leaned in and stage whispered, "Truth is, she did

far better for herself by turning to fiction writing. She always did march to a different drummer. Did things her way."

Emmaline looked at Abby with her eyebrows raised, saying, "We need to get all of this home and put away and I need to get back to work."

William, who only had one of those little plastic baskets hanging on his arm, said, "Of course, I don't want to keep you. But Emma, do get some sleep. Then call me. If you want to bring pages for my review, you know I'm happy to read them. But only if you want my input."

"Thanks, William. I may take you up on that later." And she began to push the cart toward the checkout.

Once they got the bags in the car, and seated, Freddy banging his tail like mad against the door, head crammed over the seat back, Abby said, "Grandma, that man called you Emma."

"Once upon a time I used the name Emma, instead of the rather unusual name, Emmaline."

Abby paused a moment, before saying, "To try and fit in."

"I suppose so, yes. William knew me as Emma. No reason to try and teach an old dog new tricks now."

"So, he's the boyfriend?"

"Oh dear. You make me sound like I'm a teenager. He's a senior citizen, as am I."

"You were hiding him from me?"

"Not true. I told you I was meeting an old friend in town, and now you've met him."

"Okay."

"Well, since you've now met William, what do you think?"

"He's really old."

"Other than that."

"He's tall. Really tall. And he has gigantic hands."

Emmaline said, "Anything else?"

"He had a nice face, a bit sunburned. He needs to use more SPF like Mom was saying about me."

Emmaline added, "Yes. Sorry if I forget to remind you. I don't burn like you do. But you and your mom are both right."

"What else was I supposed to notice?"

"Oh, nothing really."

Abby had questions. And Emmaline seemed to have questions for Abby. But neither one was going to ask them because neither one was going to answer them. Never complain, never explain.

When Emmaline, Freddy, and Abby pulled up in front of the house, Emmaline broke into the package of toilet paper with her fingernail, grabbed a roll, and handed it to Abby.

"Hope everything works out for you." Then she grinned.

Abby grabbed the roll and jumped out of the car, but not before saying, "Grandma, that is just gross."

And Abby, who had not really been in any sort of dire need, suddenly was. She jogged into the house with the TP.

* * *

A few days after the "grocery store incident," Emmaline had a 'come-apart'. At least that's what Sissy called it. Abby thought that description was too harsh. Maybe Abby had been too dramatic in describing it. But it was something. Abby wasn't sure yet what that something was.

Abby had found Emmaline in her bedroom, sitting at a

sort of desk Emmaline called a vanity. That was because this desk had a big mirror on it. Emmaline was only wearing her underwear, her hairbrush in her hand. She seemed frozen, staring at herself in the mirror. Abby thought her grandma had been crying. Abby stood in the doorway and said nothing. She felt bad for spying, but not so bad that she made her presence known by making a noise. In fact, Abby had backed up and hidden herself around the corner but did not leave and instead peeked around the door frame to watch her grandma.

Emmaline had not moved, but sat staring at her reflection, then wiped her eyes with the back of her hand. Abby was right, Emmaline had been crying. Abby had never seen her grandma cry. It rattled her. Something bad must have happened. Finally, Freddy went into the room, put his head on Emmaline's thigh, and broke the spell.

Emmaline knew Abby was there now. She said, "Abby?"

Abby stepped into the room. "Grandma, are you okay?"

Emmaline got up and grabbed her jeans off the floor and pulled them on.

She said, "Yes. I'm fine. I finally had a lovely shower. Long overdue. I'm sure I was beginning to stink. Time to put on clean clothes, too. Let me grab a tee shirt."

Emmaline pulled a shirt off a hanger and put it on.

"Now I just need some fresh air and I'll be fully restored. How about I walk down to the Taylors with you and Freddy?"

"Sure."

Once they were walking, Abby said, "Grandma, why were you crying?"

"What?"

"Did something bad happen?"

Emmaline smiled. "Nothing happened. How to explain? I'm writing. And the task of writing means I am spending a lot of time with my own thoughts. It's a hazard of the job."

"Introspection."

"Bravo."

Emmaline continued, "Every story I tell, every motivation I explore, every character I construct, they come not just from my study of history, they come from me. And not just the heroes of any given tale, the failures, and the villains too, they spring from the well of my own life experiences, or at least my own imaginings. Do you understand?"

"I think so. But I'm not sure all that introspection is healthy, not if it's making you sad."

Emmaline smiled, "Healthy? That's an interesting premise about writing. Writing does require a certain level of self-absorption. I suppose that could be considered unhealthy. A good story has to elicit feeling. And if my story can't make me cry, why should I expect it to make my readers cry?"

"Why does your story have to make anyone cry?"

"For verisimilitude."

"Which means?"

"To seem real, it has to feel real. It must be similar to the truth. Verisimilitude. Life will make you cry sometimes."

"Seeing you cry scared me."

Emmaline shook her head. "Ah, well, fear can be far more dangerous than sadness."

"Grandma, half the time I only partially understand what you're talking about."

"I think you understand perfectly well. You just said it

yourself, 'Writing requires introspection.' The unexamined life is not worth living."

"Did you just make that up?"

"That's Socrates; thousands of years old."

"Okay, that's freaky old."

"There's nothing new under the sun."

"Did Socrates say that too?"

"Look it up on your phone."

Abby was doing just that when Emmaline interrupted.

"Look, there's your buddy."

Emmaline waved at Sissy who was parking the gator in the shed by the barn.

Abby frowned, "You're really okay?"

Emmaline said, "More than okay, I'm refreshed by our walk. You go have a ride, and I'll see you at the house for lunch. Bring Sissy."

* * *

Abby and Sissy made their way to Chickasaw House later, they were both hungry and thirsty after their ride. Abby realized she was also sunburned. Emmaline had not reminded her to put on sunblock and she had forgotten. When they got to the house there was a truck parked next to Emmaline's car.

Sissy said, "That be Bobby Taylor's truck." She stopped in her tracks.

Abby said, "Come on."

"He ain't too partial to me, and the feeling is likewise."

"Hey, you're my friend and Grandma said to bring you over."

Abby and Sissy and the dogs walked into the house to find Bobby and Emmaline sitting at the kitchen table eating cake and drinking coffee.

Bobby said, "Hey, young'uns."

Sissy replied, "Hey, Mr. Taylor."

Emmaline nodded to the girls, "Wash your hands, then help yourself to pasta salad."

Abby asked, "Can we eat those potato chips, too?"

"You may. Then there's iced banana bread for dessert."

Abby said, "Banana bread. That's another banana dessert we should have mentioned to Daddy."

Emmaline turned her attention back to Bobby. "So, what happened next?"

"Hard feelings. That's what happened. Them horses, the foundation herd, well they all went in the will to them who had been servants. All the best lots of land, too. Piecemeal plots but added up come to a lot. Of course, them horses weren't fancy riding horses. But tough. Better than a mule really. Mules are hardy, see, but too smart. Them Chickasaw bred horses were gentle as kittens, safer to have around children than a mule. Homely though. Today you'd call them ugly. Breed died off for lack of interest."

"And the two branches of the family? Did they ever make peace?"

"Nah. But they also ain't waging war. Back in the day, though, well, it is said it got hot. That I can tell you. Not from personal experience, mind you. But that bitterness, well it carried on up until my Daddy's time."

"And you never considered just selling the old place?"

"My Daddy told me to never sell, not that he were superstitious, but his daddy had said the same to him. I took over handling the property before he died, but to be honest, I might consider selling now, for the right price, that is."

Sissy interrupted, "You ain't afraid of no curse?"

Bobby frowned, "Child, that talk were just meant to scare folks away. Kind of an insurance policy. And I guess it worked. But not on me."

Emmaline said, "The place sure needs a lot of work."

Bobby's eyes twinkled. "Are you trying to negotiate?"

"What if I were?"

Bobby smiled, "You're from California. High prices don't make you folks blink."

Emmaline said, "I've interrupted you. I want to hear everything you know about the history of the place."

Bobby said, "So, like I was saying..."

The girls had settled at the table with Emmaline and Bobby and the dogs had stretched out on the cool floor when there was a knock at the door.

Both dogs jumped up and began barking as they ran out of the kitchen.

But the barking ceased quickly, and dog nails against the wood floors tapped out a happy beat, escorting the guest into the house and down the hall.

"Halloooo! Emma! Anybody home?"

Emmaline stood up as William came into the kitchen. "William."

"Oh, I've disturbed a luncheon party."

William leaned over and gave the dogs vigorous pats.

Emmaline said, "There's more where that came from. Hungry?"

"Is that banana bread? And here I was worried that you weren't eating."

Emmaline said, "Yes, it is. I made plenty of pasta salad too if you haven't had lunch."

"I've eaten, but I won't say no to a piece of cake with some coffee."

Emmaline nodded, then said, "I'm surprised to see you out here."

"Just dropping by to do a wellness check."

Emmaline got up to get the pasta salad out for the girls and to cut William a piece of cake.

She said, over her shoulder, "Clearly, I am managing fine."

Bobby Taylor stood up and extended his hand. "I'm Bobby Taylor. This old pile of bricks belongs to me."

William took his hand. "William Campbell. I knew your Daddy. Nice to see the old home place is still standing. I haven't been here in decades."

Emmaline handed each of the girls a bowl of pasta salad, then said, "Lemonade?"

Once each girl had their drinks, Emmaline shooed them out, "You two take these dogs and eat on the porch. It's getting crowded in here."

Abby and Sissy did as they were told, but Abby dragged her feet.

Once they sat down and began to eat, Sissy said, "That Ms. Emmaline's boyfriend?"

Abby nodded.

"Must be a local fella' if he knew Bobby's daddy."

Abby said, "He was her teacher at the University."

"How long ago you think that was?"

264

"A long time. My Grandma is old."

Once they had let the dogs lick out the bowls, they headed back into the kitchen looking for cake.

Bobby was saying, "Never had trouble renting the house out to students in years past. But the kids today, they got more money than they know what to do with. They don't care about the history of the place, or its other fine points. They want luxury, and they want to be right near the corner."

William said, "Don't you want to pass it on to your kids? Keep it in the family? I remember this place. Lots of history, as well as a couple of ghosts, as I recall."

Bobby said, "Me and Emmaline were just talking about that. I don't hold to such beliefs. On the other hand, I don't want to live here. None of my family do. Not my kids, and not my grandkids. They don't have any interest in the place."

Emmaline had cut two slices of cake for the girls, fetching forks and napkins. She was shooing them back to the front porch, along with the two dogs. As soon as they had passed the doorway, Emmaline turned her back to them and walked back to her guests.

Abby put her finger to her lips and looked at Sissy. They hovered with the two dogs, who had eyes only for their plates of cake, and listened.

Bobby said something, then Emmaline said something. Abby was straining to make out the words. But she clearly heard William say, "Emma and I have many fond memories of this place, don't we, Emma?"

Sissy had by then, grabbed Abby by the wrist and was pulling her to the front porch.

When they got to the porch, Abby said, "Why did you pull on me like that?"

"Cause I didn't want to get caught spying on Ms. Emmaline. She got us out of that kitchen for a reason. And I like her too much to want to be out of her good graces."

"But you heard Bobby. If he's gonna' sell the house, that affects you guys."

"That ain't why you were spying."

Abby was quiet for a moment. Then confessed, "Yeah. But that old man, William, he just said that he and my Grandma had fond memories of this place. I swear he looks like the man in my dreams. It's him for sure."

"Why does it matter that a long time ago your Grandma and that tall fella' come out here?"

"Because she kept it secret. She kept Willliam Campbell secret, and she kept it a secret from me and from my parents that she knew this old place."

"You think she owes you all her secrets?"

"Of course not."

"Then why can't you let her keep 'em. If the time comes, she wants you to know, I 'spect she'll share them."

"What about Bobby talking about selling Chickasaw House."

"He's likely probing to see if Ms. Emmaline has deep pockets. Bobby Taylor ain't gonna' spend his dollars fixin' that place up. He'll let it fall to the ground before he fix things. But he might just try and get Ms. Emmaline to start thinkin' of the place as hers, do some work for free."

Abby looked thoughtful, "I wonder what she's up to. She's up to something. You once called my grandma sly."

"I think it was you I called sly."

"Maybe that apple didn't fall far from the tree."

"Abby Woods, what you up to?"

"I wish Mom was here."

"She sly, too?"

"You wouldn't think so, if you knew her."

"But?"

"Grandma said she didn't want old bones dug up to pick over. But I think that's exactly why she's here. What I can't figure out yet is why she's digging. And why now?"

17

Abby and Sissy threw the frisbee for a while but grew bored. Abby said, "My Grandma learned to play frisbee to get a good-looking boy to spend time with her. You think that's how we're going to get boyfriends?"

"Naw. And I think Ms. Emmaline likely could 'a done fine without ever tossing a frisbee."

Abby said, "You know, she never did get married. I thought maybe she didn't even like boys."

Sissy said, "She seems to like that old man, William."

Abby mused, "Wonder why she's been so secretive about him?"

"She might have had other boyfriends you don't know about, too."

"I doubt it."

Sissy added, "Well, she didn't find your Momma in no cotton patch, now did she?"

Abby sighed, "What's that supposed to mean?"

Sissy said, "Was your Momma adopted?"

"No."

"Well then, you can figure it out from there."

"Grandma just wanted a baby, bad, and she wasn't going to wait around anymore for a man. So, she went to a place where you can get pregnant on purpose from an anonymous source."

Even as Abby was telling Sissy what she thought to be

true, she wasn't entirely believing it herself. Sissy shook her head. "I suppose that could be true, but I know this much, women don't get pregnant without a man being involved. That's just a fact."

Abby and Sissy sat down on the porch stairs. William and Bobby were still inside with Emmaline.

Abby wondered out loud. "That Bobby, he's making himself a bit too comfortable with my grandma. And William Campbell, too. She didn't look pleased to see him. She's trying to get her writing done. They're going to wear out their welcomes."

Sissy said, "Yeah, I've noticed how grown-ups can plop down in a chair, and in a flash, they've grown roots. And they sure can drone on about nothin'. Emmaline do look tired. But maybe she don't mind letting those men drone on while she rests."

"Yeah. Maybe. She's been burning the candle at both ends."

"That's a good one. Made a picture in my head as soon as you said it."

Abby said, "What I don't get is why my grandma is making time for that old man. She hasn't needed a boyfriend all this time, why want one now?"

"You jealous?"

"No."

"Maybe she likes having some attention paid to her."

Just then Emmaline came out with Bobby and William. Abby and Sissy clammed up.

Emmaline was speaking to Bobby, "Can't we keep him a bit longer?"

"I suppose. My wife ain't too partial to him. He gets in more than his share of fights. And the sound of a cat fight, well, it will wake you from the deepest sleep, make you think you got demons right there in the room with you."

Emmaline said, "You won't get him neutered? It would cut down on the fights."

"Naw. He's never been to a vet that I know of. He's just a stray we feed. Lots of folks borrow One-Eared Tom, but nobody owns him. And I 'spect he likes it that way."

Emmaline brightened, "Is that so? Well, if you don't own him, maybe I'd like to claim him."

Bobby looked surprised. "Would you now? Cat might not agree."

Emmaline grinned, "Oh, he's already decided he likes sleeping on the furniture instead of outside. I think I can persuade him. Yes. I think we should do that. What a great idea. Thank you, Bobby."

Abby was confused. "Grandma, how are we going to take him back to California?"

Emmaline looked unfazed, "In a cat carrier."

Bobby shook his head, "Sounds like a road trip from hell to me. That old cat will scream bloody murder the whole drive and likely take a piss in that carrier. You ever smell Tom-cat piss? You'll never get the smell out of your car. You sure you ain't doing that cat a disservice, taking him out of his natural environment?"

Abby said, "Grandma, really? How about the fact that you're going to send Freddy round the bend."

"Freddy will be fine about Tom by then."

Bobby said, "If you change your mind, I'll come pick him

270

up and drop him off at my cousins. She's having a time of it with mice in her kitchen."

William chimed in, "Emma, I agree with Bobby on this one. Why not wait until you return to California and get a kitten. The dog will get to know it when it's tiny and they'll naturally bond. That tomcat looks scary even to me, and he'll likely always be partially feral."

Emmaline frowned, "I like the mystery of 'One-Eared Tom.' I like that he's been through the wars. He has character. Besides, he should be neutered and vaccinated. We can do that much for him."

Sissy added, "That ugly old cat sure likes you too, Ms. Emmaline."

Sissy and Abby watched Bobby drive off in his truck, and then Emmaline walked William to his car. Abby and Sissy couldn't hear what they were saying.

Abby said to Sissy, "My grandma asked me if I noticed anything about William."

"Did you?"

"He's got big hands and a sunburn. But that was it."

Sissy made a huffing noise.

After William drove off, Emmaline climbed the porch stairs slowly. She stopped on the porch and said, "I can barely keep my eyes open. I think I'll go have a toes-up. Abby, can you please clean the kitchen. Don't want to attract the mice, or squirrels, or roaches, or..."

"Yes, Grandma. And Grandma?"

"Yes?"

"About that old man?"

"Who?"

"William Campell."

"It's not polite to refer to someone as "that old man.""

"Did you two meet playing frisbee?"

Emmaline smiled. Then she did that funny thing with her hair, staring off at nothing. She said, "He casually joined our game on the lawn a couple of times. He was pretty good, too. Said his name was William. The next semester, there he was, in my history class. And he wasn't a student like I had assumed. He was Professor Campbell. William was Professor Campbell."

Abby said, "I feel like I've seen him before."

"I doubt that."

"But he's been here before. I heard him say that. And that you were here before too."

"Could have been. Maybe I've forgotten."

"But he didn't forget."

"I'm desperate for a nap."

"Grandma, are you really going to take One-Eared Tom to California? I don't think he would like to go, and I don't think he'd like living in the village either."

"I might have been rash. I think I just wanted an excuse to get Tom some veterinary care. He's a good old cat. I'd like to do something for him since he's done so much for us."

"You're not going to buy the house either, are you?"

"I never said I would."

"Why was Bobby Taylor even out here?"

"Why wouldn't he be out here. This is his house."

"Was he coming to take Tom away?"

"No. Although he offered to take him. He was here because I asked him to tell me more about the house, the history. I wanted to hear what his side of the Taylor family tree would say about Robert and Lucy and Charlotte."

"Whether the story checked out."

"Yes, although in Bobby's telling, Lucy was not portrayed as a victim, but as cunning. And Lotty was portrayed as someone who had been duped, which is the same thing that Mimi had said. He never mentioned the word slave or enslavement, as if it wasn't an important detail of the story. When in fact, it was central. Who knows what Lucy felt or thought. But she clearly fought for her small bit of privilege, and for her children. But Bobby didn't seem to blame Robert for the situation. He just said it was the way it was."

Sissy said, "Bobby say anything about our side of the tree?"

"No, Sissy, he did not. But he knows I'm friends with your Mimi."

Sissy said, "William Campbell. I bet he was fine looking as a young man. Tall and straight and even features, too."

Emmaline tipped her head to look down at Sissy sitting on the step, grinning. "I can only imagine what kind of story you two are spinning, sitting out here like two old biddies."

Abby said, "Biddies?"

"Gossips. Comes from the word for hens."

Sissy smiled, "You gonna' tell us to mind our own beeswax?"

Emmaline said, "Sissy, I couldn't have said it better myself!"

* * *

273

Emmaline was typing away on her laptop, and they had not had dinner, and it was getting late.

"Grandma, aren't you getting hungry?"

"What? Oh, sorry darling. I'm afraid it's bubble and squeak for you tonight."

"Bubble and squeak?"

"British for find some leftovers in the fridge and fry them up with an egg and call it dinner."

Abby shook her head, "Um, weird and also unappealing."

Emmaline looked up at Abby and frowned, "Sorry if I'm being inattentive, but I'm on a roll. Surely you can find something for dinner. We just spent a small fortune at the grocery store."

When Abby and Freddy went into the kitchen there sat One-Eared Tom on the counter, staring at his empty dish. Freddy paused at the door, eyes on the cat. He wasn't running away, but he wasn't going to go any nearer either.

One-eared Tom glared at Abby, ignoring the dog, then purposefully pushed the pottery bowl off the edge of the counter. It hit the floor and broke. "Blam!"

Abby yelled, "Hey!"

Emmaline called from the other room, "Everything okay?"

Abby said, "No! No, it isn't okay."

In a flash, Emmaline was at her side. "Oh Abby, it's no big deal. It's just an old bowl."

"Grandma, the cat did it on purpose. He looked right at me then pushed it off the counter. What a brat."

"Just put the pieces in the garbage and get out another bowl."

Abby pointed her finger at Tom, "Look here, cat, you're not the boss of me."

Emmaline said, "But I am. And I asked you to clean this up and feed the cat. Then feed Freddy and feed yourself. Just let me keep writing."

Before Emmaline went back to her work, she and One-Eared Tom had a moment. He head-butted her, and paraded back and forth on the counter, purring and arching his back to meet her hand, his tail vibrating. They only broke their lovefest when Abby presented the cat with a fresh bowl of food.

Abby said to the cat, "Don't say I never did anything for you."

Emmaline went back to her work. Freddy was still hovering in the doorway.

Abby looked at Tom again and shook her head. "You've been working my grandma, but I see right through your game. You think you're so smart. The thing is you don't know what she's got cooking. First off, you're getting neutered and vaccinated. Next, she's talking about putting you in a carrier and taking you all the way back to California. You'd mostly be a house cat. Back in California, you'd get a little collar with bells on it so you couldn't kill any songbirds or sneak up on any mice. Your killer days would be over. No more ripping out guts for you."

Tom finished eating, wiped his whiskers with his paw, then jumped off the counter onto the floor. He sauntered over to Abby and rubbed himself on her jeans.

"Don't look so smug. You think you've got my grandma all figured out? Good luck with that."

Then he walked straight over to Freddy, who was frozen in place, his eyes averted from the cat. Tom sat down. A long moment ensued, where the cat silently studied the dog who would not, could not, move. Then Tom turned and walked to the back door of the kitchen. He wanted out. Nighttime was Tom's time to prowl. Abby opened the door for him, and he disappeared into the shadows.

* * *

The next morning Abby found Emmaline looking bleary-eyed again, sitting at the kitchen table with her cup of coffee.

"Grandma, you're wearing the same shirt you had on yesterday. Did you even go to bed last night?"

"Yes. I fell face first into my pillows at some point."

"How is it going?"

Emmaline sighed, "I'm not sure at all what I'm doing or where my story is going. I have a spaghetti bowl full of story lines, and fascinating women, riveting life stories, but where is the payoff for the readers? What is the resonating resolution? Where the hell am I going?"

Abby was listening, thinking. She said, "What is the important truth you're trying to tell."

Emmaline's jaw dropped. "What did you just say?"

"You always told me that writers were liars, but liars who were telling important truths. So, then, what is the important truth you are trying to tell?"

Emmaline shook her head. "Wow. Out of the mouths of babes."

"And that would mean?"

"What you said, despite your tender years, is very wise. It's very anchoring. It's why I chose these stories in the first place. But I have a lot of work to do."

"How about this truth. You need sleep, then a shower, and some clean clothes."

"Okay. Point taken. While not nearly as profound, it is also wise."

Abby got Freddy fed, then popped a bagel in the toaster. Emmaline got up from the table and put her dishes in the sink.

Emmaline stopped and turned and said to Abby, "What happened to the story you started writing back home. Did you ever figure out where it was going?"

"No. And since I've been learning about all these real people, my story seems to me kind of silly."

"Was '*The Lord of the Rings*' silly?"

"No."

"*Harry Potter?*"

"No. In fact, both were kind of terrifying."

"True. All had moments of lightness, of humor, silliness even. But they got darker and darker. But there was light at the end. Redemption."

Abby frowned, "Redemption?"

Emmaline smiled. "Oh, yes, redemption. Redemption is a thing that saves someone from sin, error, or evil. It's a central concept of Christianity. But it existed long before then. You've heard the expression, 'beyond redemption?'"

"Yes. Voldemort was beyond redemption."

"I think you're right about that."

Emmaline added, "Abby, you've really helped me. Now, pick up your pen and tell your story of the witch and the wolf. I can't wait to see where it goes."

"Grandma, I don't know where it's going either, not exactly."

"We are in the same boat it seems. Time will tell. And when it does, you must write it down."

"I have a lot to think about first."

"Same."

"I think I'll go see Sissy, go for a ride, let my mind rest."

"And I'm going back to bed."

* * *

Abby came back to check on Emmaline after her ride with Sissy. She brought a casserole from Mimi. She hadn't exactly asked Mimi to make one, but she had told Mimi that Emmaline was looking rough, having stayed up way too late writing too many nights in a row, and that she had quit cooking. Mimi said it wasn't a big deal, as she had several in her freezer. Abby knew it wasn't Vegan, but she also knew whatever it was, it was going to be their dinner.

When Abby walked in, Emmaline was back at her computer. But she was wearing different clothes, a good sign.

Freddy ran to Emmaline doing his happy dance and snapping his jaws. She stroked his head, "Well, hello to you too!"

"Mimi sent us a casserole."

Emmaline stood up and took the casserole from Abby. "She's the sweetest. I'm sure it will be delicious."

"Bet you it has meat in it."

"You can always eat around the bits of meat."

"Freddy really misses you coming out on walks."

"Oh, I doubt that. He and Belle run all morning long, keeping up with you and Sissy on the horses."

"But you need to get outside and move around too, get

your heart pumping. Bet you've got a stiff neck and shoulders."

"You're right about that. As soon as I put this casserole up,
you can massage out my kinks."

Emmaline got seated, and Abby rubbed her hands together like Belva Ann always did, then she began to work on
Emmaline's shoulders at the base of her neck.

Emmaline dropped her head and sighed. Then she said,
"Great news from Belva Ann. She finally gave notice at work."

"Mom quit her job!"

"She did. She sounded so excited. She has a few ads left
to complete, but as soon as they are done and proofed, she is
finished. Seems like she may make that drive back with us
after all."

"So now we have One-Eared Tom and Mom and Freddy
all in the back seat?"

Emmaline said, "No. Belva Ann would sit up front with
me. We would share the driving. I could even take naps while
Belva Ann took a turn at the wheel. Sounds divine to me."

"Oh, so it's me crammed in the back with the screaming
cat, peeing in protest, next to a terrified dog. Good times."

"I ordered a fancy cat carrier. And Tom goes next week to
the vet to get the works done."

"No good deed goes unpunished."

"Hah. Well, in this case you could be right. It's just I really
like Tom, and he's earned his way into a cushy retirement. I don't
think he's a young cat, but the vet can tell us how old he is."

Just then there was a knock at the door, and Freddy
jumped up and ran to check it out. But he didn't bark. Instead,
they heard him whining. Emmaline and Abby followed.

It was William, again.

Emmaline protested, "What in the world! I thought we agreed that I needed uninterrupted time to write."

"I come bearing gifts. Hello, Abby. Hello, Freddy. Here, fresh fruits and veggies from my favorite roadside stand."

William handed Abby three paper sacks. She could see tomatoes and corn on the cob and peaches.

Abby said, "I'll wash these and put them in the fridge.

Emmaline said, "Tomatoes and peaches need to stay out of the fridge. You can put them in bowls on the countertop."

Abby nodded to her grandma, who wasn't really looking at Abby, but at William. And then, there it was, Abby noted, the hair flip. Oh my God. She also noted the way William gazed just a little too long at Emmaline. William was an old man, and Emmaline was her grandma. What was wrong with her then?

Emmaline said, "I need some fresh air. William, will you come walk with me?"

Abby realized she had not been invited to join them.

William said, "I'd love to. I recall an especially nice view. Up on a hilltop?"

Emmaline said, "The girls ride up there every day."

She also said, "Freddy?" And patted her thigh. And Freddy, without hesitation, bounced off to join them. Abby watched for a moment, standing in the door, as the witch and the wolf, and William, walked down the track, heading for the fields. Sort of like in her dream, except it was summer, not winter, and they were leaving the house, not returning to it, and now they were old. That left Abby by herself, with produce to wash and put in bowls.

Abby walked into the kitchen and emptied the bags of produce into the sink to wash. Her Grandma was a liar. But didn't she always say she was? But why lie? What about her spiel about the 'noble lie?' A lie couldn't be noble if it was self-serving. Abby remembered that part.

Abby could almost hear Sissy's voice telling her it was none of her beeswax, anyway.

What she knew now was that Emmaline and William, well, they had been an item. And they had been here, together, in this old house. Just like in her dream. Walking. Emmaline had said there had been a blizzard when she was at school. What did she know about blizzards? Nothing from personal experience. But she did see stuff on the news. She knew that people got stuck places during blizzards. Like in this old house. It didn't take a lot of imagination to consider what might have taken place in this old house during a blizzard.

She needed to talk to Sissy.

* * *

Mimi had taped directions on the aluminum foil cover on the casserole. All Abby had to do was leave the casserole on the counter to thaw, then preheat the oven and wait. Abby was on her own.

After Emmaline had come back from her walk with William, she had gone upstairs to take a shower, and she hadn't come back down. She must have taken a nap. She didn't say when she was planning on coming down either, and Abby was afraid to disturb her. Emmaline had been looking rough. Abby knew she needed her rest. But she needed to eat too.

So, Abby kept busy cleaning and doing laundry and such. The casserole needed to cook for thirty minutes, and then have the foil taken off and cook another ten minutes after that.

Abby had questions for her grandma. Like a lot of them. But she also knew her grandma was being evasive and would probably just keep lying about stuff. How much stuff she couldn't say.

Abby went ahead and fed Freddy. Then Tom showed up and glared at her until she fed him, too. Then he wanted to go back outside. This time Freddy didn't leave the room when Tom entered it. Progress. Still, Abby thought her grandma was bonkers to want to take the beat-up mouse-assassin back to California. For once in her life, Abby wasn't sure about her grandma. Maybe her Daddy had valid concerns. I mean, he had known her a lot longer than Abby. And her mom, she was not an unbiased observer. Good grief, Abby had never thought such things before.

It was getting late, so Abby finally went ahead and put the casserole in the oven. Then she went and knocked on Emmaline's bedroom door. She opened the door a crack, and Freddy, who was at her heels, pushed the door open with his nose, trotted into the room, and jumped up on the bed.

Emmaline, who had been face down in her pillow, rolled over and began to pet the dog.

"Well, hello there, Freddy."

"Grandma, I put the casserole in, so dinner is ready in like, twenty minutes."

"Bravo. I feel drugged. I think I could have slept the clock around."

"What?"

"Give me a few minutes to shake out the cobwebs, then I'll join you."

"Okay. I cleaned up the kitchen and did your laundry too."

"You can set the table."

"Done. Now, aren't you glad I came along!"

"Worth your weight in gold."

It seemed like forever to Abby before her grandma made it to the table. She was barefoot, but she had brushed her hair and had on a long sleeve blouse and her jeans.

"Grandma, I was getting worried that you had gone back to bed."

"Ah, that sounds tempting. I really am spent. I think I'm going to pass on writing tonight. I'm afraid William coming by like he did, well, it broke the spell. And now I can't think about anything but sleeping. Writing will have to wait for another day."

"Good. Then I'm glad he came by. You've been looking wiped out. Plus, I miss our evenings with Mimi and story time. If Mom was here, I think she'd have made you take more rest breaks. You'd have listened to her."

Emmaline deflected, "This looks yummy."

Abby had scooped out a hearty serving of steaming hot casserole. "Squash?"

Emmaline took a bite and closed her eyes. "Squash casserole tastes like summer. Isn't Mimi the best!"

Abby said, "She remembered we don't eat animals."

"She did. Eat up. It's delicious."

Abby took a hot mouthful. She'd never had a squash casserole like this one. It was full of some kind of cheese, definitely not vegan, and likely butter too, and it was topped with some kind of toasted crackers. But Emmaline was right, it was delicious.

Abby cleared their dinner plates and put the kettle on for tea. There was still iced banana cake in the pie safe. She told her grandma to sit still, and she would serve them dessert. And for once, her grandmother complied.

When they got settled, Abby said, "Grandma, how come you never got married?"

Emmaline laughed. "So, that's your burning question, is it?"

Abby said, "What's so funny?"

Emmaline said, "In college, I had a poster that said, 'A woman needs a man like a fish needs a bicycle.'"

Abby said, "Fish don't need bicycles."

"Bingo."

"Oh."

"But the thing is, dearest, I've learned that there's so much wrong with that statement."

"Uh, duh, yeah."

Emmaline raised her eyebrows. "Why do *you* think that?"

"Grandma, I know a bit about the birds and the bees stuff. Why the heck should I care about tossing a frisbee, except that you seemed to think it was a skill I needed to meet boys. Why should you care if I meet boys if they are so useless."

"Valid point. What else?"

"Well. Boys are different than girls. And different isn't always bad. Although the boys at Pepper Tree Elementary were brats and stupid too. Maybe they'll get smarter in time. My daddy's not stupid, but maybe he was a brat and stupid when he was in elementary school."

Emmaline looked amused. "Do you know about Yin and Yang? You can look that up later. We need male as well as female to create harmony and balance in the world. For too long in history, women were not legally allowed an equal share of control or political power. That was not fair or right or healthy and created a distinct imbalance. But we have made so much progress. Look at all the women leaders around the globe. I think the Hemings women, as well as Lucy and Lotty both, would be amazed. I hope to live long enough to see a female president of the United States. We need good men. We need men who esteem women as their intellectual and political equals. Balance, equilibrium so to speak, means we need men as much as we need women. Women need good men to work shoulder to shoulder with them on any task worth doing."

"Still, Grandma, I don't want to play sports just to meet boys."

"You don't need to meet boys at all, yet. That's for later. What you need to do now though is enjoy Sissy and riding and writing and reading stories and training Freddy and helping your grandma. And next school year, helping your poor teacher instead of making her job harder. Not a bad gig."

Abby said, "You didn't answer my question."

"Come again."

"Why didn't you get married?"

"I suppose I thought I didn't need a man."

"But you were wrong?"

"I was wrong about a lot of things. But I was blessed to have a wonderful father. And Belva Ann was lucky to have had my Daddy, too, to parent her during the years when she was growing up. He was like a father to her. You don't remember him, but he lived long enough to enjoy you as a baby. But do children deserve both a mother and a father? Yes. That is the ideal. Yin and Yang. Look it up."

"But now, you're seeing William."

"Is that a problem?"

"It's just that he knows you already."

"And?"

"And he knows Squirrel Manor."

"And now we know it was once called Chickasaw House. Which is fascinating news."

"Grandma, when I met William, I realized something. You won't believe me, but I swear it's true. My story, where you were the witch, and Freddy was a wolf..."

"Yes?"

"You read the first bit. The witch was summoning a man. Sissy and I talk about it. But we also talk about the story Mimi told, and we talk about all those Hemings women, and we think about what kinds of things must have gone on around here back in those days. My head is filled with all these stories, but maybe most of all the story I want to write. I haven't figured out yet how to include a dragon. But I will. I think about it every night as I fall asleep, I work though a scene in my head. But that isn't the bit I wanted to tell you about."

Emmaline said, "Oh my. You are my granddaughter. I never go to sleep without telling myself a story, reviewing my research in my mind and creating pictures."

"Grandma, it's this house. It's the old lady. I think the house sends me dreams. And in my dreams, I see scenes. Now that I know about Lucy and Robert and Lotty, sometimes I see them, and I see the children. This old house was full of children once, although in my dreams the children were baby squirrels, which was weird."

Emmaline chuckled.

Abby continued, "And sometimes I see this house full of college age kids, making noise, drinking, and dancing"

Emmaline smiled, and Abby confessed, "Actually, in my dreams the college kids were mice."

Emmaline said, "Now, *that's* funny!"

"But the thing is, the thing is, I saw a scene, in the snow, of two people walking up the path to the front of the house. The couple wore big old puffy down coats, not the flat kind people wear today. The woman had thick wavy hair. The man was tall. And even though I didn't see him from the front, I know now it was William. William from a long time ago. And I know it was you, even though your hair in the dream was brown. Dark brown."

Abby saw that her grandmother was listening. And there was something gratifying about the fact that her grandmother was taking her seriously. But of course, Abby was lying. Abby was embroidering what she had dreamed. Abby was lying in order to probe for more information from her grandmother, who was sly. They were cut of the same cloth. Liars both. But liars searching for truth.

Emmaline smiled. "Fascinating, darling. I don't doubt this house has many a wonderful tale to tell. Write it all down."

Abby exhaled loudly, "*Was* it you and William? In my dream?"

Emmaline pushed her chair back and rose from the table, "If you say it was, in your dream, then of course it was! I can't wait to hear what happened next. I'm off to bed. I leave it to you to run the dishwasher."

"Sweet dreams, Grandma."

"Sweet dreams to you, too. May this old house send you more marvelous dreams filled with romance and snow and parties with mice swinging from the chandeliers."

Abby said, "I'm counting on it."

18

Everyone relaxed on the front porch, plates empty, stomachs pleasantly full. The sun was nearly set. Their mugs were pretty much empty, or half-filled with second cups gone cold. The dogs were stretched out on their bellies.

Mimi was saying, "It is something to think of this old house. Everything that went on here. It was built by a rich man, built to show off. But it don't belong to a rich man now."

Emmaline said, "Good times are always gone too soon, and troubled times pass too slowly. This house saw enslavement, then war. A terrible war. And after the war, the money was gone. It's hard to come back blow after blow."

Mimi said, "I heard tales about the great depression. That was long and deep. It ran from the crash right up to World War Two. Folks sure were poor. If you couldn't grow it, raise it, or trade for it, you didn't have it. They didn't have no electric here. No indoor water in the house. 'Course, this old house always had a good well. You had to hand pump it up, but it was right in the back there. It's still good and sweet, the water all about here is. We have a good well ourselves, don't we, Francis?"

Francis cleared his throat. "We do. Mimi, how is it you know all these things?"

Mimi nodded, "And how is it you don't? I'm just saying to these folks what your Momma said to me. And your Momma heard it from Mother Taylor before her."

Francis grunted.

Mimi continued, "And that's why we know about Robert Taylor and Lucy and Lotty, too."

"Yes."

Emmaline asked, "Mimi, do you know how many children Lucy had? Did they all stay here and farm?"

"Well, I only know about the boys. I believe one was named Francis. Course, the eldest was Robert and there was James, and Charles. They had land deeded to them. Robert Taylor made it legal like, put it down in print, official. Although the courthouse burned down with all the papers. But that was long after all the folk mentioned had passed. By that time, they'd passed all that land on to their children."

Abby said, "Bobby Taylor, who owns this old house, he's probably named Robert, right? So, Mimi, are you saying the same names got passed down both sides?"

Mimi nodded, "Sure, they did. Lotty named her first born Robert Jr, after his Daddy. Even though Lucy's Robert Jr. was already alive and walking and speaking by that time."

Emmaline said, "Like a sort of competition between the two women."

Mimi said, "That's right. The law though, it already had declared the winner."

Emmaline nodded, "Makes me think about when Betsy Hemings died, she was buried next to her master, son-in-law of Thomas Jefferson, John Wayles Eppes. That was a scandal. Slaves never got buried in the white cemeteries. Never got proper headstones. But she did. His white wife, the one he married as a widower, had her body sent to her daughter's plantation to be buried. That says something. Betsy took the space that should have rightfully gone to her. Some say Betsy was fathered by Thomas Jefferson himself. I suppose it could be true. Her mother, Mary Hemings, was first rented from Jefferson, then purchased by Thomas Bell in Charlottesville. Bell had two children with Mary he had to purchase from Jefferson. She couldn't be legally married to Bell, but she lived as his wife. After Bell purchased Mary, he freed her and their children."

Abby asked, "Did Mary get buried next to Thomas Bell?"

Emmaline said, "I don't know."

Mimi asked, "Who do you think decided to give that plot and fancy gravestone to Betsy?"

Emmaline said, "The children. Perhaps as an act of redemption for all she had suffered in life. A small price to pay to soothe their shame and guilt. But I could be wrong. I see things from my own time. Perhaps they did not see the sin of slavery the way we do now. The inscription called her "beloved" Mammy. It also called her Mother, Sister, and Friend. Nothing about wife. Of course, nothing about being a wife."

Abby added, "So, her secrets really did go to the grave with her?"

Sissy shook her head, "We talking about it, ain't we? Maybe, she couldn't say it plain while she lived, but after she was gone, that grave spoke plain enough for her."

Francis said, "That second wife, the young white woman, the one who stepped into a settled house full of children, just like Lotty, well, I do feel for her. She, like Lotty, was a victim of fraud. Even the white children from the first wife, they already had them a Mammy. They likely didn't want her."

Mimi said, "Laws denied slaves a legal marriage, and laws

denied legal unions across the color lines until right recent. But laws don't always rightly reflect how folks behave. Them men were practicing bigamy."

Emmaline said, "Those wealthy planters acted with impunity. Laws that applied to the common man, they could flaunt without fear of consequences. It reminds me of that tax criminal, billionaire Leona Helmsley who famously said that "taxes are for the little people.' Such hubris."

Abby said, "Hubris? Spelled?"

Emmaline spelled it out, "H-U-B-R-I-S."

Emmaline added, "It would be a fine word for a spelling bee. The H sounds like "Hew" like chopping something up. It means arrogance, an overabundance of arrogance."

Francis said, "So, Emmaline, are you saying our famous Thomas Jefferson may have been afflicted with this trait?"

Emmaline nodded, then added, "Yet when he was in the White House, it is said that he made a point to play the common man. The foreign minister of Great Britain described his attire as "utter slovenliness."

Francis said, "But he lived like a prince, up there on his mountaintop."

Emmaline said, "He crafted his image carefully, but he lived as he wished. I doubt he ever denied himself anything he wanted. Food. Wine. Books. Travel. And if he had sex with his female slaves, perhaps including Mary Hemings, and then her younger sister Sally, well, he was legally within his rights to do so. And certainly, the Hemings women would have seen such activities normalized because of their mother Elizabeth's long relationship with Martha Jefferson's father, John Wayles."

Mimi said, "Living a lie ain't nothing new. For some, it's

about keeping up appearance, but sometimes, it's an act of self-preservation."

Sissy said, "If Thomas Jefferson had come out and said the rumors were true, if he had said, these children are my children. What would have happened?"

Francis drew his finger across his throat.

Mimi said, "I wouldn't go that far."

Emmaline said, "Maybe not literally. But Francis is right. Admission would have finished him as a politician. And socially? Indeed. Polite society, even in slave states, would not have openly condoned such use of female slaves. It would have been a taboo subject, even while the plantations abounded with mixed race children who looked just like the master.

And despite his hubris, Jefferson had an intense need to be liked. To the point that people often assumed he agreed with them totally, especially those pushing for emancipation, when in fact he did not, would not, act openly on that front. Not once while he was in politics proper and could have actually taken steps toward emancipation did he try. Jefferson, despite his brilliance, was deeply flawed.

On the other hand, he did free his own enslaved progeny, at least all of Sally's children. As he purportedly had promised Sally he would do. It was part of his moral code as a gentleman to keep his word. And evidently, he did. I suppose it was that same code that kept him from denying the rumors about Sally. That lie he never spoke. He simply chose silence and allowed others to lie on his behalf.

Francis said, "He never admitted those children were his. But I expect everyone local knew the truth. It was a lie, that was known to be a lie, but there was a gentlemen's agreement to accept the lie, superficially at least, as the truth. And only a cad, or a political enemy, would seek to reveal the lie. Jefferson was a local celebrity, and a founding father. And he wrote the words that became the bedrock of this country. Charlottesville was proud of Jefferson. Still is."

Mimi added, "I'll wager those of the planter class, they were glad to defend Jefferson, lest folks get to inspecting all the mixed-race children at their home plantations."

Sissy said, "Ms. Lotty, she had a right to be angry, though. I give her that. Robert done lied by what you call it, Ms. Emmaline, by staying silent about Lucy and the children."

Emmaline said, "A lie of omission."

Abby had been listening intently. She said, "Grandma, is lying by omission always bad?"

"No. We talked about this, right?"

"Yeah. I remember the 'noble lie.' But can a lie be okay, even a lie of omission, when it isn't a noble lie?"

"I think I see where you are going. So, here is a 'what-if' for you. What if you were asked by your best friend to keep a secret. And someone asked you to tell it. What would you do?"

"Maybe I'd pretend not to know what I know. Or maybe I'd make up a different story to put them off the scent, then tell my friend they'd been nosey."

Francis and Mimi both hooted.

Sissy said, "Girl, even I know better than to start digging a hole like that."

Emmaline smiled. "Some secrets are meant to remain secrets. And some people simply don't have a right to know things they aren't meant to know. Some secrets are meant to go to the grave. And some are meant to be revealed at a later date, when they can't do much harm. I think though, that Jefferson's secret was no secret at all to local people, people at Monticello, and to his family. But because he was so esteemed, the lies were accepted and repeated. They were protective lies. But that certainly did a disservice to his mixed-race children and their descendants. When they tried to tell the truth, they were wrongly shouted down and branded liars. But the time came when the truth was revealed."

Mimi said, "To everything, there is a season."

Emmaline added, "The tricky part, is determining when that season has arrived."

Francis said, 'Seems to me, no one determines the season. Facts just have a way of catching up with folks. Old TJ was safely abed when they caught up to him."

Emmaline smiled, "Lucky man."

* * *

Sissy and Abby stopped on the top of the ridge with Bunny and Buttermilk and the dogs to enjoy the view.

Abby noted, "Virginia sure is an alive and green place. You look down that sight line, and you'd think those hillsides were moving, but it's just the wind in that tall grass."

Sissy said, "Hay's ready for second cutting."

Abby frowned, "That's what you see? Hay?"

Sissy shook her head. "I see that it's pretty. That's why I come up here. That and I do love letting Bunny rip up that hill. She likes to stand here and catch her breath and so do I."

Abby said, "I love it here. I love the green fields and the mountains and trees."

Sissy grinned, "Virginia is for lovers."

"What?"

"You never heard that?"

"No."

"Girl, it's our state motto. You can buy a tee-shirt at the corner with that written on it."

Abby repeated, "Virginia is for lovers. You think there's anything to it? I mean, my grandma has sure been weird since we've been here. She seems way too old to be flirting with that old man, putting on makeup and flipping her hair over her shoulder. You think the place has that effect on people?"

"Man, you can't let it go that your grandma has a man-friend."

"Man-friend?"

"Seems wrong to call him Ms. Emmaline's boyfriend. He's no boy. But Emmaline ain't no girl, neither. They be old, both of them."

"What if your Mimi found herself a 'man-friend?' How would you feel about that?"

Sissy laughed. "Don't know where or how she'd scare up such a thing."

"See?"

Sissy said, "But Ms. Emmaline, she didn't just come under some spell when she got here. She come all the way here from California for a reason. And don't tell me it was just to write a book about Chickasaw House; to write about Robert Taylor and Lucy and Lotty. She only just learned about all that."

Abby shook her head, "She knew she was going to write about secret families. She was going to write the stories of the powerless. She was going to write the true stories that the powerful don't want to be told. She was going to write about women who persevered and did the right things for themselves and their children under difficult circumstances. So, she chose the Hemings women. That's why my grandma rented this house for the summer. She wanted the time here to put the story together, close to where it all happened."

"Don't go getting your feathers all ruffled. I'm sure that is all true as true can be. But why here? How'd she choose that old house?"

"How many historic homes are for rent? And Grandma went to school here. And William, he was one of her teachers."

"Them's a lot of coincidences. Just sayin'."

Abby said, "Maybe you're right. I'm glad she decided to come. I'm glad my summer camp sent back our deposit check. I'm glad I met you and your Mimi and your Daddy, and the horses and Belle. And I know Freddy is glad we came too. I'm now a Virginia-lover too."

There was a long pause before Sissy added, "Maybe you'll come back next summer. And one day, maybe you'll go to school here, too."

Abby said, "Wouldn't that be awesome! Sissy, you have to go too."

"Oh, I don't do that good at school. I'm not like you, Abby."

"I know what my grandma would say, she'd say 'poppycock!"

Then Abby cracked herself up.

Sissy said, "What's so funny?"

Abby said, "I just remembered the etymology of poppycock."

Sissy said, "It means nonsense. And I'm real glad you

think I could get into UVA. but my grades ain't good enough, and they ain't likely to be."

"But you're as smart as I am, any day of the week."

"So, what's so funny?"

"Poppycock comes from the root words that mean mushy-poo."

"You pulling my leg."

"I'm not. See, aren't words fun? Don't you want to learn a bunch of words that other people don't know? Please, please, tell me you'll work hard in school so we can both get into UVa."

"Maybe. Maybe you can rent that old dump of a house, and I can come live with you there. Then I'd still be able to take care of these old horses, and we can ride each day after classes let out."

Abby and Sissy took a moment to imagine it. And each found the idea to their liking.

Sissy said, "Come on then. Let me show you something. Let me ride you down to the pool. It's a steep trail that can get kind of slick, but the trail's probably dry enough today. Besides, I know you never have swum a horse before."

Abby followed Sissy as she turned off the grassy path into the woods. At first it just seemed to Abby that they weren't following any path at all. But Sissy and Bunny seemed to know where they were going. Abby grabbed mane and followed. The trail turned downhill, and Abby could hear the sound of water.

Abby said, "That sounds like whitewater."

Sissy said, "Don't worry. When we get to the pool the water is quiet. It's good for wading and in spots we can swim. You can swim, right?"

"Of course, I can. Daddy made me take classes. He was hoping I'd take sailing at camp this year. But I don't like the cold water much."

"Only your legs will get wet if you stay on top of Buttermilk."

They broke through the trees to look down on a flowing stream. But it was down a steep ravine."

Sissy said, "Follow me. I'll show you where the hunt horses cross."

The trail started to meander downhill, and it soon became clear where Sissy was heading. But they still had a short steep bank to go down to get to the pool below.

Sissy said, "Hold on."

Bunny nearly sat down on her haunches as she and Sissy made their way to the silty edge of the water.

"Come on."

Abby grabbed mane and squeezed her eyes shut. Buttermilk did not hesitate, but plunged ahead, Abby leaning back as Buttermilk's neck and head lowered.

Before she knew it, the two horses were knee deep in the water. Bunny got herself a drink. And soon Buttermilk was flipping her lips back and forth in the water.

The two dogs jumped in gleefully and began to swim in circles. Sissy said, "Watch this!"

She pointed Bunny upstream and there must have been a shelf of some sort under the water, because Bunny disappeared up to her chin and they began to swim. Bunny kept her head up and swam a few strokes before turning around and rejoining Buttermilk, Sissy laughing all the way.

Sissy hooted and said, "I do confess, Bunny feels as slick

as a seal when her body goes under. Makes me feel like a mermaid or something. Now, if we crossed to the other side, we could ride for hours. Like the hunt horses do. But my Daddy don't want me to go that far. He really don't like it that I get into the deep water, either. So, we just waded. Right?"

Abby nodded, and although she didn't say so, she was really glad they weren't going to go any farther away from the farm. But she also knew that if Sissy had gone, she would have followed her.

Sissy said, "Now you put Buttermilk's nose right on Bunny's tail. I want you to feel like a mermaid too."

Buttermilk went, and Abby felt "the bottom fall out" as they stepped off the invisible shelf into deep water. A strange sound, a squeal of sorts, bubbled up her throat and out of her mouth. Sissy was right in that Buttermilk's coat became slick and she felt herself become unmoored from the back of the horse. But not for long as they turned and headed back for the shallower water."

Sissy said, "Hey mermaid! Fun, huh?"

Abby was breathless when she answered, "Scary. But yeah. It was fun."

Sissy said, "We best get back. The horses do scramble a bit on the climb up. Just hold on to the mane."

Bunny did an odd hopping gait to scramble to the top. Abby clung like a barnacle with legs and arms and a fistful of mane, but she stayed on.

They broke out of the woods and into the sunny field, strolling down the hill they had galloped up. The sun felt good on Abby's wet jeans; all tension was gone.

Sissy said, "You suppose Ms. Emmaline been thinking of

William all those years. That's kind of romantic, ain't it? All them years and Ms. Emmaline never had another sweetheart. Never married."

Abby said, "Now you're the one making up a story."

Sissy said, "Virginia is for lovers."

Abby said, "Touche."

"You suppose Mr. William been keeping the flame alive all these years, too? Never had another sweetheart, never married. It's like some curse was made against them two, and finally, now that they old and withered up, the curse is finally lifted?"

Abby said, "I thought you said my grandma was the prettiest old lady you'd ever seen."

Sissy said, "Well, she is. That's true. Maybe she ain't withered up too bad, yet."

Abby said, "And I don't know about any curses. Like the curse that Lucy put on Lotty and her children. Because you know, curses, well, it's something that people do to scare others. A curse is a kind of 'bottom of the barrel' power. It's what people do when cursing is all they've got."

Sissy said, "Maybe it's a bottom of the barrel kind of power, but if it makes folks afraid, its power is still real enough. Carrying around fear, that's not a small thing. You suppose it was something like that, keeping them apart?"

"Don't know."

Sissy said, "Looks to me like the curse got broken."

Abby said, "And if it were? Emmaline is never going to tell the likes of us."

Sissy grinned, "Then maybe it ain't Emmaline we ask."

* * *

301

Emmaline and Abby sat on the front porch watching fireflies. They had eaten breakfast for dinner. They had scrambled eggs with cheese, bagels with cream cheese, and hot tea.

Emmaline said, "Isn't it lovely? The fairies are having their own Woodstock tonight."

"Woodstock?"

Emmaline continued, "Too bad we can't hear the music. The frequency of fairy music is too high for human ears."

Abby said, "Freddy doesn't seem to hear it either."

"Too high even for dogs."

The two of them sat quietly for a few minutes entranced by the flickering fireflies.

"Grandma, we swam the horses today. It was so cool. Sissy said it made her feel like a mermaid. But Sissy had also said the wet horses made her think of seals. It was like we were seals in the ocean."

Emmaline looked intrigued. "Ah. You weren't mermaids then, but selkies."

"Selkies?"

"A Selkie is sometimes a seal, and sometimes a woman."

"A shapeshifter, like in Harry Potter?"

"Exactly! I expect sailors detected something quite human and female when they spied a seal at a distance."

"Seals do have pretty eyes."

"Yes, they do. Like a beautiful woman. The Selkie, like the mermaid, could come ashore, gain two legs, and become a woman by removing and then hiding her seal coat. Some-times falling in love with a human man, even bearing him children. But she would return to the sea, to her seal-shape, by putting on her coat again and leaving, because the sea would always call her home. A man who found her coat and destroyed it, could prevent her from ever returning. But no man who truly loved a Selkie would do such a thing. Doing such a thing would certainly bring a terrible curse upon his head!"

"Grandma, it's the Disney movie!"

Emmaline gave a snort. "Believe me, the movie came long after the ancient myth. Selkie or mermaid, it matters not. But what is interesting is how your horses became sea creatures in your mind. Isn't it something how connected we are by universal myths?"

"Sissy and I were talking about curses today. Could Selkies put curses on people?"

Emmaline pointed her finger at her granddaughter. "Don't piss off a Selkie!"

That made Abby laugh. She said, "Lucy put a curse on Lotty. She put a curse on this house. And it sure turned out to be real. For Lotty and her descendants at least. But do you believe in curses?"

"Well, I suppose if you believe in the power of a curse or spell, then sure, I think they can become real, in that they certainly can impact lives and events."

"Like what you taught me is called a self-fulfilling prophecy."

"Certainly. That's a real phenomenon."

"Grandma, why do you think that it's always women making curses and spells? In the stories, I mean."

"And I'm sure you've noticed, they are often old women, often an ugly old woman. It's so unfair, isn't it? The evil witch is a crone, a hag, and jealous of some young and pretty girl. But as to your question, bestowing a curse is an act of desperation. It's an act of a powerless person. For most of history, women had little power. And in parts of the world, that is still as true as it ever was."

"I told Sissy it was to make someone afraid of you. Someone who maybe had more power than you. Making them afraid of you, kind of levels the playing field."

"Oh, Abby, you get it."

"Maybe a little."

"A curse is generally an act of revenge by a desperate person. A curse is a last resort. Even if it doesn't come true, I think it offers some satisfaction in uttering, especially when said with feeling."

"Like saying a bad word?"

"That's why they are called curse words."

"Grandma, have you ever cursed someone?"

"Have I ever cursed? Oh, yes, of course. No one lives life without experiencing intense frustration, pain, disappointment, defeat, losses. I curse. I curse plenty. And then I move forward with a new plan, because time marches on whether or not you have a plan."

Abby said, "When the bridge is burned, you *have* to march on, right?"

"Yes."

"But, Grandma, sometimes you march into something better. I could never have predicted this summer. I thought I was going to be back at that snooty camp. I really wanted my name on that perpetual trophy for the spelling bee championship. That sure seems stupid now. This is the best summer ever. Sissy is the best friend I've ever had. We're going to stay friends forever. And I'm riding horses. And Virginia sure is pretty, even if I sweat like a pig every day."

"This is a beautiful spot."

"Sissy says the state motto is 'Virginia is for lovers.'"

"While I am quite familiar with the slogan, that is NOT the state motto. But although it was created for promoting tourism, I do like it."

Before Abby could formulate a more probing question. One that would provide clues she could run by Sissy the next day, Emmaline had risen.

As she stood up, Emmaline said, "It's such a shame we don't have fireflies back home. I'd forgotten how magical they are. I'm going to go type up some notes before I come up. Why don't you get ready for bed."

"I'm not tired, Grandma."

"Go read or write then until you get sleepy. I'll see you in your dreams."

Abby replied, "Not if I see you first."

Emmaline laughed and said, "Enough with the spying. If you see me, please make your presence known."

Abby was so surprised by Emmaline's response, that she couldn't think of a thing to say, but thought to herself that she *would* look for Emmaline in her dreams. And William, too. And this time she *would* speak to them. When she closed her eyes, she even asked the house to send her dreams of her grandma and William.

But Abby did not see Emmaline or William in her dreams. And the dreams were not funny or silly this time with rowdy mice or baby squirrels. Instead, they were more like nightmares. She felt paralyzed with fear and felt her arms go goosepimples. Later, she couldn't say why she had felt so afraid. In her dream, she saw the dining room the way it must have looked when Chickasaw House was in its prime.

Above the wainscoting was a mural, with boats and flowers and animals. But she walked right through the dining room and up the stairs, following a woman with a candle, a basket hanging from the woman's arm. The hall was dark, the candle a dim and flickering light. She followed down the long hall. Watched as they opened the door to the attic. She went no further. She was far too afraid to follow. And then the hall was total blackness. Abby woke up, pulled Freddy into her, and rolled over, and felt instantly better.

19

Sissy and Abby were tossing the Frisbee while Emmaline was inside typing away at her laptop like a mad conductor. Her gray mane was only half-contained with a clip, and index cards and post-it notes were stuck everywhere. Gone were the neat columns for Act One, Act Two, and Act Three. Her printer was continually humming. Pages were stapled, then unstapled, then spread across the floor. Even Freddy stopped going into the room for visits, but instead almost ran past the doorway.

Abby had thought that for a dog, or most anyone really, Emmaline's movements appeared to be a sort of fit, or a malady. They looked like repetitive and meaningless motions, punctuated with occasional verbal outbursts. But Aristotle had said, "There is no great genius without some touch of madness." Or maybe that was just her grandma making excuses. Regardless, these days Abby followed Freddy's example.

Abby tossed the frisbee and explained Selkies to Sissy. "So, the Selkie already knew him, see, from watching him as a seal, and she falls in love, and she decides she must have him. She comes ashore and takes off her seal skin to turn herself into a woman. Then she hides the skin. Of course, he falls in love with her. She's beautiful. They get married, and they have children, and you'd think it would end there, like a fairy tale ends with happily ever after. Of course, it doesn't end happy.

But Grandma says that's not how real fairy tales end; happi-ly-ever-after."

"'What you mean?"

"Grandma says real fairy tale endings wouldn't be consid-ered appropriate for children."

"That so? So, what happened to the Selkie?"

"The sea calls them back home. And all the Selkie has to do, when that call comes, is find her seal coat and put it on, and she changes back into a seal. Then as a seal, she dives back into the ocean and leaves her human family."

"So, being human is temporary for a Selkie?"

"Apparently. But maybe that's the point. Being human is temporary for everyone. Everything is a metaphor."

"What about them children? Are they Selkies, too? Or are they humans? Bet they be different, half-and-half."

"Wow. I don't know. And I also wonder, does the husband know his wife was a Selkie? Did she keep it a secret from him? Does he think she's a human who just ups and leaves. Surely if he finds out she's a Selkie he has to keep it a secret. Something tells me the villagers would get out the pitchforks and go after her if they found out. They might even hurt the half-Selkie children if they knew. They might consider the children defective or even monsters."

Sissy shook her head and stopped tossing the frisbee. "Ain't it all the same story told different ways?"

"What?"

"That different ain't tolerated. That this 'un can't marry that 'un, and like has to stay with like. And if you break the rules, you gotta' keep it a secret."

Abby nodded, "Sissy, you're good at this."

Just then a small car pulled up.

Sissy knew right away. "Looks like somebody can't stay away."

Freddy and Belle ran up to the car but were wagging their tails in greeting instead of barking. William got out, then opened the rear door and grabbed a couple of grocery bags while the dogs bounced around in excitement.

Sissy greeted him first. "Hey, Mr. William! What ya' brung us!"

Abby rolled her eyes. "I don't think William has brought 'us' anything."

William said, "Hello, ladies. I'm just here doing another wellness check on our favorite, yet slightly deranged writer of fiction."

Abby walked up to him and held out her arms. "Thanks. I was just thinking our cupboards were getting pretty bare."

William said, "I know you don't eat meat, but you should have the makings in there for pasta primavera. And I brought some good breads and cheeses, too."

Abby said, "Yum. Thanks. I'll go put this up. Grandma is hard at it."

Abby went into the house, leaving William on the front porch.

Sissy said, "You know how to play frisbee?

William smiled, "Once-upon-a-time."

"Me and Abby are green as grass. But Ms. Emmaline, she determined we learn how. Like she considers it a necessary life skill."

William stepped back off the porch and Sissy handed him the frisbee. He lobbed her a floater that she caught easily.

Sissy's return toss was wobbly, and William had to pick it up off the grass. Sissy said, "You and Ms. Emmaline used to play together?"

He nodded, "Go long, put your hand out, and I'll see if I can still hit a target."

William put a tighter spin on the disc and threw it right to Sissy.

She said, "You got some real control. That's impressive."

"Thank you."

"So, you and Ms. Emmaline, you boyfriend and girl-friend?"

Just then Abby walked back out onto the porch.

William laughed and said, "I believe we are both far too long-in-the-tooth for such a term to apply."

Sissy blurted out, "I know this one! I know this one!"

Abby said, "New to me."

Sissy was bubbling over, "Ain't often I know words that Abby don't."

Abby said, "It's not a word, it's a phrase."

Sissy ignored her. "See, horses, their teeth never stop growing. Not their whole lives long. I mean, other than how they get worn down, they keep getting longer. So, young hors-es have short teeth, and old horses, they got long teeth. That's why you don't look a gift horse in the mouth."

William smiled, "Correct."

Sissy said, "That why looking a gift horse in the mouth is rude. Even if it turned out not to be so old, or broken down, it don't look right. You're just supposed to say thanks."

"Exactly right."

Sissy asked, "Mr. William, you know about horses?"

William said, "Ah, a wise man knows he knows nothing."

Abby cut in, "You ride?"

William said, "No hour of life is wasted that is spent on the back of a horse."

Sissy grinned, "You people kill me. You ride or not?"

William chuckled, "Not for a long time. But I used to ride to hounds. Played a bit of polo."

Sissy stared at William a moment then noted, "You are built right for a rider. Long legs and arms, upright kind of bearing."

William turned to Abby and tried to hand her the frisbee. "Don't let me interrupt your game."

Sissy said, "We can play with three. Come on, Mr. William, toss it here."

Abby stepped in and once Sissy caught it, she tossed it to Abby.

Sissy said, "So, if you and Ms. Emmaline ain't boyfriend and girlfriend, what are you?"

William said, "Old friends. We haven't seen each other in years. It's nice to reconnect."

Sissy said, "You know she's a grandma!"

William laughed. "And I'm a grandpa."

Sissy said, "Is that so?"

"It is. I have two sons, married and raising sons of their own."

"No girls?"

"Sadly, no."

"Your wife, she pass on?"

Abby was embarrassed by Sissy's probing questions. But she also had no intention of stopping her.

William said, "She did."

Sissy said, "I'm real sorry to hear that. My Momma passed too. And my Daddy he don't have no girlfriend, nor any old-woman friend. I suppose he gets lonely just hanging out with me and my Mimi. She's his mother, my granny. She ain't got no old-man friend neither."

William smiled, "Sissy, I'm sorry to hear all of that. But should your Daddy reconnect with an old friend who happens to be a woman, I recommend you not refer to her as his old-woman friend."

"I guess it's plain enough without saying so."

William grinned, "Emmaline tells me you're a Taylor. You've got deep roots in these parts."

Sissy nodded, "Can't throw a rock without hitting one. You ain't a Taylor too, are you?"

He shook his head and tossed the frisbee to Abby.

Sissy said, "They's a mess of us about, both black and white. Do you got deep roots in these parts too?"

"Not as deep as my wife's. Her family name appears on more than one building at U.Va."

"Must have been rich folk."

"Once-upon-a-time."

"Like in a fairy tale?"

"I suppose so. Delia was always treated like a princess. She did lead a charmed sort of life."

Abby piped up, "Delia?"

Sissy said, "That's a real pretty name. Was she pretty?"

William nodded. Then he looked at Abby.

He said, "I think I'll come back another time when Emma is ready to come up for air."

Abby said, "Good idea. But she might be mad at me when she finds out I didn't come tell her you were here."

William said, "Don't say anything then."

Abby said, "She'll have questions when I feed her a dinner she didn't buy."

He winked at her, "Tell her after she eats. I've always found that to be the safest time to speak to Emma. You can tell her she can call me any time."

Sissy and Abby watched as William walked back to his car and turned to wave at the girls. Sissy waved, and Abby too waved back with the frisbee in her hand.

They watched as the little car made a U-turn and slowly bounced down the rutted drive.

Abby said, "You are a brazen thing."

Sissy said, "What?"

"It means bold, and not in a good way. All those personal questions you asked William."

"You knew I would."

Abby said, "Sure, but you could have been more subtle. You'll never make a spy."

"I found out stuff you wanted to know just by asking. Mr. William didn't care; he just answered my questions, true and easy. Are you wishing I didn't?"

Abby was quiet for a moment. "No. That name. Delia."

Sissy said, "I wasn't lying when I said it's pretty. Sounds like a flower. I never heard that name before. "

Abby said, "I have."

"Really? Where?"

"I'm not sure."

"Maybe it'll come to you."

"He said she was pretty."

"And rich, too. Delia come from money. Bet that means old William still got money."

Abby frowned, "Not necessarily."

Sissy said, "Whether or not he got money, he got children and grandchildren, but they don't live here it seems. So maybe he were lonely. But with Emmaline around, he got someone to keep company with."

Abby said, "But not for long. We will go back to California in a month's time."

Sissy sighed, "Poor Mr. William. But what about me? Poor me, too! I was happy enough with my Daddy and Mimi before you come. But now I ain't so sure. I mean, I'm going to really miss you."

Abby looked like she was going to cry. She said, "I'm going to miss you, too. Grandma just said to me that 'friends are the siblings that God never gave us.'"

The two girls hugged. Sissy then giggled, "No one would ever think we be sisters, though!"

* * *

When Abby and Freddy came down to breakfast, Emmaline was already getting up from the table.

"I'm pouring a second cup and getting right back at it."

Abby yawned, "Grandma, you must have slept last night, you're downright perky."

"Belva Ann called last night, and we had a long talk. She's decided not to wait any longer, she's flying back to finish the summer with us."

"Won't Daddy be lonely?"

Emmaline paused, then said, "Isn't it funny, how when we fall in love, we want everyone else to fall in love, too?"

"A non-sequitur?"

"Hmmm? Oh, sorry. But don't worry about your dad. He's focused on that big deal right now and working long hours. Evidently, some problem came up. A fly in the ointment, so to speak. It's not unusual in these real estate deals."

"Fly in the ointment?"

"Imagine you're making a batch of ointment, maybe it's a wound cream, and a fly gets stirred into the batch. The whole batch would be ruined."

"Daddy's probably freaking out."

"I'm sure he is. He had been excited about the deal. He even mentioned it to me on their visit. But perhaps he'll find a way to salvage it. Anyway, there's nothing Belva Ann can do to help, so she might as well come be with us. And then of course, she promised to help us make that long drive home, later."

"But you're busy writing. What will Mom do all day?"

"She told me she is very interested in doing more research on the Taylors. If Mimi agrees. She really likes Mimi and would enjoy spending time with her. Belva Ann was telling me about how these online genealogy sites work these days. It's unbelievable. And people share what they know, share photos and family lore. Not to mention documents that can be reviewed online. I'm sure there are countless Taylors in the databases."

* * *

Three days later, Belva Ann was pulling up to Chickasaw House in a tiny rental car. Freddy once again acted as if Belva Ann had been gone years instead of a few weeks. He barely let her out of the car, and once she was out, he ran circles around her, snapping his jaws and yodeling.

Belva Ann called out, "Oh, Freddy, I've missed you, too!"

Emmaline, Belva Ann, Abby, and Freddy scrummed together in a disorganized celebration of hugging.

Emmaline pointed at the tiny car. "Darling, I still don't understand why you felt the need to rent a car. Seems a totally unnecessary expense."

"Because I intend to take Abby and do some sight-seeing while I'm here, and you'll want to keep writing."

"But you could take my car."

"Nope. I remember the days when you and I shared a car."

"You were in high school. And I purposefully wanted you to have to ask for the car in those days. It helped keep you out of mischief."

"What I remember is that it was hell. I want my own wheels, and as I am not in high school now, I am able to obtain them myself. I'm also no longer required to ask your permission to drive somewhere, nor tell you where I am going, or exactly the hour of my return."

"Suit yourself. Mi casa, su casa."

Belva Ann said, "As true today as it ever was."

As soon as they walked in, Belva Ann spotted the new cat carrier sitting on the floor. The front of it open. "Oh Mom, you aren't really going to take that cat?"

"Not sure. First, he has to go to the vet. He has yet to go

into the carrier. He's only poked his nose in. He smells a trap. But I *am* smitten with that beat up old hooligan."

"Mom, he can't spend three or four days in that thing. There's no room for a litter pan. For that you'd need a crate. And if you put a crate in the car, then you have no room for luggage."

"We'd have to ship our luggage and only take tote bags."

"Mom, sometimes I think Jim is right about you."

Emmaline did not protest. She just shrugged.

Abby was looking at her mom and twirling her finger next to her ear. "I think it's a crazy idea, too, for what it's worth."

Emmaline said, "Funny thing about cats, they generally like climbing into tight spaces. Especially paper bags and boxes. He'll go in. You'll see."

Abby said, "He likes to be up high, Grandma. You put that thing on the floor. You need to put it on your desk, next to your computer if you want him to go in."

Emmaline brightened, "Now you're cooking with gas!"

Abby said, "Why is it better to cook with gas?"

Belva Ann said, "It isn't really. It's just an old saying because professional chefs, serious chefs, generally preferred gas ranges. So, the ad agencies pushed the slogan, made people think that if you were serious about cooking you would switch from electric to gas."

Emmaline said, "Thank you, my marketing genius. My point was that Abby's suggestion was brilliant. If I'm serious about getting him to get into his carrier, I should put it up on my desk."

* * *

317

The next day when Abby and Freddy went down to ride with Sissy, Belva Ann walked with them. She brought her laptop with her.

Abby and Belva Ann found Sissy standing with Mimi by the pasture gate. Belva Ann greeted them and said, "Mimi, thank you so much for agreeing to do this. I can't wait to see what we can find."

Mimi said, "Aw, honey, there may not be much. I was told all the deeds got burned up when the courthouse caught fire. Chimneys were the main cause. But you think on it. Without electric, most folk used candles or kerosene lamps. They cooked on open flames too. Not to mention smoking tobacco. All it takes is a live ember to fall and catch. All the facts we got is what we were told. And I guess that don't count for much."

Belva Ann said, "Oral history counts for a lot. But you never know what we may find online. Do you have a printer?"

"Honey, I don't. Francis, he has a computer, and we got internet, but I never look on it. 'Course, Sissy is real good. If I want something looked up, she finds it for me."

Belva Ann said, "Anything you want a hard copy of, we can use Emmaline's printer. And if you find you want a lot of this printed, we can find you a printer for not too much money, then you can make real file folders. Not just virtual folders in your computer."

Belva Ann looked thoughtful before continuing.

"We can begin by building your family tree and then write down everything you can remember about your ancestors. Once we get it posted on the genealogy site, we can share it. People who are on the site who are interested can read it and add in anything they may have heard. It's like a clearinghouse for information, photos, and oral history. It's an amazing tool. Research like this isn't just for historians anymore. It's for everyone."

Abby had strangely taken her mom's hand while she was talking to Mimi. She could tell her mom was eager to do this project with Mimi. She wasn't used to seeing her mom so wound up. She could almost swear that her mom had the zoomies. Which wasn't quite right. Belva Ann was the quiet one. Belva Ann was the stable one. Belva Ann never had zoomies.

Mimi said, "I'm happy to go a searching with you. But we got's to go look at your story too. Only fair that both of us discover things we didn't know."

Belva Ann nodded to Mimi and let go of Abby's hand and turned to her daughter. "You wild things go have fun with the dogs and horses. Don't do anything too crazy. Be sure to come back to Chickasaw House for lunch. We'll make sure Mom stops to eat."

Then she and Mimi turned to go into the house, heads close together, Belva Ann speaking in low tones that Abby couldn't hear, although she stood and watched their retreating backs.

Abby thought about what her grandma had said about 'biddies." Which did rhyme with buddies. Maybe her mom and Mimi were both.

* * *

319

Belva Ann tossed a big salad for lunch. Then they had sliced peaches for dessert.

Mimi had made Sissy stay home with her to help her weed the garden she had out back. She promised later to share tomatoes and squash. Mimi said she had more tomatoes and squash than she knew what to do with, even though she made and froze casseroles and stewed and canned the extra tomatoes. Mimi said that horse manure used as fertilizer grew the best maters and squash, even if it also sprouted weeds.

Belva Ann said, "These peaches are the best I think I've ever tasted. I mean, we grow great peaches in California, but these seem to have some extra flavor."

Abby volunteered, "William got them at a roadside stand."

Belva Ann raised her eyebrows. "William?"

Emmaline said, "A friend."

Abby added, "An old-man friend."

Belva Ann said, "Abby, people generally don't like to be referred to as old."

Emmaline added, "Especially if they are old."

"So, Mom, tell me about your friend."

"He once was my professor. When I was a graduate student."

Abby added, "His wife died."

Belva Ann said, "I see." And tipped her head inquisitively.

Emmaline deflected, "How'd you get on with Mimi this morning?"

"Like a house a'fire."

Abby said, "Mom, that doesn't make sense. A burning house isn't a good thing."

Belva Ann said, "The saying means that we became

friends as fast as a house catches fire. And I guess fire was on my mind because Mimi was right about documents being destroyed in courthouse fires. It happened here more than once, if you can believe it."

Emmaline added, "I knew you two would hit it off. She knows a lot about a lot."

Belva Ann said, "She's funny too."

Abby added, "William's wife's name was Delia."

Emmaline said, "Now that's a non sequitur."

Abby shrugged.

Then Emmaline frowned, "Abby, how did you know his wife's name?"

"He told me."

"When was that?"

"When he dropped off those peaches we just ate."

"Where was I?"

"Working. He decided not to interrupt."

"Oh. Sounds like you had a nice chat."

"Sissy and I even got him to toss the frisbee. He was good."

"Seems I missed out."

Belva Ann stood up, "I'll clean up the lunch plates. Then I thought I'd drive up to Monticello, take Abby along. I know you've been many times."

"Oh."

Abby grinned, "Can Sissy come?"

"Sure. Maybe Mimi would want to join us, too. We can ask."

"Mom, you're welcome to join us."

"You go. I'll want to hear all about the Sally Hemings exhibit later. I've heard it's very moving. It's mixed media. I've seen it online. They've come such a long way from the years and years of denial."

It wasn't long before Abby got into the car with her mom. Belva Ann reached over and patted Abby on the knee. They would pick up Mimi and Sissy and then catch the afternoon tour. Mimi and Sissy had never been. Belva Ann insisted on it being her treat.

Driving to Mimi's, Belva Ann said, "I'm so excited to be here with you. You and me, Abby, off on an adventure. I can't remember when I last felt this free."

Abby smiled back at her mom. "Virginia is for lovers! Did you know that, Mom?"

Belva Ann said, "I did not."

"Sissy told me that. I feel like you and Grandma are different here."

Belva Ann said, "I feel like you're different here."

Abby said, "I love Virginia."

"It's a beautiful place. I think we should pick a day to picnic on the Skyline Drive. If we pick a weekend, Francis could join us. The photos look glorious."

"Grandma and I came over the mountains on our way here. It was pretty amazing."

Belva Ann said, "So, Mom didn't want to say much about her friend William at lunch today."

Abby asked, "She hadn't said anything to you about him?"

"Nope. Guess it's a secret."

Abby nodded, "She's been keeping it on the lowdown. She's mostly been meeting him in town. She puts on makeup and skirts and jewelry."

"Does she now?"

"And William, he knew the house, Chickasaw House. He and Emmaline went walking there years ago."

"What? She'd been here, at this house?"

"Yeah. Why'd you think she kept that a secret?"

"I don't know. Your Grandma is a sphinx. I think I'm going to want to meet this William character. Check him out."

"What does it mean to be a sphinx?"

"Mysterious."

"I always thought of her as a witch, but definitely one with secrets. But she's mysterious to you too?"

"Maybe especially to me. Mimi suggested I create a family tree for us. But you know, Abby, I know we don't talk about it, but half my tree is blank."

"Yeah. I know."

"Like some adoptions, some information is meant to stay private. And that's okay. But I sent off a DNA sample anyway. I did it after our last visit. After we talked about Freddy's DNA. The test will tell me all sorts of interesting information about my heritage, which of course is your heritage too, without saying anything that breaches anyone's privacy."

"Did you tell grandma?"

"No. You promise not to tell her either?"

"Why can't you tell her?"

"I suppose I will at some point, but she's very private about some things. A sphinx. Look, she doesn't want to tell us about her friend William. And until she does, she shouldn't be forced to tell us. If there comes a time she and William want to, um, as they say, take it to the next level, I'm sure they'll say something then. As far as my own genealogical research goes, well, she took a lot of heat back in the day for her decision to have a child on her own. It's a sore topic. Even your dad has been critical."

"Mom, grandma said something to me that makes me think even she now thinks it was a bit crazy."

"Really?"

"Have you ever heard "A woman needs a man like a fish needs a bicycle?"

Belva Ann shook her head, "That doesn't make any sense."

"Grandma said it did, until it didn't."

Mimi and Sissy were coming out of the house as Belva Ann pulled up. But she had time enough to look at her daughter and say, "Wow. She says things to you she would never say to me."

20

When Abby and Belva Ann returned from their field trip, they discovered that Emmaline had decided to cook dinner for everyone. She said she had hit a roadblock in her story and needed a break. Besides, she had to find a way to use up the tomatoes filling the bowls on her kitchen counter. So, she made multiple tomato, cheese, and onion pies. One-Eared Tom had appeared in the kitchen to supervise, sending Freddy to the doorway where he curled up, his nose between his paws.

Emmaline told Abby to call the Taylors and invite them to come to dinner. The pies were hot and needed eating.

Soon, the Taylors came up in the gator, Belle tagging along. Emmaline had set places on the front porch.

Emmaline greeted them saying, "It's a simple meal, but there's plenty of it so the family 'hold-back' rule is waived for the evening."

Francis laughed, "You think these young'uns knows what that is?"

Mimi said, "Lord no, they don't. They've never wanted for anything."

Sissy said, "I know. It's when the family makes sure company gets their fill before anyone takes seconds, even if they have to 'hold-back' on how much the family gets to eat."

Emmaline smiled, "We've gracious plenty. I made so

325

much that we each could have our own pie if we could fit that much in our bellies."

Abby said, "Grandma, I think you went overboard."

Emmaline said, "Sometimes I go on a writing jag, sometimes I go on a cooking jag. I've also defrosted two lemon loaves for dessert."

Belva Ann chimed in, "Writing or cooking, either way, Mom, you always have something to show for it."

"Thank you, darling. Help yourselves."

Emmaline began to ask questions. "Mimi, what did you think of your tour today?"

"I thought a lot of things. See, I never have gone. Isn't that an odd thing, living here all my life? Francis he's gone more than once. He's taken an interest in a way I never did. Seemed like something white folks do. Seems like Jefferson is almost a God to so many of them. People come here from all over the globe to see where he lived. I found out today they did that when he was alive too. He had admirers in France, he had admirers in Italy and all over. Folks who considered him a founder of America and a friend of liberty and such, and we learned they crowded him there, so many wanted to come. Like being a movie star today. People spying in his windows and skulking in his bushes to have a peek. He couldn't get no peace. That's why he built that getaway outside of Lynchburg."

Emmaline said, "Poplar Forest."

Francis said, "Martin Luther King, he wrote and spoke on Jefferson. How the Declaration of Independence, Jefferson's writing, was a promissory note that needed to be honored. Jefferson wrote that all men were created equal, with a birthright of liberty, a liberty he denied his own enslaved people."

Belva Ann said, "The Sally Hemings exhibit was wonderful, Mom. You were right. I got emotional watching it."

Emmaline turned to Sissy. "What did you think, Sissy?"

"I heard a lot today. But what did it make me think on? Old Robert Taylor and Lucy and Lotty and the children, black and white. Big old families full of big old problems. See, no matter how snooty and rich, people can sure make a mess of things."

Francis leaned back in his chair and put his fork down. "That's what you took away from touring Monticello?"

Sissy said, "People are people."

Mimi said, "Tell them what we learned about his death."

Sissy said, "He and John Adams, they died on 4th of July, same day, same year, like they planned it. What struck me more about the man, was that when his wife died, he went so crazy with grief that his daughter had to ride out with him for hours each day, because she was afraid for him. Afraid he might end it. And we also learned his dying wife made him promise to never marry again."

Emmaline said, "Sissy, I think that detail is very important myself. He kept that promise, too."

Sissy said, "I lost my Momma, didn't I? And my Daddy lost his wife. Made me think Thomas Jefferson, he might of had lofty thoughts and was famous for his writing, but he was also like me and my Daddy, too."

Abby added, "Did you know that all but one of his children died before he did."

Mimi said, "You mean his white children. He had three sons and one daughter the world would never recognize as his. Not while they lived. And once he sent the two eldest to DC to pass as whites, they never could come home again."

Sissy said, "Ain't that tragic sad?"

Emmaline said, "It is."

Abby said, "That's redundant."

Emmaline cut her a withering glance.

Sissy said, "Ms. Emmaline, Abby was telling me about the Selkies."

Emmaline nodded, "A legend. Similar to mermaids."

Sissy said, "Made me think about these men who made families with women they really weren't supposed to make families with. They even had laws against it. But even without the laws, people thought it shameful and wrong. And there was suffering because of it. Suffering for breaking rules."

Emmaline said, "Do you think the stories were meant to be a warning? That these are cautionary tales?"

Sissy nodded, "Abby said that in the real stories, the old fairy tales, well, they didn't end 'happily-ever-after' at all. So, maybe that's so."

Emmaline nodded. "The Disney versions could be called revisionist."

Sissy said, "The Selkie gets called home to the sea. She leaves her husband and children. Ain't that sad? And before that happens, she has to be all secret-like, or everyone would turn against her, against her children, too. But she has to leave. She's being punished. But it just ain't her that is punished. The children get punished, too."

Emmaline said, "So people who break the rules, or shall we say, societal conventions, pay a price, sometimes a heavy price. But the impact is wider?"

Sissy nodded.

Emmaline said, "Sissy, I can almost see your doctoral thesis."

* * *

Sissy and Abby were walking their sweaty horses back down the hill toward the barn when a huge horsefly landed on Buttermilk's butt. Buttermilk began to hop her hind legs up and down, grunting.

Abby yelled, "Hey! Buttermilk, stop that!"

Sissy yelled back, "Kill it! It's biting!"

"What? Buttermilk's going to buck me off."

"Slap it, hard."

"Where?"

"Behind you, you dummy."

Buttermilk stopped bucking, dropped her head, and splayed her front legs wide then twisted her neck around, teeth bared.

Abby was hanging on to Buttermilk's mane and screeching in alarm, as Buttermilk's twisting pushed her off center. She had a close-up view of the horse's distressed eye, rimmed in white, reaching over her leg with her very large teeth frantically trying to reach the huge black fly stuck to the top of her butt.

Sissy was yelling again, "For God's sake girl, smack it dead!"

Finally, Abby heard what Sissy was saying. And then she saw the bug. It *was* huge. The biggest fly that Abby had ever seen in her life. She let go of Buttermilk's mane with her left hand and went on the attack. Wondering as she did whether the thing was going to sting her.

The first blow did not accomplish anything. The thing was stuck like glue to Buttermilk's hide. Buttermilk was writhing and grunting, and Abby was gripping with her thighs and holding on tight with her right hand. She tried again. The second blow had to have killed the thing. Abby used the next blow to give it a swipe and it fell to the ground.

Instantly the frantic scene was done.

Abby said, "What the hell was that?"

"You never seen a horse fly before?"

"Sucker looked prehistoric."

Sissy giggled. "We've actually been pretty lucky this summer. Bugs haven't been too bad. A horsefly will draw blood. Deerflies too."

"Those little triangular bugs, those are the deerflies, right?"

"Yeah. You've been slapping them all summer."

"But at least they aren't as big as that monster. Must have really hurt. Poor Buttermilk. I thought I was going to be collateral damage there for a moment."

"Girl. Speak English."

"You see how she was going after that fly with her teeth?"

"She don't have hands."

"I thought she was going to either get me with her teeth or dump me on the ground."

"She wasn't after you, just the fly."

"I could've been hurt anyway. Collateral damage."

"I guess it'll teach you to kill that fly next time instead of screeching."

"I *was* slow to jump in and take care of business."

"You got two good hands."

"Yeah. Glad I don't have to kill bugs with my teeth."

That got them laughing.

Then Sissy said, "That was real nice of your Momma to take us to Monticello."

"You weren't bored?"

"Maybe I would have, except for all the stories we been hearing. Did you think of Robert and Lucy and Lotty?"

"I was thinking about all those Hemings women. Slavery times were hard, but seems to me it was especially hard on women."

"You probably right about that."

"My Grandma, she wrote a novel about Suffragettes."

"Who?"

"The women who fought for the right to vote. Women didn't use to have any say at all. Didn't get to vote. Didn't get to make laws. They couldn't do a lot of things that we take for granted now, because of strong women, brave women, like suffragettes, they made the world change. They were women who acted outside social convention. They broke rules."

"And they were punished for it?"

"Yes. But they persevered, because they were right."

"Abby Woods, you know a lot of stuff."

"Do you think it's all as interesting as I do?"

"I guess I do."

"Maybe we'll both major in history."

"You could. I'm not sure about me."

"History is telling the story of what happened. You like stories as much as I do."

"I do."

"I'd help you. But you're a good worker. You're not afraid of hard work. You're not afraid of anything."

"Well, that ain't so. Not really. But it's nice you think so."

"What are you afraid of?"

"I'd have to think on that."

"Maybe you don't think you can do some things that I do. But I didn't think I could do any of the things you do. We even have fun sucking at frisbee. It doesn't mean we can't play the game. We still suck, but not nearly as bad. If we keep at it, one day we'll be proficient."

"What you trying to say?"

"That we're going to go to UVA. You and me. We're going to play frisbee and catch some good-looking boyfriends while we're there. We'll ride horses, too. And you and I will graduate with degrees in history. Best friends forever. How does that sound?"

"But just to meet the minimums to get into a school like U.Va. would be near impossible for me. I'd have to throw myself into it like my life depended on it."

"Mimi would be so proud of you. So would your Daddy."

Sissy was quiet for a moment then said, "So would my Momma."

The two girls were silent at that. But it was a nice silence. Abby thought to herself, that her very brave friend, her very smart friend, did have things that scared her. She was in so many ways older than her years. And by that Abby didn't just mean that Sissy could drive a tractor, or earn money, or ride a horse like she was born on one. Sissy knew about death, about loss. She cared for all those old horses, and she knew her Mimi was old, and that someday she would lose her Mimi too. She had made caring for old things her occupation.

Sissy said, "William, what was his last name?"

Abby said, "Campbell. Why? What made you think of him?"

Sissy said, "Just come to me that his wife had died. What was her name again?"

Abby said, "Delia."

Sissy said, "So, her name would have been Delia Campbell?"

Abby nodded, "Makes sense."

Sissy said, "We could find out about her."

Abby shrugged, "Okay. I guess. How would we do that?"

Sissy shook her head. "Ain't you the historian? The researcher? You always looking stuff up on your phone or your little notebook computer. You of all people. There'll be something about her on the internet."

Abby said, "At minimum an obituary."

And then she remembered.

Abby's eyes got wide. "Sissy. Oh my God."

"What?"

"I've seen it."

"What you seen?"

"Her obituary. Delia Campbell."

"Where'd you see it?"

"Back in California. I was snooping around at my grandma's. I saw it on her desk."

* * *

Later when Sissy and Abby went up to Chickasaw House, Emmaline was coming out of the door. She was toting the cat carrier, Belva Ann by her side.

"Grandma!"

"It worked. Poor Tom. I fear he is not very happy about this. I think he'll see it as a gross betrayal."

Sissy said, "You sure he's in there. He ain't making a sound."

Belva Ann said, "I zipped it up myself. Mimi gave me the name of the vet they use for Belle. And I explained how we needed to make hay while the sun was shining."

Sissy said, "I know that one. If you've cut your hay and the sun is shining but rain is coming, man, get that hay in before it gets wet and ruins it."

Emmaline said, "In life, timing is everything. If you see an opportunity, take it. He who hesitates is lost!"

Emmaline got into the passenger side of Belva Ann's little rental car. "You two hold down the fort. We'll return as soon as we get Tom checked into the hospital for his procedure."

Sissy said, "Old cat going to wake up minus some body parts."

Emmaline said, "Oh, Sissy. You make it sound barbaric. Poor old thing only has one ear left. And as he is not a young cat anymore, he might fare much worse if he keeps up the battles."

Sissy added, "Hate to have to call him 'No-eared Tom.'"

Belva Ann said, "Mom, it's a good thing you're doing for him. Even if he'd rather forego the honor."

Sissy and Abby stood and watched Belva Ann and Emmaline drive away. Freddy and Belle standing beside them.

Abby kept looking down the drive. "They'll be gone for some time. Time to find out what we can about Delia Campbell. Make hay while the sun shines."

Sissy added, "He who hesitates is lost."

They walked into Emmaline's office space; her laptop was open on the desk.

Abby walked right up to it and turned it on. The field came up for a log in.

Sissy said, "You fool. You shouldn't go looking in Ms. Emmaline's computer. Besides, you know her password?"

"Yeah. Grandma uses our address back in California."

Abby typed it in, and it was rejected.

"Well, she used to."

"You think your grandma is onto you?"

"What does that mean?"

Sissy rolled her eyes. "Shut that thing off. We don't need to be leaving no tracks. We can search on your phone."

"I wouldn't leave tracks. I'd clear the search engine before I shut it off."

"Every keystroke is permanent-like. Least that's what my Daddy says. How you think they catch all them pervs."

"Sissy Taylor, why would you know about stuff like that?"

"Abby Woods, why don't you know about stuff like that?"

Then they grinned at each other.

"Let's go up to my room."

"Keep the door open though so we can hear when Ms. Emmaline and Belva Ann get home."

Abby and Sissy got up in the bed in their filthy jeans and did not even take off their shoes. Then, to add insult to injury, both dogs hopped up on the bed to join them.

Abby was already typing the name Delia Campbell into her search engine.

The obituary popped up immediately.

Sissy leaned in close to look.

Sissy said, "Ain't she pretty? How old you s'pose she was in this picture?"

Abby shook her head. "I don't know. But not very old. Nice isn't it that they used a picture from when she was young."

Sissy said, "I guess. But Delia's children never knowed that woman. Delia, the one in the picture, she don't know yet what life has in store for her. She ain't wise yet like Mimi or Ms. Emmaline. I wouldn't know my Mimi if they used a photo of her at that age in her obituary. I'd prefer to see what she looked like as an old woman."

Abby was reading the fine print under the photo.

She said, "She was old, but not super old."

"A lot older than my Momma got to be."

"I'm sorry, Sissy."

"Well, it makes me feel sad for William."

Abby said, "Here's his name. Under 'Survived by.'"

Sissy said, "Survived? Makes it sound like they was all in a car wreck."

Abby added, "And like he said, he has two sons, and three grandsons. That has to be some happiness for William."

Sissy said, "They live in northern Virginia. You suppose William will move up there to be closer to them. Now his wife is gone?"

"I don't know."

"Mr. William was Ms. Emmaline's teacher. Right?"

Abby nodded.

"You suppose they was girlfriend and boyfriend while he was her teacher? He came here walking out with her back in the day when she was a student. You know that ain't right."

Abby said, "Grandma never let on to me that she knew this place. How could anyone forget this place? I know I never will."

Sissy said, "Ms. Emmaline, she had her reasons. 'Course, she didn't realize her granddaughter was some kind of spy."

"I wasn't supposed to be coming along. I was supposed to be at camp. She kind of got stuck with me."

Sissy said, "Let me look at that obituary. When did Mr. William and Ms. Delia get married?"

Abby and Sissy leaned in and scanned the obituary again.

Sissy said, "When you say Ms. Emmaline study here?"

"I'm not exactly sure. But she was in one of the first classes when they allowed girls."

"Let's look that up. Okay. U.Va. started admitting women in 1970. Your Grandma is old, but I don't think she's that old. But maybe she is. William sure is."

Abby said, "*I'm* the spy?"

Sissy smiled. "Okay, best friend forever. Here's what I think and don't be mad at me. I could be wrong. But it seems to me that Emmaline and her professor had a thing all them years ago while he was her teacher, and she was his student. And he may or may not have been already married to the pretty lady named Delia, at that time. But that don't really matter now. Except that neither Emmaline or William forgot each other. And that's kind of sweet, ain't it?"

"I don't know. William, he chose Delia instead of my grandma."

"But Ms. Emmaline never chose another. Pretty as she is, she could have. I feel certain about that."

"Except that she thought that a woman needed a man like a fish needs a bicycle."

"Maybe that was true enough for her back then."

Abby said, "Or maybe it was sour grapes."

"What does that mean?"

Abby said, "It's from Aesop's fables. When the fox couldn't reach the grapes, he just pretended he didn't want them anyway, and said they were probably sour."

"Oh. So maybe Ms. Emmaline couldn't have William, 'cause he chose Ms. Delia over her. Either that, or he had already married Ms. Delia, but was doing her wrong with Ms. Emmaline. So, sour grapes. Emmaline decided that not only did she not want William no more, she didn't want no man at all."

Abby nodded, "But why'd she come back here, all these years later? I don't think William asked her to come."

Sissy said, "Ms. Emmaline saw an opportunity and she took it."

"Nothing ventured, nothing gained?"

Sissy sighed, "I think we done spied enough on Ms. Emmaline for one day."

Abby nodded. "My lips are sealed if yours are."

Sissy said, "I hope she don't discover how much we been snooping. But it ain't just us. Mimi and Belva Ann, they digging up bones too. I think there's trouble brewing. I think Belva Ann has found herself a bone, and she's ain't giving it up, and she ain't done digging."

Abby said, "My mom is digging up bones? With Mimi?"

Sissy said, "I think I need to tell my Mimi what we found. On the lowdown. She'll likely tell me it were wrong to poke around in Ms. Emmaline's business. But she also knows that Ms. Belva Ann is hungry to know more about herself. And Ms. Emmaline is holding back for reasons of shame."

Abby bristled. "Shame? I'm pretty sure my grandma has

done nothing to be ashamed about. She might have lived outside of what was considered proper at the time. She'd call it living outside social conventions, but that's different.

Sissy said, "Emmaline has her own story to tell, and I guess when she's good and ready to tell us, she'll tell us. Or at least she'll tell Belva Ann. And when Ms. Belva Ann is ready, she'll tell you."

Abby scowled, "When she does, I think I'll already know all about it."

Sissy said, "Just be sure to look all surprised when she do."

21

It was late when Emmaline and Belva Ann returned with an empty cat carrier. Sissy and Belle had gone home to do chores.

Emmaline and Belva Ann looked exhausted as they set the empty carrier down on the porch where Freddy inspected it fully, looking worried.

Emmaline said, "Don't worry, we're bringing him back."

Belva Ann added, "I think the dog was hoping we wouldn't."

Then she turned to Abby, "Abby can you bring us some lemonade. Mom and I need to sit and relax."

Abby brought them their drinks. They were leaning back in their chairs, legs stretched out, Freddy stretched out alongside them. Abby said, "How's Tom?"

Emmaline said, "Unappreciative."

Belva Ann added, "Mom's spending a small fortune on that old cat."

Emmaline said, "In for a penny, in for a pound."

Belva Ann said, "Not only is he being neutered, but he's also being vaccinated, and getting his teeth cleaned. Oh, and we were told that Tom is a senior."

Abby frowned, "What does that mean?"

Emmaline said, "One-eared Tom is somewhere over the age of eleven."

Belva Ann said, "I asked if it was too late to neuter him,

but the vet assured me that it's never too late to neuter a male cat."

Abby said, "Poor old cat, isn't going to know what hit him."

Emmaline said, "He has to stay inside wearing a soft collar for a week. He's going to hate that."

Belva Ann shook her head, "Mom, I think you just bought yourself a very expensive half-feral cat."

"The heart wants what it wants. Besides, I haven't decided yet whether he's going back to California."

Belva Ann frowned, "You've got to be kidding me. After all we just went through. All the money you just spent?"

Emmaline shrugged. "Maybe Mimi could use a cat." Abby snorted. Emmaline changed the subject. "I feel this house at my back. Such a nice feeling."

Belva Ann said, "I have no idea what that means, Mom."

Abby said, "Mom, grandma and I have made this old house feel better. When we got here, the house felt worried."

Emmaline added, "Fragile."

Belva Ann said, "Is that anthropomorphism, or personification?"

Emmaline smiled, "Good question. Personification is a literary device, like describing the wind whispering through the trees. Anthropomorphism is ascribing human characteristics to non-humans."

Belva Ann nodded, "And which is it, then?" Emmaline shrugged. Belva Ann said, "Fragile isn't quite the right word. The right word is decrepit."

Emmaline nodded. "I'll give you that. The house is indeed in a state of decrepitude. Foundation needs work. The floors need releveling. Everything is out of plumb. The plumbing is likely shot. Who knows the condition of the roof. Probably also shot. The rest is mostly cosmetic, although not cheap to do. Like refinishing wood floors, and painting. The kitchen though, that needs a total updating. That's hugely expensive. Then there's the outside. And the landscaping is non-existent. I know all that. Still, it feels different now to me. Solid. The house seems incredibly solid. What this old woman could tell us. And now I feel somehow protected here."

Belva Ann said, "Brick is a durable building material." Then after a few beats she added, "Mom, you are coming home, right?"

Emmaline looked surprised. "What? Oh, of course."

Belva Ann said, "Mom, the cat is one thing, but this house is another sort of project all together. Taking on a house like this could ruin a person. Financially at minimum. But projects like that take an emotional toll as well."

Abby piped up, "The Taylors can't sell it. That's part of the curse."

Emmaline said, "I suspect Lucy Taylor hoped her curse would mean the old home place would eventually go to their children, Robert and Lucy's children. But it never did. Bobby doesn't seem interested in the house. He sure isn't going to put money into getting it restored."

Belva Ann said, "Mom. What the heck is going on? You're here to write a book, not get besotted by an old house."

Emmaline smiled, "It's been a magical summer. Hasn't it, Abby?"

Abby said, "Yes. I'm riding horses now, and Sissy is the best friend I ever had. And Grandma, we both want to go to

UVA. and major in history, except that Sissy doesn't think she can get in."

"Oh, darling, that is a wonderful idea. And you tell Sissy, that if she works hard at school, she can get in. Not only that, but there may be financial aid for her through her Daddy's job. But she shouldn't worry. Her job is to focus on school, and the rest she needs to leave to the grown-ups."

Belva Ann said, "Sissy will need extra help to catch up. I think she's behind where she needs to be. I can speak to Mimi about it. She knows that Sissy is smart as can be and isn't going to go into the military, like her brothers."

Emmaline switched subjects. "You haven't said much about your research you've been doing with Mimi."

"Well, I've a confession to make."

"Oh?"

"All our discussions about DNA got me thinking about submitting my own. So, I sent mine off to be analyzed."

"I don't remember discussing this."

Abby said, "We talked a lot about it, Grandma. Jefferson. Freddy. Remember?"

Emmaline ignored Abby. "So, what did you discover?"

Belva Ann shrugged. "My ancestry is all British Isles. I don't know what I expected. The good news is my health screening was good. I do have a higher-than-normal chance of developing celiac disease. But that was it."

"Well, that at least is reassuring."

Abby said, "So, Mom, does that mean you don't have to worry about heart disease like Grandma?"

Emmaline frowned, "Who said I'm worried about heart disease?"

Abby said, "Grandma, it runs in the family, which means maybe you should read up on it, I've read up on it."

Emmaline shook her head, smiling, "I bet you have."

Belva Ann deflected, "You know Mom, your family tree *is* pretty interesting."

Emmaline nodded, "My grandfather was a very successful man. California was full of opportunities for enterprising men and women at that time."

"Yes. But of course, half of my tree is simply blank."

Emmaline said, "I'm sorry about that, darling. I know you must be curious. I'm not ready yet to say more to you about that subject. Not yet. Nor to you, Abby. We Sparks women have enquiring minds. I'm not blind."

Belva Ann looked over at Abby and then back at Emmaline. "Mom?"

Just then Belva Ann's phone played the tune that indicated that Jim was calling. Belva Ann picked it up.

"Hi! Oh, we're all just relaxing on the porch with lemonade after the big adventure of taking One-eared Tom to the vet."

"No, he's fine. Emmaline decided he needed to be neutered and get up to date on all the veterinary care that he's never received in his entire life."

"What? Uh, sure."

Belva Ann stood up and walked into the house where Abby and Emmaline could no longer hear her.

Emmaline said, "That can't be a good sign."

"Grandma, why did Mom have to go where we couldn't hear her."

"It means that whatever Jim has to say, he doesn't want us

to hear. Or more accurately, that he doesn't want us to hear Belva Ann's response to what he has to say."

Abby shrugged, "She'll tell us when she gets off the phone anyway. Daddy has to know that."

Emmaline once again deflected, "I bought makings for veggie tacos. We haven't had that in a long time. The avocadoes look perfect."

"I'll make the guacamole."

"You do such a good job at it, too."

Just then Belva Ann walked out on the porch, her face expressionless but her shoulders sagged as she leaned against one of the pillars.

She said, "Jim was fired."

Emmaline gasped, "What! That can't be! What about the huge deal he was about to close."

Belva Ann shook her head, "He got the rug pulled out from underneath him. He was asked to clean out his desk and was escorted out of the offices. His boss is taking over his accounts."

Abby added, "But I thought his boss was a bumbling idiot."

Belva Ann sighed, "Maybe a shark, but not an idiot. The problem is that Jim has no allies at work. None. So, no one gave him a heads up."

Emmaline frowned, "So, he had not made friends and allies in his peer group?"

"Mom, don't you dare. This is not the time."

Abby said, "Is Daddy maladapted?"

"Oh my God, no, of course he isn't. What a thing to say."

Belva Ann looked at her mother, "Did she hear that from you?"

Abby said, "Mom, I heard Daddy say that about me."

Belva Ann looked like she was going to cry. "You were snooping! Your Daddy never meant any of that. He just blows off steam sometimes."

Emmaline said, "Abby, you are not maladapted, and neither is your father. But really, Belva Ann, it's just, oh, you know, stones and glass houses, isn't it? I don't mean to be engaging in schadenfreude. But surely there will be some good to come of this."

Abby whispered, "Schadenfreude?"

Emmaline whispered back, "Taking pleasure in someone else's misfortune."

"Oh, like sadistic?"

Emmaline put a finger to her lips.

Belva Ann sat back down and put her head in her hands. "I quit my job. And now Jim's been fired. We have no income."

Emmaline said, "Jim will surely get some kind of severance package."

"Mom, he was fired."

"After all those years? No package? Fired? For cause?"

"Yes."

"Which was?"

"Evidently he had created a hostile work environment. They'd been carefully building a file on him for some time, on the advice of counsel. His co-workers and staff helped in that process."

Belva Ann continued, "I guess Jim *was* living in a glass house, with no self-awareness, as he chucked stones at everyone around him. All that talk about being part of a team! One of the complaints was that he was not a team player.

But worse than that, that he was hypercritical and verbally abusive."

"Mom, are you mad at Daddy?"

Belva Ann sighed, "Yes. But I'll get over it. In time. He wanted to join us while he regroups. But I told him to wait."

Emmaline said, "It might do him a world of good."

Belva Ann said, "It might do him a world of good to be alone with his own thoughts too."

"There is one team where he still belongs. Tell him to come. He hasn't been fired from this one, even if he is currently on the bench."

Belva Ann smiled, "Sports analogies? Really, Mom? Not your strong suit."

Emmaline said, "The thing is, this place is magical. Get Jim out here and help him. Forgive him."

Belva Ann softened. "Mom, that's so beautiful. I'll try."

Emmaline said, "Forgive us our trespasses, as we forgive those who trespass against us."

* * *

They ate their tacos the first night and they were so good they made more the next night. They ate on the front porch and watched the fireflies. At first there was not a lot of conversation. Abby sensed she should not ask too many questions, although she had many. The second night, the atmosphere began to relax and as they watched the fireflies perform their ballet, Emmaline and Belva Ann spoke in low tones, feet propped up on empty chairs.

Belva Ann mused, "The house does have good bones."

Emmaline nodded. "The house is substantial. And yet, the scale of it is not too large. It was always meant to be a graceful home, rather than a monument."

"The millwork is quite fine."

Emmaline's voice was also low and soft. "The fireplace surrounds and mantels are, too. And I've peeled back some of that wallpaper. I imagine the very first paper is under there waiting to be discovered."

"Mom, do you believe the story about Robert and Lucy and Lotty?"

"I do."

"After your book comes out, people will become interested in the real place, and the real story."

"I suppose that could happen."

"And I'm afraid there will be ghost hunter types coming to see if they can commune with the ghosts of Robert and Lucy."

Emmaline shrugged, "People do love a good ghost story. I know I do."

"Do you think the place could be popular as a B&B? It's not far from the University."

"I don't know. But I don't think B&B's are all that profitable. Definitely not profitable enough to make a dent in the cost of bringing the old lady back to her full glory."

"True. Just a thought."

Emmaline nodded again, "There are other considerations."

"Like?"

Emmaline rubbed at her temples. "Like as of now, there is no book. Even if I get the book to print, no one is going to know about Chickasaw House but us for a long time."

Abby said, "Mom, don't count grandma's chickens before they hatch."

Emmaline said, "Touche'."

Belva Ann said, "Okay you two, throw me a bone here. I'm unemployed and my husband just got fired. A place like Chickasaw House has so much history as well as ghosts. And this was once a working plantation. It could be educational for tourists and guests alike. I can imagine Sissy giving tours as her summer job. This was her ancestor's home."

"But you have a beautiful home already, back in California."

"That's your home, Mom. You just let us live there rent free."

"Stop it! It's your home. I am perfectly content in the guest house. I wanted you and Jim to raise Abby in that home, the way my parents raised me there. It represents stability. It represents continuity, it's our history, your history."

Belva Ann said, "It will always be Grandma and Grandpa Sparks' home to me."

Emmaline stayed calm, her voice low, "So, maybe it represents the success of my grandfather, your great-grandfather. Abby, that would be your great-great-grandfather. So, I suppose if you feel that you and Jim and Abby don't deserve it, then of course, that means I don't deserve it either, and neither did my parents."

Abby said, "Sissy said if you see a turtle on a fence post, you know it didn't get there by itself."

Belva Ann and Emmaline were both struck dumb for a moment, then began to laugh.

Emmaline said, "Did she, now? I guess that makes us all a bunch of turtles."

Belva Ann shook her head. "Sissy makes a good point. Some of us, not all, get a lift onto that fence post. It's called privilege."

Abby said, "A big house isn't all we inherited, Mom. I know words and read a lot because of my family. Sissy knows horses and dogs and riding and how to run a retired horse business because of her family. Sissy is teaching me about riding, and I'm teaching her about words and such. Seems to me that nobody gets a lift up on everything."

Emmaline added, "No man is an island."

Abby asked, "No man is an island?"

Belva Ann said, "Famous poem by John Donne."

Emmaline added, "The last line is famously used by Hemingway to title his book 'For Whom the Bell Tolls."

Belva Ann said, "Never send to know for whom the bell tolls..."

Emmaline solemnly intoned, "It tolls for thee."

Abby said, "You guys!"

"Oh, Abby, it's so much fun to be with you and Mom. I haven't quoted poetry for a long time."

Emmaline said, "The point John Donne was making, is that we are all interconnected. History is a living thing. And we have such a small part to play. But what I've learned is that even when we make a small ripple, that ripple has consequences beyond us. Whether we mean it to or not."

Abby said, "I like Sissy's saying better. It's funny. That John Donne guy sounds obsessed with death to me."

Emmaline grinned. "Touche' again, kiddo."

* * *

Emmaline set the carrier down on the floor in her study. Again, Tom was silent. Emmaline and Abby crouched down and peered in at the cat.

Emmaline said, "He hasn't made a peep. He's so dignified about it all. They told me they showed him his carrier and he walked right into it all by himself."

"Grandma, his collar is not dignified at all."

"It's a soft collar. It's supposed to be more comfortable than the old-style plastic cones."

"It's made up to look like an iced donut with sprinkles."

"I hadn't noticed."

"Look."

"Oh, you're right."

Abby and Emmaline continued to stare at the cat. Tom stared back at them in a calm and studious way. He had his front paws tucked under his chest and his tail curled around his body.

Belva Ann said, "You guys?"

Emmaline said, "Yes?"

"Someone is concerned about Tom."

Abby and Emmaline turned to see Freddy, belly-walking his way to the carrier. When he got closer, he lifted his nose a bit, poking it into the air and pulling in the smells in loud sniffs.

Abby sat back, patted her thigh and said, "It's okay. Tom is okay."

Freddy flattened himself in front of the carrier, placed his nose between his front paws, and stared. Tom remained motionless, but Abby could see his eyes had halfway closed, as if he was going to go to sleep. She reached over and stroked the head of her dog.

She and Emmaline and Belva Ann exchanged glances.

Abby cooed, "Kitty-cats are our friends. Kitty-cats are our friends." As she stroked his head.

Freddy sighed and broke his concentration to look up at Abby, worry wrinkles over his eyes.

Belva Ann said, "Looks like fear has been replaced with sympathy."

Abby said, "He knows the smell."

Belva Ann asked, "What smell?"

Abby said, "You don't smell it, Mom? Tom smells like a hospital. Freddy had the same operation after he was rescued. He probably is reliving those feelings. I think it's called empathy."

Belva Ann said, "That's a brilliant analysis, Abby. Empathy leads to compassion. Which is related to sympathy."

Emmaline said, "Freddy might not feel the same way about Tom once he's out of the carrier and back to full power."

Belva Ann said, "I don't know. I think this is a breakthrough."

Emmaline said, "Regardless, I think it best for you two to take Freddy out of here. I've got the litter box set up in the corner. I'm going to close the door before I open his carrier."

Abby said, "One-eared Tom, you are now officially a house cat."

Belva Ann added, "Maybe. Maybe not. Don't get used to it."

* * *

Emmaline said, "I've really got to get back into my work."

Belva Ann nodded, "Sure, Mom. Abby and Freddy and I will entertain ourselves, won't we, Abby?"

Emmaline gave them the thumbs up and closed the door to her study so that she could let Tom out of his carrier.

Belva Ann turned to Abby, "Let's poke around this old house, shall we?"

Abby and Freddy followed her mom up the stairs.

"Six bedrooms in all?"

"Yeah. But only one bathroom for everyone to share. I don't think people will want to stay somewhere where they have to share a bathroom."

"Good point."

"I don't know about the B&B idea, Mom. I mean, at least the house would be cared for and have people learn about its history. But it also seems wrong to me. This house is a home, not a hotel."

Belva Ann opened another door to an empty bedroom. They both stepped in. Belva Ann said, "There's really nothing special about the bedrooms."

"Mom, that's not true. Grandma's room has the sleeping porch. It's condemned now but it could be made safe. Look at these old fireplaces. I mean, they're not grand like downstairs, but they are still pretty. And look at the wavy glass in the windows. That's original. And the baseboards and crown molding. And the hardwood floors."

"How do you know so much?"

"Grandma. But y'know, a floor is just a floor, and a window is just a window, until you know about the people who walked on them and looked out of them. That's what gives them meaning."

Belva Ann smiled, "You're channeling Mom."

"Yup."

Belva Ann sighed, "A B&B is probably a dumb idea. I'm grasping at straws."

"Don't worry, Mom. Grandma thinks everything will be okay. Daddy will get a new job, and you'll end up writing your own book."

"Well, if Grandma says so."

Abby continued, "This old house does need love and care. But it's not going anywhere. We could just keep renting it. Maybe Bobby will let us make some small improvements. We could come back here every summer. And then Sissy and I will go to college here together and ride horses. And maybe someday, this old house will be my house."

Belva Ann raised her eyebrows. "That's some impressive planning on your part."

"It could happen."

"Anything is possible, I suppose."

After looking into all six rooms, Belva Ann came to an odd narrow door at the end of the hall that resembled a closet door.

Belva Ann said, "What an odd door."

Abby said, "It's the attic. There's no AC up there or electricity, so it's hot and dark. I've only poked my head in there and that was enough for me."

"Is there a floor?"

Abby nodded, "And a lot of dirt and nuts and such."

"Nuts?"

"The squirrels were raising their families up there."

"Let's have a look."

Abby led Belva Ann up the narrow stairs. Freddy trailed behind, looking anxious. A bit of natural light filtered in through the half-moon window over the front of the house."

The two of them looked at the dimly lit space.

Belva Ann said, "What a waste of space. You would think after all this time; someone would have finished it out."

Abby said, "Mom, do you think anyone ever lived up here? I mean other than squirrels."

Belva Ann said, "Maybe servants."

Abby said, "You mean slaves?"

"I suppose I do. Although it's hard to believe. It's so abhorrent and antithetical to everything we as a country, as a people, believe in as an enduring truth, as our foundational principle. It's the exact opposite of freedom, enslavement."

Belva Ann walked into the space, and began to examine it, something Abby and Emmaline had never done.

She placed a hand on an exposed beam that angled over her head. Abby and Freddy stayed by the door. Then Belva Ann pointed to the floor, "There's your stash of acorns."

Abby said, "Poor squirrels. They had to leave without packing. They must have worked hard to gather all those nuts."

Belva Ann kept walking; she pointed to the interior masonry. "Chimneys. Makes me think that this space was cozy in the wintertime. The brick in the backs of these chimneys can release a lot of ambient heat into an attic space."

Abby added, "Bet nobody could bear to stay up here in the summertime. It's pretty suffocating."

Belva Ann mused, "True. It would be awfully hot in our bedrooms too. In the days before air conditioning, we'd all be out on Emmaline's sleeping porch or on the front porch. People hung mosquito netting to keep the bugs off. Heat rises, so the upper stories were hotter than the lower ones."

Abby said, "They have bugs here like I've never seen before. Deerflies and horseflies that will draw blood. I killed one that was attacking poor Buttermilk."

Belva Ann crouched down to examine a timber. "Look at this Abby." Then she moved to the next beam. "Someone has scratched little marks into the wood."

Belva Ann said, "Do we have a flashlight?"

"I don't think so."

Now Belva Ann was squinting, getting as close as she could. Then she sat back on her heels. "When Lotty moved in, she clearly supplanted Lucy. Obviously, she took Lucy's spot in Robert's bed. But where do you think Lucy then slept? What about their children?"

"I don't know. But I bet those two women hated each other. They should have hated Robert. He should never have brought Lotty into the house."

Belva Ann looked thoughtful, then said, "Those women's fates depended on gaining and keeping favor with that man."

Abby said, "You think maybe Lucy had to live up here?"

Belva Ann said, "I couldn't say. Come look at these. These look like simple hash marks."

Abby frowned, "What does that mean?"

"Like someone counting off the days."

"You mean like a prison sentence?"

"Yes. Exactly. Like this space was used kind of like a prison. One door that could be locked. Only the light from that one measly window, too."

"Mom, I think Grandma will want to see this."

Belva Ann nodded, "Mimi too. Mimi will want to see this. I'm going down there tomorrow anyway."

* * *

Abby and Belva Ann and Freddy stood outside Emmaline's office. Belva Ann tapped lightly on the door. After a moment, Emmaline cracked open the door. "Hi. I'm hard at work, be quick, I don't want to let the cat out."

Abby said, "Grandma, we found something in the attic."

"What?"

Belva Ann frowned, "Little hash marks in the base of a couple beams. At least that's what it looked like to me. It made me think of what prisoners carve into the walls of their cells. Do you think they used the attic as a prison? To punish slaves?"

Emmaline stepped into the hall and closed the door behind her. "Show me."

Abby said, "Let me get my phone. We can use the flashlight app."

Belva Ann sighed, "Thanks, Abby. I can't believe I didn't think of that."

Once again Freddy trailed after them as they headed up the stairs. He didn't look any happier about the second trip than he did on the first one.

Belva Ann led them to the beam. They squatted down and Abby turned on her flashlight app.

Belva Ann pointed to the marks. "See. A row. How many marks in a row?"

Emmaline counted them under her breath, then said, "Ten."

"You may be on to something."

Abby said, "Grandma, where do you think Lucy slept, after Lotty came and took her place as Robert's wife."

"Often the enslaved slept on pallets on the floors. But it could have been anywhere I suppose. There would have been a kitchen house out back. She could have slept there or in a cabin in the yard with her children. Those cabins, what I've seen of them, were dirt floored and primitive. Wherever she was moved, it was a step down for her and her children."

Belva Ann said, "Mom, these marks add to the story."

Emmaline looked thoughtful. "They do. I think you may be right about their meaning. Dear Lord, it was a terrible thing, slavery."

Belva Ann said, "I found marks on some of the other beams too. What other explanation could there be? People got locked up here for days at a time."

Abby said, "Grandma, we sensed fear when we first came here. Like the house was afraid of us. Two white women coming up the driveway. Maybe it wasn't just Robert who did wrong by both women. Maybe it was a white woman came here and locked folks up in the attic."

Emmaline said, "Abby, that may be going a bit too far."

Belva Ann shook her head, "The hashmarks are real. And they are the work of human hands. Lotty had credible reasons to be both jealous and fearful of Lucy. And if she locked Lucy up there, maybe she ought to be afraid. I'd want to get justice any way I could if I had been locked up and otherwise mistreated."

Abby said, "Lucy had good reasons to want Lotty dead."

Belva Ann added, "And Lotty had good reasons to want Lucy to either die or to run away."

Emmaline said, "Lucy wasn't going to run away and leave her children."

Belva Ann said, "Robert must have been a foolish man to think he could pull this off."

Emmaline said, "He wouldn't be the first man to think such a thing." She added, "And so, I suppose, Lucy and Lotty used whatever power they possessed, which was little in those days, to try and drive the other away. Mistreatment, punishments, labors, evil eyes, what else?"

Abby said, "Poison?"

Emmaline said, "That's how George Wythe died, arsenic. Arsenic sprinkled on strawberries. But not by an enslaved person. He was poisoned by a family member wanting their inheritance early."

Belva Ann said, "I doubt Lotty wanted Lucy cooking for her or looking after her children."

Abby said, "Let's get out of here." When they turned to leave, Freddy froze, his hackles went up. Abby found her arms and the back of her neck going goose pimples. All four them, Emmaline, Belva Ann, Abby and Freddy, glanced at each other in alarm.

Belva Ann said, "Why is Freddy scared? I don't see anything."

Emmaline said, "Why isn't it hotter up here? It's summertime. In fact, I just felt a waft of cold air. Why would that happen in a closed off attic space?"

Belva Ann said, "Fear. Fear can make you cold or hot. Even at the same time. So, why are we standing here looking like deer in headlights? C'mon, move."

Abby said, "C'mon, Freddy, it's okay. Let's go back downstairs."

Freddy wasn't moving, he was frozen to the place. And it soon became clear why. Tom was in the doorway, donut cushion around his head. He walked right up to Freddy and rubbed up against his leg, purring. Then greeted Emmaline in the same fashion.

Emmaline picked him up and cradled him against her chest. "Oh, Tom. How in the world did you get out?"

22

Abby dragged herself into the kitchen for breakfast to find Belva Ann standing over the stove sprinkling shredded cheese on an omelet, while Emmaline sipped at her tea.

She was saying, "I called Jim last night and told him all about my discovery."

Emmaline raised her eyebrows. "And?"

"And amazingly enough, he stopped being miserable long enough to take an interest."

Belva Ann pointed a spatula at Abby, "Make yourself a cup of tea and put a bagel in the toaster. A cheese omelet coming right up."

"I need to feed Freddy first. Grandma, how's donut-head doing?"

"He's had his stinky tin of cat food and a lovefest with me this morning. I still don't know how he got out of my office last night."

Belva Ann continued, "I told Jim this may actually be one of those blessings in disguise. And he laughed. He said if that was true, it was a very well disguised blessing. But then I think he heard me when I said that his job was never what he wanted to do as a career. And we all knew my job was not a good fit for me. So, I think I've convinced him to come out and join us. He's stewed in his own juices long enough. And Lord knows *we're* not going to make him feel guilty about this. It's a wakeup call, is what it is."

"Daddy's coming!"

Belva Ann grinned, "He is!"

Abby said, "Wow, that means you guys can drive your rental car back to California. And you can take donut-head in your car. That way Freddy can still have his deck, and we can still take our luggage."

Emmaline said, "Not a bad idea."

Belva Ann smiled. "I'm still not sure about taking Tom, but yeah, I like the idea. It will make Jim feel useful, too."

Abby said, "Isn't it weird? How we all ended up here."

Belva Ann raised her eyebrows. "Unexpected. That's for sure."

Emmaline said, "If you do nothing unexpected, nothing unexpected happens."

Abby said, "Is that like the one about doing the same thing over and over and expecting different results?"

Belva Ann's mouth dropped open.

And Emmaline once again softly said, "Touche."

* * *

Belva Ann and Abby and Freddy had walked down to the Taylors. Abby was waving at Sissy who was scrubbing out the water trough. They all turned their heads when they saw William's car going up the drive.

Abby said, "Haven't seen him in a while."

Belva Ann said, "So, that's Mom's secret flame?"

Abby said, "What do you know about him?"

"Probably not as much as you know."

Abby said nothing in reply.

Belva Ann looked thoughtfully at Abby. "You do know something, don't you? I can see it in your face."

Just then, Mimi came out, wiping her hands on her apron. She nodded, "Ms. Belva Ann, Ms. Abby."

Abby turned to Mimi and asked, "You suppose folks got locked into the attic up there, at Chickasaw House, as punishment?"

Belva Ann added context. "We found hash marks on two of the beams up there in the attic. Like you would see someone do in a prison, to count off the days."

Mimi just said, "Lord, have mercy."

Mimi and Belva Ann turned their backs to the girls and spoke to each other in low tones as they went into the house. So, Abby helped Sissy finish scrubbing the water trough. Sissy then asked Abby to keep watch as the hose filled the now clean tank, while Sissy went to drag the field. Sissy had instructed her to turn the water off at the pump handle and coil the hose on the ground. Then she was to place the two by four that was lying on the ground, in the tank.

She had asked, "Why'd you want to do a thing like that?"

"That there is my squirrel ladder."

"Squirrel ladder?"

"Daddy taught me that. Squirrels got to drink, too. It's summertime. They get hot and thirsty. They fall in, they can't get a way to climb out. So, we be sure they got a ladder. Lots of times creatures get into situations they can't get out of. As true of people as animals. They don't deserve to drown 'cause of it."

Abby said, "I would have never thought of it."

Sissy said, "You would if you'd fished a dead squirrel out of your water trough."

The horses seemed to know the tank was just about full. They began to move as one toward the tank. Abby stepped back against the fence to give them more room, and she thought of Sissy's words. She needed to give herself a way out.

There was Bunny in the lead. And right behind her, Buttermilk. The rest of the herd seemed to step back and let the two mares go first. Buttermilk, as if to confirm her status, made a menacing expression at those behind her. But it was Bunny who drank first, lifted her head, and then decided to drink again. Her giant ears flopped forward and back a bit with each swallow. Buttermilk waited her turn patiently. Horses were still a puzzle to Abby. But she wondered if the fact that she and Sissy took these two mares out, together, nearly every day, had given them some sort of status in the herd. They certainly seemed to be buddies, outside of the ride time as well as on the ride. Just like she and Sissy were buddies. Best friends.

Once Bunny stepped back, Buttermilk stepped forward and had a good long drink. Then the herd took turns. Some seemed thirsty. Some seemed to just go through the motions. But because everyone drank, the tank took a long time to fill.

Abby finally got to shut off the pump and began to coil the hose. When she stood up, Sissy poked her in her side.

"There goes Mr. William. He sure didn't stay long."

She was right. And he was driving awfully fast down that rutted drive. Bouncing wildly.

Sissy said, "Looks like a horse that got a burr under his saddle pad."

Abby said, "Or one that got bit by a horsefly."

* * *

Sissy and Abby had to change their route on their ride. Sissy had been right. The hay was ready for its second cutting and more than one big mower was at work in their field. Sissy said they would in no ways be a welcome sight riding there today.

Abby asked, "Where can we go?"

"We can ride up to Squirrel Manor and poke around your woods. I know some deer tracks back there we can follow."

Abby said, "So, why'd you think William got mad at Emmaline? Do you think it's because Grandma's been ignoring him since Belva Ann got here? Plus, last time he came by, she was busy writing, he decided not to even go in to say hi. Maybe something was already up."

Sissy said, "Maybe she done broke it off. The way he tore out of here, like his tail was on fire makes it seem likely."

Abby frowned, "That doesn't sound right to me. My Grandma cut out that obituary for a reason. We drove all the way from California. And she looked him up as soon as we got here. I mean, really, she put on make-up and jewelry and skirts!"

Sissy laughed, "Could be like the dog that caught the car."

"What?"

"When you chasin' after something, and once you catch it, well, fun's over. You find you don't want it after all."

"I don't know about that."

"Me, I feel sorry for Mr. William. He's a sweet man. Poor man with his wife dying and his kids and grandkids moved away. Ms. Emmaline showing up was likely a happy surprise for him. Even if he didn't realize she planned it. No one does know about that but us. And we ain't tellin'."

Chickasaw House came into view. And for the first time ever, Abby felt a chill run down her spine.

"Ugh, secrets. There's the old lady. And she certainly has her own secrets. Sissy, they locked folk in the attic. I mean for days. So many days that they got marked off by scratching hash marks in the wood to count them off."

Sissy shook her head, "Girl, you know that weren't the worst of what went on at places like Chickasaw House. Rich white folk who owned people who looked like me? You surely seen some of those pictures in all them books you study."

"I have. You know I have. But I love that old house. And seeing those marks made me feel differently about the house. And it's just last night, for the first time, I wondered about what happened to Lucy after Lotty settled in as Robert's wife and took her place. Like, where did Lucy sleep at night? Where did their children sleep?"

"What did Ms. Emmaline say?"

"She said, maybe they got moved into a little cabin in the back. She said there would also be a kitchen house out back. Lucy might have slept there. But for sure she lost her place. Lotty would have made sure of it."

The girls rode their horses past the house and stopped in the rear yard. Sissy said, "Look at your bird house. And what is that feeder, there?"

"For the squirrels. Grandma and I have acquired a fondness for the squirrels here."

"Ain't you got no squirrels in California?"

Abby winced, "You mean, don't we have squirrels in California?"

Sissy grinned, "*Ain't* that what I said?"

Abby narrowed her eyes. "You're torturing me on purpose. Humor me, okay. I want you to get into UVA and be my roommate. And, yeah, we do have squirrels. They're bigger than yours, and not as cute."

Sissy said, "You don't think I can talk like you and Ms. Emmaline, do you? You want to hear my Ms. Emmaline imitation?"

"What?"

Sissy sat up tall and lifted her chin, drawing out the words. "Abby darling, please look that up on your phone, spell it, give me synonyms, and also its, etym... She turned to Abby. Um, Abby, help me out, here. How do I say the word?"

"Etymology."

"Yeah. That."

Abby chuckled. "You sounded just like my grandma."

"Don't you tell her I did that. I love Ms. Emmaline. I wouldn't want her to take offense. I sure would hate you to mimic my Mimi. Even thinking on that makes me ashamed of myself."

"I won't. And don't be ashamed. It made me think of something she said. About how we can learn dialects like learning another language. You might have to speak "Emmaline" at college. It might help you get better grades at school if you did it there, too."

"Might get me beat to a pulp at school. I'd be a big old phony. And if it weren't me we were talking about here, I'd be wanting to beat the stew out of anyone at school who put on airs like that."

"I'm the wrong person to give advice on how to talk at school. I had no friends, and even my teacher hated me."

"I get that you stuck up like a high nail amongst the other kids. I'd likely want to pound you down too, if I had you in my class. But I'd a thought you'd be the teacher's pet."

"I almost got expelled. Spent the last couple weeks in the principal's office."

"Well, knock me over with a feather. How'd you manage that?"

Abby was quiet for a moment. "I didn't fit in anywhere."

Sissy looked at Abby with her eyes narrowed. "What you do to your teacher?"

"Nothing bad."

"Which means, you did something. Weren't murder. Didn't spill no blood?"

Abby giggled.

Sissy said, "Bet you were a pain in the ass. To the point the poor teacher just had to be shed of you, or she was going to lose her ever-loving mind and commit child abuse."

Abby felt a hot wave of shame wash over her cheeks. But she giggled anyway.

Sissy whistled for the dogs and then ducked down a trail into the woods that Abby would never have noticed without Sissy's lead.

Sissy said, "Watch your head for low branches and spiderwebs. Critters that go through here ain't tall enough to clear 'em for us."

Sissy led them down a steep little deer track. Abby could barely see where they were going as she was either ducking under limbs or peeling spiderwebs off her face and arms. Buttermilk had collected her own webs that hung between her ears. They broke free of the densest part of the woods to bottom land. Sissy pulled Bunny up and silently pointed ahead of her.

It wasn't just one deer, but a group of them. Twin fawns were nursing on a doe. Her large ears swiveled around to take in the girls and their horses. Sissy looked down at Belle and whispered sternly, "Don't you dare run no deer." Belle looked up at Sissy, her lean body quivering. "I said, no!" Belle obeyed.

Sissy whispered to Abby. "Foxhounds get punished for running deer. They sure do tempt 'em though. It's a strong scent. Hah. But look at your dog. He for sure ain't no hunting dog."

Freddy had thrown himself down on the ground and was rolling in something, seemingly oblivious to the deer right in front of him.

It wasn't until the deer bounced away, white tails flicked over their backs, that Freddy seemed to sense something exciting had happened. The two old hunt horses had stood alert watching, full of attention, but frozen in place. Abby could feel Buttermilk's heart beating beneath her, moving her legs that hung along her ribcage.

Sissy said, "I haven't been down here for a long while. Bottomland stays lush. Always lots of deer and fox and all sorts of birds. It's too wet for cultivation though. And It'll suck the shoes right off a horse. But these girls are barefoot, so that's not a problem for them. We can scout us out another path back.

Sissy led the way, and a huge red-tailed hawk seemed to fly alongside them, tree to tree.

Abby wasn't sure which way *was* back. But soon, they moved out of the marshy bottomland and headed into the trees. It was all trees, deerflies, and spiderwebs and dark under the heavy canopy. They zigged and zagged above the trail they had just traversed until Abby was even more turned around than before. But Sissy seemed to know exactly where she was. And each turn found them on higher ground.

Abby ducked under one large web and spotted a gigantic spider smack dab in the middle of it. It looked like something in a haunted house. It had black and yellow on it and to her way of thinking, it was far too close to her face. She threw herself onto Buttermilk's neck shrieking, "Spider! Spider! Holy-Moley!"

Once she dared sit up, she said, "Did you see the size of that thing?"

Sissy turned around on Bunny and laughed at Abby. "Nothing but a globe-weaver."

"It could have jumped on me!"

"They barely move until the sun go down."

Abby blew through her nose like a horse and muttered. "Could have mentioned that. Thing gave me a heart attack."

They popped out of the gloom, and miraculously were directly behind Chickasaw House, near where they had first entered the woods.

Abby said, "How'd you do that?"

"Do what?"

"Find your way back?"

"I ain't going to get lost in my own woods."

"Technically, these are Bobby Taylor's woods."

"Bobby Taylor ain't hardly ever here. I been here all my life."

Abby and Sissy pulled up the horses to stare at the back of the house. The dogs flopped down, also seemingly studying the back of the house.

Abby asked, "Where do you imagine the little cabin would have been?"

Sissy said, "Where people driving up wouldn't see it. Wouldn't want it spoiling the view of the house. And we saw what them cabins were like. We saw them at Monticello. Only had dirt floors and rough chimneys. Weren't nothing like those fancy fireplaces and mantels and floors in the big house."

Abby said, "I'm glad they tore them down."

Sissy shook her head, "Not me."

Abby said, "But they tore them down because what happened was shameful."

"Sometimes, shame is the proper thing, the right thing. Ms. Emmaline wants to tell the truth story even in her made-up stories. Not the story all gussied up, with the shameful cabins torn down. Hiding the shameful truth is what folks did at Monticello for time-out-of-mind. Somebody tore down all them cabins on Mulberry Row a long time ago, so folks wouldn't feel no shame touring the grounds. Torn down, they could pretend it weren't so bad being enslaved at Monticello.

Course, now they rebuilt 'em so we could see the way it was, learn the full story. That's a good thing. We learned on that tour a lot about how they's now committed to the full picture of what life was like at Monticello. Maybe someday we'll see it full. Maybe they'll get them all built back. They should. Even if it makes some folks ashamed."

Abby said, "When Grandma and I first drove up to this

old house, we both felt like the house was a person. And we both felt like the house was afraid and sad. So, Grandma made up a story. About how the house was afraid of strangers, carpetbaggers she called us. We had to convince the house we were friendly and were not going to harm it. The old lady we called it."

Sissy grinned, "Ms. Emmaline can spin a tale."

"It felt real. And then I learned about Lucy and Robert. I thought of them as a love story. But then Robert wrecked it all by giving into pressure to marry a white woman."

Sissy added, "And don't forget about you dreamin' about your grandma and her lover, here all them years ago."

Abby said, "That turned out to be true!"

Sissy and Abby started walking the horses, the dogs hopping up to lead the way.

Abby said, "Grandma and I both felt the fear and sadness in the house the moment we drove up, and I guess we weren't wrong. This old house has seen fear. Lots of it. Maybe a place gets changed by what went on there. I thought all the house needed was for us to show some respect and care. But seeing those hash marks changed my perspective, maybe in a way that you already understood, and I didn't until now. You understood stuff when we were touring Monticello that didn't hit me until now."

Sissy said, "I don't forget that it's black Taylors likely got locked up in that attic. Got locked up by white Taylors. And if those white Taylors got too afraid to live there, well, maybe they got good reasons other than some curses put out by Lucy. Maybe it were shame. If they lived there, they'd have to live with those hash marks over their heads every night when they slept."

As they rounded the house, they caught sight of Emmaline sitting on the top step on the front porch. Her hair was loose around her shoulders. She was wearing one of her flowery skirts. Her feet were bare. Her chin was resting in her palm, elbow on her knee. Before they could greet her, before Freddy made it to her side, she rose and walked back into the house.

* * *

Sissy and Abby turned the horses back out into their field. They stood by the gate and watched as first Bunny, and then Buttermilk, rolled in a dug-up spot in the field.

Sissy said, "I keep trying to grow grass there, and they keep digging it up. I realized I was only messing with their handiwork. Fills with water and makes a mudhole when it rains too."

"They like to roll in the mud?"

"Just like little piggies. Some days the herd lines up to take turns at it."

Sissy said, "Wonder what Mimi has for us to eat?"

Abby said, "Bet my grandma has made us something back at Chickasaw House."

"I dunno. I got the feeling Ms. Emmaline don't want to be steppin' and fetchin' for us today."

"Did I tell you my Daddy lost his job?"

"Mercy sakes alive. I can't believe you waited until now to say it. Bet your momma is in there cryin' on Mimi's shoulder. They were whispering serious like this morning for good reason."

"Grandma says everything is going to be fine."

"Well, she would say that, wouldn't she?"

"Why would you say that?"

"That's what Grandma's do. They try to make everything okay for the grandchildren whilst the other grownups have a come-apart."

"But I believe her. She said that job made Daddy miserable. And Grandma was happy that Mom had quit her job. Grandma kind of pushed her into it. But now, nobody has a job."

Sissy nodded, "That's kind of scary."

"We'll be fine. Grandma owns both houses we have in California. Free and clear."

"That's good."

"She says she has enough for all of us for now. We can still pay our bills for now."

Sissy shook her head, "So, maybe Ms. Emmaline is right. But I bet your Daddy's pride is hurt."

"Yeah. It's weird. I always got the feeling that he was really good at his job. Like way smarter than everyone else there."

"Kind of like you at school. 'Cept you said you almost got yourself expelled."

Abby gasped, "Man, I feel like smacking you right now."

"Like Father, like daughter?"

Abby exhaled, "I don't see how school is like Daddy's job."

"I think maybe it is. Like maybe I'm right on the nose. Getting fired, getting expelled."

"My Daddy is very smart."

"You are too."

Abby grimaced, "Maybe it's not great, being too smart."

"They's different kinds of smart."

Abby sighed.

Abby and Sissy walked to the house, quieter and more reflective than usual. Even the two dogs seemed to share the mood.

The door was open, they walked in and were about to walk into the kitchen when they heard Belva Ann. They froze.

She was saying, "It says we share fifty percent of our DNA. Fifty percent! Mom used an anonymous donor. This means this man is my half-brother. I mean, if Mom's donor donated a lot, they could have a lot of unknown children out there. I could have a lot of half-siblings. Oh, my God. What do I do? I told mom that I had sent off my DNA, she knows about it. But I never expected this. I'm going to have to tell her."

They couldn't hear Mimi's voice, but they heard Belva Ann's reply. "No anonymous donor expected back in the day to be, you know, exposed. No one ever expected so many would have access to a huge public data base of DNA."

Sissy poked Abby in the back, forcing her to walk toward the kitchen and make their presence known.

Sissy said, "Hey, Mimi. Hey, Ms. Belva Ann. What we got to eat for lunch?"

Abby walked around to where Belva Ann was sitting, her laptop open on Mimi's kitchen table. Belva Ann mindlessly gave her daughter a hug.

"I'm sure we have plenty at home for your lunch."

Mimi said, "Sissy, why don't you girls fix you some tomato and mayonnaise sandwiches? We got some potato chips and lemonade."

Sissy said, "That sounds good."

Mimi added, "Then take yourselves and them dirty hounds outside. Belva Ann and I are busy here."

Abby cut her eyes quickly to the open laptop. A name just about flew off the page and assaulted Abby. There was a name, without any profile photo. The name was William Campbell, Jr. and it was the first name listed under a column titled, "DNA relatives."

Abby turned to help Sissy as she pulled out a cutting board, tomatoes, lettuce, mayonnaise, white bread, the pitcher of lemonade, salt and pepper and a bag of potato chips. All the makings for a fine lunch.

Sissy and Abby had their backs turned to Belva Ann and Mimi, who were not saying much to each other. Sissy tore a piece of bread in two and gave each half to the dogs. Her Mimi did not reprimand her. She and Belva Ann were too engaged with the computer screen.

Abby cut her eyes at Sissy, and Sissy ignored her. Not now. But out on the porch, Abby was dying to share what she had seen. Abby knew what Belva Ann did not yet know. She cut her eyes at Sissy again, who ever so slightly shook her head. What Abby knew was burning a hole in her stomach.

23

Abby and Sissy took their sandwiches out onto the front porch. Sissy took a huge bite out of her sandwich, mayonnaise decorating both corners of her mouth.

Abby said, "How can you eat at a time like this?"

Sissy answered with a full mouth, "This mater sandwich is the best and I'm starving. But it don't mean I didn't notice. You spied something. Written all over your face. Good thing your Momma had her back to you. She didn't notice you snoopin' like you did."

Abby said, "You heard my mom. She got notified of a DNA relative. One that shares fifty-percent DNA. That means he's her half-brother."

Sissy nodded. "I heard. She must not have realized we heard, though. Otherwise, she'd a smacked that laptop shut when you walked up."

Sissy continued, "So spill, peeping Tom. What'd you see?"

"William Campbell, Jr."

Sissy's eyes widened, "You sure about the name?"

Abby said, "I saw what I saw."

"William Campbell, Jr?"

"Is there an echo in here? I said, that's what I saw."

Sissy's eyes now narrowed. "Same name as Ms. Emmaline's old-man friend?"

Abby too was still slightly disbelieving. "Yeah. Except this one's called junior. That means he was named after his Daddy. Oh my God. That old man and my Grandma..."

Sissy said, matter-of-factly, "Had them a love child."

Abby said, "Meaning, my mom has the same Daddy as William Campbell, Jr."

"Duh. Just different mommas."

Abby said, "Junior's mom is Delia?"

"Sounds right."

Abby was shaking her head. "My Grandma is a liar. A big fat liar."

"Ain't she always claimed as much?"

"But why?"

Sissy raised her eyebrows, "Maybe she'll say. Maybe she won't. But she ain't gonna' be able to lie much longer. Cat's about to climb outa' that bag. Who gonna' be the one to warn Ms Emmaline 'bout the shitstorm what's coming down the pike?

"Me. Has to be me."

"You sure that's a good idea."

"You and I figured this out first. And we ought to come clean, so when Belva Ann lets her have it, Grandma is ready for her. And oh God, Daddy is coming. Yeah, we need to warn her."

"We?"

"Please? If you're there, she'll take it better."

"I don't know about that."

"Just stand with me. You don't have to say anything. Please? Best friend forever."

"You gonna' pull the best friend card?"

"Yeah."

"Well then, if it is gonna' be you, with your bestie at your side, you best hurry, if you gonna' beat your momma to the punch that is."

Abby's eyes got wide, she nodded, then drew a deep breath. "Drive me in the gator."

Sissy took another enormous bite of sandwich and mumbled with a full mouth. "Okay. Bring your lunch."

"I can't eat. My tummy hurts."

"If you don't eat it, I will."

"Okay, Okay, just let's go, now!"

Abby picked up her plate with her uneaten sandwich and the bag of chips while Sissy grabbed their lemonades, shoving the last of her sandwich in her mouth. Abby's stomach still hurt. But the smell of the tomato sandwich also made her mouth water.

Abby had to put both lemonades between her thighs while Sissy drove, and half of each glass splashed onto her thighs as they bounced down the drive to Chickasaw House.

The dogs trotted merrily alongside.

Once Sissy had turned off the gator, Abby handed Sissy the lemonades. Then she secured the bag of chips in her teeth and picked up the plate with her sandwich.

Sissy said, "Looks like you wet your pants." And she giggled.

Abby didn't care. Her tummy hadn't settled on the bumpy ride.

Abby pushed on the door. It still had a way of swinging itself open, like that first day. Bobby had never fixed it.

Emmaline's study door was closed. But it took very little

effort to open. It helped explain how One-eared, donut-head had so easily set himself loose.

The room was dark. No one was sitting at the desk. Freddy hung back at the door, but Belle walked right in and went behind the desk.

Then they heard Emmaline's voice, very softly say, "Belle?"

Abby said, "Grandma?" As she walked toward Belle. There was Emmaline, face down on the floor, forehead resting on the backs of her hands, her gray mane spread over her shoulders, her floral skirt splayed wide. One-Eared Tom was sitting on her butt, inflated donut collar nearly glowing pink in the dim light.

Emmaline raised herself up on her elbows. And for a moment, in the dim light, Abby saw a much younger Emmaline. The moment passed as Emmaline rolled onto her side, Tom jumping to the floor. Then she pushed herself up to a sitting position, crossing her legs and leaning forward, elbows on her knees, chin resting in her hands.

Sissy poked Abby with an elbow.

"Grandma?"

Abby handed Emmaline a half empty glass of lemonade. "Thanks."

"What are you doing on the floor with Tom on your butt?"

"I was taking a cat nap. Get it?"

Emmaline took a sip of lemonade. Abby handed her the sandwich. She said, "For me?"

Sissy said, "It was for Abby, but her tummy hurts so maybe you'd like it. I ate mine. It was mighty fine."

Abby sat down next to her grandma, and Sissy sat down too. Then Belle stretched out on the floor alongside Sissy.

Tom sat next to Emmaline. And miracles of miracles, in came Freddy, and he placed himself right between Emmaline and Abby.

Emmaline said, "Well, I'll be damned. Look at that, Abby. It's Freddy. And isn't this odd? All on the floor. All on one level. And in a circle, too. Circles are magical. Special power in a circle. It's like we three are all witches, and these animals are our familiars."

Sissy said, "Familiars?"

Abby said, "Kind of like in Harry Potter. Magical creatures that assist the witches and warlocks."

Emmaline said, "That's right."

Abby said, "It's a good time then. You would say a propitious time."

Sissy said, "Pro-pich-us? Is that one of them spelling bee words?"

Abby said, "Yeah. It means good timing. But Grandma, we don't have a lot of time to say what we came to say."

Emmaline had taken a bite of the sandwich. But her chewing slowed down. "Okay. Better spit it out then."

Abby said, "You are a story hunter. Well, I am too. You always like hunting for hidden stories. You like looking for the ones no one wants told."

Emmaline stopped chewing. "Yes."

"Turns out, I'm pretty good at it."

"Are you?"

"Don't be mad, Grandma."

"I can't promise that."

"I saw the obituary on your desk back in California."

"Snooping?"

"I wasn't looking for anything in particular. And it didn't mean anything then. But Delia is an unusual name. Pretty name. Last name was common, Campbell."

"Yes."

"Then we met William. William Campbell. And we heard about Delia from him."

"Did you now?"

"And you told us William was an old friend, and that he had been your teacher."

"All true."

"Didn't take a lot of imagining that you and William had been sweethearts. Maybe before Delia came along, or maybe not. Even though, Sissy and I know enough to know you shouldn't be sweethearts with your teacher."

Emmaline nodded.

"But now Mom is researching her DNA."

"I know."

"Well, today she discovered she had a DNA relative. His name is William Campbell, Jr."

Emmaline placed a hand over her mouth. Then said, "I see."

Then they all sat quietly for a moment.

Abby sounded surprised when she said, "That makes William my grandpa?"

Emmaline inhaled deeply, "Don't be angry at him. He didn't know until this morning."

Abby said, "Sissy, am I hearing right? The old man did not know he had a granddaughter?"

Sissy whispered, "Makes sense why this morning he come flying down the drive like he was being chased by hornets."

Abby said, "Grandma, how did you live such a lie all these years? Mimi is down there trying to keep Mom from falling apart. But she won't be able to keep her there forever. We came up here fast as we could to warn you. The chickens are coming home to roost, like any minute now. Sissy and I thought we ought to give you a chance to, y'know, gird your loins. But since she's not here yet, and until she is, you have a chance to explain yourself to me."

Sissy frowned and whispered, "Gird your loins?"

Abby and Emmaline ignored her.

Emmaline said, "You're both too young to understand."

Abby's jaw dropped open, "Grandma, yesterday we found those hash marks. People suffered here. This old house has shame soaked into every wall, every floor, every crooked door. And yet, this old house is beautiful too. We love her. We want to protect her. We want her to love us back. Even now. You and I respect old things. Things with history, history that we want to know. Not just the pretty parts, but the ugly parts. You've got to tell us the full story. Even if it's ugly. And you need to tell us now.'

"I'm so ashamed."

Sissy spoke, "But that makes you a good person, Ms. Emmaline. The opposite of shame is shameless. You ain't shameless. You got regrets. That mean something."

Emmaline's eyes welled up. Then she nodded. "You sweet, dear child. I'll try to tell it all, tell it full, just as you said, Sissy."

Emmaline, strangely enough, took another bite of sandwich, and then a swig of lemonade. She nodded at Sissy and said, "Thank you for the sandwich and lemonade. It is fortifying. Abby, darling, please take the other half."

Abby realized her tummy did feel better. The hard part, her hard part anyway, was done. The tight places in her tummy had relaxed. And her grandma hadn't yelled at her, didn't even seem mad.

Abby said, "Okay." And took the other half of the sandwich. It tasted wonderful, even though the bread had gotten soggy with mayonnaise and tomato juice.

Emmaline winked at her and said, "That's my girl." Then she shook her head, still staring at her granddaughter. "Good God, we are two peas-in-a-pod, snooping around and digging up old bones." Then she sighed, "I had an affair with a married man. There, I said, it. And like most narcissists who engage in such foolishness, I harbored the fantasy that William would leave Delia. Choose me."

Abby said, "He didn't though."

Emmaline grimaced, "The full story?" She sighed. "Delia and I knew each other. Of course, we did. Socially, at least. And she confronted me. She told me that she and William were trying to start a family, and once that ship had sailed, well, I would need to set sail as well. Like off into the sunset."

Emmaline used her hand to indicate a boat sailing away.

Abby said, "I'm confused."

Emmaline added, "It wouldn't be the first time a woman thought a pregnancy would rope and tie down a philandering husband. So, I pointed out that at that present moment, neither one of us was in fact pregnant. But two could play the same game. Stupid as hell, I know. But passion can make you do stupid things, especially in your twenties. Beware that decade, girls. I'm telling you. It's a time when the sex drive makes rational thinking a challenge."

Sissy said, "Play stupid games, win stupid prizes."

"It was a stupid game, true. But I made out just fine. Better than fine. Sissy, Belva Ann and Abby are the best things that ever happened to me. "

Abby said, "But you got pregnant. Why didn't William choose you?"

Emmaline said, "William came to tell me that Delia was pregnant, that he did love her, and that as much as I meant to him, it was time for him to grow up. He had a child coming, and he intended to become a good husband and a better father."

Abby shook her head. "Why didn't you tell him?"

"I didn't know. I promised to leave town, get out of the way and finish my dissertation back in California. I would only have to come back to defend my thesis. But the thing is, once I got home, it wasn't long before I realized I was pregnant, too. Well, I decided not to tell William, because we were both at peace with our decisions. And I surely could not come back to defend my thesis obviously pregnant. So, that was that. Time to put it all behind me and forge ahead as a single mom. I decided to pretend that I had intentionally gotten pregnant by using an anonymous source. People believed my lie. Besides, I always wanted to be a mother. Especially a mother to a girl. And I had a good home, with supportive parents who had the financial means to help. My mother knew the truth. But not my father. Never my dad. It was our secret. Mom's and mine."

Abby repeated, "A woman needs a man, like a fish needs a bicycle."

Emmaline nodded, "I believed it then. And I found I

385

didn't want another man. I was excited about becoming a mother, and then about writing. It seemed like enough."

Sissy added, "Then you saw that Ms. Delia had passed."

"Yes. And so, there was an opportunity. To see if William and I still had a chance to be together. I made a plan, to carefully test the water. Of course, it was never my plan to have you with me Abby, or Belva Ann, or Jim here. I needed time alone with William. I did want to live in this old house again. What were the odds that it was available for rent? It seemed like a good omen. And I was hoping that the magic would return once I got William out here, walking these same paths. But it's true, the arrow of time flows only one direction."

Sissy said, "Mr. William, he didn't take it well I'm thinking. When he found out he had a daughter and granddaughter you never told him about?"

The door to the study swung open nearly soundlessly. Belva Ann was framed by the light coming from the hall. She looked incredibly tall since they were sitting on the floor looking up. Her long arms hung down her sides, her large hands fidgeting.

Abby thought to herself that it was plain as plain could be. Why hadn't she noticed before? Belva Ann was a female version of William.

Belva Ann said, "Mom? Why are you all sitting in some kind of a fairy circle in the dark? Is that Freddy? Oh my God, that is Freddy. He looks so relaxed. And the cat is right there."

Abby said, "He closed the bubble. All by himself. Just like Francis told us he would."

Belva Ann shook her head, "What are you guys doing, casting spells?"

Abby said, "Grandma is helping me finish that story I was writing. The one where she is a witch and Freddy is a wolf, and she was summoning help and protection from someone. You remember the one, Mom."

Belva Ann looked slightly confused, but she was nodding.

Emmaline said, "We're not finishing it. Not yet. Not unless Abby knows how it ends. Do you?"

Abby shook her head.

Belva Ann said, "May I join the circle? It looks rather cozy."

The next moment, another figure quietly appeared in the doorway. Mimi said, "My goodness. What in the world y'all got going on here?"

Mimi added, "I was thinking maybe it weren't my place to come up here, but looking at y'all sitting there like you tellin' ghost stories around a campfire, makes me think I don't want to miss out."

Emmaline laughed. "Come on in, close the door. I don't want the cat to get out again."

Belva Ann grabbed the chair to the desk and pulled it over to the circle while Sissy scooted back. She said, "Mimi, I am not going to let you sit on the floor." Then she gestured at Mimi and then at the chair."

Mimi said, "Why thank you, Ms. Belva Ann, I think I will."

Abby scooted back so her mother could join the circle. Belva Ann found herself sitting next to One-Eared Tom, who swiveled his head around in his ridiculous sugar-sprinkled plastic inflatable donut, eyes in slits, staring at her intently. Then he lowered his head, as if bowing politely and gave her a gentle head butt.

Belva Ann instinctively began to stroke his head.

Emmaline said, "He likes you." And she reached over and took Belva Ann's hand. She gave it a squeeze.

Emmaline said, "Abby, tell your mother the story. I'm so tired of my own story. And you always make me look better than I am. You make me powerful. When the truth is that I am not. I'm more like this old house, fragile."

Abby added, "But a survivor."

Then Abby began, she told the story as best as she could. She even used her storytelling voice.

* * *

That night Emmaline ordered pizza to be delivered to Chickasaw House. Abby was glad. The three of them were spent, but at peace. There had been no yelling, no anger. Regrets. Yes. There had been sadness and shame and a few tears, too.

It was an odd sight, sitting on the front porch watching the pizza delivery car come bumping up the rutted drive. When the car stopped, Freddy ran out to greet it. The driver rolled down his window. He said, "My God. Is that a wolf?"

All three women sang out in a chorus, "He's a German Shephard!"

Then Emmaline got up and walked to the car. "He's friendly, but you don't need to get out if you're concerned."

The young man awkwardly handed her the pizza through the window, and she handed him his tip.

He said, "Thanks for the note about the driveway. I never would have found the place. Wow, look at that house, it looks old."

Emmaline turned to look at Chickasaw House in a way that was almost comical. Like she was just noticing the age of a house she was living in. She said, "I think of it as a beautiful example of Greek Revival architecture. But then the Virginia landscape is full of such examples."

The driver said, "If that old house could talk, bet it would have a mess of stories to tell."

Again, Emmaline seemed surprised and impressed by the young man. "I've thought the very same thing!" She gave the car a fond little pat, as if it was a dog, then turned and walked back to the porch, pizza box held high.

Belva Ann shook her head and sighed. "Oh, Mom."

Emmaline said, "I'll get the lemonade and a stack of napkins. We'll eat it right out of the box."

They ate pizza, reclined in their seats and said little until they had each polished off two slices. But then Emmaline said, "I know you are going to be anxious seeing Jim tomorrow. But oddly enough, I have a good feeling about the timing."

Belva Ann sniffed, "Mom, you are an optimist."

"Here me out. He's coming with his tail between his legs. He didn't have losing his job on his bingo card. He'll feel terrible. He'll likely be engaged in self-flagellation. But, when he arrives here, to all our current drama, he'll discover that there are those, such as I, who are guilty and doing penance for much greater sins."

"Good grief, Mom. You do have a way with words. Vivid image there of Jim scourging his back with a cat-o-nine-tails."

Abby was trying to listen, to catch all the phrases and words, to remember them so she could look them up. But she was struggling to keep her eyes open. And when her head fell forward all by itself, she jerked violently upright in her chair.

Belva Ann stood up and walked over to Abby. "What a day we had! Let's get you and that big goofy dog put to bed."

Abby didn't argue. She took her mom's outstretched hands and let herself be tugged up onto her feet. Belva Ann held one of Abby's hands as they trudged up the stairs, then walked with Abby into her room. She helped Abby find her pajamas, then went with her to the bathroom, and put the lid down on the toilet and sat down while Abby washed her face and brushed her teeth. She hadn't done any of those things with Abby in a very, very long time. Abby was so grown up. And so smart. And all the worries she had harbored, about Abby having no friends, about Abby not functioning at school, alienating her teachers as well as her classmates, well, this summer, this weird summer, had been just what Abby needed to find her own way to change.

Belva Ann felt the burden of her earlier fears had been lightened. Abby was exceptional. Abby had a gift. Of course, Belva Ann had to be certain that Jim understood. And maybe now that he had lost his job, been fired, maybe he had developed the capacity to see things more clearly, about himself, and about his daughter. She wasn't sure how her news would affect his attitude toward Emmaline.

They returned to the bedroom to find Freddy already on the bed.

Belva Ann went to turn down the sheets for Abby. She was horrified, "Ay-yi-yi! Your bed looks like a red-clay field, plowed and ready for planting."

Abby said, "Good one, Mom."

Belva Ann said, "Tomorrow we will wash all of this. But not tonight."

Abby crawled in, and Freddy wriggled his way up against her back, and she was gone.

* * *

After breakfast, Belva Ann and Emmaline shooed Abby out of the house to go join Sissy. When Sissy had finished her chores, Mimi handed them each a pail and gloves.

"I need you young'uns to pick me two pailfuls of blackberries from back of the pump house. Them canes are heavy with fruit. You be sure and put on them gloves. Them brambles is wicked. Don't pick any berries that are close to the ground where critters might have peed on 'em. And only bring me the ones that are fully black. I'll make a couple of cobblers tomorrow. I got to soak 'em overnight in cold water to kill all the bugs before I can use 'em."

Sissy said, "We got ice cream?"

Mimi said, "I'll tell Francis to pick up a couple gallons of vanilla."

Abby followed Sissy back behind the bee boxes, back behind the well house, and Mimi was right, up against a fence was a huge stand of blackberry canes.

Sissy put on her gloves and nodded her chin to indicate Abby do the same. She said, "I saw a big old snake back here last summer. Must have been a coach whip, long and skinny and black. Made me jump. I don't much care for snakes. I do love a blackberry cobbler though, long as it got lots of ice cream on it."

391

"I don't know what a coach whip is, but we have rattle-snakes in California and they're venomous. Mom and Grand-ma keep snakebite kits in their gloveboxes. If I see a snake, I run first and ask questions later."

Sissy grinned, "Me too."

Abby said, "I've never picked blackberries before."

"If it weren't for the cobbler, I'd be happy to let the birds have all the fun."

Sissy started plucking off berries and dropping them into her pail. "Plunk, plunk, plunk."

Abby followed her lead. Sissy was saying, "Your Daddy comes today? Are you nervous for him?"

"Why would I be nervous for him?"

"Plunk, plunk, plunk."

"He be feeling low, being fired and such. And soon I expect be finding out about William."

Abby said, "Ouch! Shit!"

"Don't go closing your fingers too firm-like, them thorns will push right on through your glove."

"Now you tell me."

Abby took her glove off, examined the spot, then stuck her finger in her mouth. She put the glove back on and started picking again. Now that the bottom of the pail was covered in berries, they no longer made a sound. She was pulling big fat blackberries off the canes. They were beautiful. Every now and then she would flush a little bird out of the bushes. She saw butterflies and an assortment of other bugs. Belle and Freddy snuffled around the lower branches. Belle even gingerly plucked off a couple of berries and ate them. Freddy didn't see the point but did lift his leg and pee on them. Which made Abby laugh.

Abby pointed at the dog and said, "Mimi was right. Don't pick from the low branches!'

She and Sissy picked in silence for a moment before Abby said, "Everyone will know everything soon, about grandma and William. And I think that's a good thing."

Sissy nodded, "Will be weird for a time. But folks will get used to the idea. You think Ms. Emmaline and William, they gonna' be a couple again?"

Abby shook her head. "Grandma said, you can't go back again."

Sissy made a noise. "That Mr. William sure looks like a lonely old man to me. But he got some territory to cover taking in the shock of the news, what with having to speak to Junior about his and Emmaline's affair. They'll be mad on their Momma's account, and you can't blame 'em."

"He said he had another son, too."

"Junior is on that website already, so Mr. William will have to answer some painful questions real soon."

Abby hadn't thought of that. "Boy, that DNA test is a tattletale. It reveals all sorts of things that used to be hidden forever."

Sissy said, "I been to Monticello. I seen the Sally exhibit."

Abby nodded, "But history isn't just stuff that's hundreds of years old."

"We just learned that up close and personal-like."

Abby raised her gloved finger. "Don't do anything you wouldn't want published on the front page of a newspaper."

"Never heard that one. Never got the newspaper delivered out here, neither."

"You get the idea."

"Yeah, I do."

It took them about an hour or so to fill both buckets. By that time, they were sweaty and despite great care, were nursing sore spots on fingers and scratches on arms. Blackberry picking had lost its charm.

The girls handed over their buckets to Mimi and raced back to the pasture to catch Bunny and Buttermilk.

Getting up on Bunny and Buttermilk felt like getting out of school. The mowers were gone today, and the fields were flattened with cut hay, perfuming the air.

When Bunny and Buttermilk hit their special hill, they flew. It no longer felt scary to Abby. Sissy had been right from the start; it would be hard to fall off Buttermilk and she hadn't. Abby no longer gripped with her knees. All her scabs had fallen off. She had not made any new rubs on her legs, either.

At the top of the hill, they stopped to enjoy the spectacular view, waiting for the dogs to catch up to them, which they shortly did. The dogs did their usual flop, then rolled and rolled in the newly cut grass alongside the path, kicking their hind legs and sliding on the hill.

Abby said, "I'm going to miss this view. I'm going to miss you and Belle and Bunny and Buttermilk."

Sissy said, "I'm going to miss you and Freddy."

Abby said, "Best friends forever. Don't forget!"

"Girl, you are unforgettable. I got a pretty good imagination, but I couldn't of made you up if I tried."

"And when they made you, they broke the mold."

Sissy said, "Now, what do that mean? What's mold got to do with anything?"

"Not mold, like green bread. Mold like when you pour Jello into a Jello mold."

"You break a Jello mold, you likely make a hell of a mess. You sayin' I'm a mess?"

"It just means you're like, one in a million."

Abby said, "You have to promise to work hard at school. I want you to be my roommate at UVA."

"And you got to promise not to piss off your teachers and get your ass expelled."

They laughed.

They got the horses put up and made tomato sandwiches on white bread again. Then Mimi gave them slices of home-made peach pie with real whipped cream on top.

After they were stuffed as full as they could be, they took the gator up to Chickasaw House. Abby had wondered if her Mom and Daddy had gotten back yet. She halfway expected Emmaline to be there, working in her study, Tom sitting next to her laptop. But no one was home.

Abby said, "You want to toss the frisbee?"

Sissy shook her head. "I want to see those hash marks, up there in that attic space."

Abby understood. She led Sissy up the steep dark stairs. She got her phone out, and found the flashlight app. The dogs got quiet, as if they understood something solemn about the moment, but dutifully followed.

Abby led Sissy to the beam and showed her. Then to another. Sissy ran her fingers over the marks, then began to wander, examining others. She looked up too. Then she pointed toward the peak where there was a small fan shaped window.

Abby said, "We should clean that thing off, get some more light in here. I wonder if it opens."

Sissy said, "Bet it don't. Just for show. Ain't no air up here. I sure do feel for anyone who got shut up here."

When Sissy got to the furthest corner, she motioned for Abby to come look. She said, "More hash marks here, too, but something else scratched into the wood, pretty faint."

The two bent down and shone a light on it. She and Sissy found themselves both bending their heads to the side.

Abby said, "Bird? Someone drew a bird?"

"Appears so."

"What with?"

Sissy shrugged, "I'm about to suffocate up here."

They walked back down the narrow stairs, and once through the door, the air conditioning and light washed over them.

Sissy drew a deep breath. "Feels good to breathe free air. Those marks, they filled me with anger."

Abby said, "Made me feel afraid."

Sissy said, "You suppose, there was enough good in this old house to come level to all of the evil?"

Abby shook her head, "Don't know."

Sissy said, "This old lady, this house, Chickasaw House, do you see a white lady when you think of her? Cause I see an old black lady. I see a version of my Mimi."

Abby said, "I see an old white lady. But white or black, not for one moment did I think of a man. Wonder what that means?"

Sissy said, "It means it was mostly the women who suffered. Old Robert, he brought the suffering to them."

The two girls sat down on the stairs, each on a different step, each with a dog sitting faithfully next to them. Each girl found themselves placing a palm on the head of their dogs, as if conferring benedictions. Or maybe it was the reverse. The dogs were bestowing something on them. And whatever it was, it worked. They calmed and became thoughtful.

Sissy said, "Each one of them women believed this house was rightfully their house. This was what they fought for, not just for themselves, but for their children. We first was thinking of some kind of love story. Then that crazy old Robert Taylor thinking he could have his cake and eat it, too. But we thought he was in love with Lucy. But I'm thinking now that the only love in this story is the love of a mother for her children. Having a home, well, that means a lot. Security for one thing. Property. Something that can't be taken away. Something to be passed down."

Abby said, "Robert, legally had the power, but not a lick of sense, clearly."

Sissy nodded, "This place that could have been right close to a heaven, he made into hell."

Abby added, "Into a prison."

Abby furrowed her brow, "He must have felt shame though. Because in the end, he deeded Lucy's children that land. Land where your house got built. Land you still farm. Trained his children in trades so they could buy their own freedom."

Sissy added, "And feeling shame, that's a sign that he weren't shameless. Man felt repentant enough to try and do right by both women in the end. I guess he weren't all bad."

Sissy nodded, "Maybe this poor old lady, Chickasaw

House, she absorbed the sadness from both Lucy and Lotty. She's a bit of both. There was pride and beauty in this old house, but shame and bitterness, too. So much shame and bitterness that neither branch of the Taylor family want to live in this old house they fought so hard for. Neither side."

Abby said, "I think I know what this old lady house needs; redemption."

24

Belva Ann handed Abby an armload of bedding, warm from the dryer. "Go make your bed. And going forward, can you please not drag the great outdoors onto your sheets?"

"Sure."

"If you must let the dog onto the bed, at least wipe off his feet."

Abby nodded, "When does Daddy get here?"

"Any minute. Mom's made Thai flatbreads and salad for dinner."

"Are you nervous?"

"Go make your bed."

Abby turned and headed upstairs with her fresh bed linens. Freddy trotted after her as if he could help. Abby tried to make her bed at top speed. The fitted sheet refused to go on and she fought with it until she realized she had it turned the wrong way. But once on, she tugged the rest together quickly, then thundered her way down the stairs because Freddy had started barking.

Freddy beat Abby to the front door, but Emmaline and Belva Ann made it there before them both. Freddy squeezed himself between Emmaline and Belva Ann, no longer barking, but now whoo-whooing with excitement.

Abby was behind her mom when she heard her grandma say to Belva Ann, "Remember, a word once let out of its cage, can never be whistled back again."

Belva Ann grimly nodded to her mother and then walked out to greet Jim. Abby knew her mom *was* nervous, but this seemed like something more than nerves. What words were her grandma afraid her mom would "let out of a cage?"

The car stopped by the front porch, and a back door opened. Jim stepped out. Freddy trotted halfway to the car, then stopped and turned as if waiting for Abby.

Seeing her Daddy again, knowing he had just been fired, filled Abby with a new sensation. Daddies were supposed to protect their children. But Abby wanted to protect him, but from what, or whom?

Abby had tried to follow her mom, but her grandma had put a hand on her arm to stop her.

"Abby darling, let them have a moment or two."

Abby whispered, "Daddy has never had something like this happen to him."

"Something better will come from it. Every new beginning, comes from some other beginnings end."

"Did you just make that up?"

"No. It's Seneca. But it is true. Keep it in your back pocket. I promise you will need it at some point in your life."

Abby briefly wondered how anyone could know what words to keep in cages, and what words to keep in back pockets. Words mattered, but man, knowing when to use them could get complicated.

Abby relaxed a little as she watched her mom and daddy hug, especially when the hug lasted longer than usual.

The driver turned the car around and slowly made his way back down the bumpy path, as her mom and daddy stood next to his luggage, earnestly talking. They weren't looking at Abby or her grandmother.

Emmaline pulled a reluctant Abby away from the doorway.

"Help me set the table." Then she called Freddy.

Freddy at least could be "whistled back." Freddy didn't have words, and maybe Freddy was considered "unstable," but Freddy never lied to anyone about anything.

* * *

Dinner was awkward. It was like they were all strangers. Abby's daddy asked polite questions, but no one talked about the huge things, the important things.

Belva Ann and Emmaline never mentioned anything about Jim being fired, or William or DNA or *any* of Emmaline's lies, big or small.

Jim, too, did not speak about being fired, or the fact that both he and Belva Ann were now unemployed.

Abby answered her Daddy's questions, but also felt confused about how much she should or should not elaborate. She was beginning to feel frustrated by the whole charade, like she should bang her fist on the table or yell something totally inappropriate, something to break the weirdness.

Instead, she focused on unsuccessfully spearing a tiny bit of avocado with her fork.

Finally, Belva Ann said, "Jim, after dinner I'll take you up to the attic with the flashlight. I told you about the hash marks, but Sissy has since discovered a faint etching of a bird. Isn't that something?

Jim frowned. "A timeless image of freedom, birds."

Abby said, "That's good, Daddy. I didn't think of that."

Emmaline said, "It makes sense though, doesn't it?"

Abby put down her fork. She said, "Yeah. It makes me think of something else Sissy showed me. It doesn't have anything to do with the house or what happened here, though."

Emmaline said, "A non-sequitur?"

"Yes."

"So, let's hear it."

"When Sissy fills the water trough for the horses, she always puts a long piece of wood in the trough."

Jim said, "And why is that?"

"She said it's a squirrel ladder. See, the squirrels drink from the trough, too. And they sometimes fall in. The sides are smooth. They can't get traction to climb out. Without the ladder, they drown."

Belva Ann said, "How terrible. But how thoughtful of Sissy to make sure they don't."

"Sissy said a squirrel doesn't deserve to drown just because it took a fall."

No one responded. Abby had that same sensation she used to have in Ms. Pierce's classroom. She knew she had said something interesting, maybe even profound, but somehow it had not landed as it should have.

Emmaline exhaled loudly then said, "I'm sure there isn't a soul on earth who hasn't needed that metaphorical ladder at one time or another. Anyone want more salad?"

When no one responded, Emmaline rose, taking the salad bowl with her.

She said over her shoulder, "I made Mimi's banana pudding for dessert, in your honor, Jim."

* * *

In the morning, Abby and Freddy came down to the kitchen to find her mom and dad sitting at the kitchen table drinking coffee. One-eared Tom was sitting on the counter staring at Jim with slitted eyes, as if he wasn't sure if he approved of him. Without the inflatable donut, he looked like the street tough that he was.

"Where's Grandma?"

Her Dad said, "Well, good morning to you, too."

Just then, Emmaline came in through the kitchen door, carrying a brown paper bag.

"Mimi taught me how to make biscuits from scratch this morning."

Tom jumped down and trotted after Emmaline.

Emmaline put the bag on the table, then fetched plates and napkins, putting a tub of butter and a jar of Francis' honey in the middle.

She said, "Butter them up while they're hot."

Belva Ann said, "Wow, Mom, you must have gotten up at the crack of dawn."

Emmaline nodded, "So worth it. Wait 'til you taste these!"

Tom then jumped up on the table and went straight to Jim.

Belva Ann quickly picked up the cat and placed it on the floor.

Jim said, "I swear, cats know I'm not a fan, and yet they come right over. I think it's to torture me."

No one said a thing in reply.

Abby put the kettle on for a cup of tea. While she waited for the whistle, she helped herself to a warm biscuit. She slathered it with butter and drizzled it with honey, noting the room had once again gone quiet.

Emmaline broke the silence. "Jim, what did you make of the attic? Did you find the hash marks and the bird?"

"I did. I felt a bit like an archeologist holding up a torch in a cave and finding drawings."

Belva Ann added, "But the cave paintings aren't dark, metaphorically speaking. Those marks in the attic, well, they are."

Emmaline breezily said, "Time flies over us, but leaves its shadows behind. That's Hawthorne."

Jim scowled, "Meaning?"

Belva Ann answered for her mother. "Slavery left a big shadow, and probably shades too. In fact, I wouldn't be surprised if this old house really did have a few shades floating about."

Jim said, "Annie don't fill your daughter's head with nonsense. Abby, there are no such things as ghosts. But there *is* history. And this house *is* historic. That's enough to make it worth studying."

Emmaline said, "I just knew you would be interested in the history of the place."

"Well, that much is true."

Belva Ann changed the subject. "Mom, Jim and I are heading out after breakfast. I thought we should check out skyline drive."

Abby started to say something, because there had been a discussion about having a picnic there, but Emmaline cut her a meaningful glance.

She said, "That's a wonderful idea!"

"After our drive, Jim wanted to try some local cuisine for lunch."

Emmaline smiled, "You mean, find a place where you can eat meat?"

Belva Ann smiled and nodded. "Likely fried."

Emmaline said, "You kids enjoy. I'll be busy all day working on my project, and Abby and Freddy will be with Sissy and Belle, Bunny and Buttermilk, roaming around these hills free as a feral child."

Belva Ann laughed, "My neat freak child *has* gone a bit feral. And now I've ruined things by washing the red clay off her sheets."

Jim said, "I may find myself going feral, too."

Emmaline chuckled, "Might do you a world of good. I've always found a bit of howling at the moon to be cathartic."

Jim smiled. It was a smile that seemed to release tension from the room. It did not last long, but Abby thought it was a start.

He said, "Yes, but Emmaline, *you* own a wolf."

And the women answered in chorus, "He's a German Shepherd!"

* * *

Later, Abby and Emmaline waved at Belva Ann and Jim as they got into their car.

Once out of sight, Abby turned to her grandma. "Does Daddy know everything? You know, the truth?"

"Yes. Well, if I left anything out, Belva Ann will get him up to speed before they return."

"Everyone is angry at everybody. Aren't they? Mom's mad at Daddy. Daddy is mad at himself."

Emmaline put her hand on Abby's head again, like she would pet Freddy.

"And everyone is mad at me."

"I'm not angry at you, Grandma."

"No, I don't expect you are. Although, I've deprived you of a grandfather all this time. Maybe someday you'll discover you are indeed angry about that. And certainly, William is furious at me. But you'll never guess who has leapt to my defense?"

"Mimi?"

"Mimi has been a wise counselor. But no. It was Jim. You could have knocked me over with a feather."

"Daddy?"

"He told Belva Ann that because of my lies, both outright and lies by omission, William never had to give my existence another thought after I moved back to California. He had no stain on his career. Plus, his guilt about 'jumping over the traces' put him on the straight and narrow with Delia, which helped in his marriage going forward. Because of my lie of omission, there would be no scarlet letter for William."

"Scarlet letter?"

"Hawthorne. You'll read it in high school."

"He never had to give you a second thought. Are you saying that William never thought of you? All those years? Really, Grandma?"

Emmaline nodded, "He said so himself. But he *was* angry when he said it, so it may or may not be true. But what is true is that when I did not finish my degree, he did not enquire why. He was, I am sure, relieved. He could move on. He closed that door with relief and tried to forget it all. And the thing is, I did not pine for him. I was in love with Belva Ann, and I had my wonderful parents. And I turned my thesis into a novel. I remember it as an exciting time."

"But now his sons will know what he did. He can't lie about mom's existence."

"There are no secrets that time does not reveal". Time and DNA testing in this case. Because I did not tell William I was pregnant, he never had to lie to his children. He did not know about Belva Ann. I'm the liar. Everyone can be mad at me."

"I think I get why Daddy defended you. You lied to protect William. You probably thought it was a noble lie. But I'm not sure it was. Doesn't your lie make you like Jefferson's family lying for him? You were protecting a man who didn't deserve protection."

"And you say this because…"

"He was your teacher. Even I know that makes him worse than you for doing… you know."

Emmaline nodded. "You have a valid point."

"I do?"

"Yes. But I am not guiltless. Now, as to your father getting fired, he is not without guilt either. For a man as good at his job as your dad was, to be fired, well, it's obvious that being good or smart was not enough. Time for introspection, for both of us. But it's what happens next that matters most."

"Okay."

"Mistakes, and I have made plenty, well, they are simply portals of discovery. 'If you dive into the wreckage of your worst deeds, you might find survivors unaccounted for.' Isn't that a marvelous quote? I can't recall who said it."

"Grandma, you're overloading my brain again."

Emmaline continued, "In order to decide what comes next, Jim and I are going to be delving into our own wrecks."

"Grandma, do you ever say anything, like, original?"

Emmaline smiled, "If I am seeking wisdom, the last person I should look to is myself."

"Then tell me why I should listen to you at all?"

"Because I can repeat more wise quotes than you!" Abby looked like she thought her head would explode. "Poor darling. Why don't you go ride with Sissy?"

Abby couldn't wait to call Freddy and head down the path to Sissy's.

* * *

It was a very hot day. Abby and Sissy didn't gallop their hill, but just let the horses walk, and Bunny and Buttermilk didn't even break into a jog. But they did stop at the top to enjoy the view. The dogs had their noses down, walking in circles and wagging their tails. But then they flopped down on the grass, bellies up to the sun, kicking their feet and rubbing their backs.

Sissy said, "Shhhhh."

Abby thought that was weird as she wasn't saying anything.

But the dogs got up and froze.

Then she heard it.

Sissy whispered, "They's giggling."

"Who?"

Then Abby heard it, too, and whispered back. "Children? Some kids are up here?"

Sissy shook her head. "Foxes. I think it's coming from that way. Maybe we can get closer." She looked at the dogs and said, "Stay."

Then she said to Abby, "Follow me."

Abby followed Sissy and Buttermilk along a ridgeline, staying in the shadow of the trees. Sissy held her hand up, and they all stopped, including the dogs, who had not stayed, but were keeping a distance. She put her finger to her lips and pointed.

Below them four foxes looked like they were playing a game of tag.

They ran in big circles, they body-slammed each other, getting rolled in the grass, they jumped in the air and reversed the direction of the chase. All the while laughing and giggling like children.

Abby felt the hairs rise on her arms. These were not dreams of squirrels and mice, although not so far from those dreams. The foxes were sounding like humans, playing like humans, but in their natural state, wild things. Sissy and Abby exchanged a glance, grinning.

Then out of the woods came another weird noise, not laughing, but sounding like a bark combined with a shriek. The four foxes darted off.

Sissy said, "Momma called them back. Den is over that way." And she pointed.

"Those were babies?"

"Teenagers, full of themselves."

"Wow."

"We got lucky to see that."

"Why didn't Belle know they were there?"

"She's a scent hound, not a sight hound Also, you got to remember I got her cause she wouldn't hunt."

"That was magical."

"I think so, too. There's much that goes on that we don't get to be a part of or know about or understand. But knowing that much, well, it makes life a wonder. Makes me feel small in this big old world."

"Humbled. Mastery begins with humility."

Sissy nodded, "I guess that's right. The best horsemen I've ever met were real humble."

"So, if mastery *begins* with humility, and the real masters are *still* humble…"

Sissy smiled. "Means the good ones never lose it. Which means they are open to the possibility that there is still more to know, that they still can get better."

"And that they still can be wrong."

"I guess that, too."

"Grandma said if you aren't humble enough, life has a way of teaching you to be."

"Okay."

"She meant *me* when she said that. *You* don't need lessons in humility. You need lessons in reading and writing. That and the old "seat of the pants to the seat of the chair" time studying until you get your fair share of that mastery."

"I do need to read and write better. But that was sweet of you to say. Thanks, bestie."

"No, thank *you* for the best summer of my life."

25

Abby had taken a shower and put on a pair of clean shorts and a tee shirt and padded down the stairs barefoot, her hair wet and pulled into a ponytail, Freddy at her heels.

She had already told Emmaline all about seeing the foxes and hearing them laughing and she was still reliving the scene in her mind. The whole thing was dreamlike, and she was afraid it would disappear from her memory the way some dreams did. If she could tell her mom and dad too, maybe that would help cement the memory, make it like a video she could replay in her head years from now.

She found Emmaline in her study, but she wasn't working, she was on the phone. Emmaline held a finger up to Abby, then said a few words and hung up.

"That was Mimi."

"And?"

"Well, she had invited us down for blackberry cobbler with ice cream tonight, but plans have changed."

"Bummer. Sissy and I literally bled for those cobblers."

"Mimi says we are in for a huge storm. Radar shows a big red blob heading our way."

"A red blob? Grandma, what does that mean?"

"It means no blackberry cobbler tonight at Mimi's. But no worries. I'm going to make veggie rollups for lunch tomorrow, and I bought enough to feed a crowd. I told Mimi to come on up midday tomorrow with Francis and Sissy and bring that cobbler and ice cream."

"You know that's not what I meant."

"A big red blob means the storm is serious enough that Francis is helping Sissy put all those horses in the old barn. Sissy worries about them getting struck by lightning. Evidently, they don't put the horses in that barn very often."

"I wish I could help."

"Well, you can help us here."

Just then all the lights went off.

Emmaline said, "Isn't that odd? It's not even raining yet."

The two of them walked over to a wall plate and flicked the switches several times to demonstrate that yes, indeed, the power was out.

"Abby, let's go look for flashlights and candles. Hey, at least we have a gas stove. All we need are matches, and we're 'cooking' with gas.'"

Abby used her phone to search through the dimly lit pantry, while Emmaline rummaged through the kitchen drawers. They did not find a flashlight. But they did find a couple large dust-coated candles. One was scented. And they found a box of matches, the long kind you use for fireplaces.

Just then Jim called from the front of the house, "Anybody home!"

Abby and Emmaline walked into the foyer, each carrying a candle. Freddy trailed after them, panting.

Emmaline cheerfully said, "You two have a good day?"

Jim answered, "We did, although this heat is unreal. The air is so heavy I feel like I'm breathing soup."

Belva Ann asked, "Is it me, or is it stuffy in here?"

Jim frowned, "Why are you two carrying candles?"

"Ah, well, the power went out."

Jim said, "Does that happen often?"

Emmaline smiled, "Nope. But as they say in the south, we are 'fixin' to have us a gulley-washer."

Belva Ann chuckled, "Oh, Mom."

Jim said, "But it's not even raining. Are you saying the power went out preemptively?"

"I suppose I am. But Abby and I found two candles and a box of matches. Hope everyone's phones are charged."

Abby brightened. "I just charged mine while I was in the shower, and I have a flashlight app."

Emmaline said, "Hooray! You are our girl scout! Let's make a big salad for dinner and eat out on the porch where we won't be so hot."

Jim said, "I hope the storm clears the air."

Belva Ann said, "Honey, let's see if we can open some windows and prop the doors open to get some cross ventilation in the house, otherwise sleeping tonight might be impossible."

Emmaline said, "You two work on that while Abby helps me make dinner."

When they finally settled on the front porch with their salads and lemonade, the air had noticeably cooled. Freddy sat next to Abby, and Tom sat in the open door to the house, his tail curled around his feet.

The wind picked up. Emmaline said, "That feels divine."

Jim said, "Sorry we couldn't get a single window open; painted shut. At least we propped open the two doors downstairs, and we did get those doors to your porch upstairs propped open."

"Thank you. That ought to cool the house down."

Belva Ann said, "I forgot to tell you that we spoke to Bobby Taylor today."

Abby said, "And I forgot to tell you about the laughing foxes!"

Emmaline turned to Belva Ann, "What did Bobby have to say?"

"Not much. We did tell him we were charmed by the house and wanted to talk to him about it."

Jim added, "I invited him to come to lunch here tomorrow. I hope that's okay."

Belva Ann interjected, "Mom, you don't need to cook anything. I can take care of everything."

"No need. I already invited the Taylors to come up. We've got gracious plenty. But you can help me fix the rollups. Mimi is bringing homemade blackberry cobbler and ice cream for dessert."

Abby was shaking her head. "Bobby Taylor?"

Belva Ann said, "You think that will work out okay? We really want to talk to Bobby, you know, privately."

"I think you'll get your chance."

Jim shrugged. "You know him better than we do."

Emmaline deflected, "Abby, tell your parents about the laughing foxes."

Abby did her best to tell her story, and to make it sound as magical as it felt. She was sure she had fallen short. But when she looked over at her grandmother, she could see the slightest nod of approval.

Abby finished her story, and her mom made the right sort of noises of appreciation. Even her dad said something nice.

Just then, Abby smelled that smell.

She announced, "Petrichor!"

Emmaline nodded, "The wind has brought us the smell of the rain. The storm is close. We'd best get inside. We can have dessert in the dining room."

Emmeline stood up, "Just stack the dishes in the sink. I'll light the stovetop. We can at least have a cup of tea with our dessert."

They reconvened in the dining room a few minutes later with cups of Constant Comment.

Tom oddly positioned himself inside the fireplace. Freddy stood next to Abby's chair looking worried. The animals must have smelled the storm too.

Emmaline brought in an iced lemon loaf cake along with forks and plates and napkins.

She said, "I want you to know this is the last of the lemon loaves Abby and I made on arrival."

"Grandma, that's sad. It means we're on the last bit of our magical summer."

Belva Ann said, "Abby, the magic doesn't end with summer."

Abby nodded, "I guess that's true. Grandma will still ask people to tell their stories, and she'll serve tea and baked goods, and she'll write things down so that those stories will get told. And I'm going to do the same. Well, I'm not sure about the baking part. But I'm going to look for stories, and I'm going to write them down."

Emmaline smiled. "Bravo. Well done, young grasshopper."

Abby said, "Grasshopper?"

Belva Ann laughed, "Cultural reference."

Emmaline said, "Look it up."

Jim took a bite of cake. "Delicious, Emmaline."

Just then Abby felt the hair rise on her head and arms. Emmaline made a startled noise and then lightning lit up the room. "KABOOM!" The noise was deafening; the house seemed to shake on its foundations.

Jim stood up, as if there were a place to go. Just then, in a flash, through the painted shut window, hissing and emitting a sulfurous odor, came a ball of fire. It was the size of a basketball. It rolled across the floor. Just as a ball would do. It traveled straight into the fireplace where with a whoosh, it disappeared.

Jim said, "Good God!"

Belva Ann shouted, "What in God's name was that?"

And everyone looked at Emmaline. As if somehow, she had something to do with it or at least had an explanation.

Emmaline hoarsely said, "Great balls of fire." As if that explained what they had just experienced.

Jim said, "Like the Jerry Lee Lewis song?"

Belva Ann said, "It came right through the closed window. I can still smell it. Sulphur. Like it came directly from hell."

Jim said, "I'll tell you what, I'll never again stand near a window in a lightning storm."

Emmaline pointed to the fireplace. "Where's Tom? Wasn't he sitting there?"

Abby cried out, "Where's Freddy? Freddy's gone. Grandma, Freddy is having a panic attack, you know he is. We have to find him."

Then, like a tap being turned on, a hard rain began outside, with accompanying lightning and thunder.

Emmaline cried out, "Oh, Tom!"

Jim said, "Now, calm down. There's no cat carcass in the fireplace. The two of them are likely under someone's bed, hiding."

Emmaline said, "Abby and Belva Ann, you search upstairs. Jim and I will look down here."

They all ran from the room in a panic, calling out both Freddy and Tom's names. (As if the cat would ever have come when called!)

When Abby and Belva Ann came back down, they found Jim and Emmaline in the kitchen, the two lit candles sitting on plates on the countertop. The room smelled of pumpkin spice.

Emmaline had put a towel over Jim's shoulders and had one of those large black trash bags out.

Belva Ann said, "What are you doing?

"I'm making Jim a raincoat."

"Mom, that's crazy. Jim, you cannot go out in that storm. It's too dangerous."

Emmaline cut a hole for Jim's head and slid it on.

Abby said, "I'll go. Daddy, he's my dog. Mine and Emmaline's. We took an oath to protect him. Let me go look for him. He's having a panic attack. He's scared. He'll come to me, Daddy."

Jim said, "I'm not letting you go out in that storm. He's probably not gone too far. I bet he's crawled under the front porch."

Belva Ann said, "Jim, Freddy will come back all by himself once he gets over the shock. I mean, we all just had a near death experience. It's not just Freddy who is shook up."

"I know all that. That's why Abby needs her dog. She needs to know he is safe."

Emmaline turned to Abby and said with a stern voice, "Let your dad do this."

Emmaline and Belva Ann exchanged a glance that silenced Belva Ann's protest.

Abby wiped tears from her eyes, and said, "Okay. Thank you, Daddy."

Belva Ann sighed, "Okay, so now I get to stress out over the dog, the cat, *and* now my husband, all being out in that storm? I'm still shaking like a leaf over that ball of fire."

Jim said, "I'll just look in the obvious places and then come back."

Abby handed her dad her phone. She said, "Use the flashlight app. Use it to scan under the porch. You might not see Freddy, he's so dark, but you'll see his eyes reflecting back at you."

"Thanks, I wouldn't have thought of that."

Jim headed out the front door into a dusk made darker by the storm. His frame was briefly silhouetted by a flash of lightning. The three women stood in the doorway for a minute, straining to see outside while Abby shouted for Freddy. Abby then ran to the kitchen and shouted for Freddy from the back door. But the wind had gotten crazy strong, and the propped open door suddenly slammed shut in her face.

The dusky sky turned a strange greenish color and then hail began to fall.

Belva Ann grabbed her phone and called Jim on Abby's phone. Surprisingly, he picked right up.

"Come inside right NOW!"

Abby yelled, "Mom, put Daddy on speaker!"

Belva Ann did, and Jim's voice came in loud and clear. "Calm down. I found them!"

Emmaline said, "Thank God."

Abby yelled into the phone, "Where?"

Belva Ann yelled, "I don't care where, just get inside. It's hailing."

"Honey, we three are down in the cellar, cozy and dry. Hey, Abby their eyes did glow in the dark, just like you said."

Emmaline said, "That cellar was locked."

Abby said, "Cellar?"

Jim said, "Oh, the door is still hanging by that padlock, but the hinges are rusted clean through. The wind must have blown it open."

Emmaline said, "You're in the safest spot in the house. Stay put."

Jim said, "Emmaline, did you know there's a fireplace down here?"

"I did."

"The cat and the dog were curled up together in the fireplace. I couldn't believe it."

Emmaline said, "I bet Tom led that panicked dog to safety."

Abby said, "Wow. Grandma, just like you always said. One day a Kitty-cat really would be Freddy's friend. It's happened."

Belva Ann said, "Will wonders never cease?"

Emmaline smiled, "Never."

Jim said, "You wouldn't believe it, but the cat is in my lap purring, and Freddy has his head on my leg. He's calm."

Belva Ann said, "Did you see the hail coming down?"

"No. I've never seen hail."

"Well, it was something to see. Sit tight."

Just then Emmaline's phone rang, and Belva Ann took the phone off speaker, turning away from Abby to speak privately to Jim.

Emmaline announced, "It's Mimi. I'll catch her up on our drama."

Abby left her mom and Grandma and went to the front door, which was still propped open. The rain was letting up, a mist was rising off the balls of ice that blanketed the ground. She realized she was exhausted. She wondered if everyone else felt the same way. She turned and dragged herself up the stairs to her bedroom and flung herself onto her bed, face down.

She dozed, but not for long. In her sleepy state, she saw the second key in Emmaline's purse. And she realized she had never wondered, never asked her grandma, what it was for. But Emmaline knew, of course she did. She knew about the cellar. She knew this house. More of her lies, although they were lies of omission. She had not wanted anyone to know that she had a history with this old house. It was a history she wasn't proud of.

Abby got out of bed and walked down the stairs. Emmaline was standing in the doorway, just as Abby had been earlier. She was silhouetted by the mist and light that framed her in the dim light of the house. For a moment, Abby did not see her grandmother. She saw the woman from her dream who was once again wearing a long black puffy coat. It wasn't her grandma, but a younger version of Emmaline standing in a mist, standing at a threshold from her past.

Emmaline turned to see Abby walking down the stairs,

and the spell was broken, she was no longer a young woman, but once again her grandma.

"Ready?"

Emmaline had made herself a trash bag raincoat just like the one she had made for Jim.

Belva Ann walked up behind her; sans trash bag.

"I want to come."

The three of them walked out, the rising cool mist from the hail swirling gently around their ankles.

Emmaline led them to the far side of the house, the side away from the woods and the propane tank and the well. She pointed to a hanging door, set into the foundation. It was about three feet tall and now only attached by the padlock, as Jim had described.

Emmaline said, "Careful of your head. There are steep and uneven stairs directly inside, and there's no handrail."

No one spoke as they made their way down. Belva Ann kept a grip on the back of Abby's shirt. Once down, they could stand upright, although the ceiling was low. The floor was bare clay.

Emmaline led them on. She said, "Jim?"

He said, "Here I am."

Jim shone the light from Abby's cell phone to show them the way.

He said, "Aren't you three an apparition. Not my first one down here, though."

Freddy threw himself at Abby doing his weird yodeling calls. She knelt on the ground and he whoo-whooed and circled her and leaned against her legs as she tried to hug his wiggly self.

Abby said, "I was SO worried about you. But Tom was your friend, he guided you to safety. You weren't alone! And then Daddy found you!"

Jim stood up, Tom cradled in his arms.

Belva Ann said, "Look who's a cat person now?"

He briefly took a hand from Tom to pat the stoney fireplace.

"Look at this old stone fireplace. Isn't it something?"

Emmaline nodded, "It's directly under the dining room fireplace. You could have a fire down here and no one would know about it from outside."

Then Emmaline stepped up to the fireplace, feeling the stones on the side, searching.

She said, "There."

Jim handed the cat to Belva Ann.

He ran his hands where Emmaline directed.

He said, "Seems the mortar has worn away between these two stones. There's a sizeable hole."

Emmaline nodded, "Once upon a time, I found a couple of pieces of broken China in that hole."

Belva Ann said, "Okay, that's odd. But what of it?"

Emmaline said, "Let me explain. You see, an enslaved person who could read or write could forge passes. You can imagine why that would be seen as dangerous. That's one reason it was against the law for an enslaved person to be literate. Getting caught with a book sometimes meant losing fingers or even a hand."

"Mom, what are you trying to say?"

"That there are other ways to leave messages. Things could mean something. Like where to go, where to hide. Who to trust."

Belva Ann said, "Mom, that's a stretch."

Abby said, "You mean, like this spot was a safe hiding spot for those escaping to freedom? Like Frederick Douglass did? And that leaving a bit of broken China was sort of like leaving a note?"

Belva Ann said, "Abby, I doubt any of that is true."

Jim took a deep breath and exhaled loudly. "Normally I would be skeptical, too. It's just, well, I sort of had an experience while I waited down here with the dog and cat."

Emmaline simply said, "Did you?"

"I had closed my eyes. The cat was purring in my lap. Freddy was leaning on my leg. For some odd reason, I thought Mimi had come in. But I must have been dreaming, because I didn't even try to open my eyes. She placed her hand on my head. I mean, I could feel her hand. And she said, I was not to worry. That I was safe now."

Abby's eyes opened wide, "Daddy, it was Lucy. It had to be Lucy. And wouldn't it make sense that Lucy would use this house to help others to freedom?"

Belva Ann said, "I suppose it could be true."

Abby said, "This old lady house, she saw some bad things. But maybe she saw good things, great things, brave and courageous things, too. Like helping others to freedom."

Emmaline said, "Redemption. William and I were shocked by those marks in the attic, but in the cellar, we found redemption for this old house. I hope I'm right, we're right."

Belva Ann said, "William?"

Emmaline blew out a long breath. "William, your father, and I found those shards of China together, right in that hole. We found those hash marks in the attic. We didn't know the story of Lucy and Lotty, though. Although William knows a great deal about such things. He *is* a real historian. I asked him if he had the other piece. He said he didn't remember. Maybe it doesn't matter.

"But I think it's past time for you two to get to know each other. I have confessed my sins; I've done what I can to redeem myself. I'm ready for reconciliation. That's why I'm here. But reconciliation is a decision that I have taken in *my* heart. I can't make anyone else take it into theirs."

* * *

The lights had come on soon after they had made it back into the house. Emmaline fed Tom on the kitchen counter. Tom ate his dry cat food with gusto.

Emmaline was cooing to him, "Tom, you are the hero of the hour."

But even though Abby said nothing, she knew Tom was not the only hero of the hour. She looked over at her Daddy and felt something new, her heart seemed to squeeze itself, like squeezing a sponge. The feeling passed and she wondered if she had not loved her Daddy enough. Not like she loved him now. It was like he had always stood outside the magic circle formed by her grandma and her mom and herself. And that circle included Freddy, too, of course.

But now he had stepped in, and was part of it, too, and just like earlier in the day, when she watched the foxes laugh and play, she felt wonder. She realized she knew so little about well, everything. She knew so little about her parents. She had known so little about her grandmother. But she had seen a bit more tonight.

Jim said, "Tonight was the weirdest night of my life."

Emmaline kept stroking the cat and said, "When you are an old man in your rocking chair, talking to your grandchildren, or even your great grandchildren, you will have the most amazing story to tell."

* * *

The next day, Emmaline made a huge platter of veggie rollups. Belva Ann and Abby made a fruit salad. The air was cooler and full of the smell of wet earth and grass. Although they had not seen any downed trees, Abby could also smell something she thought was pine sap.

The Taylors came up in the gator, Belle trotting alongside. Everyone was full of chatter over the excitement over the storm. Sissy had gotten caught out in the barn with the horses and had ridden out the worst of it there.

When Bobby arrived, he exclaimed, "Looks like y'all are having some kind of party."

Emmaline squealed like a teenager and in Abby's opinion went full "Elly May."

"Bobby, we had a ball of fire roll across the floor last night!"

"You sure about that? Ya'll weren't tipping back the old brown jug?"

Jim looked at Francis who explained, "He means white lightning."

"Cross my heart. It was a ball of fire; it rolled across the dining room and went up the chimney. Smelled like hellfire."

He shook his head, "I don't know about you California

425

people. Sounds like you was performing some kind of exorcism."

Emmaline smiled, "Well, I hadn't thought of it like that. I suppose we could have."

Jim put his head in his hand and shook his head.

Bobby said, "I'm pulling your leg. I never have seen such a thing, but I sure have heard of it before."

Jim said, "Scariest thing I've ever seen in my life."

Francis rose when he saw Bobby and extended his hand. Bobby and Frances gripped each other's hands for a long moment. Bobby said, "You get good quality hay off your fields?"

"Yes sir, I did, and plenty of it."

"Fields sure do look pretty. I think you're the last of my kin to be farming."

"I 'spect I am."

Bobby turned towards Emmaline and gave her a wink, as if he had been showing off just for her.

Abby loaded up her plate alongside Sissy and they took the dogs over to the front stairs and sat down. Both had forgotten all about the family holdback rule.

It wasn't too long before Mimi and Emmaline brought out bowls full of warm cobbler topped with ice cream.

Abby heard Bobby say, "I don't know why I haven't come by to visit with you Taylors before. I think it's high time that changed."

The grownups were chatting, and Abby and Sissy weren't paying much attention until Abby heard her mom say to Bobby, "Well, if they haven't given you a deposit yet, could we jump the line?"

Jim added, "Of course, we can give you a deposit today.

And we certainly expect to pay a pet deposit, too. It's just we'd like to be able to come and go this year and have it for next summer, as well."

Abby and Sissy worked hard to contain themselves, and Sissy even mimed praying.

Emmaline suddenly stood up and walked back into the house.

Abby and Sissy knew why.

William was coming up the drive.

The porch got quiet.

William pulled up and parked right in front of the porch. He waved then asked, "Emma here? I brought her a few things."

He opened the rear door and turned his back to pull something out. And was hit on his back with a frisbee.

All eyes went to Emmaline, who did not look the least bit guilty.

She said, "Seeking to forget makes exile all the longer. The secret of redemption lies in remembrance."

There was a sort of stunned silence, except for the sound of the dog's panting.

Sissy whispered, "Where she get that?"

Abby put her finger to her lips.

Then Emmaline announced, "I have something for you."

And she walked out to the car, where William had picked up the frisbee. He said, "A frisbee?"

Abby strained her ears but heard Emmaline say, "And some other thing."

William seemed to understand, "Ah."

Emmaline opened her fist, and he lifted out what Abby knew had to be the shard of China.

He said, "I don't suppose you want these groceries?"

"Later."

William reached back into his car, bringing out something none of them could see, something small. Abby knew. It had to be the other shard of China. He had kept it after all. He handed it to Emmaline. After she took it, she threaded her arm through his.

She said, "We'll see you folks in a bit."

Bobby grinned and said to the others, "My goodness, a lot went on here this summer."

Jim said, "Where do you suppose they're going?"

Abby said, "We know, don't we, Sissy."

Sissy nodded, "Prettiest view I know."

EPILOGUE

THE WITCH THE WOLF AND THE WING OF TIME
By Abby Woods (With thanks to Emmaline Sparks, my Grandma. She helped a lot.)

The witch drew the hood of her cape over her wild grey locks and slowly twirled while she chanted in low tones. She was not sure if her incantation was correct as she mouthed the words, words she had been carefully gathering these long winter months. She was not who she had once been, her powers had diminished.

Her black wolf began to circle her in the opposite rotation. He curled his body around her legs. His growls were low and continuous, like a song, punctuated by howls where he lifted his chin toward the sky, his golden-eyes glowing.

As witch and wolf continued to rotate in opposite directions in a dance not unlike those of native Americans, the sun set behind the horizon, and the moon appeared, as golden as the eyes of the wolf. When it broke free of the shadow of the earth, the dog and the woman stopped dancing.

No message, no magic occurred. She had failed. The witch removed her cloak and spread it on the ground. Then the wolf and witch sat side-by-side upon it, to gaze at the golden orb.

The witch spoke to the wolf, "I once was the favored one. But that was a long time ago."

And then she stroked the wolf upon his head, and he lay down and rested his chin on her thigh, sighing.

She said, "I released him. Perhaps I gave away all rights to him forever. Perhaps he has forgotten me. Or wishes to. We will try again, for the sun will set and the moon will rise, and each day is but another chance."

The wolf had rolled his eyes up to watch her, to listen. He seemed as disappointed as she. But perhaps he was only showing compassion for the one who had shown him the same.

As they rose, a large shadow and a cloud of mist scuttled across the dusky sky overhead.

The witch shivered and then said, "Yes, I felt it too. My dragon. I used to chase after it. I was young and impatient and wanted to grab its talons and fly toward the future. But now it stalks me instead. Time is not, 'of the essence' but is the essence."

* * *

The next day was sunny, the sky as blue as a robin's egg. The witch was nothing by day but an old woman with a black dog. She was old, but she was lithe, and active, willing to engage in the village with anyone who would stop and chat, usually at the coffee shop. Hearing the stories of others was sustenance for her. So many tales of courage and perseverance and triumph over calumny. The dog would stay curled at her feet at an outside table, not understanding words but knowing full well the tenor of each tale.

She loved to talk and to listen. Yet she had a need to talk to one who would not want to talk to her. Not yet.

The good book said, "Do not neglect to show hospitality to strangers, for thereby some have entertained angels unawares." She lived this as her creed and therefore had an ear to lend to whomever was willing to speak. One day she believed she would find she had indeed befriended an angel.

The spring sunshine made her feel itchy and restless, and hopeful. The winter had been dark and wet, but it had given her time to think, to plan. Now every fiber in her being said it was time, perhaps past time, to "knit up the ragged sleeves of care." But not through sleep, as Shakespeare had said, but through engineering reconciliation and restoration. She would require magic. Of that, she was sure.

Through the years, her dragon was always with her. It could never be any other way. Her perception of that constant, that dragon, well, that did change.

She and the wolf rested during the day, but the moonrise was for magic. She still had something up that ragged sleeve of hers to try, something magical.

And so, she set out once again with her wolf at her side. As the sun sank in the sky, they made their way to a bold mountain creek, climbing down a bank to reach it. The witch took off her cloak and gathered up the hemline of her skirt, tucking it into her waistband. The wolf sat on the bank watching with interest as the witch removed her shoes and socks.

She said to the wolf, "Heraclitus said, you cannot step into the same river twice. Let us test him."

The witch waded into the water.

The wolf opened his mouth and began to pant.

"We ought to be able to summon the memory of that river we stepped into long ago."

As the sky darkened, the moon went from gold to white. And the witch began to chant. It was a different chant than the previous night's. Instead of turning, she lifted her arms in front of her. She gazed at the opposite bank. Her chant had a musical lilt, a sweet song of yearning. The wolf too, added his song, a sort of vibration that was not exactly a growl as the pitch was not low but high.

The water that flowed over her legs began to slow. It was working! The water eddied for a moment, then magically reversed its flow. And there, above the bank, ripples formed in the air, like ripples in a pool of water. The ripples began to take shape, to reveal a man. A beautiful young man, long limbed, broad shouldered, spare of flesh, a mop of curly fair hair lending an air of wildness to his form.

She smiled at him as he stared at her in wonder. He said, "Why are you here?"

She saw her arms as they once appeared, firm and smooth. She saw her fingers, long, straight, and fine.

She said, "Do you ever think of me?"

He shook his head, slowly, "I banished you, as you banished me."

"Even from your dreams?"

"Even so."

"Cannot we allow memory, sweet memory to revisit us, to reanimate, to give fresh vigor to our bodies, to reawaken those divine desires of years long passed? Seeking to forget makes exile all the longer, the secret of redemption lies in remembrance."

"Redemption?" He shook his head. "I do not seek redemption. I am no exile."

And then, above her, her dragon. She heard the flap of his leathery wings, felt the hot flush of his breath on her scalp.

Instantly the water stopped flowing then pooled and eddied against her legs, then regained its former direction, as her lifted arms suddenly ached with fatigue. The young man aged before her eyes, as she surely aged before his. He cried out, was it in horror? And she felt shame. If her young form had been banished even from his dreams, her aged form must have filled him with a revulsion so deep as to ensure its permanence in his nightmares.

This was exactly the opposite of her intentions.

Her arms were now trembling with exhaustion. Her legs and feet were frozen with the cold. She struggled to climb out of the icy water and up the bank. As she collapsed upon her cloak, the wolf vigorously licked her feet with his warm tongue, the blood flowing, feeling returning. Only then could she put her socks and shoes back on, unhitch her skirt, and walk.

They went home.

The witch spent that night staring into the fire, the wolf stretched out at her feet, both weary. Heraclitus had also spoken of the ever-living fire, kindling in measures and being quenched in measures. It was ever-living. And she held onto the belief there was yet an ember alive deep in her beloved's memory. An ember that needed but the right sort of kindling.

There on her mantelpiece sat various items. Talismans, she called them. Leaning back in her chair she began to consider them. These items held magic; or once had. She stood up on weary legs, picking up each treasure, although others would see them as junk. She put each piece down in turn as it felt dead in her hand. Until she held in her hand a broken piece of China. It was a pretty thing, with bands of cobalt blue that had once rimmed a plate. The memory then hit her in a way that bent her knees. She put her free hand on the mantelpiece to steady herself. The wolf who had been dozing, startled awake, and she reassured him. "No fear, dear one. I think I know what I need to do, where I need to be, and why I cannot stay."

The next night, the witch and the wolf walked away from the village. The wolf trusted. He trusted even this night when his witch made no incantations, nor came back to their cozy place, with warm beds and full larders.

He trusted because the witch had taken him in when he was cast out, discarded, after he had been beaten and broken and bloodied for human sport. And he, a mighty wolf, as noble a creature as could be found in nature. He had been alone, unclaimed. But he was now beloved. And a wolf who is beloved cannot be anything but loyal, and truly no "lone" wolf chooses to be that way.

When the witch claimed him as her own, he was but a skeleton of fear and despair. She treated him as her everything and so she became his everything. So, where she walked, he would also. But it did not mean he no longer felt fear. It did not mean he no longer felt despair. The witch had her dragon. And the wolf had his own sort of dragon, too.

The wolf thought they were much alike. True, she was friendly to all, but where was her mate, her pack? She had perhaps also suffered banishment; been cast out. The wolf sensed that was her current quest, to rejoin one other who was beloved by the witch.

They walked for many days, until, far from the village, they came upon a burned-out bridge. They waited by its blackened timbers, gazing across the open divide at the other side. They waited until the sun dropped, and the moon rose, this time the moon was only a sliver, but a sliver so bright it cast shadows on the darkened moon's pocked surface. That tiny slice of light proved the moon to be so much more than a smooth disk reflecting light, or some sort of hole in the sky where light shone through. Its surface was terribly scarred. The wolf considered these scars to show it to be old and wise, a survivor of many battles. This explained why the witch called upon it for aid.

The witch said, "We live for the sunny days, but it is in the darkest sky that the stars shine the brightest."

And in that darkness, the bridge showed itself whole.

The witch, perhaps surprised, sat down on the ground, the wolf sat too and leaned against her side.

She fretted, "If we cross now, there will be no path back. I cannot say what lies ahead. This is my journey. You did not ask to go on it."

The wolf answered by standing up and giving a whole-body shake. Then he threw his head back and howled long and piercing as if he was howling at the stars. This was his battle cry; this was his answer.

In that starshine above them, passed a dark shape with flapping wings that moved the air. The shape circled back behind them, diving and in pursuit. The witch imagined seeing talons flexing as if to pluck her from the ground. The witch felt herself commit. It would be like jumping off a cliff, expecting to develop wings on her heels on the way down. Her heart was pounding as she looked down at her wolf and hoped he could feel the love she was sending with her eyes.

The witch said, "Let us try to cross, quickly now. We cross in the memory of what was before I put a torch to it."

The wolf sprang forward. He was nothing if not fleet of foot. He trod on air, never feeling the boards beneath his pads with his witch behind him. But they made it across. And there, on the other side of the bridge stood the beautiful young man.

He said, "Again? Leave me in peace. I do not wish to remember."

"Please, let me speak."

"Did you not burn this bridge?"

"Yes."

"Did we not agree?"

"We did."

"Then this is but illusion."

"It is."

"Ah. You are a gifted conjurer who has forced your way into my dreams. But this must only be what it is, a dream."

The witch replied, "Not gifted enough, you disappear before we can speak."

"I do not wish to speak. But if this is innocent illusion then kiss me and let me enjoy the illusion."

She nodded, then the witch and the beautiful young man clasped hands and then closed the space between them for a long kiss.

When they broke apart, the witch said, "Remember?"

He smiled and said, "That, I remember."

The witch said, "Let us make this illusion incarnate."

He said, "It is but a memory, but if you mean remember things carnal…" He lifted one hand toward her.

But before they could enjoy another kiss, came the wash of heat across her scalp. Her hair stood on end, and all was dissipated in that hot breath. It had felt real, but it was but moonlight and starshine. The young man stood there no longer. The witch had built back the bridge and crossed into his dreams, urged forward by her dragon, but it was gossamer, destroyed in an instant, like brushing away a cobweb.

The dragon had chased her across. Why? Perhaps, her dragon was toying with her. Like a cat torturing a mouse before putting it out of its misery. It had driven her across the bridge in fear, then allowed her to light a different kind of fire before snatching it all away. Of course, the rebuilt bridge had disappeared, along with the beautiful young man.

She still felt the kiss on her lips and the embrace deep in her belly, although she knew that embrace was many decades old. But the memory was strong. Perhaps that was all she was destined to ever have, memories. Yet she would not yet cede her desire to reclaim what she had long ago given away. Besides, there was no path left to her but the one that lay ahead. The dragon had made sure of that.

The wolf looked nervously at his witch, until she strode forward with intention away from the ruins. He watched her back for a moment before loping after her.

* * *

They travelled by day, an old woman and her dog, and rested each night without more attempts to cast spells. The wolf sensed they were getting closer to something. He sensed a growing excitement in the witch, perhaps confidence. Perhaps power.

But no matter how great her powers were, the dragon's powers were undeniably greater. The witch sometimes spoke aloud to the dragon. She often heard his heavy wings, felt the odd heat of his breath. His breath made her joints ache, her skin feel dry, and her hair stand away from her skull, wild and white with age.

But she and her wolf walked onwards.

The witch and the wolf warmed each other in the nights and found food and water when required.

Many more days passed, until they crossed over the blue mountains. They stopped at a big white abandoned house at the base of the mountain. The witch knew this place. The wolf did not. The house was filled with spirits. Some walked on two legs. Some walked on four. Even an abandoned old house could feel crowded. This made the wolf nervous.

But the wolf found the air to be delicious. It smelled of wildness, of pine and fox and coyote and deer. There were horses grazing in fields. Soon he met a dog. She trotted right up the front steps onto the porch, a one-dog welcome committee. The wolf thought she was beautiful. Not a trace of wolf about her. The dog was not afraid of him, or of anything it seemed. The dog did not seem to notice the dragon, but that was because she was young.

The wolf felt shy at first, but the witch urged him to go on and greet the stranger. The witch raised her voice to welcome the dog, and the dog, in return, gave the witch a polite bow. Then the dog approached the wolf and began a wiggle dance.

The wolf looked over his shoulder at the witch, and her smile gave the wolf permission to perform his own dance. Then the beautiful young dog danced her dance down the porch steps and away from the house, and the wolf followed her into the tall grass, the white tip of her tail leading him on like a flag. He would not go too far from the witch and the house full of spirits. He would listen for her call.

She did not call.

He fell in love but was back in time for dinner.

The witch always shared her meals with the Wolf. And although he seldom understood what she said, she did speak to him as if he did.

She said, "You like it here, I see. Found a lady-friend."

She bent down and stroked the wolf, and he rolled over to let her run her warm hands across his belly, his mouth hung open, his tongue slid out the side. He was enjoying the rub, but he was thinking of his new friend.

The sound of scampering feet above their heads startled the wolf. He sat upright, his ears straining, his hackles rising. Down the staircase came a mother squirrel, followed by her babies. All looked to be in a panic. They were heading right towards them. The wolf, ducked behind the skirts of the witch, quivering with fear.

She raised an arm, and the entourage slid to a halt. She said, "Stop! Have no fear."

The wolf disagreed by growling low and soft. He had fear. He had fear for good reasons. They had claws. Claws that could dig deeply, right through his coat. They had teeth. Teeth that could tear flesh. Such animals could leap upon his back, in places where he could not dislodge them with his teeth.

Once they had speared into his flesh, they could cling, mercilessly delivering wound after wound, unabated. Such things were seared into his memory.

Then weirdly, before his eyes, the mother squirrel became a small dark-skinned woman, and the baby squirrels became little children, human children. This confused the wolf. But not his witch. The children gathered around the woman's long skirt, clinging in fear.

The small woman looked shocked and angry, she pointed to the witch and said, "This house is our house, not yours."

The woman paused and squinted her eyes at the witch. "Wait, I seen you before. Ain't that right?"

The witch merely nodded.

The woman drew a deep breath, stroking the tallest of the children on the head in a reassuring manner, then gave a weak smile and a nod. She said, "Long as you don't bother us, we won't bother you." And then, just like the beautiful young man, she and her children dissolved into nothingness.

Fear drained from the wolf. He was exhausted both by his fear and his confusion. But he had learned that odd things happened around his witch, and that she would protect him.

The witch looked down at the wolf. "I'm sorry they scared you and I'm sorry they did not stay for tea. I should make cake for the children. Strange. I cast no spells to conjure these spirits. This house has many memories that have no bearing on us. Not directly. Still, they are all important. I too am a small part of its story, but we all belong. None should be afraid. Now, how do I get any of them to stay and speak to me?"

Days later, after the witch had been in a baking frenzy, they rose early to watch the sun break the horizon. It had rained in the night, and the air had cooled. The witch drank her tea, and ate her cake, and tried to summon the woman spirit and her children. She said to no one, "Come, the teapot is full, and I sliced the cake and set the table."

The wolf stood up when he saw a small dark woman and a child, walking up the front path toward them. He would have been frightened, but with them came his newfound dog friend. She bounded up to the wolf, and he bowed and sang to her, as she licked his face.

The witch said, "I'm so glad you came, and you brought your dog! What would you like in your tea?"

The wolf realized this small dark woman was too old, and the child too old to be the apparitions they had met earlier. Perhaps this old woman, too, was a witch. She showed no surprise at the place setting prepared for her, but smiled a kindly smile, dimples appearing in her cheeks. Perhaps she was the angel the witch had hoped to entertain. But they were solid forms. Of that, he was sure.

After they had chatted and eaten and had multiple cups of tea and were well away, the witch said, "Wasn't that lovely? It seems we both have found new friends."

The wolf wagged his tail and made a short happy bark.

The witch gave him a slice of cake.

The witch walked into the kitchen loaded down with cups and saucers, plates and forks, with the wolf at her heels. She stopped in the doorway with a small gasp.

A cake sitting on the counter was being savaged by mice. The wolf began to whimper, although the mice did not look as dangerous as squirrels, he deemed their numbers too great to take on in battle. Such a mob could overtake a wolf, attacking from both front and back, clinging to all four legs at once. No, they were far too dangerous a foe.

The witch raised both arms laden as they were with China, and shouted, "Begone, riotous, filthy, good-for-nothing wastrels!"

The mice instantly turned into young men, some with mouths stuffed full of cake.

And in the very next instant, they turned to smoke, filling the room with a sickly-sweet smell as well as the sour odor of beer and sweat. The wolf found the odor nearly overwhelming.

The witch made a noise of disgust. "Frat boys with booze sweats and the munchies. Old houses such as this one, well the memories are thick and sometimes odoriferous. We shall have to open the back door and get some fresh air in here."

The witch put down her dishes, opened the back door, then threw out the remains of the savaged cake while cursing softly under her breath.

She said, "Well wolf, we shall have to find a way to exorcise those devils, I was not looking for a side-quest. But this is unavoidable housekeeping as I fully intend to keep baking."

* * *

For the wolf, the days that followed were happy ones. He was in love. Daily he and his friend frolicked. They kissed and made love in the shadows of trees. They swam in the creeks, and dried off in the sunshine, rolling in soft grasses. One day, he returned to the house to find his witch away. And he paced and fretted until her return. When she came up the steps of the porch, he wanted to be angry, to sulk, and show his displeasure. But this was not possible. Instead, he nearly knocked her over with joy and relief.

She said, "There, there. I would never leave you, surely you know that. But since you were busy with your beloved, I thought to slip away to spy upon mine. You see, he lives nearby. Not the memory of him. Him."

The witch sat upon the step and the wolf sat by her side. He turned his head to study her face, and she placed her hand on his back. She talked a long time, and the wolf listened. He did not know the words, but he saw pictures in his mind. He understood.

She said, "He is still a fine-looking man. His belly is yet flat. I tried another spell. I summoned a breeze to whisper my name into his ear. I succeeded. He startled, and then looked around, and although I stood behind the corner of a building, and felt sure he did not see me, I sensed he did.

My dragon did not interfere. I leaned against the old brick building and waited for him to leave. But every time I peeked to check, he was still there, his brow furrowed. He was deep in thought. Which trapped me in my spying place.

I was not yet ready to let him see me as I am. So, I waited in hiding. This gave me time to examine my many failures. You see, when you are as old as I, you continually bring up your growing collection of failures, the ones you tried to bury. You blow the dust off them and examine and re-examine them and search for something good, and yet again find no value or lessons, but only self-pity, and humiliation.

I checked again, and did not see him. I stuffed my failures back into their dusty pile. I darted out from my hiding place, out of the alleyway, thinking already of what I should try next, but satisfied to have seen him in the flesh and looking well.

But although I am the conjurer, I forgot that he has magic all his own. Of course he does.

I shall try to explain. You and your lady-friend play. Yes, it is part of the charm of love, this playfulness. We too once played. We had a disk that we could make soar like a bird who floats on the breeze. That memory had gone dark in my mind. But as I was walking, I felt compelled to spin on my heels and look up. I watched, detached, as I reflexively snatched the spinning disk out of the air. A warm electric 'zing' travelled down my arm. I was momentarily filled with joy. A laugh escaped my lips. And in that moment, I was quick and agile and young again. And at some distance there he stood. His beauty sent a thrill through my body. A crooked smile of amusement creased his face. This was no spell of my making.

He said, "Caught you."

As I closed the distance, walking toward him, he aged. I knew I did as well. But my heart did not. It never had.

I said, "This spell is yours?"

"You've been relentless, haven't you? You've been haunting my dreams. I possessed the disk, but it had belonged to you. I dug it out of my attic and have been carrying it around in my car. When you called my name, I went and fetched it. You have unfinished business with me, I presume?"

I could feel the disk vibrate in my hand. "Ah, you kept it all this time. This disk has become a talisman."

He said that to him it was just an old plaything.

He asked why I was there. And I told him it was because she who stood between us had passed."

The witch stroked the back of the dog and addressed him. "I never disliked her. Truly, I never did. But we were in the wrong. But now? There is no need. There is no wrong. We are old, but we are not dead. His oath was only until death do they part."

The wolf half closed his eyes, distracted by thoughts of the pleasures of his day.

The witch continued, "He insisted that our time was ended long ago. But I answered that every new beginning comes from some other beginnings end. That we could not turn back the clock, but we could wind it up again."

The witch took her hand away and leaned forward, holding her head now in both hands. "He said to leave him to die in peace! I replied that he did not look sick to me. And then he said that he was merely sick of me and my bedevilment. I asked if he had found a new love, and he nearly spat at me the answer. It was no.

I had made an utter fool of myself. That is why my dragon stood back and did not interfere."

She moaned, "He left, and I said aloud to no one, that I am a stalker. A pest. A withered and fearsome crone. Unwanted and pathetic. I expressed all that, and then, as if I had given a cue, I felt my dragon descend, and heat prickle my flesh. I was terrified. I feared I would be seared into ash and blown away. And if I had allowed it, I believe I would have been. But I commanded, NO. YOU CANNOT HAVE ME. And so, here I am."

The witch rose from the step, her wolf falling behind her. When they stepped through the front door, they were brought up short by the sight of a cat sitting on the top of the newel post on the staircase, eyes like slits staring at them. It was missing one ear.

The wolf yelped in fear.

The witch startled too, then said, "Oh, my! Can I help you?"

The cat morphed into a short scruffy man in overalls. He was wearing a ball cap, a toothpick hanging out of his mouth, sporting a three-day-old beard, and indeed, missing an ear. In his hand was a switchblade. He pressed on it and the blade popped out.

"I understand y'all got a mouse problem."

The witch heard a scrabble of nails on the hardwood floors and turned to look behind her. The wolf had fled.

"Yes, we do. Brazen things attacked my freshly baked cakes."

"Can't be having that. You just leave it to me."

"Well, that's good news. How shall we pay you?"

"Unlimited Little Friskies. The salmon recipe."

And just like that, he was a cat again, and a few minutes after that, he was nowhere to be found.

It took an hour for the witch to convince the wolf to come back inside the house.

* * *

The witch took to taking long walks. Sometimes the wolf went with her. Unless he was with the dog who came calling for him most mornings. The days had gotten hotter, so the wolf and his dog spent more time wading in the creeks than frolicking.

One thing the wolf would not do is stay in the house alone. The squirrels had stayed out of sight, so he had relaxed about them, but the cat was a bridge too far. He never knew where or when the cat would appear, but that creature was a killer and proud of it. The wolf was afraid of many things, but nothing was as scary to him as that cat.

The cat proved to be a prolific murderer. Dead mice began turning up everywhere. The witch did suffer some unease about their killings. But they should never have attacked her cake. She kept a bowl of Little Friskies filled on the kitchen counter, the salmon recipe. And the cat helped himself regularly. If the witch was about, he always thanked her by purring and vibrating his tail.

* * *

The witch now fought off her dragon nearly every day. She heard its wings; she felt its hot breath. Summer was full upon the earth, hot and humid and pulsing with life, yet she sat upon the porch and felt herself becoming parched, her skin, her bones. At dusk the fairies came and danced, making pinpoint lights in the darkness and singing their songs, but at a pitch she could not hear.

Her wolf was nearly always at her side. Innocent to what lay ahead. His beloved was carrying his babes. She tried to tell him, but the words and pictures she sent him held no meaning.

She sat upon the porch one morning, feeling too tired to walk among the fields she and he had once made their own. Sitting there she could no longer summon his image nor enter his dreams. She could hardly believe it, but the piece of broken China had gone dead in her hand. This troubled her so that she had placed it in the pocket of her skirt, hoping it would come back to life. While she sat, she kept her hand in that pocket, periodically palming it, to no avail. She felt leaden with despair.

She looked down when she heard a sound to find a baby squirrel had climbed upon her shoe. The witch put her hand down and the squirrel climbed into her palm. She placed the squirrel upon her lap, and in the blink of her eye, a little girl, perhaps around three years of age, leaned against her chest, putting her thumb into her mouth, her long lashes lowered as she began to suck. She was a beautiful child, this squirrel baby.

A voice said, "I had meant to stay out of your way."

The witch looked up to see the short dark woman take the chair next to her, pulling another child up into her own lap. A little boy. An older child, a girl, leaned against a column.

The witch said, "I'm glad you've lost all fear of me."

"I 'member you more and more. Course, you never seen me back then, nor the children. You wouldn't have been able. Not back then. But I was here. And the others from before your time. I 'member how you and he wanted to know everything this old house had seen, the history. You got some things right. But there is so much more to tell. Wouldn't you like to hear it all?"

The witch gazed once more down at the little one in her lap. "I hope the fact that your children are, well children, doesn't mean they perished as children."

"No ma'am, thank the Lord. Lived to see they's great grandbabies. These is just my happiest mem'ries."

The witch began to rock the child in her lap, she tipped her head down and instinctively kissed the top of the babe's head.

She said, "I have a daughter, too."

"Yes, ma'am. I know."

"You do?"

The woman smiled, and the witch noticed for the first time she had dimples.

She said, "Not to be indelicate, but you made her in this house."

"Ah."

"But see, I come to say something important; you can stay. You come on and bring your favorite mem'ries."

The witch frowned, "That would require my death?"

"Is your child well set?"

The witch nodded, "Yes, with a good mate and a child of her own. My wolf…"

"You need not worry on his account. That old woman and child will see to his care. You ain't alone. I'll be right here. Go on."

The woman put the little boy down, then rose and picked the child up from the lap of the witch and placing her on the porch. Then she stepped toward the front door, the children gathered around her.

"Go on."

"Now?"

"Now would be fine. The old lady will find your body."

The realization that it could be now, right now, made the witch draw a deep breath and exhale loudly. She listened for the sound of the dragon's leathery wings. She braced for the searing heat. Her heart began to race, her hair stood on end. She felt no fire, no hot breath washed over her, she heard no wings.

Instead, she felt a lovely internal warmth. She wanted to stand up, but she could not. With her next exhalation, her beloved appeared, young and beautiful as he had once been. He knelt before her and stroked her knees, then slid his hands under her skirt. She was paralyzed, unable to move, unable to speak. She looked down into his softened gaze, full of love and desire as he leaned forward and found her lips. She felt the weight of him lean into her. She felt her whole body respond, awake and release. If this was illusion, it was the most vivid and intense of her life.

She realized she would die with this memory.

But then, in a sort of spasm, her hand closed on something sharp and hot and biting. She realized she was no longer paralyzed. She pulled her hand from her pocket and saw she had gripped the shard of China so tightly as to drive an edge into her flesh. Blood rose from the spot.

She was not going to die. Not now. She knew this. The dragon had tried seduction this time, rather than fear. She had almost surrendered; she had meant to, but her talisman had drawn blood to draw her back, breaking the illusion. As she looked at the rising spot of blood, her heartbeat slowed. She felt a twinge of regret. It would have been so easy. But it would have been cowardly, too.

She turned her head and saw the small woman, standing just inside the front door, the children hidden from sight.

The woman frowned, "I guess you got unfinished business."

450

The witch nodded, "I do. He doesn't know. I never told him."

Instantly the witch stood alone. No woman. No children. Not even a squirrel could be seen.

It would be a fine thing to feel the love she had once known. She had the memory. That was more than many could claim. But what she still must do was not for herself.

The witch had to make a new plan.

* * *

The witch sat on the porch watching for his car, her wolf at her side.

She no longer tried magic to summon him. She had merely left a message on his phone. She said, "You were right. I have unfinished business. Come. Now."

But it was not he who came up the path. Her wolf jumped off the porch, tail wagging. The young dog bounded up to the wolf, licking his face.

Trailing behind the beautiful young dog, was the old woman who owned her.

She said to the witch, "Your wolfdog has gotten my girl 'in-the-family-way'."

The witch lowered her gaze, "Apologies, but she did make him the happiest dog alive. Be assured that as soon as the pups are weaned, I'll take what you don't want."

The woman laughed, "You sure 'bout that? Hounds generally have big litters."

"If they're as pretty as her..."

"She is real pretty."

"Can I get you a lemonade? This heat is terrible."

"Not today. We got tornado weather."

"I assume that's unlikely.

"Maybe so, but now, listen to me. You see hail, you go on down into that cellar. You know where the cellar door is?" She pointed to the side of the house. "Door is set into the foundation. Watch your step down those stairs. It's right cozy down there. Take a flashlight or candles. If I see hail, I'll rest easy if I know you and that dog are down there. Me, I'm set up to go to our basement. It's going to be bad. I can feel it in the air. We may not get a tornado, but we will lose power."

The witch could not find a flashlight, but she found a box of matches, and a small votive candle. She put them in the empty pocket of her skirt, leaving her broken China in the other pocket.

The witch and the wolf sat alone again and waited. The air became heavy and tinted green as if it were under the shadow of a large tree.

And then he was there, climbing the stairs of the front porch. He said, "I already regret coming. If you have something you must say, say it, we are under a tornado watch."

The witch led him into the house, into the dining room, and they sat down. The wolf couldn't take his eyes off the man. Here was her beloved, in the flesh. He was no spirit. And he did not seem friendly. The wolf growled, soft and brief and leaned against the legs of the witch.

He said, "A wolf? As a pet? I am not surprised."

She ignored his comment and asked, "Have you been here since... to the house, I mean?"

"No."

452

"I've learned more about it. This house. You and I were right about some of it. Remember how we explored every nook and cranny. How we researched its history? The families that lived here? What went on here prior to the Civil War?"

"How is that pertinent?"

"Remember how we walked these fields? The glorious views?"

"Of course, I remember. But what is the point?"

The wind shook the window in its casement. He said, "And here it comes. I see what you have done, here. Is this storm a trap?"

The rain began, heavy drops, but spread thinly.

"No. I did not summon the storm. You think me more powerful than I am."

The wolf no longer feared the man. Something in the man had changed. But the wolf did fear the storm. He began to pant.

The man got up from his seat and began to pace. "Talk then. You have until the storm passes and not a moment longer."

The witch laughed weakly. "Ah, I am like Scheherazade, as long as I talk, I entertain, I live."

The house shook with lightning, and the lights flickered. The rain now blew in sheets.

He said, "Go on then."

"The memories are not just mine, but yours too."

"I banished them."

"Memory does not take orders and does not follow commands. Neither does time. If you cannot remember our love, our passion, our fascination for each other and for this house, then I have no hope for your grace."

"I do not wish to be tortured by memories."

He stepped toward the witch and leaned on the table to look straight into her eyes. He said, with passion, "To hell with those memories."

A deafening bolt of lightning crashed right above their heads, and a fireball flew through the window and rolled across the floor, sizzling and filling the air with a sulfurous odor.

Then the hail began.

The witch cried out. "To the cellar, NOW!"

The witch led them, the wolf putting himself between the witch and the man.

As they rounded the corner of the house, the witch felt the dragon at her back. The thought came to her in a flash, she would not make it to the cellar. Her unfinished business would remain unfinished. She had so little fight left in her. She was but a shell of who she had once been.

The hail was stinging her arms, her neck, but she could now see the cellar door. But then she felt it; the grasp of talons on her left shoulder, down her armpit, piercing her left breast.

She fell to the ground.

The very next thing she felt was her wolf, he was upon her back, growling and shrieking. The talon released its fearful grip.

She lifted her head, in time to see her wolf being lifted off the ground.

She cried out, "Not my dog, not today!"

And then, from nowhere, the one-eared cat hovered in the air, above the form of the dog. In the next moment, the one-eared cat, was a one-eared man, with a switchblade slashing the air. The dog dropped to the ground with a yelp.

And then the one-eared man was again a cat, who landed lightly on the ground on all fours.

In the next moment, the witch felt herself lifted off the ground, again. She felt warm arms around her, her head against a chest. Somehow her beloved managed to open the cellar door and navigated the steep steps down into the darkness.

He carried her to the fireplace and helped her into the rocking chair, one of two.

He said, "Are you okay? You took a nasty fall."

With shaking hands, the witch pulled the matches and the small votive candle from her pocket.

"Light the candle, then the fire, please."

He said, "These chairs?"

She said, "You remember them?"

"And there's wood and kindling in the fireplace."

He turned his focus on getting the candle lit, and then the fire in the fireplace. Once lit, it took no time to roar into a glorious blaze."

The man put his hand on the heavy stones of the fireplace. "I remember this cellar. It was our secret place."

The witch said, "A safe space. That's what it has always been. Even the dog and cat feel it."

The witch pointed to the animals, who had come into the flickering light of the fire.

The man said, "Your dog is bleeding."

He walked over to the wolf, who allowed him to examine a scratch on his nose. "Cat scratch. Nothing serious."

The cat walked up to the wolf, who lowered his nose, and the cat commenced licking the wound.

The witch smiled and said, "Yet you see that all is forgiven."

The dog lay down and then closed his eyes while the cat licked the dog's face.

The man looked at the witch, sitting in the rocking chair. Then he squeezed his eyes shut. "I remember."

He ran his hands around the side of the fireplace, along the heavy stack of rocks that formed it."

He said, "The chiseled-out spot between the stones. It's still there."

"Of course it is."

The man pulled out a bit of broken China and held it out to the witch.

She stood up and pulled her bit out of her pocket and came to stand by his side.

Without a word, they joined the two bits together.

And then looked up to find the small dark woman there. This time she did not have her children with her.

The woman said, "See, you could have a fire down here, and no one out there would be the wiser 'bout anyone being here. Uses the same chimney as the dining room. All a body needed to ask for sanctuary was a bit of broken China. You show that, and we know you ain't no threat, you just asking for sanctuary. Many made their way to freedom from this place with nothing but a bit of broken China."

The woman disappeared as quietly as she had appeared.

He said, "Am I going mad?"

They still held the two pieces of China together. But the witch slowly pulled her bit away.

She said, "The pieces fit together perfectly. But they could never be a complete thing. Too many of the largest pieces are missing. But they are still beautiful."

"Please, Scheherazade, continue your tale."

"I don't have 1001 nights."

He sat down in one of the rocking chairs, she took the other. The cat jumped into her lap, and the wolf leaned against her legs.

"We have a daughter."

The man slumped in his chair; his mouth dropped open. "A daughter?"

"And she a daughter of her own."

"Why did you never say?"

"You and I took an oath to forget everything. To never contact each other again."

"We did. But still…"

"I waited until she had passed away. I kept my promise to her, if not to you. Can you forgive me?"

"I, I don't know."

"I cannot charm away my own mortality. Time is not of the essence; time is the essence. My wish is to be forgiven. My wish is to reconcile. My wish is to have you by my side, to stand by my side, for whatever number of days I have left to me. There is more work to do yet. I need you."

He looked around the dim space, then at the flickering fire. The two of them gently rocked.

He closed his eyes as he rocked. "I broke my vows long before you broke yours. But you kept a promise you should never have kept."

"Have we both not paid penance enough?"

He sighed, "I think the storm has passed. We can let the

fire die out on its own and go back out. I think the danger has passed."

"Perhaps. Even so, I'd rather stay down here for a while. I feel quite safe here, just as I did all those years ago. Perhaps it's just an illusion. I know we can't stay down here forever, but I am in no rush to leave."

He took one of her hands, raised it to his lips and gently kissed it. He said, "Then stay where you are. Speak."

ACKNOWLEDGMENTS

People have asked me, "How do you write a novel?" And even though *The Story Hunters* is my seventh novel, I can't really say for sure how they all came about. But I can tell you how I went about writing this one.

Like Emmaline Sparks, I became fascinated with the history of the Hemmings women and life on Jefferson's plantation, Monticello. While reading the WPA slave narratives, reading Mary Chestnut's diary, and watching "Finding Your Roots" an idea for a story began to form.

Along with my historical reading, I had read Frederick Backman's excellent novel, "My Grandmother Told Me To Tell You She's Sorry." And somehow from there, in my mind, I met a precocious Abby Woods and her novel writing, story hunting grandma, Emmaline. They would be my story hunters, and Charlottesville, Virginia, home of Thomas Jefferson, would be their hunting grounds.

To jump start the project I signed up for NANOW-RIMO, (National Novel Writing Month) which challenges writers to take the month of November to log sixty-thousand words. I used the month of October to sketch out an outline, then hit the ground running on November first. I completed the challenge, winning the tee-shirt that "contestants" pay for!

After that first NANOWRIMO, I put the manuscript aside for a full year. When the next November rolled around,

I pulled it back out, and I used the new NANOWRIMO challenge to revise and finish the story.

Once November was history, I sent pages to Danielle Chiotti of Manuscript Academy. Danielle was my "alpha reader." I am thankful to Danielle for her excellent help in guiding my first revision. (Danielle has not seen the ending. I hope it pleases her!)

My next step was to give the manuscript to my "beta readers." Janet Salem and her mother Linda Wynn did a stellar job! Janet runs an active book club, and Janet and Linda read a prodigious amount of fiction each year. Both have eagle eyes for errors. They also made insightful suggestions that made my story better. Thank you.

My next step was to give it to my publisher, Bob Babcock of Deeds Publishing. Thank you, Bob, and thank you Deeds Publishing for once again producing a beautiful book. Thank you for your continued encouragement and support.

I was telling someone once that I had been worrying and fussing in my mind over people who I knew (in the rational part of my brain) did not exist. He said to me, "Do you think that's healthy?" We both laughed. But there is a bit of madness in creation, as well as too much isolation. I spend untold hours alone with my imaginary friends.

If I didn't know for sure that I had you, my readers, to give these stories to, I think maybe I could find myself more than a little bit "mad."

But here you are. And for that I am eternally grateful.

Karen McGoldrick is married to a UVA grad, and lives in Canton, Georgia. She is the author of the series, "The Dressage Chronicles." She rides and teaches dressage and is a USDF certified instructor who has earned her USDF bronze, silver, and gold rider medals on horses she trained herself. She's lucky enough to still have horses in her daily life, a good dog, and a large number of books in her TBR pile.

www.ingramcontent.com/pod-product-compliance
Lightning Source LLC
Chambersburg PA
CBHW031026030726
47497CB00004B/1024